4.99

On the ice planet—
where exile is death . . .

The cold fulfilled its promise of earlier in the day, biting noses, fingers, even through the gloves, and penetrating the heavy traveling cloaks. "Hurry," Karne urged, striding faster.

But finally, I stopped, my lungs burning, my breath coming in harsh gasps. "I can't go on. Let's stop, let them have what they want."

Karne's arm tightened and he jerked me into motion again. "We can't. I have only one stun charge left."

We never reached the safety of the hills. At the first black outposts, something swished over our heads and skittered through the gravel ahead of us. It was a wicked-looking spear.

Karne dropped the pack, picked up the spear, and turned to face the Runners . . .

Books in the WINTER WORLD Series
by C. J. Mills

WINTER WORLD
EGIL'S BOOK
KIT'S BOOK
BRANDER'S BOOK
ZJHANNE'S BOOK

WINTER WORLD
ZJHANNE'S BOOK

C.J. MILLS

ACE BOOKS, NEW YORK

This book is an Ace original edition,
and has never been previously published.

ZJHANNE'S BOOK

An Ace Book / published by arrangement with
the author

PRINTING HISTORY
Ace edition / June 1992

Cover art by Jean Targete.

ISBN: 0-441-89448-8

Ace Books are published by The Berkley Publishing Group,
200 Madison Avenue, New York, New York 10016.

PRINTED IN THE UNITED STATES OF AMERICA

10 9 8 7 6 5 4 3 2 1

PROLOGUE

"Prepare to debark. All passengers prepare to debark."

The sultry computer voice roused the lean, dark man from his thoughts. Karne Halarek, Lharr in Halarek, pushed his chair away from the desk, stood slowly, and adjusted his jacket so it settled more comfortably on his shoulders. It had been years since he had worn Inner World clothes. He smiled thinly. Ten years. Ten years ago the Gild had prohibited everyone from the Houses of Starker IV from traveling anywhere on Gildships and that kept everyone planet-bound, because Starker IV had no space flight, except for the rare Black Ship expeditions.

The Gild restriction had come, indirectly, because of Karne. He had been returning home to assume rule of his House and assassins from House Harlan had attempted to prevent that, only they had made their attempts aboard Gild properties. This violated the Gild's neutrality and the Gild had reacted to protect its reputation. It seemed eminently suitable that it was Richard Harlan, son of the man who had ordered the assassination attempts, who had persuaded the Gild to lift the restriction.

Karne swept the papers on the desk into a pile, tapped them into a neat stack, and slid them into a large envelope. *I never expected the bastard to keep his promise about the truce, let alone his promise about the Gild.* Karne shook his head. *It's Richard's unpredictability that makes him so dangerous. Only two days out of prison, and he sends us word the Gild had agreed to take Family passengers again. Two days! He'd signed a contract with the Gild on behalf of all the Houses, pledging no more incidents on Gild property. He backed that with fifty thousand Gildcredits of Harlan money! Unbelievable.*

Karne shook his head again. It was still hard to believe—Richard had parted with hard currency *and* had kept *both* promises he had made to a clan enemy. Karne allowed himself a grim smile.

Those Gildcredits make it unlikely Richard can afford a Black Ship expedition any time soon. I may yet have living heirs before he does. Especially considering the damage Brander did to Richard's fertility before I discovered his plot.

Karne glanced around the room to make sure he hadn't missed any possessions. Spared the military expenses of feud by the truce, his House had had time to assemble enough credit to rent and refurbish a Black Ship. A Black Ship bride brought enormous prestige to a House because of the expense she represented. Had Richard known Karne would use the truce to get an off-world wife? Perhaps that was why Richard had parted with so much cash so easily. It would be like him to plant a man of his aboard the Black Ship to Seal Karne's prospective wife before Karne could, thereby stealing her from Karne as Karne's great-grandsire had stolen Richard's great-grandsire's prospective wife. It would be a "humorous" reminder of the act that started the feud, it would come close to bankrupting House Halarek by forcing Karne to search yet again for a wife, *and* it would save House Harlan the enormous expense of a Black Ship.

Karne ran his hand through his hair and stood with head bent, hand at the back of his neck, thinking. It was not just a chance. It was likely there was a Harlan man on his Black Ship. The truce had ended when Richard left his cell, after all. Richard would not likely pass up an opportunity to humiliate the woman, perhaps to damage her, in order to humiliate and damage Karne and his House. As he had intended to humiliate and damage Kit.

Karne straightened and let out an explosive breath. The way to protect Zjhanne Verlith from Richard was to perform the ancient ritual of Sheet and Broken Seal before the Council witnesses immediately after she came aboard. He did not want to do that. But she could end up damaged permanently, or the wife of a serf, or the leman of one of Richard's allies if he did not.

The computer's voice cut in. "All passengers prepare to debark. All passengers prepare to debark. Immediately, please."

Hurry, hurry. Why did he have to have last-minute afterthoughts?

For both of them, the beginning would be unpleasant, but he had hundreds of Halareks and thousands of dependents to think about. He and his advisers had worked out over five years that this gamble was the most likely to save his House and his world. At least his House.

And this woman was not like other Black Ship brides, not a chance victim near enough to a Black Ship's landing site to be easily taken. Karne had hired an agent to find a woman who could help him pull Starker IV's society toward a less violent, less autocratic way of life before it tore itself apart, as it was beginning to do. Of the candidates Lance had found, Zjhanne Verlith seemed the most suitable. She was a specialist in Terran pre-industrial history, so she understood the sort of society Starker IV had. Zjhanne Verlith was Karne's last gamble. She had to work. He could not afford the slightest risk that Richard would take her from him. The ritual was necessary, but he would make sure it would not be painful or traumatic for her. And she would adapt. His mother had been a Black Ship bride and she had adapted.

Karne quickly smothered the voice of conscience, which whispered that his mother had not come from a society as far ahead of Starker IV as Fruhe's was.

"All passengers prepare to debark. The shuttles begin leaving from bays 10 and 20 in five minutes."

Karne strode toward the cabin door, which slid into the wall as he approached, and hurried along the corridor. He hoped Lance would come to meet the shuttle himself. It had been ten years since the Academy. Karne wondered if they would still recognize each other.

The "outside" wall of the corridor was a holo that pretended to be a window onto Fruhe, a planet of the old Empire. In it, Fruhe rotated slowly, gold and blue and pale green. Fruhe was a turn-around point for many ships, which were thoroughly cleaned and serviced in dry docks before they took off again. Its orbital dry docks and machine shops were one of the reasons Fruhe was so rich. It was also a world of high culture and absolutely no violence. Karne wondered if that would be another problem between himself and Zjhanne Verlith. No one could say Starker IV was a world of no violence. Or of high culture, either.

Karne turned a corner and there was the waiting lounge for bay 10. Humans and XTs stood or sat, read or talked or slept, waiting their turn to board. In the far corner of the lounge, a line of beings moved slowly through a door and into a shuttle. There was a holo here, too, showing the rounded metal nose of a shuttle snuggled into the dock's air lock.

Karne walked over to the holo and stared at it, but he was not really seeing it. He was wondering again what Lance would look like after ten years. He was wondering what Zjhanne Verlith looked like. He was wondering if a world where women thought and worked as actively and freely as men could provide a satisfactory wife to a man who came from a gender-divided feudal society.

Karne shook his head, as if he could shake out his doubts. Lizanne had been a docile and obedient sheep who had been unable to bear a living child and who had died trying. Charlotte had been a renowned beauty, a coup for a young man once thought certain to lose his House to someone stronger, but Charlotte had been unwilling to bear any child at all, had lain with Richard merely for the excitement of adultery, and had been assassinated by a Harlan cousin. House alliances, tradition, and Family advisers had chosen Karne's wives twice. He had made quite clear to all of them he was selecting this wife himself and, by the Guardians, this one had to work out! House Halarek would not survive another failure.

Karne turned back to the lounge, took his place in the shuttle line, and slipped the first four sheets of paper from their envelope. One more time through the background and financial reports on the Verlith family, the pix of the family and its large farm, and Lance's personal report about Zjhanne and he could fit in with the guests at the party the Verliths were giving this night.

Perhaps Lance could find some time before the party to unobtrusively show him possible landing sites for the Black Ship. No, perhaps was not good enough. Lance would have to show him. Knowing safe places to bring in the ship was part of their agreement.

CHAPTER 1

A pre-dawn fog hung over the farmyard. In the east, the beginning of sunrise made the fog glow. The painted sign at the barn's peak, "Verlith Farms," appeared and disappeared at the whim of a breeze. I love the way fog makes things appear and disappear.

Some of the dairy workers were walking toward the barn for the milking. Most days when I come home for a visit, I help. I love the warmth of a barn before dawn, and the yellow light inside, and the smells of hay and chickens and clean cows. Today, though, I wouldn't be going out there. Today Lance and I officially announced our engagement with a big party for the neighborhood and for Lance's friends and business associates. A friend from Lance's Academy days was even coming all the way from one of the more barbaric Outer Worlds for the party. The distance he was willing to come for the occasion impressed me. Lance's own family wouldn't come to Fruhe, even for the wedding. They said Fruhe was too far from Terra. But Terra was closer than Starker IV, where Lance's Academy friend was coming from. There had to be a very important tie to bring this lord from a world on the edge of nowhere. I would have to be especially nice to him because of that.

I leaned against the windowsill for a moment, imagining the welcoming warmth of the barn after a walk through the fog. I missed that, living in my city apartment. I considered, for a moment, putting off my duties long enough to treat myself to a few hours in the barn, then shook my head. I couldn't do it, and I was wasting precious minutes thinking about it. The major preparations were complete, but there was still a lot to do before our guests began arriving for supper.

Mom was a meticulous planner, so everything—foods, drinks, entertainments, even the time each dish was to be served or each singer or band was to appear—had been put on lists. So had the guests' names, with short notes beside each to make starting a conversation easier. Everyone in the family had a copy of the guest list plus a personal list of duties, even Pieter, who thought *his* short stay at home should be a vacation. Zjhaques and Sharine would help as much as a six-year-old and eight-year-old could, too, but . . . I dug my work list out of a pocket, smoothed it against my knee, and read down it. I'd start by checking if the setting-up in the sunroom and parlor had been finished.

Hours later, when I came back to the kitchen for lunch, Pieter was standing in the middle of the room, sandwich in hand, snarling at Mom.

"Watch the boys! Why can't Abby watch the boys? I'm only on Fruhe a few weeks. I have friends I haven't—"

Mom silenced him with a look, something even Dad couldn't do. Pieter's attitude was a throwback to Fruhe's settlement days. Pieter couldn't see that he was hurting Abigail when he suggested that watching his own sons for a few hours was beneath him. He only saw that Mom was telling him to do "women's" work. And telling him to eat as he went. Pieter hates eating on the run and obviously Mom intended him to start with the boys immediately or he would have been sitting at the table with his food.

Abigail *was* sitting at the table, sort of crouched in her chair, as if she expected a blow to fall at any moment. I knew it would never even occur to Pieter to hit her, though. Our people don't do that. Fruhe has no wars, no feuds, no ritual battles, and no sports that involve hurting people for the amusement of spectators, either. Still, it was a kind of blow for Abby to know Pieter thought watching two toddlers was good enough for her to do, but not important enough for him to bother with. I couldn't understand why Abby didn't just tell Pieter to shut up and take care of his kids for a while, though. Promotion to captain of a Gildship didn't make him king of the world, after all. But Abby never stood up to him. Maybe that was one of the reasons he loved her. Or maybe he would love her more if she stood up for herself sometimes.

Abby might let Pieter get away with such behavior, but Mom wouldn't. "You're away months at a time," Mom snapped. "Your boys need time with you, too. Abby needs time off from being two parents. If you weren't willing to take care of the boys sometimes, you shouldn't have had them."

That was a low blow. Pieter adored his children.

After a moment, Mom's mouth twitched upward into a smile. "Besides, you know you hate peeling vegetables and washing dishes and today those are your other alternatives. You're not a guest here, you know, so stop acting like a baby and let Abby get on with her lunch so she can help."

Pieter opened his mouth, caught the look in Mom's eyes, reddened, shut his mouth, and went up the back stairs. He would take care of the boys. I had seen Mom handle him like this before, as if he were still eight or nine. It made me think of training horses: No matter how big they got, horses never figured out that the humans controlling them were a lot smaller and weaker than they were.

Pieter wasn't really stupid like a horse. A man didn't make Gildcaptain before he was thirty if he were stupid. It was just that Pieter was inept dealing with people except on a business level. His problem. Mine at the moment was to eat calmly, and that meant not thinking of all the things I had to do yet.

By sunset, I'd done everything on my list and bathed and gone to my bedroom to finish getting ready. Sharine sat on my bed, chattering about what *she* had accomplished, while I did my hair, put on my dress, then struggled with its back press-closure. Sharine stopped her stream of words and slid off the bed.

"Let me help, silly," she said, sounding like Mom. She slid her hand inside the opening, freed the cloth that was causing the trouble, and closed the opening. She stepped back. "Turn around."

I obeyed. I couldn't help smiling. Sharine's tone of voice and her body language were so like Mom's, yet she had only lived with us since she was four.

Sharine caressed the fabric of the dress. "I *like* that color blue. It sets off your eyes, just like Dad says. And your hair, too. It brings out the red in your hair. I wish my hair was brown like yours and not brown like mine. Mine looks like dirty dishwater."

Oh, Lord, she was beginning to worry about things like that already.

I kissed her forehead, put my arm around her, and gave her a squeeze. "When I was your age, sweetie, my hair was carrot-red. I got teased so much I sometimes came home crying."

Sharine looked up at me with interest, her unhappiness disappearing into sympathy for the little girl I had been. "That must have been *awful.*"

"It was, sweetie." I kissed her cheek. "Thank you for caring." I pointed her toward my jewel box and sent her toward it with a light swat on the bottom. "Go get my garnet necklace and earrings, then get yourself ready. Come back here and we'll do your braids on top of your head and put flowers in them, so when I introduce people to my little sister, they'll think she's a queen."

Sharine wriggled and giggled and hurried to do as she had been told.

We were at our assigned post on time. Sharine stood with me on one side of the double doorway and Mom and Dad stood on the other. Zjhaques had been left in the nursery with the nanny and he had been enraged. Nothing either Mom or Dad could say, short of inviting him to the dinner, could mollify him. At six, *we* knew he was still too young to be able to behave himself for hours with only adults for company, but he didn't. Sharine behaved with the grave courtesy of a grownup. She had that ability, at times, to be as grownup as any of the adults.

Lance had warned me he would be late, because of the shuttle's arrival time. He was right. The guests had finished their appetizers and Mom and Dad were directing them to their assigned tables in various rooms when Lance's red hoverer drew up at the door. I sent Sharine to tell Mom that Lance and his guest had arrived. By the time I returned my attention to the door, the two men were there, waiting.

Lance smiled at me and my heart turned over. Just two months more and we would be married, two months more and we would no longer have to endure the traditional live-apart of his people. Among my people, a commitment to marry allows a couple to live together. Not among his, Lance had told me. Among his people, the time between commitment and marriage was a time of separation and contemplation of the rights and duties of each partner. Because of this, we had never lain together. Wondering what that would be like created internal tension high enough I sometimes wanted to jump out of my skin.

Lance kissed me, a cool kiss, as is given before strangers. He motioned toward his friend. "Zjhanne, I'd like to introduce Karne Halarek, Lharr in Halarek. Karne, Zjhanne Verlith, researcher in Terran pre-industrial social history. Your people live like many of those she studies."

I thought that was a particularly clumsy remark, but if the Lharr thought so, he hid it well.

The Lharr was only a few centimeters taller than I. From the stories Lance had told about him, I had expected him to be big and powerful. He was lean and wiry instead, with eyes as gold as a cat's.

"Gentlefem," he said in Galac.

That surprised me. Somehow, I hadn't expected a feudal lord to speak either of the trade languages. Dumb, since I knew he had trained at the Altarian Naval Academy for five years. He probably spoke Sternlangue, too.

His long, slender fingers closed around mine but, instead of shaking my hand, the Lharr lifted it toward his face and kissed the air just above my skin. It was a custom I had only read about.

I felt as if the kiss disturbed a thin shell of air above my hand and I shivered. I looked at him more closely. There was nothing sinister about him. I told myself the shiver had just been a silly reaction to a man I knew had been trained for a military life. Though Lance *had* said Lord Karne's training had primarily been in peace negotiation. It would not have been only that. He lived on a world famous for its wars and feuds. He could not have survived ten years there without skill in weaponry and tactics. And killing.

Lance took the Lharr a little aside so I could greet three more stragglers without extra introductions. He pointed out to the Lharr some of the curiosities Dad had picked while selling our farm machinery on other worlds. I couldn't pay proper attention to the new guests. I found the presence of a man who lived daily with war and death very disturbing.

I glanced at the lean, tanned Lharr. Lance had said the lords of Starker IV were *very* touchy about slights to their honor or courage. Would the Lharr anger easily? Would he attack other guests if he took some social comment for an insult? I had studied societies where infinitesimal insults had led to duels and feuds that lasted generations.

I scolded myself for silliness. Lance, proud as he was of Karne Halarek's most violent adventures, would not have brought him here if the man weren't fit for civilized society.

Mom, in the door to the sunroom, was beckoning to us impatiently. Lance directed me toward her with a hand in the small of my back. His friend followed close behind. Mom had gone to our table and was standing behind her chair. I could almost see her foot tapping. She did not believe in holding up parties for late guests, even a guest of honor such as the Lharr Halarek.

We sat, Lance on my right, the Lharr on my left, with Mom, Dad, Pieter, and Abby in the other chairs. The caterer's helpers brought in the soup. I watched the Lharr Halarek out of the corner of my eye, not knowing what to expect. He ate his soup like everyone else, though. I felt mild surprise. I had half expected him to drink from the edge of his bowl, like a lord from Terra's Middle Ages, or to slurp when he sipped from his spoon, in spite of his years on Balder. Balder isn't all that civilized, either, but at least there the violence is ritual, regulated by law, and seldom deadly.

We on Fruhe draw a line, you see, between civilized people, who do not kill other sentient beings, and uncivilized, who do. Balder is on the borderline. Starker IV is centuries on the wrong side of the border. But the Lharr looked like a civilized person. He ate like a civilized person. Perhaps my preconceptions were too narrow. I hadn't had much experience with beings from the Outer Worlds. They didn't come to study at the university, so I met none at work. Dad must occasionally host one at the plant, but he never brought any home as guests, though Old Empire and Inner Worlds' foreigners came often. Pieter sometimes brought Gildsmen or XTs to dinner, but not people from the Outer Worlds. I would have to talk to the Lharr, though, perhaps even dance with him, because he was Lance's friend. I didn't like the idea. This man had killed.

One of the caterers leaned over my shoulder with the main course. The main course already, and I'd talked to no one. I was being as rude as I'd expected a feudal lord to be, but I couldn't eat and talk to a man who had killed other men. Even thinking about it made my stomach heave. Later. At the dance, I'd make conversation with him. Right now, memories of Lance's stories about the Lharr Halarek interfered.

Lance enjoyed telling us Karne Halarek's adventures. It was a vicarious enjoyment of what he thought was an exciting life, I supposed, but perhaps part of his morbid interest in such stories came from envy. The Lharr led a dangerous life. Lance had left the Academy under circumstances he would not talk about, and he considered his life as a commodities broker quite dull. That had always surprised me. I knew a number of brokers and dealers whose ulcers or asthma betrayed how exciting and stressful that career was. Even our Fruvan training in internal self-examination and healing can't overcome *chronic* stress.

Lance told these stories whenever the opportunity presented itself, which was in almost any group that included off-worlders.

During his first few visits with us, he thought to amuse and, perhaps, to impress us with his friend's adventures. He was angry when we got up and left the room the moment blood started to flow and men started to die. He had no understanding of the way Fruvans feel about violence and death then. He never noticed how pale some of the more violent details turned people or how angry others were to have such stories forced on them.

I glanced at Lance and he smiled that crooked, boyish grin I loved. We had so many common interests. Lance's lack of empathy was his worst flaw. Otherwise he was clever, witty, charming, tender, and sexy. I could put up with this one unpleasant trait.

Lance had a stock of perhaps ten different Karne stories. My family and I heard sanitized summaries of these from off-world guests, many of whom seemed both appalled at the violence on Starker IV and fascinated by it. At one time, I'd thought that if I listened a little bit further into a story each time he told it, I'd get used to hearing about blood and killing. Unfortunately, as I learned later from guests, the Kit story I tried to sit through was the worst of the batch. It was about the capture (which involved killing hundreds of people), ritual rape, and impregnating of the Lharr's sister. An enemy clan's attack on the sister's wedding procession and death after death after death came right at the beginning. My stomach began to churn and my head to feel light and unsteady. I had to run from the room before I threw up. I was very, very sick and had nightmares for weeks afterwards.

This incident almost made me back out of our engagement, but Lance was so bewildered when I accused him of really brutal insensitivity, and so contrite, and he comforted me with such tenderness, that I forgave him. I had chosen to sit in that room and listen, after all. I knew what his stories about the Lharr were like.

Dinner had reached the pause before dessert. I glanced at the Lharr again. He was leaning back in his chair, his eyes closed, his hands lying quietly on his thighs. He looked very tired. And very sad. I felt a twinge of sympathy for him. He had tried to break free of his people's savage way of life by going to the Academy.

The nanny came quietly across the room and whispered something in Pieter's ear. He grinned at us ruefully, got up, and followed the nanny out of the room. Last night, Pieter had listened to the story of the Lharr's sister's kidnapping all the way to the end, but Pieter's job exposes him to other cultures all the time. Pieter also likes to think nothing can ruffle him. Even he was rather green when he came out of the parlor at the story's end, however.

Pieter came back in a very short time. He sat and spread his napkin across his lap. "Nightmare," he said to the table in general. He turned to the Lharr. "I'd like to hear how you came to be here, Lord Karne. The Gild has refused to carry passengers from Starker IV for ten years. I once met Captain Telek, who commanded the last flight there. What happened?"

The Lharr's face hardened. "To Telek? He was sentenced to ten years in the mines at Arhash as an accessory to murder."

Pieter, being Pieter, didn't apologize for the misunderstanding, but plunged ahead. "I meant to the ban. Something major had to have happened. Gildcentral doesn't reverse itself very often on matters that concern its neutrality." Then Pieter caught the tension in some of the rest of us. Finally. "Or maybe you'd rather not talk about it."

The Lharr stared at him with those odd yellow eyes. The corner of his mouth twitched upward. "I don't mind." He sat up straighter. "Five years ago, House Harlan, a long-time enemy of my House, made a truce with us that was to last five years. It did. This impressed the Gild, because it was House Harlan that ten years ago hired the assassins that caused the ban."

"Assassins?" Sharine cut in. "What are assassins?"

Mom gave her a shut-your-mouth look, but Sharine ignored it. The Lharr looked at Mom with what could have been apology, then answered.

"Assassins are people hired to kill other people for political reasons, or for money."

Sharine swallowed hard and looked down at the tablecloth. "Kill" she understood, intellectually, at least. My opinion of the Lharr improved a little. He had answered Sharine's question honestly, a courtesy many adults would not offer a child, and he had phrased the answer so Sharine could understand it, but he had also kept it as brief as possible, which avoided offense, as much as the answer to such a question could. He really was a diplomat, then, and a man who respected children.

Sharine looked at him, at Mom, at the Lharr again, and took a deep breath. "But why? Why?" she whispered.

I heard a soft thump, which was probably either Mom or Pieter kicking her under the table. I was a little curious about the answer myself. We have nothing like assassination on Fruhe and those I study are so old that their impact on the victims' families or on the societies that permitted them has been entirely lost.

The Lharr looked at Sharine. "You don't really want to know, little one. The details make even strong, grownup Fruvans like your brother sick."

"Thank you," Mom whispered.

Sharine looked thoughtful for a moment. "Okay," she said finally. "I believe you. I'll wait till I'm a grownup to ask."

The Lharr smiled at her, a sudden, stunning smile. He then turned to Pieter. "To finish your answer. The truce wasn't enough, of course, but it showed the Gild Harlan's good faith. At the time he signed the treaty, Lord Richard proposed to lift the ban, promising that no House would bring feud onto Gild territory again and pledging fifty thousand Gildcredits to back the promise. Fifty thousand Gildcredits is a great deal of money on my world, where most trade is by barter, but Gildcentral didn't trust him. With good reason. Lord Richard's House doesn't keep its word unless it's advantageous to it. He did keep the truce, though, as I said, and a few months ago the Gild lifted the ban with the restriction that only two Houses at a time could have passengers aboard a Gildship. The World Council accepted that restriction."

Pieter nodded. "Sounds reasonable to me."

"Why would anyone violate Gild neutrality?" Sharine was treading on dangerous ground again, but with a brother in the Gild, she knew how important absolute non-involvement in planetary politics was for the Gild.

The Lharr looked at her seriously for a long moment, then looked at Dad, then Mom. They hesitated, then nodded. She would have to learn that there was violence and death in other places. Best, perhaps, to hear why some societies thought them reasonable from a man who had already shown he would be careful how he explained such difficult things.

"My world is ruled by nine families of noble blood. Do you understand what that means?"

"Like kings and queens?"

"Sort of, only our central power is not a king but the World Council, which is made of voting members of the nine Great Houses, and the minor Houses, and the Freemen, who are merchants and craftsmen and such." He paused.

Sharine nodded eagerly. I had to admire the man's care.

"Noble houses pass leadership by birth—the oldest son rules after his father and if he dies, the next oldest and so on." He paused again. "My sire—that's what we call fathers on my world—

had four sons. I was born third. I wouldn't ordinarily have been expected to become Lharr, especially since my sire favored the other three over me."

The Lharr shut his eyes very briefly. His voice had been even enough, but perhaps there was pain in that admission. The moment passed so swiftly I might have imagined it.

"So I was sent away to school, where I learned how to lead people to settle arguments peaceably. Everyone here learns that, right?"

Sharine nodded eagerly. "We start when we're five or six."

"I didn't get to my school until I was nearly twelve—"

"*I'm* nearly nine," Sharine said, interrupting.

The Lharr smiled slightly at her enthusiasm and went on. "On my world peace-making isn't a useful skill. It's considered cowardly. I learned to be good at it because I never expected to have to go home again. Then my sire and all my brothers—died. My mother, and the Council I told you about, called me home to be Lharr. I was the only possible ruler left. Do you understand that?"

Sharine nodded again.

"I didn't want to go back, but if I didn't, my mother and sister, all my aunts and cousins, all the children and the servants and the serfs would die."

Sharine went white. "How awful," she whispered.

The Lharr's face was quite bleak. "Yes," he said softly, "how awful." He spread his hands on the table and studied them as he continued. "So I started home and the Duke of Harlan, Lord Richard's father, sent assassins to kill me. Before I had even left Balder's Orbital, they tried to kill me. And, after the first try failed, on the ship home."

Sharine was biting her lip. Mom looked close to tears. I felt such pity for that boy that I almost cried, too. The Lharr levered himself up from the table and excused himself. Lance stopped him before he was more than two or three steps away.

"Aren't you going to stay for the toasts? They're next on the agenda."

"Toasts?"

Lance came to me and rested his hands on my shoulders. "Zjhanne and I are announcing our engagement tonight."

The Lharr shot Lance a look I could only call deadly. "You should have told me. I would have brought a gift." There was an edge to his voice that I couldn't explain.

Lance turned rigid. "Didn't I tell you about that?"

The question seemed feeble to me. Quite clearly he hadn't. Just as clearly, the news was a shock to the Lharr, and I wondered why.

CHAPTER 2

The Lharr left the room. Something subterranean was going on. Lance knew what it was. The Lharr Halarek knew what it was. My family didn't, and that worried me. But the toasts were made without incident and our gifts opened and the dancing begun. My first dance was with my intended, of course, and then my father, and then Pieter, and then—

And then the Lharr Halarek cut in. "I have business to attend to and must leave early," he said quietly beside my ear. "I didn't want to miss a chance to get a little acquainted with Lance's wife-to-be."

The band was playing a waltz and the Lharr danced it well. He led me in smooth swoops and turns. I felt almost as if we were flying. I hadn't expected to find such skill in a petty ruler from the edge of nowhere. I felt uncomfortable with the silence between us, though, and my topic of conversation, the lifting of the Gild ban, had already been explained.

"You have business here, my lord?" It was a stuffy sort of question, but it was all that came to my head at the time.

"My House deals in furniture-grade orak stone and orak carvings. I wanted to take advantage of my time here, but that means I'm going to have to get up very, very early in the morning to get where I'm going."

"Orak. That's a creamy, translucent stone, isn't it?"

He nodded.

"It's very rare here."

The corners of his mouth tipped up just a little. "That's why a trade connection would be so profitable."

I looked up to see if he was being sarcastic. His golden irises were arresting.

"It never occurred to me that the ruling lord of a royal house would tend to business like a merchant, Lord Karne."

He gave a soft laugh. "Then you don't know much about my world, gentlefem. Unlike the lords of pre-industrial Terra, the lords of Starker IV can read and write, so they take charge of their own businesses. How did you think our Houses survived? We have hundreds, sometimes thousands, of members and dependents. Feeding and sheltering and educating so many requires economic transactions of some kind."

To tell the truth, my mind had stopped thinking about Starker IV when it ran up against the feuds and the wars. I was supposed to be a student of such societies. How could I have let my own culture lead me astray about this one? I was embarrassed.

"My lord, I—I didn't mean to be either patronizing or insulting."

"No insult taken, gentlefem."

"I was also surprised you knew about my studies."

He smiled a little bit and executed a fancy turn. "It's only courteous to know a little about one's host and hostesses, so one can carry on a conversation. I pumped Lance for helpful information."

The music ended. We stopped at the edge of the dance floor. The Lharr stared down into my face.

"You know, I haven't seen blue eyes in years. Since Balder. My friend Egil Olafsson, from Balder, has blue eyes, but I haven't seen him since I was eighteen. Your eyes make me think of him. All my people have brown eyes."

I stared right back. He had to be pulling my leg. "You don't."

"I'm a half-blood. Thank you for the dance." He bowed with a little click of his heels and walked away.

I danced with him again later, but only as part of the pattern of a circle dance. He watched me, though. I caught his eyes on me often during the course of the evening. I was used to men watching me from a physical interest and I knew how to handle it if their interest wasn't welcome. This wasn't like that. It was a strangely assessing look and it made me uncomfortable.

Dad announced refreshments, which meant the dance and the evening were over. Lance and the Lharr were standing at the far edge of the crowd waiting to get into the sunroom, where the punch was. I couldn't hear what they were saying, but the Lharr's face was taut almost to rigidity. His lips made a thin, angry line. Lance's face was flushed and he seemed to be arguing or trying to persuade the Lharr of something. I watched them for a moment, wondering what was happening, yet knowing whatever it was was none of my business.

The crowd got smaller as more and more people succeeded in getting into the sunroom. Lance saw me and started toward me. The Lharr gripped his shoulder and made him stop. Lance turned redder and wrenched away. Because there were fewer people between us, I could hear them if I listened carefully.

Lance said, "I've explained enough."

The Lharr saw me, too, then, and made a visible effort to control his anger. He released his hold on Lance.

"If you're lying to me, Lance, you've made a very, very expensive mistake," the Lharr said. He brushed past Lance and crossed the distance to me quickly. He touched his right hand to his head and heart, our gesture of respect or farewell. Then he looked straight into my face and I was struck by the power of his golden eyes. "We have a saying that you should memorize, gentlefem," he said in a taut voice. " 'Watch your back.' " He turned his eyes on Lance and they grew cold as a cat's. "You have violated the spirit of our agreement, Lance." His face grew hard. "If this shipment weren't vital to my House, I'd refuse it because of what you've done to get it." He spun away and left the house.

I looked at Lance for an explanation, but he was looking after the Lharr. Fury and fear mingled in his expression. "How *dare* he!" Lance muttered, almost too quietly to hear. "How *dare* he criticize *my* methods? It took a lot of time and effort to find what he wanted. And his method of delivery isn't the most ethical in the universe. How dare he judge *me*?"

We followed the others into the sunroom in silence. Lance clearly did not intend to explain what had happened, at least right now. "Watch your back." The Lharr had warned *me*, not Lance. What could he possibly have meant? He didn't know me at all. Still, the memory of that warning made the hair at the back of my neck prickle.

Lance picked at his food, though I had planned the buffet around his favorites. He seemed tense. When guests began leaving, his goodbyes were abstracted to the point of being curt. It seemed as if he couldn't wait until the last guest had gone, and some of Mom and Dad's older friends lingered and lingered. I assumed Lance wanted to talk to me in private about his upsetting conversation with the Lharr, but, when the last guest had been seen out the door, what he asked me to do was walk down to the park with him. He went to the still-open door. He was *assuming* I would go, and me so tired all I wanted to do was sit down with a glass of punch, put my feet up, and shut my eyes.

"I don't want to take a walk. I'm really tired."

"I'm so tense, I've got to work some of it off. Please come with me." He was very hard to resist when he used that tone.

"What's wrong, Lance?"

"Karne and I had a business deal and he thinks I've cheated him on it."

I felt a sudden dread. "Did you?"

"No. Not exactly."

"Not exactly?" That didn't sound good.

"He wouldn't let me explain. He didn't—" Lance spun away and stared out into the moon-bright darkness. "I can't talk about it, Zjhanne. It was a secret arrangement."

This sounded worse and worse. "Was it illegal?"

"N-no."

I felt the warm, loving life I had dreamed of having with Lance slipping away from me. A secret arrangement. Maybe an illegal arrangement. And even if not that, he had shortchanged the Lharr somehow, or outright cheated him. And I'd found out about it only by chance, and by the Lharr's warning. I'd thought I knew Lance. The man I thought I knew wouldn't cheat on a deal. He wouldn't be so evasive with the woman he had promised to spend his life with, either. How dishonest or illegal was this "business"? Would I ever find out?

"Are you coming?" The question was almost plaintive.

He would be more likely to talk if we were alone. I sighed and wondered if it were still warm enough outside to go barefoot, because my dress-up shoes hurt my toes. It probably wasn't. It was well after midnight. I might as well go, though. I wouldn't be able to go to sleep anyway, not until I knew what was going on. What I could imagine had to be worse than anything Lance could really have done.

Lance put his arm around me and I could feel his mood lighten. We walked slowly toward the park. Maybe things would turn out all right.

The park's trees stood like a dark hill beyond the farm's grain fields. Moonlight edged all the trees' leaves with silver. It cast our shadows sharp-edged on the ground and washed away all color. A few bats skimmed silently past.

We entered the trees. The park stretched for many kilometers toward the city. A breeze whispered past, making leaves rustle. The moon silvered the path and that made the bushes and trees on either side seem blacker. I slipped my arm around Lance's waist, partly for warmth, partly for comfort. More tension melted out of him. Maybe I'd been exaggerating how important this problem with the Lharr was. Maybe everything *would* be all right.

He didn't talk, though. Here, far from listening ears, he said nothing about what was going on. He didn't even murmur silly lover things as he usually did on such walks. His silence let me hear the park's silence. It was unnaturally silent. The birds that usually objected in sleepy voices to our passing, the small animals that usually rustled and squeaked in the bushes and the grass, even the owl that usually sailed across our path at least once to inspect us didn't appear. A gust of wind rattled through the branches.

I shivered.

"Cold?" Lance tightened his arm around me.

"A little." It seemed considerably colder here under the trees.

A bird called once. I stopped to listen. That call didn't belong to a night bird. Behind us, another answered.

Lance was listening, too. He looked down at me. "You're still cold. Wait here a minute. I'll run back and get a shawl for you."

It was our park, a friendly, well-known place, but suddenly I didn't want to stay there alone. "I'll go w—"

But Lance was already gone. The mist hid him in seconds. Mist. My spine prickled. The mist was as unnatural as the daytime bird crying at night. It was too early for mist. Spring mists come just before dawn.

Bushes rustled, though there was no breeze. There had to be somebody in the bushes. I wasted no more time figuring the situation out. I spun and ran toward the farm.

"Lance! Lance! Wait for me!"

He didn't answer. He couldn't already have gotten too far away to hear me. Maybe the mist muffled my cries.

My feet seemed to tangle in each other. I stumbled, caught myself, ran on. Black-gloved hands lunged from a bush beside the path and clutched at my arm. I twisted free. Someone clutched the back of my dress and pulled me back toward the bushes and the dark.

"Lance!" Panic blurred my vision for a moment. My dress ripped then, and the pulling pressure was gone. Relief gave me a spurt of energy. I raced toward the moonlight just ahead. The unnatural mist rose higher. I wanted to look over my shoulder to see how many attackers there were before mist concealed them, but didn't dare risk the time. Our fields and the moonlight lay only a few meters away now. If I could reach them, I could see my assailants. I heard heavy boots thudding on the path. Maybe Lance had heard me and was coming back. No, the footsteps were coming from deeper in the park and there was more than one pair of them. The mist swirled around my head and shoulders now. It smelled funny. Bodies crashed through the bushes beside me. The path disappeared, appeared again, undulating like the sea. It didn't seem to be under my feet anymore. Gas. The mist was some sort of gas. I wasn't going to escape whoever attacked me. Oh, where was Lance? Surely he heard me screaming his name! I looked over my shoulder. Black shapes with misshapen heads were right on my heels, shapes that wavered and undulated like the path.

"Lance—!"

Rough hands muffled my scream, grabbed my body, held my arms, threw me to the ground. I tried to fight, but my assailants seemed to flow like water and my muscles refused to obey me. They bound my hands and gagged me. Someone barked an order, then another, in a language I had never heard before. The funny-smelling mist filled my nose and head. I felt weaker and weaker. Black arms, black-gloved hands, hooded heads with gas masks surrounded me. Several men hauled me to my feet. One man threw me over his shoulder and they all trotted back into the park.

Away from the mist, my head began to clear, though my muscles still would not obey me. Gas masks! The misshapen heads were gas masks. The men's breath soughed through them like wind through dry grass. These men weren't from Fruhe and they were taking me away. For rape? For . . . ? Stories of black ships that snatched women from their worlds forever flashed through my mind. No one knew where they came from or what happened to the women they took. Slave markets and brothels on pleasure worlds were two ideas. But slavers would take more than one or two women at a time.

The men stopped at the edge of a large clearing. A sleek black interstellar racer crouched on the grass. My mind, beginning to clear, went as black as the ship for a moment. They never came to the worlds of the Old Empire. Not now. No, not now. Not me!

Terror gave me strength. I kicked and twisted and knocked the man carrying me off balance. More men rushed toward us. Sibilant voices whispered urgently. I almost fought free, though four of them held me. Then came the hiss of gas, and the trees and bodies began whirling and fading, fading, until all was mist and then darkness.

CHAPTER 3

Someone screamed. I struggled out of sleep in panic and sat up, my heart pounding. I stared into the darkness. The room outside the closed bed curtains was quiet. Only then did fragments of the dream float back—the quiet walk with Lance, the park, attackers, a strange language, rough hands grabbing, the futile struggle against sleep gas. I realized it had been my own terrified screams that had awakened me.

Someone stirred.

Poor Jaklene, I thought. She had come running at first, but that was many nightmares ago and many lost nights' sleep. She didn't wake up right away anymore.

My heart still pounded frantically. I scootched back against the pillows at the head of the bed. There would be no more sleep this night, not for me, at least. The nightmare stayed too close for sleep. I needed something to take my thoughts off the dark woods and the gas and the grabbing hands. I could will another inch or so of hair to grow while Jaklene was coming, perhaps. Long hair was one of the prerequisites for getting out of these small rooms. Why did they insist I have long hair? Because women here always had long hair. It was the custom. It was a rule. They made peculiar rules for their women in this place, but, willy-nilly, the rules were mine, too, for now. I closed the concentration-of-changing around myself like a wall. All awareness of my surroundings faded.

Jaklene had to raise her voice to rouse me from my trance. Through the gap where she had pushed the bed curtain open, I saw that she had set the Torch in its stand. She stood watching with heavy-lidded eyes while I pulled my translit from the night table and slid its chain around my neck.

"I'm sorry, Jaklene," I said softly, so as not to waken the others. "Why don't you go back to sleep?"

Jaklene pointed to her bare neck, then to my translit, and said something in her language. It was a question.

She has to have been deeply asleep to have forgotten her translit, I told myself. Well, at least she can understand me. "I'll look at my window," I said.

Jaklene nodded and pushed the curtain the rest of the way to the head of the bed. I sat on the edge, recognizing the beginning of the morning ritual and hating every moment of it and of the class distinctions it represented. Jaklene was of noble blood and I had been carefully taught that that was important on this world. Many of the rules I was required to memorize before I could leave these rooms made very clear how important noble blood was, yet Jaklene was waiting on me as if she were of the servant class, just because I was the intended bride of Jaklene's lord. Bride, for the love of Heaven! As if my wishes about the matter made no difference!

Though I was a tall woman, the bed was also tall. Sitting on its edge, my feet barely touched the fuzzy rug. I watched with distaste as Jaklene slid slippers on those feet. There wasn't any point in resisting the ritual, though. I had tried and had always lost. There were too many of them and just the one of me. That had been made very clear to me from the beginning, that I was far from home, and alone, and beyond the reach of Federation law.

I could never go home. Lady Agnes said again and again that I could never go home. She couldn't seem to understand why I didn't feel honored to be snatched from my life to become the unwilling bride of a feudal lord on a world I would only willingly visit for research. I didn't even know which world it was. All I knew was that the people called themselves the Gharr.

Alone. Outnumbered. Without friends or allies. Those thoughts always gave me a chill and sometimes made me wish I could go noisily crazy. That way, I wouldn't miss home so much and I would be no use as a wife to the lord who had kidnapped me.

My chill this morning came from the room, too. The room's temperature went down at night, a holdover, I had been told, from the times these people's ancestors had lived on the surface of another world. The cities here still kept a cycle of "day" and "night," just as if the sun could reach into buildings cut many meters into the stone of this world.

Jaklene helped me into a velvet-lined robe that felt good against the cold. I wrapped it close. Jaklene curtseyed and went behind the curtain that divided the room to awaken Tamara.

I didn't understand the secrecy about where I was. What could I do with knowledge? The door to my suite was guarded day and night. I had seen no com equipment since I had awakened here. I knew no one who would help me.

The world was feudal, clearly, which made me suspect the Lharr Halarek had been a spy for some other lord. Maybe this was even Starker IV, though I'd never heard that the people there lived completely underground. Maybe the secrecy and the deep-buried rooms and the servants who didn't understand any language I spoke were all part of a plan to make me grateful to this lord when he finally released me.

I slid from the bed to stand for a moment on the fuzzy rug, then I walked across the room to the window. My slippers shushed against the cold stones of the floor. I slid my hand over the wall control and an imitation sun rose and sent a glow over an imitation horizon. Gradually its light gilded the artificial landscape, an alien landscape of barren plains, rocks, mountains, and bluish trees. I rested my forehead against the glass. The illusion of reality was skillful. I had believed I was really looking out the first time I saw it. Now I knew my quarters were tens of meters underground, burrowed into stone. My heart ached for the real trees and sunlight and fresh air of Fruhe.

I straightened and stared at the strange plants. *I will get home, even if Dad can't help me. The letter—* I shook my head. *If he'd been able to help, he would have answered by now. But I will get home, somehow. I'll outwit these people, this lord, and get home.*

The door to the hall opened and shut quietly. I turned. Lady Agnes, my tutor, stood beside the door. She bowed slightly when she saw my eyes on her. I nodded and the gaunt old woman bowed again, very slightly, because I was a member of the lord's family now, and came forward. I wondered with more than a little irritation what the lesson would be today. More history of the Gharr, perhaps. It was a bloody, tangled history, but then most feudal history was. I hadn't yet been able to find out why their society had stopped developing at this stage.

Or maybe Lady Agnes had an etiquette lesson in mind. She had so many rules about proper behavior for a Gharr noblewoman that

I found remembering them all impossible, yet remembering them and acting on them was a condition for leaving my tiny quarters. That I wanted no part of their life bothered neither Lady Agnes nor the lord who employed her. I was a woman, therefore I was to obey the lord's orders, even in his absence. And he was away from the manor. Lady Agnes had told me that many times.

I realized I was keeping Lady Agnes waiting. "Good morning," I said in strictest courtesy.

Lady Agnes replied in a voice less sharp than usual. "Good news, Lady Zjhanne. Your waiting is almost over. Your lord has come home."

She sounded so pleased! I wished Lady Agnes would stop calling him my "lord." I stiffened, just thinking about that. No man was my lord. I was Zjhanne Verlith, freeborn, a citizen in my own right of Fruhe and the Federation. My life was for no man's ordering.

If Lady Agnes noticed my anger, she ignored it and continued. "You'll wed soon, I'm sure. My lord has waited four winters to take another bride. It's past time. This House needs a son." Lady Agnes lifted a length of my hair and fingered it critically. "Almost long enough," she said. "A week more, I'd say, at the rate it's been growing, will be enough. Your lord will decide that tonight, though. You're to have a private dinner with him."

She turned to the curtain I had hung across the room early in my imprisonment, over Lady Agnes's protests, to give myself some privacy. They had expected me to live months in a single room with total strangers, where even the most intimate details of life had to be done in open view.

"Jaklene! Tamara!" Lady Agnes's voice was sharp.

The two young women hurried out, fastening the clasps of their translit chains as they came.

"Your lord is home again," she told them with the same pride and pleasure she had shown when she told me. "I'm on my way to tell him the Lady Zjhanne has learned her lessons well enough. She can continue practicing after the wedding. And her hair's almost a modest length. He'll announce a wedding date after his dinner with her tonight, I'm sure. Dress her appropriately." She turned to me. "We'll forgo your lessons today." She bowed slightly and departed.

The news was no less of a shock the second time I heard it. I had to get out. As soon as possible. This morning if possible. I licked dry lips. I was to meet the kidnapper tonight, was I? Not if I could help it. I ran over the few plans I'd been able to make, ignorant of the manor and world outside my suite as I was. Jaklene had told me we lived at the edge of the manor house and freecity of Ontar. Cities had Gildhalls. I hoped that, if I could reach a Gildhall, the Gildsmen would protect me from this kidnapper and his soldiers, even though he was a lord among the Gharr.

I almost wished I dared risk a meeting with this mysterious lord. I'd convince him he'd made a very serious mistake by kidnapping me. I'd tell him what I thought of forced marriages, marriages between strangers, and men who didn't dare risk revealing their identity. I'd—

But I didn't dare take the risk. This was an arbitrary man, who lived in a society that treated women as chattel. In such a society, my defiance could only make matters worse. Also, I didn't want him to see me. He had been on the ship that brought me here, Lady Agnes had said, but he had not been near me since I regained consciousness. She had frequently assured me that he would set a wedding date very soon after I knew enough of the rules of Gharr society not to shame him. I had considered shaming as a way to make him let me go home, but considerable thought on that subject convinced me such a tactic would more likely result in my death.

I didn't want to be around after Lady Agnes told him I was ready to wed. His last wife had died five years ago. After five years without a woman, he might be just a little impatient, and not just for a marriage. I felt a small shiver of disgust. To be thought of and used just as a vessel for an heir! The very idea was demeaning. I tossed back my hair and its weight brushed against my shoulders and back, a feeling I did not like.

Tamara picked up a hair brush. Jaklene lifted a brown marno dress from a hook on the wall. I endured the slow, awkward process of getting dressed with impatience. I wished they'd let me dress myself. But that battle, too, had been fought out and lost. Noble ladies did not dress themselves here. Jaklene began the long rows of buttons on back and sleeves. Buttons! They were such awkward, primitive fasteners!

Tamara arranged the long brown folds of the skirt, then motioned me to sit at the dressing table. She began brushing my hair the moment I sat down. Four extra hands on my body never failed to make me feel twitchy and irritable.

There was a knock on the door. When Tamara said, "Come," the sentry outside pushed the door open and a servant brought in the fast-breaking cart. Jaklene and Tamara turned to admire the young soldier for a moment. I could not see his appeal. I did take advantage of their inattention, though, to slip the tiny key to the jewel chest into my pocket.

Tamara resumed brushing. "Your hair has grown so fast, milady. I've never seen the like. Is it natural for your people?"

"Only when we wish it. We can control many of our bodies' functions when we wish it. Hair growth is one, preventing wrinkles or conception—" Suddenly I did not want to talk about anything connected with home. "Jaklene, hand me the gold pendant, please."

Jaklene went obediently to the wardrobe and lifted down the jewel chest, but couldn't open it. "Milady, the key's not here."

I snorted in disbelief, hoping the sound was convincing. "Don't be silly. Look underneath." I let my fingers lightly press against the key in my pocket. The "lost" key would get me out from under my ladies' sharp eyes for a while.

I caught Tamara's brush hand. "Help Jaklene look," I said. "I'll do this."

Tamara hesitated. Ladies of the Nine Families did not take care of their own hair. On the other hand, a lady-in-waiting did not argue with her lady. I took the brush from Tamara's hand and stroked savagely through my hair. How I hated that heavy mane! The brush hit a tangle with a yank that made my eyes water. I jerked the brush out of my hair and laid it on the dressing table with a crash. I clutched the edge of the table with whitening knuckles. God, forgive me, but I hated the lord who made me a prisoner! And to be *married* to him—

I straightened and stood slowly. He wasn't dealing with an ignorant, subservient Gharr woman now!

The ladies still searched for the key. I watched them scurrying around the room impatiently.

"Look in the common room," I ordered.

Jaklene and Tamara drifted toward the door with what I grudgingly admitted was the grace of women used to long skirts. I urged them in my mind to hurry.

To hide my own disappearance from their sight, I walked to a chest well out of their line of view and opened it, carefully leaving the metal hasp up so it clanged noisily against the stone wall. Moments later, I heard the women opening chests, too. I looked cautiously through the door. They had their backs to me at the moment and even if they turned, they would not be able to see the hall door from where they were. I could go if I left quickly.

I threw a glance around the room to locate things I might need before I found a Gildhall. I tossed the breakfast breads and fruit into a napkin and tied the corners to make a bundle, slipped a knife from the cart into my pocket, snatched up a cloak one of the women had tossed across a chair when she came in from chapel the night before, and crossed the room to the outer door.

I leaned against it, listening tensely. The sentry should be beyond the door to the right. I couldn't hear him. I looked apprehensively over my shoulder. The common room was not large and the ladies-in-waiting would soon be in line-of-sight with the hall door. I closed my eyes to visualize for a moment the hall outside. I had been down it only as far as the chapel, but whatever lay beyond that had to be better than this luxurious prison and a marriage I didn't want. Lance waited for me at home, probably out of his mind with worry and grief.

I slid the knife carefully through the crack along the forward edge of the door, then upward. It clicked faintly against the metal latch. I caught my breath and held it, listening. There was no response outside. I lifted gently and pushed the door open a tiny bit. The sliver of brighter hall light fell into my room. I let the latch down a little, experimentally. It fell clear of its staple. A few tension-tight muscles loosened. The first small step was finished. Moving as quickly as I dared, I eased the latch the rest of the way down, then slipped the knife into the bundle under my arm.

Hurry, hurry, part of me urged. Your ladies must be nearly around to the door.

Go easy, another part cautioned. You don't know where the soldiers are.

I flipped the cloak's hood over my head. I was so much fairer than the Gharr I would need all its shadow to escape notice. I pushed on the door. It was heavy and swung slowly. I stopped it half-open and peeped out. There was no one in sight. I took a gulp of air and launched myself down the empty hall. But the door's half-open bulk didn't shield me from view as long as I had hoped.

"Mistress Tamara!" a man shouted. "Stop!"

A soldier popped around a corner ahead, near the end of the hall. I dodged into the nearest corridor and ran wildly, hampered badly by the long skirt. Heavy boots pounded after me, sending echoes jarring along the bare walls. The cloak flared out behind and dragged at my neck. My heart pounded with fear. I must not be caught!

I whipped around corners and flung myself blindly from one featureless stone corridor into the next. At last I realized no footsteps pounded behind me and my panic lessened. Panting, I flattened myself into the small recess of a doorway. Behind me doors banged and men shouted, but the sounds were not as close as they had been and I scolded myself for allowing my fear to control me. I rubbed the soft sole of one velvet slipper against my leg. It was a good thing I didn't have sturdier shoes, because I would have worn them. With these, though, I couldn't be found by the sound of my running feet.

I looked cautiously out into the hall. No one moved along it. My breathing slowed and I tried to plan. Since everyone here lived underground, to go out, I must go up somehow. The barren hall offered no suggestions. I walked to my right, away from the sounds of search. When I came to an intersection, I turned right again. Ahead was a wide, sentry-guarded door, but beyond the sentry I thought I saw flowers. Was it possible the soldier hadn't heard yet about my escape? I looked at him sharply. He was looking at me. If he knew who I was and I ran, he would pursue. If he didn't know, walking past should be safe. I had to risk walking past. Those *were* flowers beyond him.

Do ladies-in-waiting leave their cloaks on for soldiers? I wondered. They must. They're nobility. Go slowly, act tired, any excuse to walk head-down. The napkin may look suspicious, but trying to hide it will only attract attention to it. Keep calm.

My modestly downcast eyes saw the military boots and blue-black pants. I let my shoulders sag more.

"Tired this morning, Lady Tamara?"

I nodded as if weary and passed into the bright courtyard. Every nerve hummed. Any moment the sentry might notice the differences between me and my woman. I was considerably taller than Tamara, for one thing. I lifted my head just a little. The brightness was not from a skylight, as I had hoped, but from light fixtures in the very high ceiling. I was intensely aware of the sentry's eyes on my back. Ahead, a huge door led into the dimmer interior of a large building. Above the door, balconies edged with boxes of red flowers projected over the courtyard. Entering the building was probably risky, but it offered immediate hope of going up, and maybe out. Once outside, maybe I could risk asking someone directions to the city.

I walked slowly, tiredly through the door. Inside there were no soldiers in sight. I let out a deep breath, relieved to be out of the sentry's sight. I looked around. A corridor ran between the outer door and the door to an immense room. To the right, beyond the immense room, doors lined the hall. To the left, at the end of the hall and past more doors, were deep shadows. One of them might conceal a stair. I started toward them. Halfway there, I froze. A woman was turning the corner. I looked frantically for a hiding place. I couldn't go back and with my limited Rom vocabulary, I couldn't answer the woman if she spoke to me. The woman's clothing was of a kind with Tamara's cloak, but of poorer quality. I prayed the woman ranked lower than Tamara.

The woman came even with me. I held my breath. The woman half removed her cape respectfully, murmured a formal Rom greeting, and passed on, apparently expecting neither recognition nor reply. I let out a deep, silent sigh and a prayer of thanks. I might not be so lucky the next time. I hurried toward the deep shadow. It was a stairway, a narrow one that went up, turned back on itself, and went up again. I lifted the front of my gown and darted up and around and up and stopped on the landing at the top. The stair opened into a hall much like the one I had left.

Just as I was about to step into the hall, I heard the heavy, important tramp of military boots. They might be looking for me. It seemed likely they would be. If a Gharr lord was willing to risk a galactic incident when he wanted a bride, he surely wouldn't allow such expensive property to slip away. I retreated to the first landing and waited in the shadows, ready to dash the rest of the way down if necessary.

Three men in the dark-blue uniforms marched past. I listened until their sound had faded, then headed for the nearest hall door. It was locked. So was the door next to it and the door next to that. But the door across the hall was different—wider, taller, and ornately carved.

It opened into a large library. I slipped in and shut the door very quietly. There was a heavy desk near the door with two stacks of books on it, a large masonry fireplace, a view-screen, a spiral iron stair that ran around the room on a rail just below the ceiling. The stair had been stopped with its landing at a door on the next level. Someone obviously had his own entrance to the library, and it was most likely the lord. Maybe his suite had windows to the outside.

I hurried up the stair. It was much sturdier than it looked, though it vibrated under me. Recklessly, I pushed open the door at the top. The room was empty, dark, and barer than mine. I scanned it quickly. Time was my enemy. I had to get out soon, because if I stayed in the manor, the lord's soldiers would eventually find me.

Of the room's three closed doors, one had light coming under its edge. I tried it. It opened into a hall just like the others. At the hall's end was another stairway. I didn't take time to close the door, but ran to the stairs and up. At the top another bare hall waited. My escape was becoming a nightmare. I saw myself running and climbing forever, up, up, up—

I forced that fear away. A more realistic fear was of the soldiers that seemed to be everywhere. They knew the house. I didn't. What might happen if they caught me I tried not to think about, but my insides tightened sickeningly. Then anger flooded in—anger at the monstrous building that went up and up without windows, anger at the Gharr lord who had kidnapped me, anger at myself for risking discovery by letting fear and frustration keep me standing frozen in a stairwell.

I shook off the sense of nightmare just in time. The soldiers I had seen, or others like them, had entered the stairwell at the level below, filling the space with voices and the clank of equipment. I turned to run but forgot to pick up the front edge of my long skirt. I tripped over it and sprawled on the cold floor. My bundle skittered across the hall, slammed into the corner, and burst open. The soldiers had reached the landing between levels. I scrambled clumsily to my feet, scooped up the fruit, and ran, hoping to be out of sight before the soldiers reached the head of the stairs, but I had lost too much time.

"There she is!" one of the men shouted.

"Lady Zjhanne, stop!"

They were not just stopping a person for security checks. They knew who I was. The pound of feet behind me changed rhythm from patrol to run. "Catch her. It's your hides if she finds a way out!"

I thought for a moment I would not be able to breathe, I was so frightened, then I put on a burst of speed, threw myself around the corner, and flung myself against the first door. Locked. Over my shoulder I saw the dark-blue uniforms. I ran past several doors, hoping to regain some of the distance, but I had been indoors and inactive too long. My muscles burned. My breath came in gasps. The soldiers were close enough I could hear their rapid breathing. I flung myself around another corner and tried to spurt ahead, but my energy was gone. Just ahead was a stair . . .

It went only down. The thud of the soldiers' feet and the rattle of their weapons were closer. Just ahead, on the corner, was another door. A hand caught the end of my cloak. Desperately I threw myself at the door. It flew open, into a room full of sunlight and plants. The hand on my cloak lost its grip. I slammed the door, dropped the latch, and braced my back against the wood, panting. The room was bright and open and filled with real sunlight. But I was not alone. A man stood with his back to me. In the seconds after the door slammed, he whirled and the gun that hung at his side seemed to flow into his hand.

CHAPTER 4

A gun on one side. Many soldiers on the other. My panting was harsh in my ears. The soldiers outside pounded on the door until it trembled. I spun and braced my hands against the door, knowing even as I did it that all my strength couldn't hold it against so many if the latch gave.

I looked down at the latch and the vibrating wood. The shouted words from outside were beyond my very limited Rom vocabulary. The man behind me shouted something. The pounding stopped. The soldiers tramped away. My own terrified panting rasped through the sudden quiet. I would have to face the man with the gun and deal with him somehow. I turned slowly, reluctantly, and looked up at the man's face. Lean, brown, with cold golden eyes . . .

"You," I whispered.

The Lharr Halarek relaxed a little and slid the gun back into its case, but his face remained cold and tight.

I had run right to my worst enemy. The men who had captured me so roughly had been Karne Halarek's. My terror in the park, the physical pain, and the wrenching agony of being torn from Lance—they were this man's fault. Hate surged up in me, hate such as my people had spent generations learning to diffuse, because it led to war. I fought the feeling. It was unworthy of a Fruvan, even after such a crime as this man had committed.

I shall not hate. I shall not kill. There is no cause righteous enough, or strong enough, to permit hate and killing.

I repeated the litany until the boiling in me cooled. There was no hope I could escape this room. The Lharr knew me. But perhaps he hadn't recognized me in Tamara's cloak and hood. Perhaps I could still get away. Had he noticed my "you" was in Sternlangue? Had he recognized my voice? Perhaps he hadn't heard me at all. I had whispered, more to myself than to anyone else. I had to try to escape him. I wouldn't be worse off for trying.

I stepped away from the door's support and curtseyed deeply, keeping my eyes demurely on the floor as Lady Agnes said was proper. Carefully concentrating on the awkward Rom syllables, I said, "Your servant, my lord."

He replied, but I didn't understand. I should have thought of that. He repeated, at the same rate of speed. I was lost. Tamara would have understood and answered immediately.

The Lharr said slowly, "Come here, woman."

I obeyed, trying to keep my eyes properly lowered. He hadn't recognized me, or he would have switched to a language I knew. I had a chance!

But there was sunlight and fresh green air. I had been almost a month without real sunlight and I let my longing for them betray me. I couldn't resist lifting my face to the brightness pouring through the skylight. As I did, the hood fell from my head.

The Lharr started. "Lady Zjhanne!" He recovered quickly and continued in Sternlangue. "Had I known you, my greeting would have been more cordial. Your cloak belies your rank, madam."

"So I had intended."

A tense, awkward silence dragged out between us. His golden eyes observed me gravely. I wondered how much I dared say. Finally the discomfort of his inspection forced me to say something.

"I want to be sent home immediately."

"A natural wish, madam, but one I can't accommodate."

He stated that so calmly, as if kidnapping were a legal and natural way to get a wife. I swallowed my anger. I had to think clearly. I had no power here. Words were my only tool. "I will *not* marry you. Even if I knew you and liked you, your method of arranging a marriage would make one impossible between us. It's barbaric. It's a thousand, no, thousands of years out of date!" I heard my voice rising. I felt myself trembling with rage and fear.

The Lharr ran a brown hand quickly through his already rumpled dark brown hair. He didn't look at me. "I understand your anger. Believe me, this is not a method I'd choose if I had other choices.

I didn't have other choices." He turned away and looked up at the skylight. "I brought you here in hope that, together, your ideas and my ideas could save my world."

"You expect me to stay here?"

"You have no other choices, either. Your world won't risk war for you. You know that."

"Send me back!"

He laughed, if one can call that bitter a sound a laugh. "Send you back? I spent everything I'd saved over the last five years and everything I could borrow for that one trip to Fruhe for me and for that Black Ship and crew. My future and my world's future depend on modernizing our society quickly. I can't do it alone. I've tried. I *had* to have help. Lance recommended you because you, with your research background, seemed best suited to understand what was happening here."

"No!"

"Yes!" He took a deep breath. "I gave Lance a list of what I needed in a wife and paid him to find one. He did. Then I checked you out myself before closing the deal with him. Romancing you was not part of his arrangement with me. *Absolutely* not part of the arrangement." He set his hands on my shoulders, much more gently than I expected. "Didn't you wonder why he didn't lie with you after the commitment had been made? It's usual on your world. It's usual on his."

"On his? That's not true." But doubt nibbled at me.

The Lharr's fingers tightened just a little. "Oh, but it is true. If he had lain with you, you couldn't have been my wife. Worse for him, he wouldn't have gotten paid, and he was to be paid very, very well."

"It's not true," I whispered.

"Your 'fiancé' is a snake, madam. From the moment I saw what game he was playing with you, I wished I'd never hired him, but by then it was too late."

"It's not true. It's not true." But the tears were coming, and doubt, and the memory of Lance running away as soon as he heard those birdcalls. Lance had known what those birdcalls meant.

Pain. Dear God, the pain!

"Believe me, madam, I didn't want an unwilling wife but, as I've said, I had no other choice." The Lharr tipped my head back. His golden eyes were full of concern and—regret? "My mother was a Black Ship bride and she learned to like living here. You could, too."

I'd believed Lance loved me. I'd believed Lance would wait for me. Yet now every suspicion I'd had that last night, every doubt, argued that, whatever the Lharr's reasons for kidnapping me, he spoke the truth about Lance.

I didn't know what to do with myself. Outside were soldiers. Here was a man who intended to wed me by force. Lance—I couldn't keep my faith in Lance. My life shattered in front of my eyes.

"I want to go home," I whispered.

"I know," the Lharr said, his voice unexpectedly gentle. "But you can't go home. Ever."

That was too much. I threw back my head and glared at him. "I'll find a way home. I *will*!"

"You can't. The Gild won't take you without my permission, not even your brother, and there is no other way to leave."

"Your *permission*? I'm a free woman, a citizen—"

"On Fruhe. In the Federation. Not here. Here you're only a woman. The wife of one of the Nine, true, but only a woman. Women have to have a man's permission to do such things."

"Dear God!" I hated the whimper that came out.

The Lharr pulled me toward him as if to comfort me. Comfort! When he was the cause of my grief? I shoved his arms away. He let me, but he lifted my chin with one hand until I had to look at him. He was not so much taller than I. I thought I saw pity in those golden eyes.

Pity only made matters worse. I wanted to howl with grief and fear and anger. I wanted to hide from this lord and his omnipresent ladies-in-waiting and his cold gray house. I wanted, in violation of all my beliefs and training, to pound on him until he lay bleeding on the floor. Trapped. Trapped. Trapped. Forever. I struggled with the anger until I had my voice under control again.

"You've taken everything life has ever been to me. My world, my family, Lance. Why should I help you?" Savagely kicking the skirt away from my feet, I spun from him and walked swiftly to the door.

Before I could open it, his hand closed gently but firmly on my shoulder and turned me around. His voice was steady, but I heard the strain of keeping it so. "You don't know what you say. The Gharr can't stay five centuries behind the rest of the galaxy while our contacts with it increase. Our serf-technicians and laborers, even the Freemen, resent the restrictions on their lives more every year. Change must come soon or Starker IV will blow apart from the inside. This is no whim, no light experiment we're taking on. My Family and our allies, we risk all we have, our very lives, for change."

I tried to shrug off his hand. "It's not my problem. You can't force me to help. I've failed today, but I *will* escape."

"Madam, you'd try the Guardians!" He shook me sharply. "How long do you think you'd last on the surface? There are no roads up there, no cities, no *people.* I may not be able to protect you even here, in my own house. My second wife was assassinated in this house. If you could reach the surface—and I don't intend you to be able to—I'll find you. If I can't, the Duke of Harlan will. My wife would be a valuable hostage, and what Richard does to prisoners, especially prisoners of my House, is extremely unpleasant. The truce between Harlan and Halarek is over, remember? That's how I could get to Fruhe." He gave me another hard shake. "If you were a Gharr woman, I wouldn't even try to explain this to you!"

"But a Gharr woman would be no political use to you, would she, Lord Karne?" I twisted to free myself and failed. "Take your hands off me! I'm not a child to be shaken!"

"You're acting like one." But his grip loosened.

"Because I dare oppose you? No, Lord Karne, I resent being made a pawn in your game. I more than resent it." I still couldn't break free, but I didn't have to keep looking at him. I stared angrily at some vines far to my right.

His hand gently and insistently forced me to look at him. I resented the feeling of smallness in even such a slight looking up and tried to turn my head away again. He wouldn't let me.

"You'll hear me out." His voice softened. "I love life and I love the Gharr. I can't watch my world tear itself apart. I married you because you can help me bring my people into the present. I'll marry you in public so there can be no doubt in friend or enemy that the ceremony was well and truly done. The Lord knows, I wouldn't marry a temper like yours of my own pleasure." He lifted a strand of the hair I'd spent so many hours forcing to grow. "Your new quarters are ready and your hair has grown a modest length. We'll wed tomorrow noon."

The blood drained out of my face, leaving cold emptiness. I felt dizzy and faint. *So soon!*

I must have wobbled, because the Lharr swiftly caught my elbows. I submitted for a moment until I had collected my wits. Then I straightened and tried to back away, but he didn't let go. His golden eyes, filled with concern, looked down at me disturbingly.

"I'm all right now," I whispered. "Please let go. The shock—somehow I couldn't believe you meant to carry out this insanity." I turned to go.

"You weren't dismissed." The Lharr's voice was cold.

I whirled, furious with him, his plans, his insufferable masculine superiority. "I'm freeborn. No man keeps me or dismisses me like a servant or a robot!"

He stiffened. "As my wife, your place is to be as obedient to me as any of the servants."

"You won't live long enough to see that happen!"

"We wed tomorrow."

Tomorrow! Again I felt the heat that comes before fainting. I gathered myself and forced away the weakness. "Never!"

He gripped my shoulders with steely fingers. "You'll change your mind before tomorrow noon, or by the Four Guardians, you'll wish you had! You're too important, too expensive, to be allowed the luxury of rebellion. Let your imagination work on the possible alternatives to marrying me, madam."

The cold anger in his face, the icy intensity of his voice, terrified me. A Gharr lord's power was absolute. He could do anything he wished to "persuade" me. And I didn't know enough about Starker IV to know what he meant by "alternatives," but I was sure they would be very unpleasant. Anger was my only defense against my terror. "I'll never consent to be your wife!"

"You are already my wife, madam, by the ancient ceremony of Sheet and Broken Seal, properly witnessed."

I gasped. Broken seal. That was clear enough, if combined with the sharp discomfort I felt after I awakened from the sleep gas. My trap only got deeper and deeper. I struck back, knowing it was useless. "In Federation law, I'm not bound by a ceremony I wasn't aware of."

"You're not in the Federation now. Our law binds, and after tomorrow, the church."

I couldn't breathe. I couldn't think. He was snatching away every hope. "The church requires my consent."

"Aye. And you'll give it, madam, or by the Guardians, I'll force your vow from you. You'll play your part here, eventually, as my mother learned to. Perhaps later you'll like it here, as she did. I'll make your life as easy as I can."

"You really expect me to cooperate."

"Of course. Women always have."

"Well, *I* won't."

He laughed harshly. "What else is there to do? Even if you could escape my Holding, what would you do? The Freemen here won't violate their precious neutrality to help you and I can assure you you don't want to fall into the hands of others of the Nine. You must ask my sister Kit about that sometime."

"Could they do worse than make me a prisoner for life? Raped at my husband's pleasure?"

Brown sparks flared in his eyes. "By my Mother's Blood!" He caught my arm to prevent me turning away and forced me to meet his strange, compelling eyes. "That once, on the ship, was *necessary,* for legal reasons. I won't bed you by force. By the names of the Allfather and the Four Guardians, I won't bed you by force!"

I stopped struggling. Angry and frightened though I was, his eyes and face convinced me. I believed him.

I said nothing. After a few moments the Lharr propelled me out the door with a firm hand on my elbow, down the hall, and into a lift. We rose silently through a shaft of solid rock. Then the door opened onto a large, curved garden. Beyond the open side of the curve, mountains reared blue-green and black. Far to the left they faded into yellow-green plains. Wind rattled through trees and bushes just leafing out and shoved gray clouds across the gloomy sky. The Lharr led me out onto the frost-crisped lawn. He waved his hand toward the mountains.

"This is my Holding. The land from here to the third range belongs to my House, and the plains far beyond the horizon." He looked out across the forested hills and rocky ridges to the mountains that filled the sky. "Much is so rocky and dry that only the wildest and strongest animals survive. To your right, that flat area between the mountains and the hills—that's the pass into the Desert of Zinn. We sentence our worst criminals there and escaped serfs go there to hide. Only a tiny percent survives. We patrol its borders."

In the following silence, the wind clattered loudly through the trees. Above the mountains thunder rumbled.

"The spring rains are coming. They'll complete the thaw." The Lharr waved toward the barren foothills and empty plains and continued. "The plains are dry and cold by Fruhe's standards, but our herd animals do well. Caravans come in summer when the forage is good. The nearest Holding is almost two hundred kilometers away and the next town half that far, so we almost always travel by flitter."

It was daunting. I didn't want to admit it, but the landscape was daunting. I spun away from him and headed toward the open lift. Two hundred kilometers to the nearest neighbor. And where was the nearest Gildhall? Hope slid away.

The Lharr followed silently, a silence he didn't break until the lift door slid open onto the hall near my quarters.

"Your level, madam."

I summoned all my will to keep my voice steady. "Goodbye, Lord Karne."

But he followed me into the corridor.

"I'll find my room," I said, my control on the verge of shattering. "Please, I want to be alone. *Please*, my lord."

A shadow crossed his face, but he said, "Go nowhere alone."

I remembered what he had told me about his second wife. Assassinated. And Lady Agnes had said the Larga Charlotte's quarters had been near the ones I now occupied. The Lharr took my arm and walked me to my rooms in silence. A soldier started from his post at an intersecting corridor as we approached, but the Lharr waved him back.

He turned to me at my door. "Madam, we'll forget that dinner tonight. Tomorrow I'll send your retinue to you, three hours after fast-breaking. Be ready."

He started to leave, then turned back and his voice had less of an edge to it. "I'd like us to be friends, but at the very least remember this: My enemies are many and powerful. Only by keeping a truce between the two of us can either of us survive."

He pulled my door open, bowed gracefully, and strode away. I watched him go.

Tomorrow. I was supposed to marry him, tomorrow. A stranger. And the man I had thought to marry had apparently betrayed me into the hands of this one. The agony of believing that was just beginning to twist inside me.

My ladies burst into the hall, questioning, scolding, demanding. Their yammering was more than I could stand on top of everything else. "Get out!" I snarled. "Leave me alone!"

"But such ill luck, milady, seeing him too soon. I'll say a prayer to protect you."

"Maybe if you sleep with your head at the foot of—"

"That old thing's never worked. My mother told me—"

My anger boiled over. "I told you to leave! I don't want any of your confounded charms! Nothing bad will happen just because we saw each other before the wedding! Get away from me! I want to be alone. Go away!"

"You mean, without any of us here? No one at all?" Tamara's voice was injured and confused.

"Exactly. Now get out!"

They left obediently, but with unhappy faces. I realized, watching them, that what I needed so desperately apparently frightened them. Only later, when I was calmer, did I realize that all their lives my ladies had never been alone, just as I wasn't really alone as long as they were on their side of the curtain. I hadn't been truly by myself since leaving Fruhe.

A few minutes later I was standing in a hot shower. It relaxed me but it couldn't wash away the pain. I knew what the Lharr said was true without knowing how I knew.

Lance! Lance! The pain was beyond anything I could have imagined.

My choices spun round and round in my head, pursued by the pain. Refuse, consent, escape, refuse, consent, escape. Slowly the relaxing water eased the knots in my mind. If I refused, I'd never find a way home. And the Lharr had pointedly shown the impossibilities of escape, at least without help. Maybe I could talk to Pastor Jarvis. He seemed kindly at chapel. Perhaps as a leader in The Way . . . Then I thought of the rituals here, gone a thousand years from the services of The Way on Fruhe, and decided that the first loyalty of any Gharr chaplain would be to his lord.

Reluctantly I stepped out of the stream of hot water and into the steam-filled bathing cubicle. I must marry the Lharr, though it wouldn't be a true marriage. It couldn't be.

CHAPTER 5

I didn't sleep well that night. A wedding meant that by law and The Way I would be bound to the Lharr until death took one of us. The Lharr had said plainly that if I didn't say the vows willingly, he would force them from me. Did I want to find out what he meant by that? If I cooperated, it might convince the Lharr I'd given up hope of home. He would at least release me from confinement. Free, I could surely find somewhere to go and someone to help me. But if I cooperated, I'd be married to this backwater lord for the rest of my days. Home or here, he would still be my husband.

Although my thoughts chased each other dizzily all night, I saw no alternative to cooperation. Yet I dreaded the emptiness of a Gharr noblewoman's life.

Jaklene awakened me in plenty of time. She, Tamara, and the tiring women scurried about for hours, preparing me and chattering.

"How lucky, milady, to wed such a great and good lord." Tamara yanked tight the boned corset and cinches.

"He'll never beat you. The Lharr Odonnel pounds his wife regular." The little tiring woman pulled several layers of woolen ceremonial petticoats over my head.

"You'll have handsome children, milady."

"House Halarek is the best on Starker IV."

"He'll be generous, too, milady."

"He so wants a child, milady. His little girl died of the Sickness, you know."

"How would she know, Tam? That was seven years ago."

Jaklene helped me into the heavy white brocade wedding gown and fastened the wedding necklace of massive jade beads around my neck. Their weight reminded me again that this was not a bad dream, but reality. Then Lady Agnes and Tamara fastened a long, fur-trimmed velvet cloak around my shoulders and arranged it over the long brocade train. Jaklene carefully brushed my hair into a veil over my shoulders and back. Then she set on the headdress, a tall cone covered with gold beads and velvet from which a jewel-encrusted veil hung, reaching from the peak almost to the floor.

I walked cautiously across the room. The dress was very stiff and made me stand very straight. I could keep the cone balanced, though, if I moved slowly and carefully.

The bride's military escort arrived, wearing the green shoulder patch of the Lharr's personal Lifesguardsmen. Then came the bride's retinue—female relatives and friends of the family, I supposed. I didn't know any of them. Once everyone had assembled, the procession to the Great Hall began. Afterward I would remember little about that long walk beside the noise, the expensive clothes, the perfumes, and Lady Agnes reminding me of the differences in the ritual of The Way here and murmuring the Rom words to familiar prayers and responses.

Suddenly, among the faces that lined the street, I saw a familiar one, a Gild friend of Pieter's. I couldn't put a name to the face, but it caused a spasm of longing for my family.

A sharp pinch from Lady Agnes brought me back to the present. "Madam, you disgrace your lord by this unseemly staring."

I looked desperately toward the Gildsman. He recognized me with a tiny smile and a tinier nod of his head. Aware now of the whispers around me, I continued the slow march to the main gate and then to the Great Hall, trying all the time to keep my eyes sedately on the ground in front of me. Ahead, a ragged boy darted out of the crowd and snatched at the gold bangles on a noblewoman's sleeve. He got nothing, but he eluded the grabbing hands and disappeared into the crowd. I envied him. I would melt into the crowd and disappear, too, if I could. Later, if the Gildsman would help me, if I could find a way to book passage, if, if . . . My future was a frightening question mark. Even if I got home somehow, I could never marry. Tears of grief and frustration stung my eyes.

Lady Agnes pinched me again. "Madam, pay attention! The entire company stands, waiting for you to proceed to the altar."

The tears slid out, and through their mist I saw a huge hall crowded with people. My tears blurred their faces. As I stepped through the door, they all knelt. The scent of the flowers they wore mingled with the thick pungency of incense floating down from the gallery. Eyes appraised me as the eyes of the common people outside had not. I stared fixedly at the rough wooden cross suspended in the haze of incense at the head of the Hall. When I could not manage both balancing the heavy headdress and looking at the cross, I returned my eyes to the stones in front of my feet.

My companions fell back and the buzzing of the guests faded. I stood alone and afraid. I looked up at the bishop and the man beside him and tried to hide my trembling. The Lharr stepped forward and gently took my icy hand in his warm one. From that moment to the passing of the kiss time passed as in a dream. The words Lady Agnes had gone over so many times came without thought. The kneeling and other ritual motions she had also taught well. When we rose for the last time, the bishop blessed us both and kissed the Lharr on both cheeks and on the mouth. The Lharr, now forever my husband, gave me the three kisses. Then we marched through the silent, fragrant crowd to a dais at the back of the Hall.

"I'm glad you made this decision," the Lharr said. "I would've kept my promise." He gave my hand a little squeeze. "I'll do what I can to help make getting used to us easier."

He beckoned to my ladies and turned to greet the guests that swept toward us. My ladies drew me into a small alcove under the gallery and began the tedious task of braiding my hair into a sort of circular nest for the headdress.

I hadn't realized how the heavy cone was straining my neck until Lady Agnes lifted it off. I sighed and dropped gratefully into the chair Tamara pushed forward. Tamara and Jaklene braided my hair and wound in flowers and aromatic leaves. Lady Agnes resumed her lecturing, this time about Gharr etiquette at banquets. I listened with only half an ear.

When Lady Agnes had concluded her lecture and set the cone into the nest prepared for it, I motioned Donna, the little tiring woman, to hold a mirror for me. In it I saw reflected a woman considerably overdressed, with lines of tension around her mouth and between her eyes. However, there was nothing I could do to change the picture. Brides of House Halarek had dressed this way past memory.

Lady Agnes led me to my place at the Lharr's right hand. He was in the midst of the ceremony of renewing homage, but he interrupted it long enough to give me a brief, approving smile and to kiss Lady Agnes affectionately. When the next vassal came forward and knelt, the ceremony resumed.

The vassal placed his hands between the Lharr's and said some words. The Lharr said some words, raised the man, kissed him on both cheeks, and sent him away with a small, elaborately wrapped package. None of the men wore translits, so I understood nothing they said. The parade of men who owed homage seemed endless, although there couldn't have been more than thirty. The ritual for each man was slow and carefully done. I tried to stand still, as Lady Agnes had told me I must, but my neck and shoulders ached, my nose itched, and my wool petticoats became hotter and more uncomfortable every minute. Just when I was sure I could be still no longer, the oaths of fealty had all been made. My husband led me to the head of the Hall, where the altar had been, and seated me at the center of a long table.

That was apparently the signal for the banquet to begin. Servants in the deep-blue livery of the House entered bearing huge pitchers of wine and ale, meat pies, long platters of roast pig and venison, tureens of gravy, quantities of breads and butter, jellies, salads, vegetables. I lost count of the courses. Like us, the guests sat paired, man and woman, each pair sharing a long platter. I ate mechanically. The food tasted like paper, like a last meal. My old life was dead. I would never be free of the Lharr, never. Until he died. The Allfather knows I couldn't kill him or cause his death, either. But this was a very violent world. Perhaps I wouldn't be bound to him as long as a lifetime.

Such thoughts come hard to Fruvans.

Soon I had eaten all my stays would allow, but still the food came. The Lharr talked quietly with his guests, occasionally pressing me to try a little fruit pudding or meat salad or carameled potatoes.

The noise in the Hall increased as guests began reaching their appetite's end. People conversed at high volume between tables. Some guests had brought dogs, some children, some hawks. The children and dogs played and fought around and under the tables. Overhead, hawks screamed and struck small birds that had flown from a pie. I wondered vaguely how the cook had baked the crust and not the birds. On the floor of the Hall, masters shouted at their hawks and, between gulps of ale, made wagers at the top of their lungs. Under the bridal table, a hound loudly crunched a bone. Suddenly he snarled and a muscular body shoved against my legs. I drew my feet as far under my chair as I could and tried to ignore the noises under the table. A page offered the last of a long line of meat pies. The Lharr wanted to take a piece for me.

"Come, madam. You've eaten almost nothing. Take some pie, and ale to wash it down."

I shook my head. "Thank you, my lord, but I've had too much for comfort already."

Lord Karne waved the page on. Another page placed a bowl of fruits and cheese beside us. The Lharr offered it. When I shook my head, he selected a hard rectangular fruit and motioned the page to pass the bowl on. He looked at me.

"Since you've finished . . ."

The Lharr motioned to Gareth, his seneschal, who motioned to the musicians and called out, "The dancing."

The Lharr pushed back his chair. "Come. We lead the first round." He stood and extended his hand.

Under the tight stays, my stomach churned. Besides, I didn't want to be close to this man if I didn't have to be. But I must be polite.

"My lord, I've eaten so much . . ."

He beckoned me up. "Come, madam."

"I know none of your dances, my lord," I murmured.

The Lharr's face registered an interesting combination of irritation and amusement. "That I know. But the first dance is a necessary part of our wedding ritual. Come." He thrust his hand closer. "We've replaced the traditional trakka with a—well, you call it a waltz."

When I still didn't stand and come, the Lharr closed his hand around my wrist. "Our guests are waiting." His voice and eyes had gone hard. No refusal would be accepted.

I was sure that if I didn't stand, he'd pull me to my feet and drag me onto the floor. I stood reluctantly. He unclipped my velvet cape and train and sent them away with a page, then led me onto the tiled dance floor. He moved smoothly into the music, performing the ancient steps easily and with grace. It brought painful memories of my engagement party and Lance—

Guests joined the dancing, two or three couples at a time, and many of these danced with the vigorous, graceful whirling I had always associated with waltzing. Even with a skillful partner and no spinning, I couldn't enjoy the dance. My meal shifted unpleasantly. The headdress pulled the muscles of my neck and was giving me the beginnings of a fierce headache. I wanted to sit down.

"My lord . . ."

But his expression was withdrawn, as if he didn't hear me, and my question faded away. We danced on. More and more guests followed the pull of the music until the floor was crowded. The musicians increased the pace and everyone spun faster and faster. It was too much for me.

"Lord Karne, I must sit down or I'll be sick. Please."

He glanced down at me, perhaps to see if I were telling the truth. "Of course, my lady."

He released me and led me back to my chair. He politely helped me sit. "I hope you'll be better soon, madam," he said. "In the meantime, I must play host." He bowed and left the table.

Soon I saw him weaving through the crowd toward two middle-aged gentlemen who were drunkenly swinging away at each other with their heavy mugs. Above the laughter and shouting and music, hearing what he said to them was impossible, but the men hunched their shoulders and shuffled their feet, then shrugged and laughed and shook hands.

Across the Hall, a juggler tossed shimmering silver balls in a circle over his head. On a small platform near him a troop of acrobats bounced and tumbled. Their flexibility so fascinated me that I wasn't aware a man was standing beside me until he spoke.

"May I have the honor of the next dance, milady?" he said in Sternlangue.

When I turned to look at him, he bowed gracefully and extended his hand. He had a smooth, pleasant face, with what seemed to be the typical deep-brown eyes and hair of the Gharr. He wore a forest-green tunic and the furs and jewels of a nobleman or rich merchant.

I smiled and shook my head. "I'm sorry, sir. I'm not feeling well. Perhaps later . . ."

The man made a sympathetic grimace. "Could I cheer you with a song, then? 'A song can soothe the savage breast.' Or is it 'beast'?" He didn't wait for an answer but called to one of the roving jongleurs to bring his lute.

I did not want company. "I'd rather—"

He smiled charmingly, turned his face toward the lute, and began to stroke the strings and sing softly. His voice was a pleasing mellow tenor and the song was quieting, though I couldn't understand the Rom words. The regular flash as he touched the strings of the green stone in the ring on his right hand was also soothing. I relaxed and closed my eyes. The stranger sang on and on and the noise around us faded before the song. I had almost decided he was an entertainer who was wealthy enough and popular enough to be a guest when he put down the lute. There was a silence, a spate of applause, then laughter and shouting began around us again.

"Better now?" His voice held polite concern.

I opened my eyes and smiled at him. "Aye. You sing beautifully."

He smiled back and handed the lute to its owner. "A lovely compliment from a lovely lady. I was well trained. Now I claim as payment a dance before your lord gets here."

He was more observant than I. The Lharr was coming rapidly through the crowd toward the head table. His face looked strangely forbidding. I assumed I had broken some rule of female etiquette by speaking to this man, but I felt too calmed by the song to worry about it.

I turned to the singer. "A dance for such a song is small payment. But something slow and gentle."

He laughed and bowed with quick grace. "As you command, Larga."

It was the first time anyone had called me by my new title. The stranger helped me to my feet. I assessed my situation. I was still uncomfortable, but no longer sick. It would be all right.

The man talked easily and joked as we walked to the musicians' platform. The leader bent down and smiled ingratiatingly in response to the stranger's whispered request.

"Immediately, my lord."

My wits, made sluggish by too much food, roused a little at the title. This was not a merchant or an entertainer, but a man of the Houses. Maybe the Lharr looked grim for good reason. Lady Agnes had made very clear how alliances shifted here and how dangerous political mistakes could be. I was in no position to make stupid mistakes. I touched the stranger's arm.

" 'My lord'? Who are you?"

"What's a title between friends? Call me Richard." He swept me onto the dance floor. "My mother came here as you did," he said, giving me no time for further thought, "though her people are close cousins of the Gharr. But why talk about me? I don't think there's one person of the Nine Families who isn't wondering about you. Karne's kept you hidden so carefully away that you're a mystery of the first magnitude. I'd love to be the first to know more about you than that you're a Black Ship bride. How do you like your new home?"

"Home? Fruhe is my home, my lord."

"Hmmm. Interesting. How do you like it here?"

Something told me he already knew the answers to his questions. I didn't like feeling set up. I'd give him little he could use for gossip. I touched the translit on my neck.

"I'm lonely, because no one speaks my language or Galac or Sternlangue, not without one of these, at least. Except the Lharr. Have you ever lived anywhere that you longed to hear your native language and no one spoke it?"

"As a matter of fact, I spent a year off-world at school. Before the Gild embargo on Family passengers. I know what you mean." He led me through an interesting and difficult spin.

It was a mistake, if he intended to pump me for information, because my head began to spin, too, and my stomach disliked the effect. "I have to sit down, my lord."

He smiled, danced us to the edge of the floor, and set a hand on the small of my back to steer me back to the dais. "Tell me about your family," he said.

I saw no way that that information could do any harm and it felt good to talk about home on a day when my life had been altered forever and without my permission. "Pieter, my older brother, is twenty-eight and captain of the Gildship *Phoenix*. Zjhaques is six and my younger sister Sharine is eight."

"You must be very proud of Pieter."

I managed a weak smile. "We are."

Richard steered me around a group of acrobats. "Have you moved into your new quarters yet?"

The sudden change of subject confused me. "New quarters?"

"Aye. Now you're wed you've moved into the manor proper, haven't you?" His voice had taken on a curious intensity and his eyes—

It had been a mistake to talk of home and family. I felt on the edge of tears. It had been a mistake to leave the table with this man. His hand had slid from an impersonal touch at the small of my back to a weight around my waist. I couldn't remember doing anything that, on Fruhe at least, could have been interpreted as flirting, but somehow he had misinterpreted my interest in him. If flirting with strangers was improper for a married woman on Fruhe, it probably earned weeks on bread and water here.

"Your hand is out of place, my lord. Take it off me." I intended for my tone to be sharp and convincingly firm, but it came out wobbly, betraying both my illness and my impending tears.

Richard laughed and dropped his hold. He also abandoned his new line of questioning. Over the music floated the thin clear song of a jongleur and the jingle of gloxinells. Near us, a man shouted exultantly as his dice came up winning. I marveled at these people, who could eat four times an ordinary amount of food, then play and dance and drink, when all I wanted to do was sit down. I trembled with nausea and weariness. We walked under the gallery arcade toward the dais. It seemed like the bridal table was a long way off.

Richard bent so his mouth would be nearer my ear, so I could hear him better over the noises in the Hall presumably. "Have you seen Lord Karne's Lifesguardsmen yet?"

"L-Lifesguardsmen?" I stalled for time. I remembered the terror of waking in the Black Ship's cabin with soldiers around me, the Lharr's personal soldiers. "Aye. I've seen them. I think."

"I've heard they're very good. Highly skilled, smart." Again there was that prodding tone.

I did not need to come from a military world to sense that this also was private information. I shrugged elaborately. "Fruhe has no soldiers, so I can't say. Tell me about your ring, Richard. I've never seen one like it."

That was a clumsy shift of subject, but it was all my spinning brain could manage. The tiny upward twitch at the corners of Richard's mouth showed he saw right through my request, but he honored it and held his hand where I could better see the ring. A golden snake with ruby eyes coiled up out of the depths of a deep-green stone.

"Green and gold are the colors of my House. I saw this in the window of a jeweler on Rigel IV. The craftsman bound himself to make this design only for me. I take the ring from my finger, thus"—he demonstrated—"and give it to someone I wish especially to honor. Or to think I honor him. Then I put another just like it on. I give very few, so I don't think anyone's caught on yet." He extended the ring toward me. "Here, you may have—"

"My wife accepts no gifts from you, Richard."

Richard and I both jumped. The Lharr put his arm possessively around my waist. "I'd like to speak to the Larga. Alone."

Richard slipped the ring back onto his finger as if he had just been showing me the carving and waited several seconds, to show the Lharr his icy stare wasn't impressive, before he bowed courteously to me and strolled away.

The Lharr's set face frightened me. I spoke quickly to defend myself. "His face, his bearing, his whole manner say he thinks he's irresistible, don't they, Lord Karne?"

"Is that why you spent so long with him, madam? Why the two of you avoided me? He charmed you?"

"Avoided you?" I shook my head. "I can't see how you can interpret anything we did as avoiding you. As for Richard, he amused me, and I was a challenge for him. He knows his flattery impressed me little."

The Lharr pulled me into an alcove. "What did you talk about?" His preemptory voice got my back up.

"I don't see that that's any of your business."

"My bitterest enemy woos you, singing and dancing. He questions you, offers gifts, and you say it's none of my business?"

"Our 'truce' won't last long, milord, if you don't try to trust me. I have quite enough sense to refuse a gift from a stranger. And I'm not used to being thought stupid. Richard got no information he couldn't easily have gotten from someone else, and probably more accurately, too. What do I know of your world that's of value to your enemies? He was only testing me. Surely you can see . . ."

But he could not see. His face got harder and colder.

I threw up my hands. "Milord, it never occurred to me that anyone would invite an *enemy* to a wedding." I felt like counterattacking, saying that he could have pointed out dangerous people to me, for instance. But I didn't dare. This was his world and I didn't know what punishments were handed out to wives who talked back.

The Lharr took a deep breath. I could almost see him pushing his anger out of sight. "We're safer, you and I, if he's here," the Lharr said finally, "because he's never on a Holding when his assassins do their work. He learned that years ago."

Assassins. Dear God! It was one thing to deal with them in books, quite another to be told there might be one near.

"You're sure?" I didn't let my voice tremble. The Lharr would've taken trembling for fear, which it was not. It was more horror at a world that allowed such things to go on.

"Sure enough. Though I've taken precautions."

How calm he was about "taking precautions" against killers! But I would have to learn to talk about such subjects. I would perhaps be here a long time. "If he hates you, wouldn't he want the pleasure of killing you for himself?"

The Lharr's arm tightened for a moment. I had made the right response by his rules, apparently. "He does, and he'll try, but not until he's quite sure he's destroyed my House. Killing me isn't enough. He wants to see my House in ruins first."

I shut my eyes and swallowed the bile brought up by such a concept. Destroy *hundreds* of lives? To satisfy one man's hate? I forced myself to go on. I would need to know a lot more than I did now to survive here. "What made you hate each other so?"

The Lharr pushed a hand through his hair. "It's hard to explain to someone like you." With a light hand under my elbow he directed me out from under the gallery and back into the light and noise of the Hall. "We shouldn't have been gone so long." He steered me skillfully around a drunken guest who sagged, snoring, against one of the columns. "Our grandsires began the blood feud, great-grandsires to be exact. They went with the first Black Ships. The tenth Lharr, my great-grandsire, thought it'd be a great joke to Seal the only woman they captured on that trip, the Duke of Harlan's captive, and make her his. The rest is rather complicated. As a result, House Harlan, meaning Richard, won't be satisfied with less than total destruction of everything the Halarek stand for. Richard, in fact, thinks he has personal reasons for destroying us." The Lharr shook off the thought. "But this is supposed to be a happy evening. I shouldn't have said anything about the whole bloody mess."

We had arrived at the dais. He helped me up onto it and pulled out my chair. "Try to forget I said anything and have a good time."

I looked at him. He was serious. He truly thought I could have a good time at a forced wedding and after being told there could be assassins in the manor. At least, when Lord Richard wasn't here.

The Lharr answered a whispered question from Gareth, then sat down to enjoy a piece of fruit. Guests and more guests came to the table, sober and drunk, male and female. The women politely complimented my costume, congratulated me on my luck, extolled the Lharr's virtues. The men wanted to dance and I had to dance with some of them. It was the ritual. There were so many of them that their faces and names merged hopelessly with their pipe smoke and sour breath, with the heat of my petticoats and exercise, with the dragging weight of that tall headdress that made my head pound painfully. A stay wore a raw spot on my hipbone.

I was dancing with a Gild official when the strain on my neck and legs staggered me against him. He was sympathetic, in an inebriated way, and unsteadily helped me back to my place at the table. Because I had told him I had business with the Gild, he slowly and carefully printed the address of the Gildhall on my napkin, handed it to me with a flourish, and departed. I sat for several minutes with my eyes closed, trying to will away the pain in my head. When I finally looked out at the Hall again, it was nearly empty. While I had been dancing interminably, most of the wedding guests had gone home or to bed. The Lharr relaxed beside me with a mug of steaming liquid. My head still throbbed painfully.

I stood, a little unsteadily. "Excuse me, milord. I'm going to bed."

"You're not excused."

My headache had increased until most of my attention centered on it. In my weariness and pain, I snarled at him. "I wasn't asking permission, Lord Karne. I was being polite."

The moment the words were out, I knew I had spoken too sharply, especially in front of guests, but I was too tired and miserable to care. If I could just get away from everyone, to someplace where I could concentrate, I could get rid of the pain. I turned to go.

The Lharr flowed to his feet and closed his hand on my wrist. "You will *not* leave. Not until the last guest has either gone to bed or fallen under the table."

I tried to twist free. "I've been polite to drunken men. I've danced my legs off. I've endured racket and stink until my head's splitting. That's all you're getting from me tonight."

The Lharr's grip tightened. "You're mistaken, madam. Sit down."

He pressed down on my wrist hard enough to bend my knees, but I strained against the pressure. Tears hovered in my eyes, which made me angrier, because I didn't want him to see me cry. "Let go!"

His eyes had gone cold again, and his voice as well. "Do as you're told."

"I'm not staying here!" I struggled to free my wrist and to escape those cold golden eyes.

His grip tightened. "Behave yourself, madam. You shame me."

I glanced around the Hall at the remaining guests. Here and there a candle sputtered and drowned in its melted wax. A portly man fell off his bench with a sodden thud and lay still. "Those drunks wouldn't notice if the ceiling fell in. Let go of me!"

I tried to push his hand away, but I couldn't. I stared at him hotly, biting my lip to keep back the tears. He pressed down firmly. When I did not sit, he slapped me. I gasped in astonishment. He'd *hit* me! My cheek stung fiercely, but the pain faded before my anger. He'd *hit* me!

I slapped him back with all my strength. His face went white and his eyes and mouth narrowed. He imprisoned both my wrists in one of his hands and whipped his free hand back and forth across my face. The pain in my head doubled.

But the pain just then was nothing compared to my shock. I had hit someone. I had *hit* someone. Calm, controlled, civilized—my image of myself wavered. I had let anger control me. Not only that, I had wanted to hit him *again*. No adult should treat another that way, yet I'd wanted to hit him again! The pain, and the horror at my own behavior, overwhelmed me. I began to cry and couldn't stop.

Some minutes later, I realized the Lharr was speaking to me. I looked at him, but although I could see and hear him speak, in my throbbing head the sounds meant nothing. He raised his hand again, but dropped it and released my wrists. I had needed that little bit of support. My knees gave way. I was falling when he threw an arm around me. I collapsed against him and that startled him. He whispered something in my ear, but the familiar Galac words meant nothing—I saw, I heard, but I couldn't understand. The Lharr lowered me carefully into my chair, then eased the heavy headdress out of its braided nest and dropped it onto the table.

I drifted into a state both deeper and lighter than sleep. Quiet there was, then low voices, gentle arms lifting, a shoulder that cradled my pounding head. Later gentle hands loosened my stays and let down my tightly braided hair. The relief cleared my head a little. Men discussed something in Rom—some insistent, the Lharr denying. As I slipped into sleep, someone finished preparing me for bed and drew a blanket over me. A hand lightly brushed my cheek and then the bed curtains swished softly shut.

CHAPTER 6

I stretched luxuriously and snuggled into the comfort of the bed again. The drawn bed curtains muffled the familiar rustling of ladies-in-waiting dressing for the day. I opened my eyes slowly. Light slipped through a small gap in the curtains. This was not my bed. It was bigger and the curtains were Halarek blue.

"Lady Zjhanne, are you awake?"

They all tittered. I rolled over and propped myself up on my elbows. Tamara peeked through the curtains.

"Oh, you're alone."

"Who . . . ?" Then I remembered last night and noticed for the first time that the other half of the bed was rumpled. I didn't want to think about that. When Tamara shoved back the bed curtain, I sat up and looked around. The room was much larger than mine, but my tapestries brightened its stone walls and familiar rugs lay scattered on the stone floor. Most welcome was my imitation window, through which morning sunlight flooded. Tamara set slippers for me beside the bed.

"Wasn't it kind of Lord Karne to bring your things to your new quarters, milady? You would've missed your window. The rest of the manor is so—so gray compared to this."

I looked at my lady disbelievingly. "Lord Karne ordered this?"

"Aye. He selected your things before you came, even designed the window for you. He wants you to feel at home, milady."

The tiring women did their work quickly for a change. I sat down at the dressing table and Jaklene began brushing my hair.

"How late did I come in last night, Jaklene?"

"I don't know, milady. You and milord were asleep by the time we came in."

"You—you didn't get me ready for bed?"

"No, milady. It must've been his lordship."

I thought of the gentle hands and flushed. Jaklene was still running on. "We met the witnesses as we came up. They said the two of you were alone."

"Witnesses?"

"Aye, milady. It's usual after Family weddings. But they said Lord Karne sent them away. He told them the Sealing had been witnessed on his Black Ship before it left Fruhe orbit."

I sat stunned. Not only had he taken my maidenhead without my consent or knowledge, but others had *watched* him do it! The barbarity of such a ritual left me speechless. That sort of thing had been common among the noble families of Terra in ancient times, but that was thousands of years ago.

Anger followed the shock. How could he expect a "truce" if he were going to make his contempt so obvious? How could anyone demean another person like that?

Someone rapped loudly on the door. I was still too furious to answer, so Tamara acted for me.

"Who's there?"

"The Lharr. Is the Larga ready?"

My anger burned higher. He had possessed me as if I were a thing. He *owned* me, had proved it in front of witnesses! I didn't trust myself to say anything.

Jaklene hurried to the door. When the Lharr walked into the room, she and the other women curtseyed deeply. He wore a leather jacket over riding clothes and tall, shiny boots. He looked questioningly at the women. Then his eyes met mine in the mirror.

"Why aren't you ready?"

I didn't know what he was talking about, but clearly he had made some sort of plans without asking me or even telling me about them. This was my owner speaking. He didn't need to be courteous to his wife. I wasn't considered merely inferior because I was female; I was a possession, a thing with no more rights than a cow or a dog. That knowledge cast a black shadow over my future.

Then anger, and a lifetime of being treated like a human being, came to my rescue. I might have to live for now on a world where women were treated as children or chattel, but I didn't have to accept such treatment for myself. I lifted my head as haughtily as any of the women who had inspected me so coldly last night and looked at the Lharr with all the chill I could muster. "Ready for what, Lord Karne?"

He stiffened. There was a long silence. My women began shifting restlessly or fidgeting with whatever they held in their hands. Had my request for information made *them* anxious somehow? Finally Donna, my tiring woman, took a few steps toward the Lharr, opened her mouth, hesitated, closed her mouth, made a deep curtsey. From the bottom of the curtsey she said, "Beggin' your pardon, lord, but we wasn't told Larga Zjhanne was goin' out. Nor about wakin' her."

Donna was trembling and her eyes, though lowered humbly, flicked nervously from side to side. I wondered what the Lharr would do about her forwardness. Order her beaten? She was only a serf.

"We're hunting with the Earl of Justin today. I told the sentry to have the Larga awakened at shift change. He'll be punished for forgetting. And you were out of place, Miss. Don't be so again."

Donna sank even closer to the floor, touched her throat, and murmured something in Rom.

The Lharr spoke sharply. "Never turn your translit off in your lady's presence, Miss!"

Donna, blushing furiously, obediently flicked on the tiny switch and scurried out of the room, forgetting she had not been dismissed. Jaklene spoke quickly.

"Forgive her, please, milord. She's young and has much to learn."

The Lharr chuckled. "Her clumsiness has charm. She's forgiven. Mistress Jaklene, Mistress Tamara, dress your lady for hunting immediately."

I stood then, my heart pounding. "I don't hunt."

I bit my lip to keep it from trembling and waited. What were the consequences of refusing one's husband's wishes here, when even asking him for information upset my women so?

His mouth tightened. "You'll learn to, then. Ladies, do as I ordered!"

My women jumped at the sharpness in his voice and hurried to obey. I summoned all my courage. I had to stand up for myself now, at the beginning. I'd learn the consequences here, now, in private. "I don't hunt, because I don't kill. None of my people do."

The Lharr looked at me as if I'd said nothing at all. I felt as if I'd been made nothing. I knew he was giving me a clear if subtle warning. If he hadn't heard what I said, he didn't have to do anything about it. I'd defied him openly at the wedding feast and he had had to punish me for it. That's the way this world worked. My anger wilted. He was giving me a chance to obey. He could force me to. He probably *would* force me to if I fought his orders. I turned away from his calm, neutral face. I would have to look at the necessity for obedience from a different angle: Every person and place I visited might be valuable later. That would have to be my compensation for going on a hunt.

Tamara brought out a bright, deep-blue skirt with matching hat and jacket. Jaklene moved to help me out of my dressing gown. Tamara brought a pair of pointed boots and knelt, ready to take off the soft slippers I was wearing. The Lharr made no move to leave or turn away.

"Stop," I ordered.

The women looked from me to the Lharr to me and back again. I controlled my temper with effort.

"Will you leave, sir!"

The Lharr's face registered surprise and puzzlement. "You're my wife, madam."

I opened my mouth to retort, thought of the hovering ladies-in-waiting, the gentle hands in the night, and swallowed the words. He probably knew what every inch of me looked like.

But that didn't make matters different for *me*. "You're still a stranger to me, my lord. I won't undress in front of you. It would be too embarrassing."

The Lharr shrugged and turned away. He did have the courtesy not to mention the previous night. A small voice inside me whispered that he had kept his promise: He hadn't forced me, he had only occupied the same bed for appearances' sake. That only made me angrier. I didn't want to hear good things about this man. Any good things. He had robbed me of my future. He had robbed me of love and family.

The women took up the movements my "Stop!" order had frozen them in, but all those hands touching me gave me an irritating twitchy feeling inside.

I brushed the hands away. "Stop! Go away! I've been dressing myself all my life. I can finish faster without you."

There was shocked silence.

"Milady . . ."

"It's never done . . ."

"You can't . . ."

I remembered the arguments we had had about this before. I addressed the Lharr's back. "You won't be angry with them, milord, if it will be faster?"

Without hesitation he shook his head. The women joined Donna in their room and I dressed myself for the first time in months. Immediately I felt more cheerful. I spun toward the Lharr and felt an unexpected pleasure in the swirl of heavy blue fabric around my legs.

"I'm ready, Lord Karne."

The Lharr turned and smiled. "You enhance the color of my House, Larga. Shall we go?" He opened the door, bowed, and let me pass through ahead of him.

The flitter was an odd, triangular craft. We climbed a short ladder onto a wing and stepped into the cockpit. After we had settled into the contoured seats, the Lharr pulled levers and turned knobs. Many levels above us, two huge doors slid aside. The flitter floated up and soared out into the sunlight. Lord Karne whistled tunelessly as he fiddled with the controls. Satisfied at last, he turned away from the instruments and tipped his seat back. Black one-man flitters, their wings bearing a narrow green band on either side of a wide, deep-blue one, passed between us and the bare trees far below, closing in a circle around the ship.

The Lharr sighed. "It would be so good to fly alone, without guards or force shields." He looked out at the escort ships, his face grim.

I looked at them. This was my life now, too, this thin protection from violent death. I thought of my own unrestricted childhood and, for a moment, pitied this man, who had been surrounded by rules and bodyguards all his life.

"Have you ever been free of this, Lord Karne?"

He looked at me as if he wondered why I was asking. He looked out the window to answer. "Once, for a few years, when I was a cadet. I'd never think of being alone if it weren't for that. Readjusting to Family life was hard." He looked at me with sympathetic eyes. "I guess I never thought till now how hard it might be for you, who's never lived here." His voice trailed away. He sighed again and avoided my eyes. "You do ride, don't you?"

"I've sent Gareth enough requests to be allowed to these dreary months."

I immediately regretted my tone. He had told me something personal and important and I had been sarcastic in return. I felt ashamed. I reminded myself it would not do to antagonize a man who held the power of life or death over me. I redid my response. "Yes, I ride. My brother Pieter and I went everywhere a horse could go when we were kids. You hunt from horseback?" That would make the long blue skirt no pleasure at all.

"For birds, always."

He looked at me as if it were my turn to say something. That reminded me I'd been ordered to come watch birds killed for sport. The pity I'd felt so briefly vanished. I didn't feel like talking with my kidnapper, my owner. The silence crawled on. The Lharr's hands twisted between his knees and a pair of lines appeared between his eyes. Clearly he didn't know how to make social conversation. In any other situation, I would have felt sorry for him.

Eventually, since he had nothing to say, I decided to tell him how I felt about rape and witnesses and being given orders. And it had been rape on that ship, even though I had been gassed so there would be no pain. Or no struggling. "Milord, I—"

Just then a rapid beeping began and a blue light on the control panel began flashing. The Lharr turned to the instruments. "Later, madam."

The flitter nosed down. Below lay a landing pad, already crowded with flitters and a few larger craft. As the flitter turned to land, the mountains we had left came into sight again, large jagged lumps on the horizon. The flitter settled lightly and we stepped out onto the wing. The Lharr jumped down and reached up for me, but I avoided him and jumped off the other side. I didn't want him touching me. He looked puzzled.

He should remember I'm on this world and in this place against my will, I told myself. I am his wife only because a Larga's life offers hope and a serf's doesn't.

The Lharr's Lifesguardsmen surrounded us. One of them handed the Lharr a heavy glove and a gun of some sort. Another gave him a hooded falcon. The bird shifted restlessly from foot to foot and her bells tinkled thinly.

"Easy, Jessika." The bird quieted at the Lharr's voice.

Two liveried boys brought horses for us. They were horses only by courtesy of their long faces and manes. They also had thick, curly hair, horn ridges, and two short, sharp horns, like goats. I looked at the side-saddle with dismay, but there was nothing I could do about it. I was a guest. I could use the wretched thing for an afternoon. The Lharr made a mounting block of his hands and boosted me onto my horse's back. Then he mounted and we walked the horses toward a stony mound surrounded by people and more horses. The Lharr stopped just at the edge of the crowd and turned to me.

"An earl heads House Justin. House Justin was once our ally. No more. But the earl's unaligned as far as I know, so don't alienate him with undisciplined behavior," he said softly.

Why bring me if he thinks I'll disgrace him? I asked myself angrily.

The Lharr might have read my thought. He smiled grimly. "Richard is out of—prison—after ten years and our battle is closing, his and mine. The powerful House of Justin will do much to determine which side wins. Lady Agnes has taught you our rules of proper behavior. You can show everyone that a woman raised without rigid restrictions needn't be a disaster. Or the opposite. So save your arguments and disobedience until we get home, please."

The guard opened a path for us through the crowd.

As we neared the flags and massed riders at the edge of the mound, the Lharr leaned toward me and said quietly, "Offer the earl your hand, touch fingertips with his wife. And act proud. You're Halarek now."

I stiffened my back and lifted my head to something of the angle of the other women's. A page presented us to the earl and his lady. The earl gravely kissed my hand. His wife touched her fingers to mine, but the coldness of the touch and of her face was not from the weather. I looked at the Lharr. He didn't appear to have noticed. We moved away from the earl's receiving area. Immediately our Lifesguardsmen closed around us.

The Lharr surveyed the crowd. "Mostly neutrals and minor Houses, with some Harlan allies. No one of ours. I don't like the looks of it. Say, there's Paul." The Lharr prodded his horse forward, stopped, returned. "You're wearing a translit, so you'll be understood. I'll translate what others say to you." He reached across and squeezed my hand gently. "Relax. Have fun. Life here is deadly serious most of the time." He wheeled his horse away, calling as he cantered off, "I'll be right back."

He was, too, bringing with him a small, pale (for the Gharr) man several years younger than himself. He introduced Paul IV, Duke of Druma. Lord Paul bowed and dutifully breathed on my hand, then he and the Lharr spoke rapidly and quietly in Rom. The duke bowed to me again, said something in Rom, and rode off to the head of the hunting party, which was beginning to move across the snowy plain. The Lharr's party fell in at the end. The Lharr brought his horse so close to mine that our lower legs brushed as we rode.

He kept his voice low. "Paul says something's afoot. With so many witnesses, it's not likely to be serious. If Justin is allying with Harlan, it would explain the social ice. How you impress the neutral Houses is still important but, within reason, you may as well do as you please." He chuckled and lifted his rein hand a little, as if toasting. "Here's hoping your idea of 'within reason' is near mine."

Several minutes later one of House Halarek's Blues came riding from the head of the hunt. He spoke to the Lharr, who shrugged. The Lharr turned to me.

"Sergeant Kranz says my absence from the fore of the hunt is much talked about. They'd looked forward to seeing Jessika at work." He tapped one of the bird's bells so it tinkled, then smiled at me and said, without looking at the soldier, "Tell them, Sergeant, that I'm spending the day with my lovely bride."

I blushed and that embarrassed me and I blushed more. It was a political statement. It had to be. But I remembered with a stab of pain that not even Lance had ever called me lovely.

The Lharr appeared to be considering something. "There's no reason why Jessi shouldn't hunt today, though. Sergeant, take her back with you and show them a champion at work."

The day flew by after that. The Lharr followed his own advice and relaxed. He joked, and teased the soldiers. Here, away from the gloomy stone manor, I discovered unwillingly that the Lharr could be good company. He pointed out the merits of a good bird and a good strike so clearly that I could soon see the differences that made Jessika the best bird in the air. He talked at length, fascinatingly, about falconry and hunting. A light wind tossed my hair and tingled my cheeks pleasantly. Our horses danced over the new spring grass. For the first time in months I was outside, and I savored every motion of the horse, every ray of sunlight, every cold puff of wind.

At last I could resist the exhilaration no longer. "I'll race you to that little hill, my lord, and win." Without further invitation, I touched heels to my mare.

The mare was willing and bounded away. Over the rush of wind and the pounding of her hooves came the drum of hooves from behind. The Lharr came even, then drew ahead. A tree at the halfway point approached, passed. The Lharr led by half a length. Then I thought I saw him pull in a little. I would make him regret giving me a handicap I hadn't asked for.

I leaned forward and shouted to the mare. I hit her once with the loose end of the reins and laughed as she burst past the Lharr. I caught the surprise that flashed across his face as we passed, and the determination, but it was too late to correct his mistake. His horse drew up as far as my stirrup, then as far as the mare's surging shoulder, but he couldn't get farther, and in a few seconds more the mare had skirted the hill. I let her slow down gradually. The Lharr looked like I felt—cheeks glowing pink, hair blown in all directions, eyes snapping.

"You misled me, madam." His face was reproachful but his golden eyes danced.

I laughed. "Nay, lord, I led you truly, right across the finish line."

"Witch," he said, but there was a laugh in his voice.

Our guardsmen caught up quickly. The hunt was riding toward us. A page broke away from it and rode quickly to meet us. He saluted the Lharr by removing his cloak, then said something. The Lharr sent him scurrying back with a few sharp words. He turned to me.

"Lord Richard wished to speak with you, alone. He's presuming on the freedom you allowed him yesterday. I told the boy anything the duke wishes to say will be said in my presence."

In a few minutes the hunters arrived and Richard rode forward. I didn't extend my hand, not wanting anything to spoil the Lharr's mood. Richard ignored the omission and swept my hand from the mare's neck to his lips. He looked across it at my husband.

"You'll regret not allowing us to be alone, Lord Karne," he said in careful Sternlangue.

"Could you do more harm in front of witnesses than you could with the implications of being alone with her?" the Lharr retorted.

He could. Before I realized his intent, the duke had flipped my hand over and was opening my fingers so he could kiss my palm. That was a liberty permitted only to lovers, even on Fruhe. I sat stunned by his impudence only seconds, but that was enough. Although I snatched my hand away before his lips could touch it, the damage had been done. My lord's face and those of the other guests had hardened against me. A woman whispered loudly and, though I couldn't understand what she said, I made out the Rom word for "hussy," a favorite of Lady Agnes's. Knowing looks passed between others in the party.

I turned fully toward the Lharr. "Surely, my lord, you don't think . . ."

But his closed face completely hid what he thought. I turned back to the duke, grateful that my translit made what I said understandable to everyone.

"I've given you no grounds for such familiarity, milord."

The duke spoke, in Rom. A page translated to Sternlangue. "As you say, milady." Richard bowed mockingly.

I was trapped. His tone implied more than his intended caress, and he spoke in Rom now and not Sternlangue, because his real audience didn't speak Sternlangue. Anger at being so cornered made me helpless and the Lharr's silence increased that anger. But the Lharr's eyes were blazing and his knuckles were white where he clenched his reins. Our fury only amused the duke and his friends. Our friend Paul had slunk to the rear of the hunt and now kept his eyes carefully turned away.

Richard watched us with a mocking smile. I wondered how I could for a moment have thought him attractive.

"Have any of your letters gotten through to Fruhe, Larga Zjhanne?" Richard asked, the page translating. "I mean the ones to your leman asking for ships to take you away."

I knew enough to conceal my shock. I lifted my head proudly and looked down my nose at him. "I sent no letters, my lord duke." Which was technically true. I'd sent only one letter, before I knew the danger.

Lord Richard cocked his head and looked at me speculatively. "Then the name Lance van Tibe means nothing to you?"

I couldn't react fast enough to conceal the pain that name caused me, and neither I nor the Lharr could conceal our surprise that Lord Richard knew anything about Lance.

Richard Harlan nodded. "Ah, I thought it would." He looked around as if to say, see what kind of woman Halarek's brought us.

I swallowed. "I once knew the man, milord. A commodities broker from Terra." The words were brave, but I knew my voice wavered. Lord Richard was skirting the edges of an accusation of treason. Letters off-world. To my "lover." Asking for an off-world ship that was not a Gild ship, though it was just to take me away.

The duke turned to the Lharr. "Your bride's told you, then, of her requests for rescue?"

The Lharr's face hardened. "Your questions have two edges, Richard. How could Larga Zjhanne have told me plans she hasn't made? She *has* spoken of her homesickness, but even you can't make treason of homesickness."

"I accused no one of treason, Lord Karne." Richard's voice was smooth and even, but his eyes glittered.

The Lharr's anger broke free. "Don't fence with me! You know a call for off-world help is treason. And that means death, for both of us. Say your charges plain."

The duke sat easily on his horse and said nothing. I hated his handsome, smiling face. I hated the avid attention of many of the other guests.

They're after blood, I thought. They want to see someone lose and someone win. They want someone to get *hurt.*

I looked at my husband, who didn't look like he was going to say anything against Lord Richard's slander, then at the other guests. It seemed odd, if I understood the social structure here, that I would have to defend myself. I let my eyes touch everyone nearby. "On my world, such slander usually ends up in court. Is it custom here that one person may slander another unchallenged, without proving the truth of the charge?"

Some of the male guests had the grace to look embarrassed. The duke continued to smile with satisfaction at his successful ambush. That was more than I could stand. I slapped his smile away with all the strength I had. Lord Richard's eyes dilated and his features twisted with surprise. A very red handprint blazed on his cheek. I spun the mare around and kicked her into a run toward the landing field.

Later, sitting alone in the flitter, I had time to be ashamed of losing control. Again. Twice in two days I had actually *hit* someone. How little it took to provoke me to violence. I blamed my inner turmoil and confusion, but I knew blaming them was just avoiding taking responsibility for what I'd done, for looking honestly at myself. I had betrayed my faith, my family, and myself.

Such self-examination is not a pleasure and I soon turned to wondering what the duke had had in mind when he accused me.

Maybe this wasn't just a random striking out against an old enemy but part of a bigger plan. Whatever I did, it would have looked bad.

How did he know about Lance? No one but the Lharr knew. And the letter I sent Dad? Even the Lharr doesn't know about that.

The Lharr stooped to enter the flitter and slumped into his seat. His face was more serious than usual. I turned away, angry with myself for caring that the happy companion of earlier in the day was gone, angry with the Lharr for doing so little against the lies. Again I felt the antagonistic eyes of Justin's guests and sickened a little inwardly. Night made a mirror of the forward window and in it the Lharr's hand idly fingered a switch. Around and around it his fingers slid monotonously. At last he broke the silence.

"You're angry." It was a statement, not a question. "You had cause, yet even so your behavior was extremely rude. Don't be so again."

"Rude! Should I let lies pass as truth? At home I'd have courts to defend me against slander. Even here, I shouldn't have to defend myself, by myself, against lies. I expected a number of people to back me, once I stated the issue."

The Lharr's voice was low and intense. "You don't have to defend yourself, madam. I'll defend you, but when the odds are even. Tomorrow dawn, on Council ground." He threw his head up and fixed me with his strange golden eyes. "Would you rather I'd taken him on here, among so many hostile witnesses? I'd be dead and you'd be free, like you want to be. Only you wouldn't be allowed to go home. Richard or someone else would take you."

I looked at him, astonished. They were going to settle the matter with weapons! And apparently one must die. I felt sick. "By all the worlds' gods! I didn't know you settled such matters here by *killing*! I can't be party to killing, my lord. Just let it pass. Lies aren't worth a death."

"Surely Lady Agnes taught you—"

"She taught me the major laws. I knew Lord Richard was hinting at treason. She didn't talk about the consequences of treason. I assumed life in prison or something like that." I looked at the dark outside. "Where do *you* come into it, anyway? It's my problem. The duke was accusing *me*, not you. You're certainly not acting out of love."

"Love, madam, has nothing to do with this."

I spun to look at him. "There would be no other reason for you to—"

"Don't be naive! I challenged the duke because your honor is mine. If *you* commit treason, *I* pay for it." The Lharr threw the switch he had been playing with and the flitter lifted sharply. "You *belong* to me, body and—"

"Body, perhaps. You've taken that with barbaric indecencies . . ." Just thinking of the degrading Sheet and Broken Seal ritual sickened me.

He looked blank. "Indecencies?" He sounded genuinely puzzled.

"Last night. And on the ship. You and your 'witnesses,' milord! As though I were a prize heifer and not a human being."

The Lharr still had a puzzled frown on his face. "Witnesses customarily attend the Sealing of a Family marriage, and, these days, that customarily happens on the wedding night. I sent them away because they weren't needed. I've already told you I Sealed our marriage before we left Fruhe orbit and why."

I looked out at the landscape flowing past in the dark below and anger fought with humiliation inside me. "The location doesn't change the barbarity of it."

"Would you really rather be bride to Richard? Or to one of his serfs?" That, too, he seemed to be asking in all seriousness, entirely without sarcasm.

"Would that be any worse?" But I knew now that it would be infinitely worse. Especially with Richard. The Lharr, at least, saw me as a human being some of the time. To Lord Richard, I'd never be more than an asset.

The Lharr began fiddling with the controls again. "Richard knew about my Black Ship. All of Starker IV did. That's one of the reasons for financing a Black Ship, having everyone know you have the hard cash to do it. I'm as sure as I can be of anything that Richard had a spy on that ship. If I hadn't so claimed you immediately by Sealing, before Council witnesses, that spy would have, in a way as humiliating to me as possible. A fitting revenge for the 'joke' my great-grandsire played on Richard's."

He stared out at the shadows with lighted windows that escorted us. The mountains drew closer. A blue, wrinkled moon peeped over them and stars stood out sharply in the cold air. Still looking out of the window, the Lharr added softly, "The old man would've thought the joke worth all the blood it's cost since, too."

Could I ever understand such people? I sighed and leaned back in the seat. The Lharr's puzzled eyes indicated he couldn't understand my reaction to such a simple, necessary ritual. Bride-snatching for political profit or revenge! Ritual rape, witnessed. At least I hadn't been conscious for that. At least the Lharr had done that much for me. I shuddered at the alienness of it all and turned to my window again. What would tonight be like? And the nights after?

Suddenly the window went black.

"My lord?" I said in sudden fear, my anger and humiliation forgotten for the moment.

The flitter settled, bumped against something gently. The Lharr switched off the engines. Lights came on outside the craft as the last escort flitter came to rest.

"We black out the hangar at night and come in on guidance. An open hangar well-lit is too easy to spot from too far away." As he lifted me from the wing he added, "You'll come to the duel tomorrow, and you'll stay to the end.

"Don't look so surprised, madam. When your champion fights for you, it's your duty to be there."

Again the alienness separated me from the laughing man of earlier in the day. "It's like a game with you, isn't it, this feuding and killing?" I kept my voice low and it trembled with strain. "And over something that could be settled in courts, without blood, without death." I stopped, choking on the horror of the idea of willful killing. "So appropriately barbaric!" I started toward the door, but the Lharr grabbed my arm and pulled me back.

"That's the third time today you've called me barbaric." He, too, kept his voice low.

I glared at him. "Aren't you?"

Jerking free, I swept past the curious soldiers standing around the flitters. I expected the Lharr to order me to stop. He didn't. I reached the door into the manor, but the soldier there pretended he didn't see me. I had to wait there for the Lharr.

CHAPTER 7

With soldiers ahead and behind, we walked toward our new quarters. At the lift the soldiers split, some going up the stairs to check the hall above, some waiting in the hall to take the lift when we sent it back down. The lift came down and the Lharr and I stepped inside. We had only passed one level when the intercom buzzed. The Lharr flipped it on and an unfamiliar voice came out.

When he finished talking, the Lharr turned to me and summarized the message. "That was Nik, Nicholas von Schuss, commander of the manor forces. Someone's just spotted an intruder, so we won't go to our suite now. I told him we'd be on level 4."

He looked at the lift door for a long moment. "Nik has been my friend ten years now. I've saved his life and he mine. He saved my sister from the worse-than-death the Duke of Harlan planned for her, so we let him marry her, against all political sense, because they loved each other, had for years." The Lharr looked down at the rust-brown floor of the lift and shook his head. "Nik's the Heir in House von Schuss, you see, and it's very dangerous for a lord of the Nine to love his wife. I'll have to tell him about Justin's turnaround as soon as this intruder's taken care of."

I thought about the Blues everywhere, the escort flitters on the way to Justin, the Lharr's warning to go nowhere alone. I didn't need the Lharr to tell me that an intruder would most likely be an assassin. An assassin. Death. In the Lharr's own manor house. And all his soldiers could do nothing to prevent it, apparently. What use were the soldiers, then? Death. I didn't want to think about it.

The lift stopped. We stepped out and its door shushed shut behind us. We started down the hall, our heels echoing in the silence. We had only gone a few steps when the hall went dark. The Lharr stopped so suddenly that I bumped into him.

"If a Harlan man has gotten to the generators . . ."

I noticed that he assumed he knew who was responsible, without evidence.

The Lharr took a step. A beam of white light shot out of the darkness. The Lharr flung his arm against me and pushed me back against the cold stone wall. A blast of heat followed the light. Another flash of light shot past, within a hair of where I'd been. The heat from it tightened and dried my skin. I began shivering violently. Someone was trying to kill *me*!

Something scraped against the stone wall of the gallery stair. The Lharr spun me around, whispered harshly, "Run, as fast as you can," and pushed me hard into the hall.

I ran, intensely aware of the thump of my boots against the stone floor. Could the gunman hunt by sound? Then the Lharr was beside me, an arm around my waist, pulling me along, zigzagging erratically, our bootheels making crazy echoes in the empty corridor. The white light flashed again and the wall we passed glowed red. Lord Karne pulled me with him into a deep doorway and pushed my head into the hollow of his shoulder to muffle my panting. His heart pounded heavily under my ear and I felt the tenseness of his listening. I heard nothing.

"Damn! Lifesguardsmen, at least, should be here already. Where are they!" The Lharr's voice was barely audible, but it shook with fury.

We stood long minutes in silence, waiting for a patrol that didn't come. Finally the Lharr took my hand and led me down the hall toward a small yellow light.

"Damn!"

The lift had stopped between levels when the power went.

"We'll have to walk. Come on." He started up the stairs.

I hung back. "Won't our boots make too much noise?"

In the dark the Lharr's hand touched my shoulder approvingly and seconds later, our empty boots on the floor of the hall landing, we were climbing the black stairwell. Only when we stood on the landing at level 6 did I realize I was crushing the Lharr's hand.

"I'm going to the wardroom for weapons and a light," the Lharr whispered. "I'm leaving you in the conservatory. Lock the door and open it only for me, Lord Nicholas, or Captain Tomas Oroark."

We stole down the hall. A sliver of light showed under the conservatory door. I stiffened and stopped.

"The moon," he whispered.

This didn't reassure me. It didn't require soldier's training to know bright moonlight was good enough to kill by, and I had no desire to die. The Lharr cautiously opened the door and guided me through it. I wanted to protest being left alone. He must have sensed it, for he pressed two fingers against my mouth.

"You're as safe here as you can be. I'll be only a moment."

I shut the door and locked it, then leaned against it and listened intently. Moonlight whitened the plants and the floor. It was very quiet. The shadows were very dark. Even the silence was threatening.

A knock. I couldn't move.

"Larga Zjhanne, open the door."

I obeyed. A blaze of white light blinded me. After several seconds I could see the Lharr, a Torch in one hand and two objects in the other. He pressed a short knobby tube into my hand, then ran a finger gingerly over the knobs.

"These control the width of the beam. The biggest one is the widest beam. Just be careful; it doesn't take much pressure and it doesn't have to be aimed much. When you need it, release the safety"—he pointed to a faintly glowing red switch—"and fire."

I stared down at the tube in my hand and then at him. The tube wasn't another light, it was a weapon; its beam would kill. Knowing how I felt about killing, he had given me a weapon! I dropped the tube. It bumped noisily into the darkness.

"You can't expect me to *kill*?"

The Lharr thrust the other weapon into his belt beside his hunting knife, then he gripped my wrist so tightly my bones ached. "That's exactly what I do expect! We die or he does. There's no peaceful choice here. We'll discuss at a better time just how many innocent lives your pacifist principles can cost. For now"—he moved a few steps aside to pick up the knobby tube, dragging me with him—"at least carry this so I can use *my* weapon." He forced the tube into my hand.

I held it reluctantly. I wanted to drop it, but was I ready to die in order to stand weaponless? The Lharr knew this world and its ways. I knew the assassin was aiming for me.

The Lharr stood in the doorway so the light from the Torch flooded the hall. He motioned me through. "If it'll make you less afraid, I've never seen a heat beam with the range of a Torch. He'll have to come into full light to have a chance of hitting us."

"It's not because I'm afraid that I won't kill!" I snapped. "I'm no more or less afraid than you." I hoped this was truc, but I wasn't sure. He was used to this and I was not.

He was already moving down the hall. He stopped at the stair. I laid a light hand on his arm.

"We can't afford to be angry right now, milord."

He looked at me searchingly. "We'll go down in the dark. We'd be sitting ducks otherwise." Then he smiled and brown flecks glinted in his eyes. "Chin up. We have a chance now."

He enjoys danger, I thought. For part of him life wouldn't have spice without it.

We slipped silently down two flights of stairs. At the level 5 landing, the Lharr pressed me back against the wall before he started forward. But he forgot the boots and stumbled over them.

A heat beam leaped through the doorway and splashed on the stairs. The temperature in the small space shot up and the steps glowed angrily.

"We can't stay here!" I cried.

"We can't go back up, either. And to go down we have to cross that light." He glanced over his shoulder at the glowing stairs.

The glare of the next beam passed so near me that my heart lunged and stopped. Lord Karne jerked and said with feeling several harsh Rom syllables.

"Much too close," he said savagely. "We fry next time."

The darkness returned as the heat spread upward and the glow dimmed and that only increased my fear. I wished I could stop shivering. I wished I could see the assassin. I wished I could see the Lharr.

"We have to gamble, my lady," he whispered. "Get down!"

He activated the Torch, hurled it down the hall, and threw himself and me flat on the floor. The force and speed of his arm knocked the wind out of me. A heat beam flashed over us, exactly where we'd been standing, then we heard someone running down the hall. The Lharr edged carefully to the door, then stood and motioned me to follow.

"There."

I caught a glimpse of cloaktail and boot disappearing around the corner at the end of the hall.

"He'll wait for us in the dark somewhere between here and our suite. Where are the Lifesguardsmen? They have to know something's wrong!" He shook off his fury. "*We* have to kill him, then. It's too late for anyone to help. And I have a good idea where he's going." The Lharr bent, picked up the Torch, and turned it off. "We'll sneak up and trap him in the light. If he gets me, you'll have to kill him."

"My lord, I can't—"

"Our lives or his," he snapped.

He took my hand again and we slid swiftly along the wall to its end. In the silence my rapid breathing and the smooth sliding sound of his leather jacket seemed very loud. Could our hunter hear? Was he moving in on us? I tried not to think what that white heat could do to a human body.

We were around the corner. The Lharr stopped me and went on alone. The heat gun flashed again, missing me narrowly. The glare faded quickly, but the hot, hot stones glowed enough to hold off darkness for several seconds more. The hunter had had time to get a good look at me and, in the momentary illumination, I had had time to see the Lharr, crouching close to the floor and out from the wall. Metal scraped against something in the library-supply doorway. I wanted to move, to get out of range, but my feet were frozen in place. I dropped the knobby tube. If I were to die, it wouldn't be with a weapon in my hand. Taking a deep breath and holding it, I tried to face death calmly. So close, so gruesomely deadly. The Torch flared. The Lharr's gun hissed.

The Lharr aimed again as the man staggered toward him, but another shot wasn't necessary. The man collapsed facedown in the center of the hall, twitched, and lay still. The Lharr rose and approached him cautiously. Holding the gun ready, he turned the body over with his foot. He cried out in pain and anger.

"Nik! Why you?" The Lharr's voice broke and he knelt beside the body.

The man's eyes opened briefly. "Harlan's work. Odonnel has Kit . . . Jemmy . . ." The man closed his eyes and struggled painfully for breath. "No choice. Your wife or mine. Forgive—" He gasped in agony and died.

The Lharr looked up at me, but he didn't see me. His eyes were hard and hot with anger and grief. He composed the body of his friend and stood. He looked down at the body for a long time. Neither of us noticed when the lights came on again.

"He did what he had to do, because he loved her," the Lharr said finally.

The lift finished its trip and some of our escort of Lifesguardsmen stepped out. The rest of them came down the stairs, and a Blues patrol appeared at the end of the hall.

"Just in time." The Lharr's voice was bitterly sarcastic.

"Milord," one of the Lifesguardsmen protested, stung by the bitterness, "we were trapped between levels."

"Lord Nicholas said the assassin had been seen running up the stair to level—" The other Guards officer drew breath sharply and stared down at the body. "My God! It's Lord Nicholas!"

"Aye." The Lharr turned to the approaching Blues. "Call the undertaker."

"Milord," the brasher officer began, "the Lady Kathryn—"

The Lharr stiffened. "My sister will bear this as a Gharr woman should. He died in the line of duty. Is that understood?"

The men nodded. "Yes, my lord."

The Lharr took my elbow and steered me toward our suite. "I must bring Kit back, before Harlan's spies report Nik's death, or Kit will be dead, too. And Jemmy, who is Heir in both Halarek and von Schuss. I don't know how long I'll be gone, so I must leave you in charge of the manor. You'll abide by Lady Agnes's advice, of course." He paused, then added harshly, "This is the price they paid for loving as lovers do, that Nik could be used against me for Kit's sake."

"It was me he was aiming at, wasn't it?"

He stopped walking and looked down at me. "Aye. I thought it would frighten you more to tell you. I knew he *wasn't* trying to kill me and *I* was afraid."

"Refusing to kill doesn't make me a coward, my lord."

"My mistake." His tone was dry and unbelieving. He resumed his brisk pace down the corridor.

I had to scurry to catch up. "Why me, Lord Karne?"

"Jemmy, my nephew, is as important as Kit. Baron von Schuss and I have no other named heirs. My last first cousin, Ronnif, was killed in a duel a year ago. One murder would give the Council two vacancies to fill and Richard Harlan has the votes to control the selection."

The Lharr halted an approaching patrol and spoke rapidly in Rom. The soldiers took off on the double. The Lharr continued. "Even an unborn child is a legal heir. Richard intends to kill you before you show signs of having one. That's what House Harlan did to my second wife. Killed her when she was pregnant."

The horror of what he was saying, piled on top of what had just happened, was too much for me to absorb. I heard the words, but they had no effect.

The sentry outside my door saluted and we entered. My ladies-in-waiting rose respectfully.

"There was an intruder. Lord Nicholas has been killed," the Lharr told them. "Mourning for him begins now." Then he drew me aside. "Forty days of mourning will relieve you of giving or going to parties, so you'll have more time to adjust to life here before you must socialize. Kit may want to mourn longer than that. I'm going now to get my sister and my Heir back. I'm leaving my best officer with you." There was a slight hesitation and I knew he was thinking that until a few minutes before, another man had been his best officer. "If I'm killed, put yourself under Gild protection immediately. The Council will be no help to you. Don't leave the manor; do it by tri-d. You'll remember?"

"Yes, milord."

He looked at me oddly for a moment. "You were brave tonight," he said finally. He touched his hand to my cheek quickly, lightly, and was gone.

I sat at the dressing-table bench for a long time, sorting out all the things that had happened since this morning—the hunt, the challenge, the attempted assassination. How tired I was! I took a nightgown from the wardrobe and looked toward one of my ladies. "What time is it, Tam?"

"One hundred hours, milady."

"I'm going to bed. Have Lady Agnes come immediately after fast-breaking. I want to meet the staff and see the house."

CHAPTER 8

Hours of sitting with needlework, listening to the inane yak-yak of uneducated superstitious women! I stabbed the needle angrily into the taut material on the embroidery frame and tried to ignore Jaklene and Tamara's unsubtle attempts to turn the conversation to babies. Already!

The house. I'd think about the manor house. It was obvious after this morning's tour that I couldn't run it. There were armies of servants, hordes of servants. And millions of details that could be taken care of by computer and weren't. That was one of the problems of Starker IV, people doing work fit only for robots or computers.

A knock on the door cut off the chatter. Tamara admitted a tall, gangly young man in a Blues uniform. He moved awkwardly, but he had a puppyish charm. I wasn't the only one who noticed it. Jaklene was frankly making eyes at him. He knelt at my feet and flushed when he discovered he didn't know what to do with his long, thin arms.

"Cap—Captain Tomas Oroark, at your service, Larga. I—I've brought messages from his lordsh—from the Lharr." His flush deepened as he realized how disjointed his words had been.

I smothered a smile, which would have embarrassed the young soldier more. "Stand up, Captain. Having men kneel to me is embarrassing. Get up."

He stumbled to his feet and his dark eyes hid behind thick dark lashes.

"Captain, the messages," Jaklene wheedled, and held out her hand.

I could see Jaklene's thought as clearly as if she had spoken it. I couldn't read Rom and Jaklene wanted to be the first to see what was inside. Oroark looked at me uncertainly.

He's so young to be a captain, little more than twenty, I thought. "Read them to me, Captain," I said. *At least that way everyone will hear the news at the same time.*

The young man fumbled at his belt and finally extracted two plastic sheets. He glanced at me again, to make sure, and then began. The first said the Lharr had flown to a minor holding of Lharr Garren Odonnel, hoping to be in time to save Lady Kathryn and Lord Jerem. He might be gone as long as two weeks.

How could I endure two weeks in my ladies' company without even a fight with the Lharr to break the tedium?

The second letter introduced Captain Tomas Karel Oroark, newly a captain in the Blue Guard and commended for bravery and exceptional judgment. The boy blushed as he read this, but he stumbled through to the end.

"My—my lady, if you'll do me the honor to accept my service . . ." He moved to kneel again.

"On one condition," I said. Oroark paused in mid-motion and looked up. "That you never kneel to me."

He apparently expected something much more difficult. He grinned with relief. That grin lit his homely face and made him almost good-looking. He touched the narrow blue oval on the sleeve of his tunic. "We'll make your sign mean the best soldiers in the Starker system."

I did not have the heart to embarrass him by revealing how I felt about the "honor" he offered. "That's a gallant thought, Captain."

He blushed deep red, but he was plainly pleased. Before he had completely regained his normal color, the sentry admitted two more men, Tane Orkonan, the Lharr's secretary, and a long-nosed, somewhat older companion. I nodded recognition toward the secretary.

"Good day, Frem Orkonan."

He bowed. "Larga, I wish to present Kurt Weisman, the librarian and my assistant."

" 'Frem' Weisman?" I examined him more closely: So this was the man Tam had bribed to take my letter to the Gildhall so many months ago.

"Aye, Larga," the man was saying in a high, brittle voice. "I, too, am a Freeman."

Orkonan slipped a stylus from the binding of his note tablet. "What are your orders for the manor tomorrow, Larga?"

I felt a surge of anger at the immense dark prison that was the manor and, in anger and resentment, I answered in violation of all Lady Agnes's rules. "The manor? I can't find my way around in it, let alone manage it! I don't even *want* to manage it. You and Lady Agnes know what must be done. See that it is."

"As you say, Larga." Orkonan almost succeeded in concealing his surprise at my blunt refusal. He slid the stylus into its place, bowed, and backed to the door.

Weisman followed. But Weisman lifted his head as he reached to shut the door and his eyes held a peculiar glint, almost like triumph.

Captain Oroark left soon after. My thoughts returned to my tour of the manor and to the squalor and emptiness of the lives of the manor's servants. If the lives of servant-serfs were so miserable under the Halareks, what was the life of a serf like on an Old Party Holding?

For the next week I walked through the manor, memorizing its halls and rooms, corridors and lifts, work sites and residences, exits and entrances, and always accompanied—Oroark, Jaklene, Lady Agnes, and a squad of Blues—whenever I left my quarters. I knew that if I were to manage this house eventually, I must know it well, yet I could talk to no one except Family and the servants directly responsible to me. These wore translits. The more I saw of the manor and the hundreds of servants and tasks necessary to keep it running, my inability to understand what anyone said increasingly disturbed me. What would happen if something went wrong with the translits? What if I didn't have one when I needed one? What if a servant brought warning of an assassin? They were apparently fairly common on this world. The extra seconds required for translation might be the difference between life and death.

The manor house presented other problems: the crowded servants' quarters, the clinic—which was dirty, disorganized, and staffed with untrained serf women—the thin, pale servant children playing all day in the halls outside their parents' bleak rooms. I had to do something to improve the lives of these people. They lived little better than the animals of Fruhe. But when I confronted Orkonan with specific ideas for changes, he met all my suggestions with "It's always been this way."

"Surely the Family doesn't use the clinic the way it is?"

He looked at me as if I'd said something unthinkable. "Of course not! Dr. Othneil comes from Ontar City to treat Family members in their quarters. The clinic is for servants."

Insufferable blindness! As if serfs were less than human. "Some of those servants are fighting and dying for this Family, Frem Orkonan! Clean the clinic up and have trained people, this Dr. Othneil among them, on duty at all times. If Dr. Othneil doesn't want to serve there—"

"But the Lharr's seal is nec—"

"Today, Orkonan!"

He blanched and bowed. "Yes, immediately, Larga."

"Also, many of the servants' children are too old to be in the halls playing. They should be in school."

"It has always been so, my lady. Each child is apprenticed to its father's trade at twelve. And once a year I select the smartest ones and send them to technical schools in Ontar or other cities."

"Well, all of them should learn some reading and writing before that."

"Larga! Even the females?"

I sighed and turned toward the view outside my "window." "All right. Just the boys. But set up some kind of school for them. Half-days if they're needed at home, but at least that."

"This needs the Lharr's seal before—"

I slammed the edge of my fist into the wall beside the window. Orkonan stopped in mid-sentence, horrified at my unseemly emotional display.

Unseemly, I thought. That seems to describe everything about me here. I sighed. "I know about the seal and this is no emergency like the clinic—the clinic *will be done*! But you can plan schools for the children. I don't know much about the Gharr, but I'll be glad to help."

He looked at me in shocked amazement. "Larga, these matters are nothing for a larga to concern herself with." But his eyes said, No woman can think this out.

Saying anything more would have been pointless. My hope of using these projects to escape my ladies for longer periods each day died.

And escaping my inane female company became more desirable and more necessary to my sanity with every hour I spent among them. I had never liked "female" conversation, and my ladies talked an endless round of lovers, babies, clothes, scandal, lovers, babies, and, when those got stale, they told fairy stories! Then there was Lady Agnes and her constant "This isn't proper" and "Larga, that isn't done." She permitted me no useful work (everything useful was "beneath a Larga's dignity") and even censored the news from the fighting because it might "unsettle" my delicate Fruvan sensibilities. Of all the restrictions, this one infuriated me the most. It was true that Fruvans didn't like to hear about death, especially willful killing, but they had been front-line medics and chaplains in all the Empire's wars. My life hung with the Lharr's. I needed to know how things went with him and no one would tell me! I knew only that many casualties were coming into the hastily upgraded clinic.

I finally reached the end of my patience with Lady Agnes and sent her to visit her daughter on Kingsland Holding, halfway around the planet. As soon as the old woman had left, I sent for Oroark.

The moment he entered my quarters I sprang my question on him. "How goes the battle, Captain?"

"My lady . . ."

"I've been put off too long, Captain. Tell me."

"The battle goes badly for us right now." Then, as if he had read my mind, "Our wounded show it, Larga. Your Fruvan stomach couldn't take the details."

"It's not the wounds I can't stomach, Captain. My people have worked as non-combatants on the front lines of the worst of Terra's wars, and then the Empire's. It's the senselessness of war." I resolved to visit the wounded, from which the household seemed to have been protecting me through some misunderstanding of Fruhe's philosophy, as soon as possible. If the battle was going badly, though, there was a more important matter to be attended to immediately.

"If the battle goes badly, then I must see about putting myself under Gild protection, as the Lharr ordered. Take me to the nearest Gildhall, Captain." Since the Lharr wasn't dead, his command to talk to the Gild by tri-d didn't apply. Or so I convinced myself.

Oroark bowed and began backing toward the door. "I'll begin assembling a proper retinue at once, milady, but it will take some time."

"Retinue?" I had turned to look for my cloak, but his words made me spin around to look at him. "I'm the one in danger, according to the Lharr, not my ladies. We will *not* take them."

"But you—it's against all custom for a woman to go out alone!" He glanced from side to side as if to find support from superior authority, but for the time, I was that authority.

I shut my eyes and counted to ten in three languages. Captain Oroark was obeying his society's rules and the rules of this House. I opened my eyes and looked at him. I kept my voice low and polite. "I won't be going out alone. I'm going with you and however many soldiers you think necessary. But I *am* going. Now." I picked up my cloak and started toward the door.

Oroark hesitated only a second between propriety and the Lharr's orders to stay with his lady. He ordered up the watch and selected four soldiers from it.

The freecity of Ontar began just outside the manor walls, which surprised me. From what I had been told, I assumed the Freemen stayed as far away from the nobility as they could manage. This was clearly not the case. When I thought about it, I could see near was better than far if one wanted to trade, and the noble Houses were the Freemen's best customers.

We entered Ontar through the hovercar garage, just outside the main gate. It was a much larger city than I had imagined. The hovercar, weighted with soldiers as it was, was almost as slow as walking, so I had plenty of time to think—about boredom and women's talk and war. Oroark worried silently in his corner of the car. I wondered about the Gildsman I had seen during the wedding procession. Where had I met him? What was his name?

All at once, the block in my memory fell away. Home, on Fruhe, that was where I had seen him. Pieter had brought him to dinner. And once more when the whole family had gone to see Pieter off. Tremo was his name, Sam Tremo. He'd been a lay chaplain then. I had a starting point for conversation with the man, at least. Whether such short acquaintance would help me enlist his aid in an escape was another question. The Gild was very strict about its neutrality. The Gharr were very rigid in what a woman was allowed to do and what she was not.

The car wound through narrower and narrower rows of shops. Pedestrians pressed against the buildings to avoid being bumped, yet I was apparently the only person who thought the proceeding arrogant. It *was* arrogant, and no way to treat Freemen.

"How far from here, Squadman Whitten?" I asked the driver.

The soldier squinted at the names of the shops as we passed. "Perhaps a kilometer, Larga."

"Stop the car, then. We'll walk."

Oroark blocked exit with his arm as I rose from my place. "Larga, it's not fitting."

"I'm tired of hearing what's 'fitting' and what's not!" I brushed past his restraining arm, ducked under the edge of the roof, and stepped down onto the cobbles.

The driver looked at Oroark, who shrugged his shoulders helplessly. They left one soldier to guard the car and walked with me. The walkways became narrower and more crowded. Many people, when they slid off their cloaks to salute the Larga Halarek, stopped and stared. Oroark kept close beside me, so close I nearly walked on him. Then we turned a corner.

I stopped in dismay. We were in a tiny stinking lane filled with twisted faces and clutching hands and the smell of filthy clothes and bodies. Voices rose, pleading, demanding. More than ever, my ignorance of Rom frightened me. Oroark jerked my arm to get me moving again. Old people and whining children pressed close. They reached for alms or whatever they could take. Some began pulling my hair.

"Move back. Move back," the soldiers kept saying, shouldering a way through the sudden crowd. "Treat the Larga with proper respect, Zinn bait!"

"Cover your hair, Larga," Oroark ordered urgently. "They'll keep trying to take some until you do."

I obeyed hurriedly. The crowd moved away reluctantly, muttering. Oroark shoved me forward, out of the congested alley. The white line around his lips showed how hard he was trying to control his anger. He wanted desperately to scold me, but that was one of the things that was "not done." It might have been funny if the situation hadn't been so frightening. Oroark compensated for holding his tongue by sending one of the soldiers back for the car. I would not be allowed to walk back. Then, ahead, I saw the red rocket and gyro of the Gild hanging over the street. I gripped Oroark's arm.

"Captain, look."

"I see," he snapped.

In moments he was vigorously banging the knocker on the plastex door. While we waited for an answer, Oroark's eyes ceaselessly searched the street and the buildings along it. The serf who came to the door recognized the Blues uniforms. He swung the door wide.

"House Halarek." The porter, wearing Gild red, bowed very slightly and swung the door open wide. "Welcome."

Oroark ordered the Blues to stand guard in the entry hall. Then he turned to the porter. "We've come to see the First Merchant."

The porter motioned toward a huge room across the hall. Sam Tremo, now wearing the red and gold uniform of the First Merchant of a Gildhall, came quickly through a door on the far side of the room. I made the slight bow that is proper greeting on Fruhe and touched my hand to head and heart, then I gave the greeting of this world.

"Peace in your house, First Merchant."

"Grace, Larga, and peace."

We shook hands. Oroark growled at the familiarity. I turned a little and put a hand on his arm. Would the Gildsman's being a family friend make matters better or worse in Oroark's eyes? I wondered. I couldn't guess, but I had to say something.

"Captain Oroark, shaking hands is custom on Fruhe, where I met the First Merchant years ago."

The open hostility left Oroark's face, but his rigid watchfulness showed he hadn't changed his opinion of the handshake's impropriety. Sam, in his diplomatic way, bowed deeply over my hand and kissed the air above it in the Gharr way to appease Oroark. Then he stepped back and looked at me.

"Good health, Zjhanne Verlith."

The familiar Fruvan salutation and speech, even with Tremo's guttural Rigel IV accent, almost made me cry with homesickness. "Good health, First Merchant. Do you—"

Oroark moved warningly. I wanted to ask about home and family and—

But I had been allowed to come to learn how to get Gild protection. I reluctantly changed to speaking Sternlangue, a language the captain understood. "My lord has told me to seek Gild protection if he's killed, First Merchant. The battle goes badly for us, I'm told, and my lord doesn't trust Council to protect us."

Sam's face became grave. "You came here to do this?"

"I thought—" My mind raced to find a plausible explanation for risking a trip through the city. "There's a deep spy in our House, First Merchant. I was afraid if the spy overheard the transmission, he'd find some way to cut that link with the outside."

Sam nodded slowly. He was going to accept my explanation. "You have risked much for something so simple. You had only to ask. No advance preparation. No paperwork."

"That's really all I had to do? Call?"

"That is all. If your husband is dead, your legal ties here, including your citizenship, are cut—if you have no children—and anything that happens to you after your petition is Gild business. That should make you as safe as is possible on this world."

As safe as is possible on this world. That was the best I could hope for. I could rely on the Gild's reputation to protect me, even if the next lord of Halarek would not allow Gild people into the manor. And who would the next lord be?

I didn't want to think about that. I didn't want to go back to Ontar yet, either. Perhaps Sam had heard something from my family. Surely, even if the letter I'd written hadn't gone through his hands, Sam would have given my parents some word of where I was. He had seen me in the wedding procession. He knew Pieter. He was a chaplain and used to giving families bad news. And surely giving an interplanetary kidnap victim's family word of her location wouldn't be considered untoward interference in Starker IV's affairs by Sam's superiors, would it? I steeled myself against the possibility that no one I loved knew where I was or what had happened to me.

"Is my family well, First Merchant? How have they taken this?"

"This know I not, Larga. But perhaps . . ." He rummaged through the pockets of his surcoat. "This arrived last week. Usually Frem Weisman picks up the mail. But of course you—"

"Sam!"

He looked startled, but didn't finish the sentence. If Oroark had learned that I had sent a letter off-world, his duty would require him to tell the Lharr and then . . . I felt a tiny shiver of apprehension. I hadn't known it was treason when I sent that letter. But Tam must have, and Weisman, who carried it. If the Lharr found out, if anyone else found out, Lord Richard's slander about treason would become true.

"—well, anyway," Sam was saying, "when I called about this, Weisman said he'd be too busy for several days."

Sam shrugged and handed me a bulky envelope, addressed to the Lharr Karne Halarek in my mother's familiar scrawl. I started to open it, but remembered in time Lady Agnes's lessons: I must wait and read it aloud in front of my ladies or I would irreparably damage my reputation.

"Who knows what damage an indiscretion could do," Lady Agnes would say, sternly.

And what would Lady Agnes say if she knew I had almost opened a letter with the Lharr's name on it? She would probably have had conniptions. Thanks be she was gone.

I was irritated enough at the restriction on letters and the restriction on shaking hands and the restriction on speaking a foreign tongue to a man not my husband that I continued my conversation with Tremo in Fruvan. "Sam, does the Gild have linguatapes? I'm in deadly danger and I know no Rom. It terrifies me, Sam."

"They could come on the next ship, Larga."

"Good. Order them. Sam, I'm so afraid!"

Oroark shifted his feet and cleared his throat. He spoke carefully, in Sternlangue. "You must speak so I understand, Larga. It is not proper for you to converse privately with a man."

I felt myself tighten all over. Rules. Restrictions. "Proper." I was suffocating! "I'm not talking privately," I snapped. "You're here, Squadman Whitten at the door, the porter who let us in—"

Oroark's angular face set stubbornly in a way the past two weeks had made all too familiar.

Poor boy, I thought, I constantly shocked his so-narrow ideas of propriety.

"The Lharr would not permit you to remain if you insist on being secretive, my lady. I will have to take you back to the manor." Oroark stepped closer, stiff with determination.

He meant it. I had to convince him I was being circumspect or this one chance to talk to the Gild would disappear. "I'm not being secretive, Captain! I want to speak my own language. Would you be happy if you never heard or spoke Rom again?" And I did want to speak and hear Fruvan. God knows, I wanted to!

Oroark's face set even more. "You must speak to the Gildsman in Sternlangue or Rom or not at all, my lady."

I stood ramrod stiff and put all the ice I could manage into my voice. "Just what do you suspect me of, Captain Oroark?"

The young man blushed violently and I regretted the need to corner him. I touched his arm lightly. "I'm sorry, Captain. I know you're only doing what you see as your duty, but who would tell?"

Oroark nodded toward the far doors. "The Gild guards, perhaps. Or one of our men. Or the porter. He surely does not live so well he would snub a bribe, perhaps lie to earn it."

I sighed. He could very well be right. There were always people around me—guarding, watching, listening, maybe spying, for the Lharr or for his enemies. The Lharr had mentioned a spy in his house when Lord Nicholas died. I would yield for now. I turned back to the First Merchant. "I'll expect to hear from you soon, Sam."

Sam bowed gravely. "The Lord be with you."

"And with your spirit," Oroark and I responded, as is Gharr custom.

Sam waited politely until we reached the door before he turned to leave the room.

I wanted very much to be alone with the letter. But, as Oroark's stubbornness at the Gildhall had reminded me, defying custom on this world could be dangerous. To prevent any distortions by my gossipy companions of what the letter said, I asked Freemen Orkonan and Weisman to join me and my ladies in my quarters to hear the letter read. I read slowly, translating the words from Fruvan into Sternlangue because Sternlangue was all my translit understood. I omitted the passages in which my parents told of their shock and grief at my disappearance and stopped in shock myself when I reached the place where Mom thanked Lord Karne for his letter. I let the hand holding the letter fall to my lap.

This wasn't an answer to my letter. Mom made no mention of my letter. Lord Karne had written to them as soon as he returned to Starker IV and told them what had happened to me, where I was, that I was well and legally married to him. He had assured them I would be treated as a very valuable asset to his House. A Black Ship captain has never, never shown such kindness! Women taken by the Black Ships just disappear.

I couldn't fit what I knew of the Black Ships with what Lord Karne had done. Why would a kidnapper who wanted no ransom report *anything* to his victim's parents? And why hadn't the Lharr told me he had written a letter? Kindness and a Black Ship. They did *not* fit together. Mom's letter showed Karne Halarek in a new light.

I realized suddenly that I was sitting silent. I quickly summarized what I had read.

A small page burst into the room, his face flushed with excitement. "The Lharr's back!" he cried. "He wants one of the ladies to attend Lady Kathryn."

I stood, slipped the letter into a pocket, motioned Jaklene to come with me, and followed the page. The Lharr waited outside the Great Hall. Jaklene and I curtseyed, then waited, not knowing what sort of response to expect from either the man or the thin, gray-faced woman beside him. The Lharr smiled wearily and took my hands in his for a moment.

"Thank you," he said softly. "Your personal attention to this is more than I expected." He turned to the woman with him. "This is my wife Zjhanne, Kit. Zjhanne, this is my sister, Kathryn von Schuss, and her son, Jemmy. She already knows about Nik's death. Keep her with you and be gentle with her. I'll take Jemmy."

He and the thin dark woman were clearly brother and sister. They had the same slightly curly hair and wiry build. Kit's eyes were gold, like his, with a lot of brown flecks in them. She drooped now against a pillar, one hand protectively on the head of a boy of about five years who slept in a heap at her feet. The Lharr picked up the child; Jaklene and I helped the exhausted Kit to the lift and then into the room across from the Larga's quarters. Jaklene helped Kit prepare for bed. She was asleep before we left.

Kit kept to herself for several days. Only after First Day services did she respond to questions about her time in Odonnel or invitations to join activities. Very soon after that, she eagerly took over the household duties Lady Agnes had despaired of ever teaching me. Kit said work would keep her from thinking too much about Nik or about Jemmy's danger. Her hatred and mine for a system that would murder a child for political reasons was our first common bond.

The Lharr was graver than ever after his return, and more restrictive. He doubled my personal guard immediately and enforced the order that I (and later, Kit) go nowhere in the house without a four-soldier escort. He often missed the evening meal to continue working on some political problem, which left me to preside over the Great Hall, full of Halarek Family resident cousins, mostly male. When he did eat with the Family, the Lharr pulled out my chair for me, then Kit's, said grace, and inquired politely how our day had gone. After that he seldom spoke.

Kit and I were sitting in the library, waiting for dinner to be served, when Kit finally decided to press her brother to give up the formal evening meal with the rest of the Family and make a much smaller family meal in the unused room next to the library.

"You need to slow down, Karne," she urged. "I've been here a week and haven't seen you take any breaks at all. If we eat next door, you'll still be so near the library that Weisman can bring any information you might need."

Obedient to Kit's look, I added verbal reinforcements. "You'll be right across the hall from the tri-d room instead of downstairs," I said. "That eliminates *that* excuse."

I watched thoughts flit across the Lharr's face. I strongly hoped he would agree. If he did, I would no longer have to sit in the Great Hall, either, trying to eat in spite of the prying, judging eyes of the unattached males of the Halarek clan.

The Lharr gave a tired laugh. "All right. All right. Shall we start tonight?"

I hadn't realized I was clenching my hands until the Lharr laughed and I relaxed: The nail prints in my palms stung.

From that night on, the three of us, along with my ladies (who now served Kit, too), Orkonan, Oroark, and sometimes others who had urgent business with the Lharr, ate dinner in the personal-family dining room.

Talking the Lharr into letting Kit and me go horseback riding on the surface was much harder than talking him into eating apart. What finally seemed to convince him was Kit's argument that any enemy could be seen approaching on the surface or in the air for many kilometers away, so it was safer on the open plains than in the manor.

The day we finally got outside, the sun was shining and the wind was sharp, but the air smelled of green grass and the bluepines on the foothills. I hadn't counted on being required to wear a long skirt, though, or having to use a wretched side-saddle, both of which considerably dimmed my pleasure. Worst, the large number of new men in our escort reminded both Kit and me every moment of the high casualties Halarek had suffered in the battle to free Kit. All in all, the first afternoon was a fiasco.

I didn't want to ride side-saddle, but, now I'd been allowed out, I couldn't stand being shut away from fresh air all the time, either. So, with the Lharr's approval, Kit, Jaklene, and I rigged schlakball nets in the barren garden. Schlak is an easy but vigorous game played across a net with rackets and a rough-surfaced hide ball. It can be played in the required long skirt. The Lharr refused to join the fun. He had too much work, he said, too many tri-d meetings with Freemen and the lords of other Houses. So Jaklene teased the reluctant Oroark into learning how to play. He became skillful and as his skill increased, his shyness and awkwardness decreased. "Captain Oroark" gradually became "Tommy" to the residents of the Larga's quarters.

Other Blues assigned to us eventually joined the games and we had many happy afternoons running around in the sunshine and batting balls. It could have been as much fun as playing at home, except for the long heavy skirt that wound around my legs and tangled with my feet.

Then the Lharr called Lady Agnes back from her daughter's. He was going to spend several days and nights at the Summer Council and thought that I, with my off-world ways and with rumors from Justin's hunt still nibbling at my reputation, needed a chaperon in his absence, someone everyone recognized as strict and absolutely incorruptible. Lady Agnes immediately complained to the Lharr that Kit and I were being "hussies" for playing with the soldiers, especially Kit, who was still in mourning. She made such a fuss about our reputations that the Lharr made us quit before he left for Council.

After Council, the Lharr continued flying from holding to holding, urging reforms, talking, arguing, listening. I wished he would explain what he was working so hard to do, but politics is not a subject Gharr men discuss with women. The Lharr talked to Kit sometimes, though. That's how I knew the little I did about what he was doing. I only saw his long hours of preparation. And some nights, when he'd come in very late, I'd wake up and see him in the wing chair beside my bed. Sometimes he would be asleep, his face at rest both very tired and very sad. He apparently sent my ladies to sleep in Kit's quarters so they could neither watch nor overhear. He didn't waken me. He didn't touch me. Most nights I didn't know he had been there until the next morning, when my ladies started questioning me. Those nights that I was aware of him there, I pretended sleep, primarily out of cowardice. We didn't talk about this in the daytime. In the daytime, the Lharr was almost never around. I came to think he was deliberately avoiding me.

Thank God I had been trained since childhood not to talk about bedroom matters, or I would have spoiled his plan the first morning. As it was, my ladies expected what they considered excessive modesty from me and accepted my evasions and then flat refusals to discuss details of our "bedplay." If there had been any doubt in my mind why he had been doing this strange thing, my ladies' eager and bawdy questions would have laid doubt to rest. He was keeping his promise and yet protecting my reputation and his own. No one would question my lack of a pregnancy, either, because the Lharr was known to be unlucky when it came to children. His first child, a girl, had died soon after birth of something called the Sickness, his second with his second wife.

Forbidden to play on the surface, left out of political conversations, and without research or teaching, I became dreadfully bored, almost as bored as during the winter. So I set my seamstress to altering my wardrobe. That is, the seamstress altered until Weisman, horrified by a pair of trousers, tattled to the Lharr. I found out what Weisman had done when the seamstress came at her usual time, but with only the velvet dress I was making for the approaching holidays.

The seamstress laid the dress carefully across the bed, but she wouldn't meet my eyes. "I'm sorry, milady," she said, her voice low and wavering. "The other things are gone. The Lharr ordered them destroyed."

"He what?"

"He said they were brazen and shocking and entirely unsuited to your station and that I wasn't to help you ever again with anything like them."

I looked down in disgust at my long, heavy skirt. "I won't need you today, then. You may go."

The wardrobe matter would not have seemed so important if I had had more to do, but I didn't, so I stewed about it. If I couldn't design comfortable clothes, what could I do? I had no research projects, nor did I consider starting any, since I could never get them published. Besides, I was too intimately involved in this society to study it objectively. I had already run through the library's small collection of books in Sternlangue. Weisman was very sympathetic about that, but swore he could not order books in Fruvan without the Lharr's seal. The tri-d was fascinatingly realistic, but quite useless, since I couldn't understand the words. Kit was helping me learn Rom, but it went slowly with neither linguatapes nor computers and my tapes from the Gild still had not come. And Lady Agnes kept saying things like "You'll have plenty to do when Advent partying starts" and "You're breeding, aren't you? That explains your absurd moodiness."

I always turned away when Lady Agnes got to that point, afraid my face would betray how wrong she was. I wasn't breeding. My people have internal control of fertility, as I had told the Lharr from the beginning. My "moodiness" was a result of having nothing useful to do.

Obviously, I frequently told myself, the Lharr is trying to turn me into a meek, domestic mouse by boring me into submission. If he'd just take a little time to provide some intelligent conversation, to pay some attention, to give me work! What kind of gamble am I if I live like all the other women on Starker IV? But the Lharr was never around to ask about that.

One evening, after an afternoon of this sort of thinking, I felt much too upset to eat dinner. Making a scene would help me not at all, so I didn't go to dinner. But I made Donna, Jaklene, and Tamara go. Relieved of their chattering and prying, I relaxed a little and lay down. I had no sooner begun the mind-clearing concentration my people use to calm themselves when the Lharr entered unannounced. He hadn't even been on the holding the last I'd heard.

"Are you ill, madam?"

"No, I just don't feel like eating. Leave me alone." His interruption added irritation to the self-pity I had already worked up.

A corresponding sharpness replaced the concern in his voice. "I'm reaching the end of my patience with you. I have enough worries without having to keep an eye on a woman who insists on behaving like a spoiled child."

"Spoiled child! Reaching the end of *your* patience!" I sat bolt upright. "My lord, I didn't volunteer to come to this hole in the ground. I'm an 'experiment,' a 'gamble,' remember? Send me home when your patience gives out. I hope it's soon!"

He gripped my arm bruisingly. "You are my wife, before God and the universe. That puts obligations on you as well as on me."

"Mostly on me."

"Sarcasm doesn't become you, madam."

I pulled free of his hand. "It wasn't meant to. What are *your* obligations? Even the rare times you're here, you ignore me. I'm just an object here, a *thing* with some obscure social and political value, like Ontar and this desolate Holding."

"You're still alive."

"Breath in the body isn't life, Lord Karne, it's existence. How can you expect me to be satisfied with that? Send me home!"

He laughed bitterly. "I hoped you'd help me, but you'd prefer to destroy me."

"That's not true! I just don't care. How could I? Even *if* I knew what was happening."

"I wish I *could* send you home. But we're married. On this world, that's a lifetime commitment." He rammed his hands into the pockets of his jacket and turned away. "Even if we could dissolve the bond between us, even if I could finance a return trip, do you think you'd be safe on Fruhe?"

"Why not? My father has the means to guard me."

"Even against friends like van Tibe?" He paused to let all the painful reminders of that betrayal rise in me. "Do you want to spend the rest of your life under guard? Here, I know the danger. I know Richard's mind. Can you say that of your father?"

I stared at him in amazement, anger for the moment checked. "What does the duke care where I go, as long as I leave you?"

"Are you that stupid?"

"I'm not stupid! You're stupid! *You* make the restrictions. *You* make me fight you, you—, you—"

He turned and froze me with his eyes. "If, madam, you were as clever as you think you are, you'd see your danger. Since the War, only one man has killed women, no matter how deadly the feud. We have too few. But our unwritten law didn't stop Richard from killing my mother, and my second wife, and trying to kill you. He can't destroy House Halarek if you carry its seed."

"But we never—"

"Not quite never."

"You don't have to remind me. You took advan—"

"When it was necessary to protect us both."

"That's what you say!" I don't know why I said that, because I hated myself for it the moment the words were out. I understood the necessity of that Sealing now and knew he told the truth.

"Grow up, madam! We *are* married. How many times more can I come here at night, do you think, before one of your women discovers that I just sit beside the bed while you pretend I'm not there?"

"Have you been, Lord Karne?"

His hand darted forward and slapped my mouth. "You know I have, though you pretend to be asleep."

This, too, was truth. I threw myself facedown on the bed and cried. It had been stupid, pointless defiance, and he knew it. Why had I said it? No one had ever provoked me into arguing for perversity's sake before.

"Go away!" I cried at him fiercely. "Go away and leave me alone!"

He turned me roughly onto my back and jerked me to my feet. His voice was frighteningly quiet. "I've had enough of your nonsense. I don't like to force what could be freely given, but I've waited four months for you to show any signs of willingness. I'll wait blessed little longer to bed you, madam. I will have a son!" He punctuated each sentence with a hard shake.

I glared at him. "No Fruvan woman will conceive an unwanted child, milord. Surely your pre-selection information included that fact. Bring a child into this life? I'd rather die!"

"That may be precisely your choice, madam." He spun abruptly and left.

CHAPTER 9

Dear Kit, she sensed something was the matter, but she couldn't find out what. For nearly a week she insisted on going with me on my household inspections, which took several hours. Kit also suggested we work intensively on teaching me Rom and introduced me, by tri-d, to some of Ontar's "neighbors." Visiting by tri-d was one way the Gharr brightened winters and winter was coming. It was a sort of joke among the Gharr; winter was always coming. "Yes, we had summer on a Ninth Day last year" was one of the ways they put it.

Seeing people on tri-d is almost like having them in, the image of them is so lifelike. My favorites among the neighbors were the son and daughters of Councilman Duval of Lews—Kendar, Elspeth, and Adrian—whom we were to visit the first few days in Advent. The Duvals were gay, witty, enjoyable people, although the girls' interests seemed rather narrow. That appearance was deceptive, Kit told me. Adrian had been her lady-in-waiting and a spy for Halarek during Kit's first marriage, when she had been unwillingly a Harlan wife and living in Odonnel.

Sam Tremo called during this boring period to tell me my order was in. That was good news. I needed the tapes badly. I didn't want to send the prying Weisman for them, though, so I tried to find a safe time to slip away for them myself. I managed to reach the hovercar garage, but I underestimated Tommy's capacities as a watchdog. I was just settling myself into the driver's seat when Tommy and six of my Blues blocked the exit door.

"Lord Karne forbids leaving the manor, my lady," Tommy told me stiffly.

"But I need—"

"I'll send someone."

I felt as though I were strangling on restrictions and togetherness. "Captain—Tommy, please, I've got to get out for a while."

Oroark shifted his weight back and forth several times and blushed when he realized what he was doing, but he didn't yield. Perhaps, if he had been alone, he would have, but he had his men to set an example for. In the end, Weisman picked up the tapes a couple of days later. As soon as he got back, he offered to thread the tape through the machine for me, curiosity clamoring in every line of him. But I didn't want spectators. I ordered him away.

Kit and I had decided that the library would be the best place to study. We wanted to start with the tapes that very evening, but we had great difficulty persuading Weisman he really didn't have to work in the library all the time. He pretended he had pressing business there. Kit thought his excessive interest very funny. He reminded me of a boy I had known in grammar school, a nosy child who thought his prying curiosity was friendliness and who could never understand why the other children avoided him. Weisman had apparently never outgrown the same stage.

The memory weakened my exasperation and I resolved to have more patience with the poor man. But the next day, Kit and I made Weisman, and Frem Orkonan, promise to keep what we were doing a secret. We wanted to surprise the Lharr with my ability to speak in his language.

The day after the tapes arrived, Kit burst into the library at lesson time. "Oh, Zjhanne, let's skip the lesson today and go riding instead."

"But I thought—"

"Aye, Karne hasn't changed his mind about us going onto the surface, thanks to Lady Agnes. But he said we could use the arena. He's had horses brought down."

"When did he get back?"

"Oh, late last night." Kit closed the book she held. "Come on. We can do this later." Her face glowed.

She's keeping something a secret, I thought, and with difficulty.

Curious, I dropped my book onto the worktable and followed her. She went to the arena on level 1, below the kitchens. It served for military drilling, tourneys, army celebrations, riding, and athletic contests. Kit stationed our soldier escorts at the doors. She turned to me, her hand on the door.

"Stay here now, and close your eyes."

"Kit . . ."

"Don't argue. You practice that enough with Karne. Come on, don't spoil my fun."

I obediently closed my eyes. I heard Kit open a door and felt the chilly air of the arena sweep out. After several minutes I heard hooves thudding hollowly on the bark of the arena floor. I opened my eyes.

Kit laughed her rare, silvery laugh. "You weren't supposed to look till I told you to." She rode forward and handed me the reins of the "horse" she led, a small, graceful animal, with large dark eyes, short black horns, and thick, woolly, reddish fur. It was beautiful. "A gift from my cowardly brother," Kit added.

I had no words to adequately express my appreciation. The "horse" rubbed its soft nose up and down my blouse. I caressed its head, rubbed behind its horns, and ran my hands down its neck to the saddle, a real saddle, a beautiful, beautiful saddle, across which lay a richly embroidered divided skirt. The Lharr had given me a magnificent gift. It was also a magnificent apology for our quarrel. I looked up at Kit, wordless.

"The saddle's a real surprise, no? Karne ordered it from the leather shops of Deneb." Kit leaned across her animal and stroked a line of embroidery on the divided skirt. "Put it on. No one will come in. Silly man was afraid to give these to you himself." And she chuckled a little at her brother's cowardice.

After my last display of bad temper, I can hardly blame him for being afraid, I told myself. It's a very generous apology. How can I show *my* regret?

There would be time to think of that later. Right now, I was going to use my gift. I exchanged my day-skirt for the riding skirt and swung into the saddle. I felt so much safer and so much more myself astride. I named the horse Gordie and he was a joy to ride—spirited, gentle, beautifully trained. I'm afraid that in my enthusiasm, I wore Kit out.

Karne was still home for nightmeal, and he presided over it with his customary formality. When he pulled out my chair to seat me, I thanked him, warmly I thought, for his gifts. He bowed gravely in acknowledgment, but said nothing. He said grace as usual and the meal began. On this particular night, neither Orkonan nor Captain

Oroark had business to discuss with the Lharr while we ate, and the Lharr himself was unusually quiet. Jaklene and Tamara tried in vain to wheedle out of him news from the holdings he had visited. Even Kit could pry loose only monosyllables. I didn't try. He and I always had a wall of polite silence between us. He was around too seldom for us to have found topics of mutual interest and, even if he had been home more, my kidnapping and continuing captivity stood between us.

On this night, the silence was different. I could feel it, tight and waiting. Sharing a plate with the Lharr had changed from an everyday, impersonal custom into something frighteningly intimate. I felt his eyes on me often and I dared not meet them. When Donna entered timidly, curtseyed several times, and announced Baron von Schuss was calling, I excused myself with relief, glad for a chance to attend to one of my few duties.

The man on the tri-d screen was fiftyish and portly, with a jovial, mustached face. He seemed within touching distance. I curtseyed respectfully.

"Peace in your House, Larga."

"And in yours grace and peace, Baron."

"Outstanding woman, aren't you?" The baron leaned forward as if to examine me more closely. "Your hair, you know. So different."

I could only stare at him. He acted as if we knew each other. That and the uncanny nearness-to-reality of tri-d pictures stopped my tongue for a moment while I reminded myself he was not really standing at the far end of the tri-d room.

The ends of the baron's mustache twitched. "Sorry. Forgot how many people you met. Wedding, you know. Kathryn's uncle-in-law. Wondered if you'd have room for an old bachelor this week. Advent's only twelve days away, you know. Kit's mourning will be over. Lots of parties. No time for an old man then."

My mind raced. I was larga in this House. Did I have the authority to agree to the visit? The man was a relative, after all, and the message *had* come to me. "Of—of course you can come, Baron."

He could have been reading my mind. "Don't you think you'd better ask Karne? Extra work for the soldiers, you know."

I hesitated only a moment. I would take this responsibility. I was not just an ornament here. "I'm sure it would be all right, my lord. May we expect you tomorrow?"

Baron von Schuss looked faintly surprised, then he laughed and I heard the faint clink of his neck chain as it bounced on his chest.

"Hoped you'd make it soon. Till early afternoon, then. The Lord be with you."

"And with your spirit."

He snapped off his transmitter. I stared at the empty screen. I wasn't yet used to seeing people who seemed "here" suddenly disappear. I turned to the little serf, who hovered uncertainly by the door.

"Donna."

She curtseyed quickly. "Milady?"

But after looking at the faces of the technicians who maintained the tri-d equipment, I changed my mind. I would not send her with a message. I would tell the Lharr myself what I had done.

Everyone looked up from their food when I opened the door to the dining room. I had thought I was getting used to eyes always on me, but even twelve pairs still unnerved me. I blurted the message and retreated to my room, all appetite gone. This time, the Lharr did nothing about my absence. When Kit came up later, she was all excited at the prospect of the baron's visit. The baron was a relative, not a guest. He would provide the fun and fresh conversation she so desperately needed without making her break mourning. As if a ritual period of mourning had anything to do with the grief Kit felt daily.

The baron's stay was fast and fun and too soon over. He was as jovial as he looked and more grandfather than great-uncle to Jemmy. Jemmy's and Kit's faces showed how much they adored him. In fact, Kit gave Jemmy's tutor the week off so Jemmy could spend as much time as possible with the baron.

Because he was a guest, the baron had the choice of what we did each day. He played chess with the Lharr, teased Kit and me, and roughhoused with Jemmy. One afternoon he and Lord Karne staged a mock tournament for Kit and me and the rest of our household, relatives and servants both. Lord Karne won on horseback, but lost both ground battles.

Evening meals were as lively as the days. Baron von Schuss sat on Lord Karne's right, in my usual place. I sat to his right and was honored to eat from the same plate. His hilarious stories of adventures as a youth in the Imperial Navy broke Lord Karne's preoccupation and I heard him laugh, really laugh, for the first time. But at the end of every evening, when the Lharr walked with me back to our suite, he was just a gentle impersonal hand on my arm and an occasional polite question.

The days went so well that I couldn't understand why the nights did not. Was the Lharr angry with me about something and didn't want the others to know about it? I was afraid to ask. Maybe I was reading him wrong. Maybe I was relying too much on what I knew of Pieter. I had seen how well trained the Lharr was at hiding his feelings. The Academy's doing, Kit told me.

Also, I hadn't yet said how much *I* regretted our last quarrel and the longer I dallied, the harder it was to apologize. Especially after the magnificence of his apology. Maybe my own guilt was part of the barrier between us. I sighed, thinking of this, and the Lharr looked at me sharply. He squeezed my arm, but said nothing. I started to say the words of apology, then glanced at his cool, stiff profile. He looked so unreachable that my words died. At my door he bowed gracefully. "Sleep well, my lady." He went into his room through his own entrance.

The baron left with the same enthusiasm he had exhibited all during his visit—a toss in the air for Jemmy, a pinch for Kit, a hearty kiss for me, and a scolding for Lord Karne.

"Got to have a son, Karne. Can't afford to dilly-dally, you know. Been too many years already."

The Lharr laughed awkwardly and carefully avoided looking at me. I know I blushed furiously. The baron chuckled, bounced into his flitter, and took off.

In the days after that, because Advent had begun, the Lharr was frequently at home and the tension between us was more than I could endure for long. The baron's parting words seemed to have changed something. I was intensely aware of the Lharr and didn't understand why. Nothing had changed. I was still his prisoner. I was still bound by his world's rules into a boring, depressing, joyless life. I felt confused, desperate. It couldn't be love, that tension. It couldn't be desire. I was his *prisoner*.

The tension in me built rapidly. I had to talk to someone to help figure out what was happening, but I didn't know Kit well enough yet to discuss personal matters with her and I didn't trust even one of my ladies to keep anything I said to herself. I couldn't write home without the Lharr or Orkonan reading the letter first, which meant the questions I most needed answered couldn't be asked. I couldn't call home for the same reasons, and because any request for help could, and probably would, be interpreted as treason. My feelings piled on top of each other, crowding, crying, overloading my ability to control them. I *had* to talk to someone before I came to pieces.

Sam Tremo. Sam was a chaplain of The Way. He was a neutral in Starker IV's politics. He seemed to be the only person on this world I could trust. I tried several times to leave the manor for the Gildhall, but Tommy's men or the regular sentries always prevented me.

The baron hadn't been gone a week when I could stand the pressure no more. I bribed a Freewoman who came in to sew for us to let me wear her clothes and use her in/out pass for a few hours. I justified my behavior to myself with the intensity of my desperation: I could trust a Gildsman not to betray me. And Tremo would understand my confusion and despair as no native of Starker IV could.

Sam was in a business meeting when I arrived without any escorts. The Gildclerk showed me into a small side room and closed the door. I had time to think in that small room. What I was doing was a scandalous impropriety *and* against the Lharr's wishes. It was also very dangerous. I should leave before Sam came. I should leave. But I owed Halarek nothing and I felt like I was going crazy. I *had* to talk to Sam.

Sam Tremo entered, somewhat upset. "Larga Zjhanne, you should not be here without your lord. You risk much."

I felt a rush of relief at his presence, in spite of his warning. I closed my mind to the apprehension that followed the relief. Here I had help at last. "I had to see you. You were a lay chaplain for years. Advise me."

"The manor has no pastor now?"

"Aye, but he'd betray anything 'improper' to the Lharr and what I have to say is quite 'improper.' Besides, he's never lived anywhere else. Please, Sam, I'm at the end of my string! I'm going crazy and I have nowhere else to turn. *Please!*"

His face saddened and he sat down heavily. "Tell me."

In a rush, I told him, in Fruvan, about my forced marriage, the rigid rules, the insipid women, the inactivity, the stifling atmosphere of masculine superiority, the boredom, the quarrels, even the cumbersome dresses and tangle of hair and the new, frightening tension between me and my husband. At the end I laughed a little, embarrassed.

"I feel better just having gotten it all out, Sam. I wouldn't dare talk about any of these things to people in the manor."

He sighed heavily. "I hope your visit here doesn't cost you dearly, Larga Zjhanne. Confession is sacred and the right of every person, but the Gharr's rules are strict beyond understanding. You may find that their rules are more important to them than The Way's."

I shook my head. "I can't help that. I'm dying inside of boredom, yet, to the Lharr, I'm just a tool that doesn't work the way it's supposed to. And we antagonize each other so. I want to go home!"

"No one can help you to do that, Zjhanne, except your lord. You're Family now, not Zjhanne Verlith of Fruhe. The Gild must deal with you by Family rules. Surely your lord told you that."

I took a deep, shuddering breath. "There must be some way, Sam. I don't want to live another day on this worse-than-backward world. I don't want to live with Karne Halarek."

His mouth tightened. "There is no way for you to leave, no way at all. If you should find a way, it would be called 'treason against the planet' and your husband and many in his House would pay with their lives for it. Stop thinking about it!"

"What can I do then? He doesn't even want to be *friends* with me."

"You and your husband do not get along. How have you tried to change this?"

"I don't know how, Sam. I've never met a man who treats me as he does. He's so distant and formal. And lately this tension . . . I feel like a bomb about to explode whenever I'm near him."

Tremo's taut features loosened a little. "You aren't so innocent that you don't know what that tension likely means, are you, Zjhanne?"

I flushed. I knew what he meant, but I couldn't possibly desire a man who took me for political reasons, a man I didn't love, didn't even like very often. What about him? We'd been married for months, the man had had two wives already, yet he had not tried even once to entice me into bed. *He* had shown no signs of desiring *me*. Was his promise really holding him back or was I physically undesirable to him?

But he *had* selected me from among several candidates, and he had checked me out himself. If I were undesirable, he wouldn't have chosen me. Besides, it seemed rather perverse on my part to care why he didn't bed me. I didn't want *him*. Or did I?

I didn't like where those thoughts were leading me. The Lharr had promised not to bed me by force. Clearly, he was keeping his promise. But what kidnapper ever did that, especially a Black Ship kidnapper? And what kidnapper wrote a reassuring letter to his victim's parents?

Just talking to Sam had opened doors I didn't want to look

through. My inner confusion deepened.

That must have shown in my eyes. Tremo's mouth ends tipped up the slightest bit. "I can see you are thinking about this now. Good. You should have thought before coming here. Go home. Think some more. If you still need to talk after that, send for me. Do *not* come here again without your lord." He stared at his hands, resting in his lap, for a moment. He looked up. "Would it help to pray before you go?"

I sighed and nodded. "It would, Sam."

I knelt and Sam began the beloved ritual.

"Lift up your hearts."

"We lift them up unto the Lord." *I'm so afraid, Lord.*

"Almighty God, to whom all hearts are open, all desires known . . ." How good the words felt, saying them again as I had learned them at home. ". . . cleanse the thoughts of our hearts . . ." As the familiar Fruvan words flowed out, calm flowed in, calm in which I would be able to think straight. ". . . amen."

I stumbled getting to my feet as I rose, and Sam extended a hand to help me up. At the door I shook hands with him and turned to go.

"Larga."

I stopped. Tremo hesitated.

"It may mean nothing, but a story is going around that Lord Karne played coward after Justin's hunt by avoiding a duel with Lord Richard. He should know of this."

"I'll—I'll tell him."

"The Lord be with you, Zjhanne."

"And with your spirit."

The street I stepped into was darkening, indicating "night" was coming. The reddish glow of "sunset" was fading and streetlights were blinking on one by one. I had been longer than I thought. I hurried to the borrowed hovercar and drove back to the manor, worrying the entire way.

Surely, since I was getting back safe, the Lharr wouldn't be angry. That had been the Lharr's main objection to leaving the manor, that it wasn't safe.

But I had flouted his orders, lured a Freewoman into my plan, worn a disguise, seen Tremo in private. The Lharr would be angry. Very angry.

What was it about the Lharr that made me act like a fool when it came to his orders?

I left the car at the manor gate and entered through the servants' entrance. I turned the key and pushed open the door. A grim-faced Tommy was waiting inside. He moved now with the deadly grace he had used in that crowd in Ontar. He pulled the Freewoman's headdress from my hair, took the key from my hand without a word, shut the door, locked it, pocketed the key, and took my arm ungently. He steered me to the nearest lift.

"You don't have to tell me where you've been, but the Lharr will have to know," Tommy said as he selected level 5. His voice was harder than I'd ever heard it. "*You've* acted very stupidly. *I've* failed in my duty, because you got out. I'll give you one day to tell him where you've been, then I must. I risk my career delaying at all."

"I just—"

"Don't talk to me! The Lharr said you couldn't be trusted and he was right. I may have lost my captaincy as it is."

Tommy rapped sharply on the door to my quarters. Kit opened it at once. She must have been waiting, too. She looked questioningly at Tommy. Tommy tightened his hold on my arm briefly, then stepped back, saluted us both, and left.

Kit frowned. "What was that about? And where have you been? I looked all over for you. We're leaving in the morning for the Duvals. I know I told you about it."

I glanced quickly after Tommy. One day. I had to report my own disobedience to the Lharr in one day's time or be turned in like a misbehaving child. "Tommy and I've just been having a difference of opinion."

Kit's expression showed she wasn't satisfied with my answer, but she didn't press me for more and I was grateful. She and I spent the next several hours packing. Kit was very particular about the clothes we should wear and our ladies-in-waiting, who should have done the packing, were so excited about being taken along that they were nearly useless. While we packed, I decided my Christmas gift to the Lharr would be an embroidered surcoat like the one Kit was folding so carefully for Jemmy's trunk. It would be a lot of work to do in a short time, but time was something I had plenty of and such a gift might approach in quality the apology he had made.

The expectation of a visit away should have been exciting, but Tremo's warning kept jangling in my head. It was just a rumor, I told myself. But I couldn't convince myself it wasn't important. The Lharr should know. Soon. I was the only one who knew. He should know as soon as possible. I couldn't put off admitting my visit to the Gildhall for even as long as one day. And the Lharr would be so angry! I dreaded the consequences of that anger. In the morning. I'd tell him in the morning. A few hours wouldn't make any difference.

The trunks were packed, the ladies in their beds, and I was almost asleep when someone pounded on my door. Jaklene got up and let Weisman in. The Freeman's entire body vibrated with his excitement.

"Larga, there's an emergency message for you. From a starship! He says it's urgent." Weisman's high voice squeaked and broke.

"Who says? Where?"

"The starship captain. In the com center, at the pad. You'd better run."

So I knotted my robe, hiked up the front edge, and ran.

It was Pieter calling! Pieter! I wished passionately I could see him!

"Zjhanne, are you alone?" Pieter's voice faded in and out.

"I will be." I motioned impatiently for the technicians and Weisman to leave. The librarian dawdled unnecessarily, it seemed, so I gave him a threatening look that sent him scurrying out. "Is something the matter at home, Pieter?"

The twelve-second transmission lag hung my question in the air of the com center.

"Let me talk, Zjhanne. There's a storm coming and I've got to get out of its way pretty quick. I'm also paying three hundred credits a minute for this, minus lag time, of course. I'm within a Jump of the Starker system, probably the only time I'll be this way for years. I can have a shuttle coming down for you in about four hours."

"Pieter, that would mean your commission!"

Twelve seconds. Pieter had never wanted to be anything but a starship captain.

"Damn the commission! I'm a good engineer. I can get another job."

"You worked so hard!"

Six seconds to go, six to come back. If the lag was nerve-wracking, it also gave me time to think.

"Stop worrying about my commission! The storm's breathing on me. Can you get free?"

My mind raced. Just short of the hills would probably be the safest place for the ship's shuttle to land. If I left immediately, Gordie could manage it in four hours. Then I thought of the irrevocable ceremony that cut me off forever from all other men.

"I married him, Pieter."

He had been told, hadn't he?

"You were coerced. It's void by galactic law. Once you're out of that system, you're free."

Relief made me light-headed. Free! Never again wearing these restricting clothes or bending before ridiculous rules or suppressing my abilities because Gharr women didn't show their abilities. Seeing the beautiful greenness of Fruhe . . . "Oh, Pieter, to be home again!"

Then between me and my goal came the memory of the ugly scene at Justin's hunt. I already lived under Lord Richard's shadowy accusations of infidelity and suggestions of treason. If I escaped off-world, treason would be proved. The Lharr and many or most of the people in House Halarek would be executed for what *I* had done.

"I'm setting course."

Hope of home and freedom when I'd given up hope. I felt as if I were smothering. At last I forced through a rebellious throat the words I had to say. "Don't, Pieter. I can't. Taking your help is treason. The Lharr would pay with his life for it. Many people would die. I can't do it. I can't."

Did he hear the last, whispered words? The unendurable time lag.

"Roger." And he was gone.

I sank to the floor and buried my face in my hands, too numb even to cry. It was done. He was gone and hope was gone. I had committed myself forever to this world.

"Larga?"

A tech had his head around the partially open door.

I wanted to be alone, but it wasn't right to keep the comtechs from their jobs. "Has the door been open all the time?"

"Aye, milady. It can't be opened except from the inside and we were pretty sure you didn't know how."

The techs had honest faces. They probably didn't understand Fruvan, anyway. Weisman was nowhere to be seen. I asked the sentry to call me an escort.

In a few minutes I was on my own level. Because I wanted quiet, I paced the hallways around and around the central cluster of rooms. My four Blues stayed a respectful distance ahead and behind, but they stayed with me. I noticed every time I passed the Lharr's quarters that there was no sentry outside his door. That meant he wasn't inside and that meant I could shake my escort by going into my own quarters and then go through the Lharr's room to the library. I desperately needed time alone and in silence.

My plan worked easily. My ladies were asleep. The Lharr was gone. I slipped through his room and crept down the iron stair in the dark, because I didn't know how to turn on the lights from the upper level. In the library, I decided dark suited me. I waved the fire on—it didn't make much light—curled up in a big soft chair, and stared at the artificial flames, thinking. I had traded death sentences for the Lharr, Kit, Jemmy, and many others for life in prison for myself. For a long time this was the only thought my numbed brain could muster. Life in prison.

When I woke up, the light coming in under the main door showed that "day" had already begun. I stretched and found stiff places. There was no point in mourning about last night. I had made the only possible choice. There was already enough killing on this planet.

I got up and stretched again. I'd better tell the Lharr Tremo's warning before I lost my nerve. But when I went to look for him, he had already gone off somewhere with Oroark, who would be in charge at the manor while we were gone. That left me with hours before departure in which to anticipate the Lharr's anger when I told him, and mine, which always followed his.

Even if Tommy had already told him I'd gone into the city alone, I'd still have to give Sam's warning. Waiting made the doing harder. I delayed going to the flitter pad like a naughty child. Finally I had to go.

There were few people in the halls, some soldiers and a young page. As I passed the kitchen, I heard two scullery women shouting over the clashing of the dishes they were washing and among the words they used was my name. I hovered outside the kitchen door, welcoming an excuse to delay seeing the Lharr a little longer and wanting to test my new knowledge of Rom.

"Humph! All these months and no sign of a child," one said. "I thought his lordship was more a man than that."

"Well, you can't tell by looks, *I* always say. You know what his sire used to say about *that* one. Womanish, he said."

"Nay,'t isn't the Lharr's fault," the other woman said with vigor. "He's man enough. Too much sense to leave bastards about, but he could've had a slew of 'em. It's the wives he picks. Remember, his first wife couldna carry a child to term and his second was murdered just before her time."

The second woman's voice softened in sympathy. "Aye, I

remember now. That witch led him a merry chase, too. Sleeping with Lord Richard for spite and all."

"Still, this House's got to have an heir, and soon. Lord Karne's not gettin' any younger."

"Aye, eight and twenty winters last 10 Aden."

"Do you suppose—"

I hurried away. So the servants thought me barren, and some of them thought the Lharr impotent. Because I would not lie with him. Because even if I did, I wouldn't let egg and seed unite. I had learned enough about Gharr politics to understand what their gossip meant for my husband's political position if more than just servants believed it. And my visits to Ontar, which led to knowing about the rumor of cowardice, which could be even more damaging—all my crimes cried for recognition at once.

When I finally reached the pad, everyone was in the flitter but me, and the ladders had already been pulled away. The Lharr waited to lift me onto the wing.

You made a bad bargain, lord, I told him silently. Look what trouble I've been.

When the flitter was airborne, Kit, Jemmy, and Weisman started a game of cards. Orkonan buried himself in an account book. I hesitantly touched the Lharr's arm. "Milord?"

He rested his golden eyes on me gravely. I lowered my voice.

"There's a rumor going 'round that you played coward after Justin's hunt and avoided the duel with Lord Richard. Can it hurt you?"

The Lharr straightened. I could feel the focus of his attention turn to me. "It can hurt. Where did you hear this?"

"Fr-from First Merchant Tremo."

His eyes narrowed. "The First Merchant hasn't been to the manor since our wedding. I'm assuming you didn't wait that long to tell me."

He was not going to make this easy. I lowered my eyes. "Yesterday, milord." He opened his mouth to speak and I put my hand lightly against it.

"No, milord, let me finish. I was wrong to deliberately disobey, but I was so confused and frightened and despairing. I desperately needed spiritual advice that Pastor Jarvis couldn't give me. Sam was once a lay chaplain, and he wasn't raised on this world." I looked away, ashamed of my impulsiveness. "Please say you won't punish Captain Oroark for what I did. I tricked him."

"By all that's holy—!"

I met his angry eyes. "Milord, I was dying inside."

"If anyone saw you— Do you have any idea what a scandal your perversity may have started? By my Mother's Blood—!"

I cut through whatever else he had been going to say. "My lord!"

At my low warning, he stopped glaring at me and followed my eyes. Weisman was watching us intently. When the Lharr looked at him, he began busily arranging his cards and talking, a little too loudly, to Kit.

I summoned all my courage and broached the hard part. "Milord, punish me if you will, but don't blame Captain Oroark."

He did not reply and his silent scrutiny made me uneasy. At last he turned away and fiddled with the switches and buttons on the control panel. Fascinated, I watched the muscles flow under his smooth brown skin. I'd never noticed how strong those lean hands looked.

After a long time the Lharr spoke resignedly and without looking up. "At least you have the sense to recognize Oroark's quality. It would be hard to find a better man."

There's one better, I thought sadly. The one who keeps his temper now, when he has every right to lose it.

I couldn't even interpret his silence for the rest of the flight as a sign of the anger I'd expected; he seldom had anything to say to me.

The flitter came down in the snow of a city pad. Sunlight glittered on the caps of snow that partially hid the signs posted at various places around its borders. The only one I could read said, "Lock your craft."

We waited until all four of our military escort craft were down before anyone got out. When at last I stepped out on the wing, the Lharr stood waiting for me on the ground. I tried to avoid him, still too ashamed of my behavior to want any help from him, but he followed me along the wing. The heat of my face told me it was red with aggravation and embarrassment.

"Larga, you've played enough," the Lharr said gently. "Come down."

What could I do but let him lift me down? He didn't let go right away. He looked at me steadily, which embarrassed me even more, and the weight of his long hands felt welcome, a feeling I didn't want. He took my chin in his hand and forced me to look up. "You have courage, madam," he said quietly. "Foolish, too, you have been, but you told me about it honestly and without being forced.

Expecting grim consequences, I imagine."

The woman I saw reflected in those clear golden eyes had been very small and stupid indeed. I looked away, squirming inside.

He brought my face back with a gentle jerk. "With courage, there's hope. I admire a woman with courage, madam."

CHAPTER 10

The Duvals were a merry group. After we exchanged the ritual greeting with everyone, the men went into conference and Mrs. Duval showed the women around the house. Their home was much smaller than Ontar manor, of course, but very elegant and tasteful. After dinner Kendar joined us as our official host while the Lharr and Councilman Duval met with the Freemen who governed the district of Lews. The Lharr was looking for support of a measure abolishing slavery and setting maximum sentence for serf crimes, Kendar told us.

It might have been interesting to talk about, I thought, if he had given more than the dry outline. But apparently women were not expected to discuss deep topics.

In the course of that first afternoon, though, Kendar and I discovered a mutual love of music. Music was something Ontar manor had very little of, so Kendar spent much of the first two days of our visit teaching me Rom ballads. Once I had the words and tune right, Kit and I and the Duvals sang together. Occasionally our ladies-in-waiting joined us.

Because Starker IV has a five-month very-cold season, and because for three of those months no one at all goes to the surface, its people knew lots of games and other indoor amusements. They keep a child's delight in simple games like riddles and forfeits, so the Duvals and Halareks played those and blindman's buff and chess. We talked a lot, too. In the evening everyone, except for the younger Duval children, gathered for storytelling.

On the third day the Lharr finished the last of his conferences with Freemen, this time with city representatives, and could spend the last day of the visit entirely with the "youngsters," as the Councilman called us. That day discussion left topics "suitable for females" and turned to the issues of freedom and individual responsibility. Positions ranged from Elspeth and Adrian's, which was the traditional belief that women should be seen and not heard, to mine, which was too often far beyond anything the others could accept.

The discussion heated quickly. Here, the Lharr didn't have to struggle to think of something to say to me. His formality fell away, his eyes and voice took fire as he argued, and he addressed points to me as easily as to Kit or Adrian. But for all his work toward freeing slaves and educating serfs—male serfs—and broadening franchises, he couldn't admit the possibility that women could be as intelligent and as able as men.

"You men can't justify your opinion of females by the example of Starker IV's women!" I insisted finally, frustrated and angry. "Of course they're childlike. They've been taught that's the way a woman should be. But if you educated them, if you gave them the responsibilities they have on most other worlds, truly you'd see how wrong you are. Women have a human right to control their own lives!"

Kendar smiled indulgently. "Gharr women have never wanted responsibilities. They like their lives as they are."

I shook my head. "How can a woman want what she's never known? How can a woman want something more than domestic duties if nothing else exists, or is permitted?"

"You sound like you're advocating a life outside the home. Women can't handle life on their own," Councilman Duval put in.

"Aye. They're like children," Kendar added. "You can't give them important responsibilities."

Kit twisted the end of her veil, hesitated, looked around the group, then spoke. "Nik—Nik let me do the work Frem Orkonan does for Karne, Frem Duval. That's an important responsibility."

Duval nodded. "Aye, but you're not an ordinary woman, Lady Kathryn."

Kit blushed prettily, but said nothing else. Kendar had opened a topic for me, however.

"The other Gharr women—it's education, not ability, that they lack. Given education and a chance, women manage their lives as well as men, better sometimes."

"Some women, perhaps, could do as well as a man, but most . . ." Councilman Duval shook his head.

"How well have you done, Lady Zjhanne? Tell us honestly." Kendar was only half teasing.

"I did very well until I was brought here. Since then I've vegetated." I turned to the Lharr. "But I won't ever be like Gharr women. I've been on my own too long to like dependence. I'm a scholar. I know what I can do. My work is respected by men as well as women. I'll never be a 'good' wife as the Gharr define it. There's not enough in housework to keep a trained mind busy."

I thought I saw a flash of understanding in the Lharr's eyes, then Kendar spoke.

"If women have the abilities you say, why have they stayed so long happily dependent?"

" 'Happily,' Kendar? You give them no choice. Even the clothes women wear here are restricting and prescribed by law and custom." I looked at the Lharr to see his reaction to my opposition. He looked interested, but nothing more. Maybe I had misinterpreted the flash of understanding. "You control your women the way you control your serfs, by force of arms."

I realized the moment the words were out of my mouth that I had made an awful and unfortunate pun. Everyone laughed and I knew that after a laugh like that, no argument of mine would bear any weight. Kendar stood up, still laughing.

"Let's break right here and eat."

Elspeth dropped her kitten back onto the floor and bounced up. Adrian took a last look at the mirror that hung from her belt and patted her dark hair carefully into place before she languidly left her stool. I made a mental note of the gesture. I had thought the dangling mirrors that were so fashionable were for bright decoration only.

"Madam—"

But the Lharr was too late. I had already accepted Kendar's hand up. Did he look a little disappointed? I shook my head. I was only a political and business asset to him.

Even the Duvals' lavish home grew chilly when evening came. The Councilman waved at the huge fireplace and, looking more amazingly authentic than the one in Ontar manor, illusory flames sprang up, giving light and heat and the fragrance of burning wood without changing the logs. The Councilman and his wife withdrew after a few minutes of polite after-dinner conversation, leaving the "youngsters" to amuse themselves. We six sat on cushions or low stools around the fire, sipping tankards of mulled cider and enjoying for a little while quiet, flames, and friends. There is a deep animal satisfaction in the wood's snap, the spicy scent of cider and smoke, the smooth warmth of fur and velvet.

Adrian's husky voice began an ancient romance. She spun the tale with great skill, her voice changing with the characters, her emotion drawing everyone into the tale. I could believe I was seeing as well as hearing the tragedy. Her five listeners paid tribute at the tale's close with moments of silence.

Kit started a tale. She must have been long out of practice, because she hadn't reached the middle before she stopped and confessed she couldn't remember the end.

"A serious offense, Lady Kathryn," Kendar warned sternly. "What should her punishment be, gentles?"

"Riddles," said the Lharr sternly. "Three, right now."

"Four," Adrian drawled.

"Four it is. If you fail this, Kathryn, we shall think of something *much* worse." Kendar's voice was the voice of doom.

There are advantages to living with a small boy, and a lot of experience with riddles is one of them. Kit escaped the worse fate.

Elspeth took her turn. She lacked Adrian's skill and magic voice and the tale suffered for it. My mind wandered. Somewhere I had heard that story before. I searched for the time and place. It slipped just out of reach and then I had it: an ancient Terran romance!

Then I heard the silence and realized the story had ended while I was thinking. I felt flustered. Had someone said something to me? Behind me somewhere Tam giggled. Kendar grinned wickedly.

"It's your turn. What's the story?"

I shook my head and mumbled something I hoped would pass for an answer. Elspeth whispered to Adrian and they both giggled. I suddenly realized the Lharr's place was empty. That must be why they were laughing. I didn't intend to look around for him, because that was obviously what they wanted me to do. Before I could decide what *to* do, someone put hands over my eyes and pulled me back against legs that hadn't been behind me before.

"You miss me so little, my lady wife? How long was I out of the room?" The Lharr spoke close to my ear and his voice was warm with laughter. His breath raised prickles along my neck.

My mind raced. How much time had I lost? "Fif—ten minutes, my lord."

He laughed. "Shouldn't she pay forfeit, cousins? She hasn't paid attention and she can't tell a story."

"Make a song."

"No, she must be our slave for an hour."

"No! No! A kiss! A kiss!" Elspeth was bouncing on her cushion with glee.

"A kiss for each of the people she wronged." Kendar passed the sentence as solemnly as if it were for life in solitary confinement.

Elspeth ran over immediately to collect hers. Kendar leaned toward me and puckered his lips comically. I kissed the end of his nose. Kit offered her cheek. Adrian deferred hers so neither of us would have to get up. And the Lharr. Would he come down for his, I wondered, or must I get up and turn around?

Don't make me come to you, milord.

"You heard the sentence," he said by my ear. He straightened. "Come. My forfeit."

He pulled me up onto my knees and bent over me. His kiss was long and warm and very gentle and I felt empty when it ended. I sank back onto my cushion, laughed to hide my confusion, and turned to watch the fire. Was this bold, teasing person the same man who was so formal and aloof at home? The man who seldom spoke to me except in politeness or anger? Yet he had been good company at Justin's hunt. Was he at ease with me only in a group? Did he really have to be away so much, or did he just not know what to do with me? The possibilities were disturbing.

His hand shook my shoulder playfully. "Hey, pay attention. It's my turn. Shall I claim forfeit again?"

I looked up at my husband and feigned abject terror. "Oh, no, my lord! I'll be so very good!"

Everyone laughed and the Lharr wove a complex romance about a husband's cruel revenge on his wife and her true love. It ended with everyone dead. It was so typical of the Gharr's attitude toward women and love that I could not contain myself.

"Even your stories show your double standard." I appealed first to Kendar, then to the Lharr. "Can't you see? It's so unfair." Putting just the proper note of petulance at the end started conversation again.

"Why not?" Kendar argued. "Marriage is for profit or politics. Love you find somewhere else."

"At least give women that same freedom, then."

Elspeth and Adrian gave gasps of horror. After a few minutes of recovery, Adrian entered the discussion for the first time.

"True love isn't impossible in marriage. My parents love each other."

I saw Kit and Karne trade glances and remembered his bitter words about the price Nik had paid for loving. The discussion ended in no agreement, of course.

The question it had raised was still troubling me when the Halarek party left for home. A double standard pervaded everything, even the fun. It was grossly unfair. As for love, the memory of it still stung. What had loving gotten me? Pain and betrayal. Knowing it was, in the end, only my pride that Lance had hurt didn't stop the pain. A rat like Lance didn't deserve even that kind of remembering.

It was very late and no one felt like talking. Kit curled up in the back of the flitter with Jemmy in her lap and went to sleep. I sat beside her, waiting, but sleep wouldn't come. The flitter glided along the rough slopes of ancient mountains. Beyond them the younger mountains of Halarek Holding rose, silvered by moonlight, their snow smoking in a stiff wind, then settling in quiet sparkling expanses. Over those glittering fields slid the bleak shadows of our escorts.

I studied the back of the Lharr's head. He was an educated, sensible man. How much of the idea of courtly love did he really accept? Or of the belief in female mental and physical weakness that lay under it? Was there any chance of changing his ideas? Could I endure with grace a lifetime of being thought inferior? I knew the answer to that one. Was it possible for two people with customs so alien even to get along for a lifetime? We'd have to find a way, somehow.

Advent parties filled most of the evenings in the three weeks that followed our return from Duvals'. All of these were large and I met many people. But the parties were also very dull, each one like every other. The Halareks went to them primarily because Karne had political business with the men. Everyone wore elaborate clothes, ate elaborate foods, watched elaborate performances by actors and acrobats, jongleurs and jugglers; but eventually, inevitably, the hostess passed around the room, collecting the women and carefully separating them from the men, often into a different room. Always, always the men had just begun arguments about politics and reorganizing Gharr society—fascinating, exciting arguments—and I was not permitted to join them, even to listen. I tried once and the hostess made a very rude fuss.

So I was exiled with Kit to "my lord" this and "my husband" that, "my little boy's tooth . . ." and "Did you hear about Margaret's operation?" and "My little girl had such a fever and I . . ." On and on and on, as if there were nothing else in the universe to talk about. I did try to be interested for a while, but at different parties the same women told each other the same gossip. Fortunately, an appearance of boredom was fashionable. Even the women soaking up gossip most avidly *looked* bored.

After all those nights and early mornings of small talk and dancing, I had no more friends than before, only a collection of faces with names attached. I asked the Duval girls about it one afternoon in a tri-d rehash of one of the livelier affairs. There had been dancing, though not for me, because the Lharr had been too busy trying to convince the lords of some minor Houses that ending serfdom would benefit everyone eventually, and it was required that a married woman give the first and last dance to her husband.

"What am I doing wrong?" I asked the Duvals.

Elspeth twirled a curl that hung in front of her ear. "It's not you, it's the Lharr. A lot of women are afraid to risk being friendly, Zjhanne, because of the feud. What would happen to them socially if Karne loses to Lord Richard?"

It sounded true to what I had come to expect of the Gharr. "That seems awfully cold-blooded."

Elspeth threw up her hands helplessly and shrugged.

"If you want to know what I think," Adrian drawled, "they're jealous."

"Of me?"

"Why not? You have the best man. My, the social climbers that had their traps out for him! Such a challenge because he's so aloof and so busy. And so attractive, because the poor, poor man has had such bad luck with his wives. But he chose you. At enormous expense. And you're more free—you've a room of your own, you sleep alone if you choose, you ride astride, you have the most beautiful clothes, you have no children. And you speak at least five languages."

"But I never talk about those things."

She laughed. "No, but your women do. You haven't been here long enough to know that 'news travels fastest by waiting-woman.' Everything you do gets around."

"You don't know how they talk, Zjhanne!" Elspeth added.

Perhaps they were right. I had no way of knowing. At least the Duvals were friends.

Winter began. Soon it was too cold and snowy to spend much of any time in the open, or so Jaklene told me. I found that hard to believe. She told me all the fliers and flitters carried crash kits with survival equipment in them now, including complete body suits and masks to keep out the wind. Coming back to the manor from First Day service one week, Jaklene told me the snow above was already close to a meter deep. I laughed. I'd been out at a party only three nights before and had still been able to see grass poking up through what snow there was.

"You're teasing me. Snow can't possibly pile up as fast as that."

The Lharr overheard me scoffing. "It's still Drak," he said. "It's still warm enough and wet enough to snow a lot. After Uhl, it will be too cold to snow. The winds of Arhast, Koort, and Nemb blow the snow of Narn and Uhl; they have none of their own."

"Too cold to snow? You're both telling me tall tales. Only I'm not gullible enough to believe them."

A shadow crossed the Lharr's face. He slid his hand under my elbow and he bowed very slightly to Jaklene, Tamara, Lady Agnes, and Kit. "Excuse us, ladies. My wife needs to be shown that I don't lie to her."

Why should my doubt bother him? I was curious. I didn't resist being guided into a lift and taken up to the surface.

He had opened the lift door. It was true, what he and Jaklene had said. Snow stood for a moment a third of the way up the opening, then sagged into the lift. The fountain in the center of the garden had disappeared under a white blanket. The bluepines drooped with their load of whiteness. The wind pinched my nose and made my eyes sting.

"I won't lie to you, ever," the Lharr said. "I brought you here in part to show you that. I also want to give you an idea of what winter is like here, in case you have any ideas of skiing away, or riding off on one of the horses or even of walking. That is, assuming I haven't already convinced you how little you want to be found by Harlan or Odonnel or Justin. This is very early winter. In midwinter, we spend three months entirely inside. No one travels on the surface. No one flies. The Gild doesn't even make deliveries from orbit because of the winds. I'm sure you've been told that already, but I wonder if you believe it."

I looked out at unbelievably deep snow, and this planet had two months of snow to come. A wind like a knife whirled around inside the lift. Had the Lharr needed to show me that their tales were true, or to warn me not to try to escape? For some reason, the idea that he still believed I'd try to escape hurt. Then I felt angry, as if he'd betrayed some trust.

The Lharr's finger hovered over the lift's control. "Have you seen enough?"

"Yes, Lord Karne."

"Do you believe me?"

"Yes, Lord Karne."

"Shall we go down to dinner, then?"

"Yes, Lord Karne."

He pressed the button for level 4 and dinner, then he turned my face toward him with a feather-light hand on my cheek. "Must you be so formal with me?"

His voice was soft and just the slightest bit apologetic. Perhaps he had warned me about the weather to keep me from endangering myself. It would be easy to die out there, even without enemies. For now, I would believe his intent was to protect me. I looked into his golden eyes and smiled and made my voice light and self-mocking. "Yes, Lord Karne."

He smiled, that stunningly brilliant smile I had seen only once before. It made me quiver inside. In that moment, alone with him in the lift, I remembered he could, by law, have bedded me every night since I came to this world, and he hadn't.

Did my thought send him some signal? His eyes dilated and the tip of his tongue slowly wet his lower lip. It was very seductive. But I didn't want to lie with a man who had taken me by force from all I ever knew and wanted. I didn't want to lie with a stranger.

At level 4, the Lharr did no more than gently direct me out of the lift and toward the dining room. I was as safe in my bed that night as I had been every other night.

The Lharr informed me we were going to have a family Christmas, which meant just the Lharr's personal family—Kit and Jemmy and their noble servants. The Family and other servants would have their own celebration in the Hall. Since it was custom in the House for one of the ladies Halarek to read the Christmas story on Christmas Eve, Kit had decided this would be the best way to surprise the Lharr with the secret of my knowing Rom: I would read the story this year.

Keeping the language lessons secret had been easy enough when Lord Karne was away a lot, but avoiding discovery for that last week of Advent, with him in the house all the time, was not easy at all. Kit planned carefully. Jemmy would play chess with the Lharr before being put to bed. While they played, Kit and I would slip away for an hour or two of practice.

The first evening Lord Karne came home from deVree much too late for chess with Jemmy, so we had to skip the practice. The next evening we watched the game begin and then retired to the library. Kit sat by the fire and examined the surcoat I had almost finished. I pulled the big Halarek book from its shelf beside the fireplace and, leaning against the mantel, began reading aloud. Although Kit was examining the surcoat's embroidery carefully, she was listening just as carefully. She didn't have to correct my pronunciation once. The Lharr must have stood for several minutes at the top of the iron stair before he spoke.

"You read Rom well, lady wife."

We both jumped. His voice was hard and cold. Kit hurriedly stuffed the surcoat behind her and I closed the book just as quickly. I know we both looked guilty.

"Are you a fast learner, madam, or have you known Rom all along?" His voice was, if anything, colder than before.

"My lord—"

"Karne!" Kit's tone reproached him. "I've been teaching her. We *were* planning to surprise you."

"Sorry, Kit." He rubbed the back of his hand across his eyes. "I've survived by suspicion too long, I guess."

"It's Zjhanne you should be apologizing to," Kit snapped. "I've given you better grounds for suspicion than she has. After all, *my* husband betrayed you." She bit her lower lip hard and stared intently at the ceiling, clenching her hands in her lap.

Kit's defense surprised me. She wasn't supposed to know how Nik died. Besides, I would never prod *my* older brother like that, especially at such cost in memories.

But the Lharr has more grace and gallantry than Pieter. He turned to me. "Kit's right, Larga. My remark was unjust. Please forget it." He smiled wryly. "If you learn anything about tactics from Kit, madam, I won't stand a chance against the two of you."

But the stiffness in his words betrayed reservations, reservations he wasn't going to bring up in front of Kit. That night, as my ladies prepared me for bed, I learned just what his reservations were. He dismissed the ladies abruptly before they were through. He spoke Sternlangue to me still.

"Kit can't be the only help you've had. You've mastered Rom in too short a time. No woman can—" He gripped my arms. "Who else?"

He was so close! I felt his anger flowing over me in waves. I took a quick breath to steady myself. "I have a natural facility with languages."

He shook me once, roughly. "Don't be flip with me. I'm in no mood for it."

"Kit and the linguatapes—"

"Tapes? I authorized no tapes. Who ordered them without my seal? Who?" The Lharr punctuated the last question with another shake.

"You don't really expect me to betray him, do you?"

"Someone from here had to take the order, someone in the Gild had to accept it. Who?"

I made my face and voice as cold as my fear allowed. "I won't yield to shaking, milord. I'm neither your child nor your servant to be treated so." I pushed one hand away and rubbed the red marks it left.

"Remember your place, madam."

"I do. I'm Zjhanne Verlith, freeborn, citizen of Fruhe and the Federation, a respected specialist in Terran pre-industrial history. That's my 'place.' As long as you try to force me to be someone else, I'll fight you every way I can."

"Is this the way wives behave on Fruhe?"

"No, milord, but there a husband respects his wife for what she is, not for what she might be if he applied pressure and a little violence."

He dropped his other hand and for a moment despair replaced the anger in his face. "Why were the tapes so important? I've explained so many times . . ." His voice sagged. "I'd have ordered them if you'd had good reason."

"I've been making my own decisions for a long time."

"Madam, I'm straining to be reasonable. Don't you realize how threatening this would look to Old Party men? You, sending an unexamined, unsealed message off-world, with the help of unknown accomplices! Try to imagine the political consequences!"

"How can I? You tell me so little about anything. I was alone, among strangers, frightened about the threats to my life. I had to learn, quickly, what people were saying. Your library was no help. I was afraid to ask you. Orkonan said he couldn't authorize the order. Oroark said he couldn't. Weisman refused. What choice had I? I was *terrified*."

He stood tensely, clenching and unclenching his hands. I suddenly wanted very much for him to understand.

I softened my voice consciously. "My lord, you're angry about an action long past. Try for a moment to see how your contempt provoked rebellion."

"I don't hold you in contempt, Larga."

"I'd never know it from your actions. You selected a woman from Fruhe because Fruhe is very different from Starker IV, but you haven't used that difference. I had a career, I was respected in my field, I earned my own way, I lived my own life. How can you expect me to quietly accept uselessness and ignorance and dependence?"

"You gave me a glimpse at the Duvals of what you've lost." He sighed and the sadness of the sound hurt me. He shook his head slightly. "Believe me, I'm still discovering the great differences between Mother's world and yours." His face changed and he looked at me with a blaze of gold. "But whatever my fault, the gravity of your action is the same. If you visit a man without proper chaperons or write anyone without my seal, no one needs other proof of—of your adultery. You know that any Old Party man would accuse you of just that to stop me."

"Yet I may escort male guests to their rooms, even help them bathe if they so wish—"

His face darkened. "Any man who betrays his host deserves Zinn sentence."

"You trust strangers so much and your wife so little?"

The Lharr flinched. "It's not that. Personal treason—adultery—is second only to treason against the planet. And treason has always meant death."

"Aye," I whispered, looking away. "That I know too well."

He turned my head back toward him. He hesitated a moment, then his fingers tightened on my chin. "What can I do to make you see that every—every rebellious act of yours increases the danger for us all?"

"Fear is no excuse, milord, but I was terribly afraid. That one person would deliberately kill another . . ."

The Lharr released me. I watched him close off his feelings behind that damnable mask he was so proud of. He reached inside his jerkin and pulled out of a pocket a folded plastic sheet, which he handed to me. His voice was deceptively steady. "What excuse do you offer for this? A request for an off-world ship! Were you afraid when you sent this, too? If this had fallen into Old Party hands—" His voice hardened. "This is the worst kind of treason!"

I unfolded the plastic. It was the letter I'd sent to Dad early in my captivity. No wonder he never answered it. Someone had been holding on to it. What could I say? That I hadn't known the rules then?

The Lharr turned away from me and fingered the raised design on one of the tapestries. "I'd hoped you'd tell me about this, but I've waited two weeks—"

"Two weeks! Milord, I wouldn't knowingly risk your life! This supposedly went home more than a month before we were married."

"Before we were married?" Then his shoulders sagged. "It doesn't matter now. What's done can't be recalled." He whirled and pointed a rigid, vibrating finger at me. "Why can't you be constructive?"

"Me? Me?" The egotistical barbarian was blaming *me* for his world's insane rules! "Why don't you help me?" I blazed back at him. "You could tell me how things are so I could make good decisions!"

Without replying he strode to the door into his room, his back and shoulders stiff and angry. If I hadn't been furious, I wouldn't have done what I did next. I sprang after him and gripped his arm hard.

"Milord, don't leave with this problem unsolved."

He looked back and down over his shoulder at me and the rage in his eyes made my mouth go dry with fear. "Milord, if you were even a little bit a friend to me—"

He spun with a sharp explanation and his fingers dug into the bones of my shoulders. "Friend?" He laughed harshly. "By the Four Guardians, you ask too much! Why do you think I stay away so much? Because I like to? No, madam, because I need your help too much to antagonize you more than I already have, and forcing you to bed, when I'm so repugnant to you, seemed the quickest way to end any possibility of you helping." He gave me a hard shake. "How long do you think I can stay in this house, living near you, hearing you move around your room morning and night, knowing you're my wife, wanting you, without doing something about it?"

He shook me again, so hard that the rug under my feet slipped. I lost my balance and started to fall. He caught me against him and his mouth came down savagely on mine. He kissed my neck, my throat, the skin deep into the V of my dressing gown, my mouth again. A wild, frightening surge of desire swept over me and I responded passionately to his kisses and insistent hands.

Someone knocked on my door and broke the spell.

"Damn the conference," the Lharr whispered. But he released me and went to the door. I watched him dizzily, every nerve on fire, wanting to beg him not to go. Repugnant? Oh, milord, not at all!

He turned with one hand on the latch. "If there were any way I could cancel this tri-d conference, madam, believe me, I would. You have a reprieve, but only for tonight." He slammed the door hard behind himself.

I turned down the lamp by my bed and sat in the dimness, stunned by the fire in me. How could I have allowed self-concern to so blind me to the terrible strain his restraint had to be for him. And who could have foretold how deeply his passion would stir me?

I couldn't sit still. I paced and argued with myself. Hope of home had made me foolish and selfish. The rationalizations I'd used to keep the Lharr at a distance before Pieter's call no longer held. Marriage was no longer a temporary arrangement. I had committed myself to this world and this man. True, I'd been kidnapped, but the Lharr had had no other choice as he saw it, and he wasn't responsible for Lance's methods. I had little privacy here, true, but more than other noblewomen. I was dominated and lonely, but the Lharr had given me everything he could think of to amuse me, including Gordie, and had planned my room to make it seem more like home. And he could've forced me to endure his lovemaking, knowing, rightly, that I'd fight him harder for being forced. The whole mess was very sad. In any other circumstances, in any other place, we probably would've liked each other.

The realization of what his reticence and my pigheadedness could have done depressed me. Surely he could've thought of something useful for me to do if only he'd trusted me. Yet, I remembered ruefully, I hadn't shown myself very trustworthy. And that made me think of Weisman, who now had my money and his master's praises. I prayed those were the only praises he had.

I finished preparing for bed, but guilt and regret and a strange restlessness plagued me. Hours after the quiet night-talk of the ladies-in-waiting had faded into sleep, I lay awake, tossing and thinking. Finally I threw a salk-fur robe over my nightgown and went to the library, accompanied by a squadman of Blues, of course.

The light was still on, but no one answered the squadman's knock. He opened the door and I stepped in. A movement caught my eye. The far door closing? Then I saw Frem Orkonan, lying across his desk, a huge charred hole in his back. His tunic still smoldered, and the stench of burned flesh—

My stomach surged violently. I clapped a hand over my mouth and quickly looked away. They told me later I screamed and screamed and screamed. I remembered only fighting down the nausea, then being cradled against the Lharr's chest while I sobbed uncontrollably. He alternately gave rapid orders to the soldiers who were all over the room and awkwardly patted my shoulder.

When he could do no more for the moment about the murder, the Lharr carried me to the lift. Upstairs he carefully set me on my bed and turned to go. The possibility of being left alone with Orkonan's horrible death on my mind and the murderer still loose in the house terrified me so much I clutched at the Lharr's arm.

"Don't leave me, milord, please. Please! I—" Heaven knows I didn't want him to see how afraid I was, but I couldn't help it.

The Lharr stroked my loose hair soothingly. "I'll stay, all night if it eases you, milady." He was cool and remote again.

He tucked me in and pulled a chair up beside the bed. I slept badly, but he was there whenever I woke, dozing perhaps, but there. If I moved, he opened his eyes and smiled reassuringly at me.

Early the next morning, Oroark tapped softly on the outer door, then stuck his head around its edge. I motioned him to be quiet. The Lharr was sound asleep, sagged wearily in the chair, his head against one of the wings. Oroark made a shooting motion with his hand, then shook his head and shut the door quietly. I crept out of bed and dressed. Then my brush caught in a snarl and jumped out of my hand. It landed with a sharp crack on the stone floor. The Lharr started. His eyes flew open and he looked so guilty I had to laugh.

"I don't grudge you your nap, milord."

He pushed out of the chair and stood groggily. He shook his head vigorously to clear it and then ran a hand through his rumpled hair in a cursory combing. "What time is it?"

"About two hours before fast-breaking, milord."

He turned his head toward my ladies' sleeping room. "Tamara!"

Tamara stumbled in sleepily, still fumbling with a robe. She was too groggy to be surprised that her master was still in her mistress's room at this hour of the morning. Her first words were typical. "How have I offended you, Lord Karne?"

He shook his head again and staggered a little with the effort. "No, no, what made you think you had? Oh, well, I'm sorry I shouted. I'm not awake yet. Get Captain Oroark."

I held up a hand. "Wait, Tam." I looked at the Lharr. "He's already been here, milord. There's no news. Why don't you sleep until there is?"

"Can't. Has to be someone in the manor. There's no time—"

"Lord Karne, listen to yourself. You're so tired you're mumbling." I motioned Tam toward Kit's room. "What can you do right now that Captain Oroark can't?" I motioned again, impatiently, to Tam. "Haven't you told me he has exceptional judgment? Well, let him use it. When he needs your help, you'll have to be alert, which you certainly aren't now."

I put my hands firmly against his chest and began pushing him toward the bed. "You were awake most of last night and the night before you were wooing the Duke deVree and the night before we were at the Earl of Kingsland's interminable party. You can't go on at this rate, milord."

Protesting, he weakly tried to brush my hands away. I backed him against the bed.

"See. In this state, even I can bully you. And here come reinforcements."

Kit had dressed hurriedly and her hair still hung in dark tangles over her shoulders. She quickly sized up the situation. "Karne, do what you're told for once. When Zjhanne is being so wifely, too."

So her sharp eyes had seen the tension between us. That stung. I had thought at least our public behavior— How many others had noticed?

"I've got to help find him. It's someone in the manor . . ." The Lharr still fought to do what he felt was his duty, but sleep glazed his eyes and his hands shook visibly.

"Lie down, dolt!" Kit pushed him down onto the bed.

"All right, but only a few minutes. No. Don't touch my boots, Kit. I'm not going to be here that long."

He was asleep almost before he finished the sentence. In sleep his face softened and I saw what he might have looked like as a boy. He's younger than he seems, I thought.

I posted a sentry outside the hall door with orders to let no one disturb the Lharr for at least eight hours. Kit and Jemmy and I were finishing our midday when the Lharr joined us. He slid into his high-backed chair with a hearty yawn. He looked at Kit and me severely.

"I told you I was going to rest only a few minutes."

Kit laughed up at him. "Aye, brother, but you didn't say *we* were supposed to wake you."

He tweaked the end of her nose and started on the warmed meats the serfs brought in. "You were calculating, ladies, but not calculating enough. You didn't count on Jaklene waking late and squealing when she saw me in the bed instead of her lady." He made a face. "That sound would wake a hibernating Zinn bear."

But he was too tired still for the good humor to last long. When he had finished eating and the adults had adjourned to the library, he crumpled into his big chair and covered his face with his hands. "What do I do now? Tane was the only person I could trust with the job and now he's dead."

CHAPTER 11

"You ask *us* what to do?" That seemed to trouble Kit. "Why not ask Uncle Emil or General Wynter?"

The Lharr shook his head. "You know our problems and our people better. We've known for years someone here works for Richard and the risk of making that man secretary . . ."

"Weisman's been with the Family longer than Tane was," Kit suggested tentatively, "and he knows the work."

The Lharr shook his head. "He's not much with complex math and he can't handle either of the galactic languages. He couldn't talk to the Gild."

"General Wynter?"

"I need him where he is. Would you take it on, Kit? You did some of the same kind of work for Nik."

She shook her head. "I have Jemmy and I'm managing the manor. Besides, it's not women's work." She glanced at me. "At least, not a Gharr woman's work."

Lord Karne sighed and rubbed his face and chin. "Maybe with tutoring in Galac Weisman could handle it. What do you think, Zjhanne?"

For a moment my mind went blank. He was asking my opinion, *my* opinion. He hadn't asked me to come here only as courtesy, then. In the moments it took me to think of an answer, there was a discreet knock on the door. Weisman entered humbly.

"Excuse me, milord, but First Merchant Tremo wishes to cross-check his listing of our export account with his." Weisman hunched over a tangle of books that had been torn from their cabinet during last night's search.

I leaned toward the Lharr and spoke very quietly. "My letter, milord. He took money to carry a letter he, at least, knew was treasonous. He hasn't shown himself completely loyal to you, milord." Then I remembered that in the Lharr's eyes, Weisman had done exactly the right thing. I rushed on. "*I* have the qualifications you need, milord. Let me help."

His eyes drilled into me. "The letter was *yours*. Weisman only carried it. And to me."

I swallowed. I had done wrong, but it was hard to say that to him. "I know my fault, lord. Now. Now I know my life hangs with yours. Has anyone else such a motive for complete loyalty?"

Weisman straightened suddenly, a thick book in his hand, and shot me a venomous look. So he *had* been listening. He opened his mouth as if to speak, but spun and went out instead, slamming the door. The Lharr jumped.

Kit laid her hand on the Lharr's arm in concern. "Must you decide now, Karne?"

He patted her hand lightly and his eyes gave her a kind of thank-you. "I should, Kit. The next Council's only two weeks away."

Perhaps now, while he was still very tired and in need of help—I caught his eye. "Then show your principles, milord, and let me work for you." I dared to add, "I'd be easier to handle, my lord, if I didn't feel so useless and bored."

The Lharr responded with a wry smile. "As Kit said, it isn't a woman's job, but what can I do when principle and necessity point to the same conclusion? Shall we get started?" He shoved himself out of the chair.

I could hardly believe it. He'd given in. Just like that. Without even an argument and in spite of my grave error with the letter.

Kit looked at me significantly. "Tomorrow, Karne," Kit said. "You've been working too hard. No, don't argue now. Go on upstairs and I'll fix you a very special All Night."

He hesitated, then nodded and slowly climbed the iron stair. Kit shook her head at his silent obedience, then pushed aside a plasti panel and manipulated the complex series of dials and buttons inside. In seconds a steaming tankard appeared behind another clear panel. She pulled the tankard out and held it out to me.

"You take it up. I want to look in on Jemmy."

"But—"

"Zjhanne, you're my sister now, so I must speak. You've cheated Karne too long of what before God you promised him. Go to him now, while he's too tired to be rough or angry. If you don't, Zjhanne, he'll bed you by force and then the trouble between you will never be righted." She looked down into the swirling steam above the cup. "He had to force his first wife, every time. She eventually killed herself—not because of the forcing—and now Karne carries as much guilt as if he were to blame. That's an important reason why he's left you alone. And he knows what being forced is like for a woman, because it happened to me." She looked down into the cup. "I know about the promise he made to you. We've always been close." She looked up at me. "It will be very hard on both of you when need makes him break that promise. Don't make him wait that long, Zjhanne." Kit shoved the tankard into my unwilling hands and hurried away.

I don't know how long I stared into the steaming All Night, though it could not have been as long as it seemed.

Kit's right, I told myself. This you must do.

I thought of the violence of the Lharr's desire and of how long he'd been holding it in. I bit my lip. If rape was what I met upstairs, it was mostly of my own provoking. I gathered the front of my skirt into my free hand and went up.

You don't have to tell him no child will come of this, I told myself. But I knew I did have to tell him.

When I reached the top of the stairs, I turned off the library lights to prevent retreat, then knocked on the Lharr's door. The knock was so timid that I knocked again, louder, to encourage myself. I waited. The herbal aroma of the All Night floated in the air around me. The tankard would stay steaming hot inside until all the liquid was gone.

Finally from within, "Come."

I opened the door hesitantly. I hadn't seen the Lharr's room since the day I tried to escape the house; on the night I'd snuck through to the library, it had been quite dark. It was only dimly lit now. The Lharr sat on the edge of his bed, his head in his hands. He didn't look up. I waited for some signal to come closer, but when he still didn't move, I carefully crossed the room and held out the tankard.

"Your promised drink, milord." My voice wavered.

The Lharr's head snapped up and in a moment a mask of alertness was over it, but I had seen the lifeless eyes and the deep lines gouged around his mouth. Sympathy stirred in me. So he had hidden the depth of his exhaustion even from Kit.

"Kit was to—" He nodded curtly toward a rok-hide chest. "Set it there."

I obeyed. That done, I had to say something, to tell him why I'd come, and the words stuck in my throat.

"What do you want?" he demanded. "If the door to your room is locked, it's from your side."

I took a deep breath and willed my knees to stop trembling. I stared down at my empty hands and the most voice I could produce was an unsteady whisper. "It's what you want of me, milord. I've denied you what is yours by right and by my promise."

I paused to steady my voice and looked up. The Lharr was standing now, tensely, his arms straight down his sides, his hands clenched.

Harshly he ordered, "Go on."

I rushed out the words. "I give you myself, Lord Karne, but no child will come of it, nor of any like meeting until peace comes, at least between us. You know I can control that. I won't give you an heir, milord."

Still he stood, watching me. I was bewildered. What more did he expect?

"Milord, what more should I say?"

"The first words were yours, Larga. There can be no going back if the first move is also yours. I want no recriminations or accusations later."

He was making it so much harder! Truly I'd behaved badly if he believed such a precaution necessary. I fumbled with laces and buttons. At last my dress settled around my feet with silken whisperings and I stood before him in my flimsy shift.

"You lift some of my weariness from me, madam," he said softly.

He came to me then, and I had no reason after to regret my yielding.

With the morning I felt rested and happier than I had for a long time. I stretched and snuggled deeper into the warm bed. A light hand touched my shoulder.

"Are you awake?"

I rolled over and smiled sleepily at my husband.

"It's long past fast-breaking, lady wife. The chrono—"

I opened my arms to him and it no longer mattered what the chrono said.

Kit presented her theory about the murderer's escape at midday meal. Murder as a mealtime topic apparently bothered neither Lord Karne nor his sister, but my Fruvan stomach had great difficulty with the subject of violent death, even when discussed as impersonally as they were discussing it.

Kit passed Lord Karne a platter of rolls. "Remember the secret passages Father showed us, Karne?"

Lord Karne smiled, remembering. "Of course. We used to play in some of them. But it's been years."

"Well, there was supposed to be one into the library."

Lord Karne laughed and turned to me. "We must've spent a month doing little else but look for it. Our sire didn't want children invading his workroom and wouldn't tell where that passage was."

Kit nodded agreement. "I think the murderer's found it."

The corners of Lord Karne's mouth pulled down and he frowned thoughtfully. "You may be right. I'll put someone to work on it." He stared thoughtfully across the room a moment.

A page came in with a bowl of fruit. The meal was over. Lord Karne selected one of the rectangular fruits, laid his napkin beside our shared plate, and stood to help me with my chair. "Time to get to work, Larga."

As I stood, Lord Karne's hand seemed to glide across my shoulder, lightly, as if in wonder. I quashed my own swift physical response to that probably imaginary gesture and followed my husband to the library.

Weisman cheerfully left his work to get out all the information Lord Karne required. I might have dreamed the man's black looks of the previous night for all the resentment he now showed.

Lord Karne and I spent hours looking through files and account books that day. Livestock and exports—blown glass, luxury fabrics, fine orak carvings and furniture—brought in much money, but House Halarek spent a lot, too. The sum just for the long list of live-in relatives was staggering, and added to this were the costs of servants—housing, wages, health care, the new school—maintenance of the manor and the Holding, support of The Way, and a quantity of gifts and bribes.

I looked up from the columns of figures. "You come very close to not breaking even, milord. Are all these gifts necessary?"

The Lharr rubbed his hand through his hair and grimaced ruefully. "When reason can't convince, money often can."

"Could some of these relatives go home?"

"They could and, if necessary, they will."

"I can see why you couldn't afford to send me home, milord."

He lifted his eyes from the ledger in front of him. "It's the political cost I can't afford. Would you care to see just how much that spacing out cost, though? *You're* one of my biggest investments."

His look made me uncomfortable. It seemed to say he was at last getting at least part of that investment back. I didn't want to think about that. I didn't want to admit how deeply my kidnapper's touch stirred me or how much I was already looking forward to the night. I had always thought love and desire were connected.

I shook my head. "I don't think so. Might make me conceited."

He laughed. "Not likely." Then he looked at me more closely. "Why did you speak of going home in the past tense?"

I stared at the accounts in front of me. "Because I've given up all hope of home."

"Why? You didn't give up when *I* told you return wasn't possible."

"I talked to the First Merchant myself. The Gild won't touch me without your permission."

"Why aren't you looking at me, madam?" Lord Karne's tone had taken on a hard edge.

I had to explain, though I felt sure merely talking to someone off-world would be just as great a crime here as sending a letter off-world. He had trusted me with important work. Concealing Pieter's call was almost the same as lying about it and we couldn't work together, I and my husband, with lies between us: I had to have the work for my sanity's sake and he had been betrayed too many times to trust easily.

I took a deep breath, closed the account book, and looked up at him. "I was trying not to tell you everything that's happened, milord. Hasn't Frem Weisman told you my brother Pieter called here?"

I looked at Weisman's busy back. Its rigidity said that he was listening and his refusal to turn at the mention of his name told me my suspicion was true. Lord Karne followed my eyes. He told Weisman to leave and I waited until he had gone before I took a deep breath and continued.

"It was the night before we went to Duvals', my lord. Pieter was a Jump away and said he'd take me home." The saying brought that terrible sense of loss back to me and I stopped, choking again on grief.

"But you didn't go."

It was a quiet statement, no more, and disconcerting because I had expected anger, as he'd been angry about the letter. All the voice I could get out was a shaky whisper. "To escape would be treason. Treason means death, lord, and I was sure that here the sentence of death would be particularly painful and bloody. You, Jemmy, Kit, perhaps many soldiers . . ." I paused, remembering the horrible things these people were willing to do to each other. How could he understand? "It—it would be like murdering you with my own hands. I couldn't have lived with that on my conscience."

"Zjhanne . . ." But he didn't go any further and I couldn't interpret the expression on his face.

We sat in silence for many minutes. Then Lord Karne began, slowly at first, to tell about his years of struggle to save the Gharr from the revolution the Old Party's politics was provoking. Soon all the frustrations of the stalemate rushed out. He had talked and talked, to noblemen and Freemen, but so many wouldn't listen. And too many more would, after all that had happened, still "wait and see."

He rubbed the back of his neck and stopped with his hand still resting there. "No one wants to be on the losing side. Most of the minor Houses (the lower nobility) are waiting to see which way to jump." He looked away. "The rumor you heard from Tremo—about my 'cowardice'—probably went out before we'd left Justin. And it has done damage, but, knowing about it, I could at least talk to people about it. Now Orkonan's murder shows Richard's spy in the manor has become active again. He hasn't done anything since Charlotte's assassination. As far as we know." The tightening of Karne's features showed the pain Charlotte's betrayal still caused him.

I felt a surge of compassion for this man who had lost so much in what appeared to be a fruitless struggle to modernize his world.

"How could anyone believe you a coward, my lord?"

"No one has to *believe* it." His voice turned harsh and bitter. "Doubt, the slightest uncertainty about me, and they hesitate to help. Many Freemen see they won't long be free if House Harlan controls Starker IV, but they value their ancient neutrality so much that they wait, hoping that something or someone else will bring Richard down." He slammed a fist down on the table. "By the Guardians, why can't they see that with every delay I'm likelier to be dead than pushing reform! Then who'll take the risk and try again? I won't make it easy, but Richard can make his dream come true. He has the power now."

"Milord, your friends—"

He gave a harsh bark of laughter. "Friends? Not enough, and time's on Richard's side. Soon, if no one else joins us, I won't have the money to force anything. And without money, the end of House Halarek comes rather quickly." He rose and began pacing restlessly. "I've presented two proposals to Council. One would abolish slavery and set maximum punishments for serfs. Harlan and Odonnel have begun handing slavery out as punishment for rebels."

"Which only makes things worse, doesn't it?"

"Which only makes things worse."

"And then?"

"If the slavery proposal doesn't pass, the other one hasn't much chance, not unless we have more big uprisings in between." He looked down at his boottips. "It probably doesn't have much chance, anyway. It frees all serfs between sixteen and thirty, until there are no more serfs. They'll adjust best to a new life at that age. Meanwhile, it sets a maximum on the crop a lord can collect from them as rent and taxes. Sometimes a serf can lose a quarter of his crops to taxes and half to rent. Starker IV is ready to explode. Most of the Houses have had revolts of various sorts: Gormsby put down an ugly one just before we went to deVree's party and there were six other major armed rebellions before the snow. There'll be more in the spring when the lords begin demanding their boon work." He made a small, grim sound that couldn't quite make itself a laugh. "Yet even the younger sons of minor Houses refuse all but upper management positions. Someone has to keep our factories running, but too few Houses realize that you can't give men the technical training to run factories and then expect them to endure near-slave status."

The heavy rhythm of the watch passed one door, then the other. "I can't even keep my own home safe," the Lharr said bitterly.

He looked so tired. No man should feel so responsible for a world's problems.

He took a deep breath. "Win or lose, the Families can't rule the way they have been much longer."

"Knowing that, why do you keep working?"

"Because it's right," he said simply. He rested the heels of his hands against the mantel and stared down at the logs. He shook his head angrily and turned back to me. "I can't even redeem that rumor you told me about. I've renewed the challenge, but Richard won't meet me. Before he takes chances with his life, he wants to be sure he's ruined mine. His assassins won't kill me, either, not all at once. A shattered kneecap, perhaps an arm burned—"

"Lord Karne!" My stomach lurched. How could he talk about such things, let alone so calmly?

"I'm sorry." He brightened with effort. "The next Council will be interesting. You can watch it on the tri-d, you know."

I conquered my heaving stomach with difficulty. "I'm afraid I haven't had much interest in politics. It hasn't been necessary," I said in a muffled voice.

Lord Karne sat down and pulled his chair a little closer to mine. "Of the Nine Great Houses (usually called the Nine), you've met Druma, Justin, Ingold Kingsland, the deVrees, and Emil von Schuss, of course. He's officially neutral, for Jemmy's sake, though that probably means nothing to Richard. The Marquis of Gormsby is a very thin, very old man who has always stood with Harlan. Garren Odonnel has reddish hair and will be the lord who echoes Richard or makes moves for him. DeVree and Kingsland aren't saying who they stand with."

He looked at me to be sure I was still listening. "We have to watch Paul. He's weak and the Family Druma will be easy to pressure financially."

"Why do you say I can watch it on the tri-d, milord? I'm your secretary now. Why do I watch the Council from here? Shouldn't I be with you? No, don't say it's not for a woman. I've been told many times your mother had a place there as your regent. I'd be very careful not to embarrass you. I could take notes—"

"The Freemen record everything. Weisman can do anything else I need."

Suddenly it was very important to me to win this public expression of his trust in my abilities. "Please, milord, you married me to be an example. So far you've wasted your money. Let me show you, and everyone else, what help a free woman can be. Free me to be myself, milord!" I read the thought that flashed across his face as easily as if he'd spoken it. "I know I've been more hurt than help till now, milord. Give me the chance to make up for it."

He sat in silence for several minutes, then stood and gravely offered his hand to help me to my feet. He looked deep into me, as if trying to see my motives. "I'll sleep on it, madam, and tell you my decision in the morning."

CHAPTER 12

Christmas wasn't anything like what had been planned. The murder ended the party spirit. Tension in the house increased as the remaining days passed and no one found further clues to the murderer's identity. Some long-time resident relatives packed up and flew home to their own holdings, believing they would be safer there. Lord Karne and I worked through the week, right to the afternoon of Christmas Eve, orienting me to the holding's business at home and in the galaxy. Lord Karne spent any free time playing with Jemmy, who was free of lessons for the week. Sometimes, during particularly rowdy games, their shouts and laughter could be heard in the library.

On Christmas Eve, Kit came to the library to scold us. Christmas Eve dinner was to begin in less than an hour and we were still working. We hurriedly put everything away and went upstairs to change clothes. I had decided to break Gharr custom for married women and wear my hair down, merely tied back with a ribbon redder than my hair. I turned once before the mirror before leaving to meet Kit and was pleased with the festive reflection. My pleasure buoyed my sagging spirits and the fluid swirl of velvet around my legs felt elegant and feminine. These dresses weren't so bad for partying.

I walked across the hall, enjoying the admiring glances of the soldiers stationed there. The Lharr was boy-sitting while Kit finished dressing. When I entered, he was holding Jemmy up in the air and the boy was squealing with delight. The Lharr heard the door close and looked. He put the boy down without taking his eyes from me. He looked for a long moment and the expression on his face was compliment enough. He walked slowly toward me and took my hands.

"Words are hard to find, madam."

The intensity of his admiration brought warm blood to my cheeks.

He squeezed my hands lightly. "I'm a lucky man to have such a handsome dinner companion. Do you know how stunning you are?"

I responded to his smile. "Now I know, milord."

He turned Jemmy toward Kit's curtained dressing area and gave him a pat on the behind. "Scoot in there and tell your mother that if she wants to be noticed at all tonight, she'll have to get downstairs ahead of us."

Lord Karne turned away long enough to pick up a small brushed-gold box from the arm of a chair. "I was going to take this downstairs for giving tomorrow, but it seems better now."

I touched the front edge and the lid flew up. Inside lay a magnificent necklace of smoky blue stones.

"Oh, milord! It's so beautiful!"

"I—I wanted something to match your eyes," he blurted.

I looked up at him curiously, both because of the unusual awkwardness of his response and because I hadn't thought he noticed much of anything about me. "Will you fasten it for me, milord?"

I held out the open necklace. He walked behind and lifted my trailing hair out of the way. I felt the clumsiness of fingers long unaccustomed to such tasks, then the small snick of fastening.

"Thank you very much, milord."

He smiled and made a little bow, but he said nothing else to me until we were seated in the Hall and well into the meal.

The Family feast, the Christmas story, and the Boosh (a huge rolled cake frosted to look like a log)—we progressed from one to the next slowly, savoring the temporary peace and relaxation. When no one could eat another bite, servants pushed the tables back and there was folk-dancing. Then those who wished to stayed for caroling. For me, the evening was more than nice and the admiration of my husband and other members of the Family made me glow. It was early morning before the last of the relatives had gone to bed and the host and hostess could finally retire, yet this night, I found even my tiredness pleasurable.

The Lharr nudged me gently awake. "Wouldn't you rather sleep upstairs?"

"I suppose so."

"Come, then." He gave me a hand up, then put an arm around my waist.

I didn't object. The weight of his hand felt good and his arm around me was so different from his customary formality. I rested my head against his shoulder and we walked slowly upstairs, he whisper-whistling the refrain of the last carol.

My ladies were already in bed and my quarters were quiet and dim. Lord Karne and I stood in the center of my room, enjoying the last minutes of peace and happiness. By a slight pressure of his arm, Lord Karne swung me around in front of him. His kiss was of a mood with everything else, warm, gentle, asking nothing.

"Good night, my lady," he said softly.

But it wasn't the kiss he could've given me. His golden eyes smoldered. After our passionate lovemaking just days ago, could he still think I only endured his bedplay? I couldn't guess his thoughts, but it would be so easy to make the evening as perfect for him as it had been for me. I pressed closer and reached up to kiss his lips. He held me tighter and kissed me with gentle fire. I slid my arms around his neck and yielded to a kiss that seemed to draw my soul right out of me. Slowly he began unbuttoning the back my dress.

The next morning, Lord Karne began preparing me for the Council meeting, which was only a week away. The morning of that meeting came all too soon.

We flew to Council ground and, surrounded by Lifesguardsmen, walked to the door of the Council building surrounded by Lifesguardsmen. Since no private soldiers were allowed inside, because no weapons were allowed inside, we went on from there alone.

Council Chairman Reed greeted everyone ceremoniously at the door of the huge blue-green Council chamber. As Lord Karne and I went through the door, a page announced, "The Lharr and Larga Halarek." Heads snapped around and a murmur swept across the room, approving or disapproving, I couldn't tell. Councilman Duval, standing with an alderman in the Freemen's section across the chamber, approved and winked slyly at me.

Lord Karne threaded through the crowd to the Halarek prep table. The men sitting on the rows of benches behind the table greeted Lord Karne casually. I didn't recognize any of them, but knew they had to be Halarek or they wouldn't be there. Karne pulled a chair out for me. When I was seated, he, too, sat down and began fingering his nameplate. He glanced around the room.

Chairman Reed came to stand behind the desk at the center of the round chamber and rapped vigorously for order. As the uproar lessened, Lord Karne whispered to me, "Remember, just your being here is unusual enough. You're here as my personal secretary only, to observe and remember. Under no circumstances say anything while Council is in session."

He turned his attention back to the chairman, who was reading the agenda—a new trade agreement with Antares III, a recommendation that Black Ship raiding be ended, a bill to free slaves . . .

Suddenly there was silence. The Duke of Harlan and some of his vassals stood at the door of the chamber. Richard walked down an aisle toward his seat, smiling at the Earl of Justin two seats down. The earl looked away. Harlan laid a friendly hand on the shoulder of a man sitting behind the Marquis of Gormsby. The shoulder shrugged him off. He bit his lip and looked across the room.

"Lily-livered bastard," muttered someone to my right.

I thought I saw faint signs of satisfaction on Lord Karne's face, but he showed no other sign of having seen his enemy. Perhaps his efforts to redeem Richard's vicious rumor about the duel had gone better than he thought.

At least the duke is getting some of the tar he wished to spread on Lord Karne stuck to himself, I thought, with some satisfaction.

"If we may continue . . . ," said the chairman bitingly.

Richard nodded gracious consent and sat down. The chairman picked up where he had left off and finished the list. The meeting began. I understood very little of the terms of the new trade agreement. The Council discussed it without enthusiasm and approved it. Then Reed called for the next order of business. The Marquis of Gormsby rose.

"Lords—and lady—the Order of the Horse recommends that the Black Ships be grounded at once, permanently. You know us, and not as cowards. We have fought often and well when there was need. I myself had a foreign wife. Yet we feel that the risk of an alliance against us of aggrieved planets increases with every raiding ship that leaves Starker IV. How much longer, gentlemen, can we expect our neighbors to submit docilely to such blatant violations of their territory and sovereignty? How much longer will they endure the theft of their people, even if only of women?"

The emotion in his voice and the lack of introduction to the subject implied that this had been much discussed before. I wondered why, then, I had the feeling that the marquis's remarks were pointed at me.

Reed next recognized Lharr Garren Odonnel, who was about Karne's age. Odonnel bowed ceremoniously to the old man. "I agree with my noble colleague. The Order of the Horse has long proposed this change. Since this last venture"—here he looked significantly at Lord Karne—"which resulted in the death of my wife's cousin and of several other good soldiers, I, too, have come to support this proposal." He paused for effect.

An expectant silence closed over the room and several heads turned to see the reaction of House Halarek.

Lord Karne growled angrily under his breath, "Odonnel's been separated from his wife more than a year. And he hated her cousin Charles like a Zinn Runner."

"We asked the Lharr Halarek not to make this flight," Odonnel continued, "but he ignored us and attacked a peaceful agricultural planet only half a light-year away—"

A man in his early thirties stood up from the ranks of House von Schuss. "Mr. Chairman, may the record show that 'we' means only House Harlan and House Odonnel, not the Council as is implied."

Reed nodded approval. "Granted, Lord Karel."

The man sat down again.

Odonnel exhaled in irritation. "As I was saying, attacked a peaceful—"

Lord Karne sprang to his feet. "I did not attack Fruhe! We landed at night and subdued the few people we met with sleep gas, painlessly and harmlessly. The three soldiers Odonnel refers to got drunk, fell into a lake, and drowned. Tell full truth, not half, milord."

Odonnel stiffened. "I haven't yielded the floor, nor will I to one who calls me liar."

"I haven't called you that, Odonnel. Yet."

Odonnel continued as if Lord Karne had said nothing. "I have explained my change of position." And he sat down, smiling a small, satisfied smile.

A very young man of House Kingsland rose hesitantly. "How does the Order of the Horse suggest we find wives, then?"

"Take a Gharr woman, of course." Duke Richard didn't wait for Reed's recognition.

A young man of House deVree exploded to his feet. "By the Four Guardians! You know there haven't been enough women for all of us since the War and the Sickness of '04!"

The duke leaned back in his chair and clucked in exaggerated sympathy.

"Then why haven't you a wife, milord?" This impertinence came from a young man of one of the minor Houses.

"Yes! Where are *your* sons, milord?" This from House deVree.

A wave of red swept up under Richard Harlan's dark skin and he glared around him. "I'll take a wife, suited to Starker IV." He looked significantly at me. "But only when I'm ready."

"Does that mean you'll space out to get her?" a voice from House Justin shouted.

"Aye. Why not? Harlan's no minor House. I can afford a Black Ship."

"That remark about minor Houses won't make any friends for him," Lord Karne murmured in my ear.

Lord Richard wasn't through yet. "Always wives for the Nine have come from worlds like ours, or from less advanced ones. Why now a change? Why a woman from the planets of the old Empire? Have the Families been wrong all these years?"

From the muffled murmur that rose, I gathered Lord Richard had made a social error in criticizing me in my presence.

The Earl of Justin turned toward me and said, "Please don't judge all of the Old Party by the bad manners of Lord Richard, Larga. We have no part of his remark."

The chairman recognized a young man of House von Schuss. "Harlan's question is not to the point, Frem Reed," the man said. "The question is not where, but if, raiding continues." He looked toward Reed, who nodded. The young man continued. "What are the chances of provoking another war, Frem Chairman?"

"Our observers report, as they have since the War, that the Federation will under no circumstances rearm. Not as long as member worlds can see ruins and radioactive burn."

I knew this was Fruhe's feeling. No provocation was worth the death and destruction of another War. On Fruhe, as on most of the Inner Worlds, active non-violence was taught from babyhood.

"What about economic reprisals?"

"Entirely possible, though no world has suggested them as yet."

"Then I say, don't stop the Black Ships," a young man behind Justin broke in. "I have no wife nor is there a woman here of proper birth and age. Am I to die without sons?"

A mutter of agreement from the younger men followed this statement. Justin rose with dignity and was recognized.

"I move, then, that the Black Ships be permitted to leave as often as necessary to ensure that the Families survive." There was a low cheer from the younger men. "Unless the Freemen . . ."

Reed shook his head angrily. "Freemen would cease to be so if they married into your Families and your quarrels. Is there a second?"

There was and the motion passed rousingly. The next items were Karne's bills. The debate was hot and windy and here the Freemen entered for the first time. For what seemed like hours to me, though it was only a little more than one, the attack and counterattack continued.

At Baron von Schuss's request, the proposals were divided and voted on separately. After vigorous argument the resistance of the Old Party was beaten back and slavery legally abolished. But the Freemen, so essential to the passage of the first part, kept out of the debate on the second, the limitation of serf-punishments. The list of permissible punishments—mutilation, beating, solitary confinement in chains, Zinn—horrified me. No arguments could persuade the Freemen that it was in their interest to take part. They owned no serfs, so they didn't feel involved and no one could make them see that as long as some men were unfree, no one's freedom was secure. After much shouting and many harsh words, the vote was taken. Lord Karne waited tensely for the ballots to be counted. The result was against him.

I knew Lord Karne's disappointment must have been bitter, because now I knew how much the issue meant to him, but he hid his feelings well, as usual. I tried to offer consolation. "At least they didn't succeed in increasing the list of criminal acts, milord."

"Aye," he said wearily, "at least we stopped that."

Then Chairman Reed cleared his throat nervously and began to read the next proposal. "Be it resolved that from this day onward, no woman of Family shall leave her house without her husband's consent and the company of at least two women of rank. Be it further declared that no woman of whatever rank shall expose her ankles or upper arms or more than one inch of neck. And be it also resolved that no person shall teach a female more than to read and write her name."

I could not immediately believe what I had just heard. There was no world I knew of in the entire galaxy that discriminated so severely against women. On the backward worlds, where women did not read or write, it was because no one did. The proposal made extremely clear how much worse my already restricted future could get. *This* sort of male arrogance was what I had let myself in for when I told Pieter to go away. *This* was why my husband had hesitated to bring me to Council.

If this stupid resolution passed, I, for one, couldn't leave the manor if Kit or Lady Agnes couldn't. And they wanted to make female clothing even more restricting! Lord Karne must have sensed my escalating emotions, because he beckoned to Oroark, who left his post near the door and escorted me out.

In the hall I strode angrily up and down, kicking my heavy brocade skirt ahead of me viciously, biting my lip to keep from pouring my feeling out in the hearing of the soldiers and Freemen in the hall. The beautiful murals were just blurs, the low voices of the clumps of soldiers only unintelligible intrusions on the angry words boiling inside. These Old Party men were at the Lharr's throat all the time, making victims of women and serfs just to get at him.

"Larga?" The tone implied Oroark had said something before.

I stopped and looked at him. He flushed and shifted his weight to the other foot.

"It's nothing to get upset about, Larga. It's no disgrace. You're a woman."

I clamped a lid on my boiling rage. Oroark was young, and he had never known another way of living. "That's not the problem, Tommy. More restrictions are the problem. Isn't life for women stifling enough already? Can't talk, can't think, can't *move* in these clothes, and they want to keep women from *reading*, too! The whole situation is infuriating! But Lord Karne was right. I couldn't've stayed quiet a minute longer."

Oroark looked at me, a perplexed wrinkle deepening between his melancholy brown eyes.

"You don't understand how I feel at all, do you, Tommy?"

"Sort of. Well, not exactly. No."

The door of the Council chamber opened and the Freemen and lords flooded out. Lord Karne came near the end, talking seriously with Duval and Chairman Reed. Paul IV Druma joined them for a few quick words and went on his way. The three stopped in the chamber's doorway and talked quietly for several minutes before splitting up.

Lord Karne leaned against the wall beside the door and I could see him consciously relaxing his taut muscles. He stayed there for several aggravating moments more, watching me, teasing me, before coming to me to answer my unspoken question.

"Relax. We defeated that one." He turned away for a moment to greet several passing men, then continued. "After all, custom and personal wishes already require modest dress."

"Whose wishes?"

"Mine. Any husband's."

"You don't sound very progressive now."

"Sometimes progress just means not going backwards. This was one of those times. That proposal's shelved for four sessions. That's more than a year. By then, one party or the other will have won."

"One inch of neck! I can't find a word bad enough to describe the blindness and masculine imbecility—and I'd begun to think you were different. Oh!"

"Keep your voice down," Lord Karne warned, but his voice was amused.

His amusement increased my anger, though I did try to keep my voice low. "Prove your words about reform, my lord. Free me. Let me be myself."

He smiled and shook his head.

"If I were a man you wouldn't dismiss me like that."

"If you were any other woman, I might consider it. But I can see you cutting your hair and wearing skirts up to your knees, conversing freely with any man who interests you and befriending serfs. No, I can't take the chance that you'll shock reform right out of existence. Its life here is precarious enough. And you don't have the patience to make little changes. Let's go home and get back to work."

With Oroark ahead and five soldiers alongside and behind, we walked quickly back to the lift that whisked us to the surface and the flitter pad.

CHAPTER 13

There would be no more Councils until spring. Two months of snow had been only preliminaries. Winter descended now with full weight. Wind and cold and blowing snow on the surface made flitter travel too dangerous even to think about. I had dreaded having to spend three months with only the Halarek household for company, but with work to do the prospect didn't seem as bad.

And Lord Karne had given me something to think about: patience and little changes. He was right. A big change would be too shocking. I was determined to show him I could learn patience. And somehow I'd think of something that would make up a little for the serious mistakes I'd made at first, even if it took years.

The door from the Lharr's quarters burst open, breaking my thought. In hurtled a large, furry dustball, followed by a loud exuberant noise, followed by Jemmy himself, still yelling excitedly. He scooped up the pale gray fluff and only then noticed where he was.

"Aunt Zjhanne, look what Uncle Karne gave me!" He extended the fuzzy object toward me.

I accepted it with hesitation. It seemed to be purring. It wriggled in my hands until two bright black eyes faced me. I rested the small body on one arm and felt through the long soft hair. It was round and, as far as I could tell, tailless and neckless. It seemed to have four legs, until another pair of legs, or arms, emerged and fingered the smoky gems of my necklace curiously. I tentatively stroked it. It now most definitely purred.

"She's an uhl-uhl," Jemmy said proudly. "That's what she says when she's frightened. Her name's Wiki."

He held up his hands and his pet squirmed to be returned to him. He clutched her against his chest. From her squashed position, Wiki purred even louder.

Jemmy looked down at her proudly. "Isn't she something?"

He dropped her onto the floor. She took off at once with Jemmy after her. Around the bed, behind the chest—Wiki waited until Jemmy almost reached her—then around my legs twice and back out the door, narrowly missing a collision with Donna on one side and the Lharr on the other. Lord Karne watched, laughing, as the chase continued noisily through his room and out into the hall, where Jemmy apparently caught his pet, for the noise stopped.

"I'd say the uhl-uhl is a success," Lord Karne said, still chuckling. "Jemmy needs someone to play with. No one will risk fostering a child with us, or fostering Jemmy."

The noise began again across the hall.

"But I didn't come to talk about that. I have a tri-d conference in a few minutes and the First Merchant may bring a tape from Chairman Reed while I'm busy. Would you wait for him? I don't want Weisman 'accidentally' opening it with the rest of the mail."

"Of course, milord. Anything you say, milord." And I curtseyed with exaggerated depth and humility.

Lord Karne accepted my teasing with a smile, a smile that started in his golden eyes and spread quickly down his thin face to his mouth. I found it a strangely compelling change. He pulled me to my feet.

"Propriety itself," he said, with the smile still in his voice.

My Blues escorted me to the library to wait. Weisman had his restoration materials spread out on one of the tables and the smell of rok hide and fixative filled the forward part of the room. I retreated to the rear and explored a row of unused cabinets. Most of them were quite empty and heavy with dust, but one held a heavy square which, when cleaned, revealed a chess board of green and white orak.

After dinner that night, I took the board to Kit's quarters and we began a game. Jemmy watched the first hour's play, then was sent to bed, protesting, "But, Mama . . ."

A few minutes after we had resumed play, Jemmy pushed open the curtains around his bed and looked up at us, his eyes squinted against the light. "Mama, I can't go to sleep."

A few minutes after that, "Mama, I'm thirsty."

Kit held a very brief whispered conversation with him. We had no more interruptions. Lord Karne came in as the endgame was beginning. When I pounced on Kit's king, he, too, seemed pleased. He held out a hand.

"Come downstairs and play a game with me?"

I accepted the offer and the hand gladly.

After that the two of us relaxed over chess in the library many evenings before going to bed. Lord Karne could talk to me easily about politics. Playing chess, he talked as easily of other things. Eventually he was at ease with me without either politics or chess. Sometimes if we had worked late, Gareth had an All Night sent in and we lingered over it to talk. We talked about a lot of things that winter. About his boyhood, free of danger only for the five years in school on Altair, about his deep love for the Gharr and for Halarek Holding, about his mother, whose unusual abilities won from Council a regency, about the ten hard years since he had become Lharr in fact. He showed me what his life had been and I thanked God again for my own carefree childhood. Sometimes I told him about Fruhe and worked out some of the homesickness that had been festering inside. As we worked and talked, we discovered each other as persons and we liked what we found. I found myself looking forward to our times together. And feeling a traitor to my family for it.

Often the two of us finished an evening with a story. Lord Karne usually asked me to read. We settled in front of the fire and I read from galactic literature as it pleased my fancy. Because Lord Karne's eyes drew me, I usually read while sitting on the hearth rug, leaning against his legs. The reading aloud, which I had considered a childish custom when I first came, became a pleasure. Sometimes, to balance all the romances and epics, I recited ancient stories from Terra, such as the Franklin's Tale, stories that showed happy, married lovers. In too many marriages on Starker IV I saw indifference, cruelty, hate, infidelity.

In the time I wasn't being a secretary, I thought out and began a project I hoped would permanently change life for Gharr women. Conversations at the Advent parties and tri-d visits afterward had shown me that Gharr women weren't as satisfied with their lives as their men thought. I was sure these women wouldn't take suggestions from "that brazen foreigner," though, so I had to think of some way to sneak around their pride and the suspicions of their even more conservative husbands.

With the Lharr's permission I ordered five small household computers. The Gild flew a heavy freighter over Ontar and dropped them through the flitter gate. It was late in Uhl, but such things were still possible in Uhl. Kit and I worked almost a month doing a household inventory, then I entered the lists into one computer's memory, showing Kit how at the same time. After that, the computer kept track of supplies, orders, expenses, repairs needed, repairs completed. After I entered a list of the meals Kit had planned and served over the past six months, the computer even planned menus. This eliminated hours of work every day for Kit.

Then Kit and I whiled away afternoons having "tea" by tri-d. We experimented with the Duval girls first, to test our sales method. We talked about the usual this and that. Then Kit casually mentioned our new "toy." The girls were immediately interested. They had to see it. We pooh-poohed its usefulness. They insisted. So, hiding smiles from the Duvals and from our own soldier escorts, who carried the portable tri-d transmitter, Kit and I showed the computer at work. When we returned to the tri-d room, Elspeth was wriggling with excitement.

"Wait till we tell Daddy! Could you get one for us?"

"Mom'll be very interested," Adrian drawled. "We'll see you soon."

They flicked off. Within a week, after demonstrating for the older Duvals, they bought. That was the only sale I and Kit made for two weeks, but we roused interest in a lot of women. Our intense reluctance to even consider parting with the remaining three computers—a vital part of the sales strategy—only increased the desire for them.

One evening Lord Karne came laughing to dinner. "I've let you two set up your business and I've resisted asking questions till now. But I can't resist anymore. Why the sudden demand for those cute little machines? The Duchess of Druma *must* have one. Councilmen have called. Even the lords of four minor Houses have asked about them. Six calls just today! And nothing can be delivered anywhere now till spring!"

"Would you order more, Karne?" Kit sparkled with pleasure at the discreet uproar our plan was causing.

Lord Karne grinned. "Maybe, if I knew why you're so eager to part a lot of men from their money."

That was a question I wanted to answer. "Milord, there's so little I can do without being shocking, but if I can free fifty Gharr women from routine work, they'll start looking for something new to do and that will lead to changes. I don't have much patience, I know, but I think I can wait for Gharr ladies to make reforms of their own."

"They will, too, Karne," Kit put in eagerly, "as soon as they start wondering what to do with the extra free time they have after they've done everything they *used* to do in their free time."

"Little devils," Lord Karne said, but he was smiling.

Kit laughed and kissed his cheek. "Aren't we? Look what I do with my freed time. I'm learning Sternlangue. I'm painting like I've always wanted to. And I'm helping make more women dissatisfied with the way they live."

Lord Karne looked at me. "If I'd known you were this crafty, I'd've had you working for me sooner. Look at the change in my conservative sister."

I couldn't tell if he were teasing and I needed to know. "Will this really help, milord?"

He set a hand lightly on my shoulder. "There's no way to say yet, but if it works the way you think it will, it's well worth trying."

His praise warmed me. I liked him so much. And I didn't want to. He had no right to liking, let alone more. I was a political act for him, nothing else. And I didn't want to be hurt again. Lance had claimed to love me just to get what he wanted from me: cooperation. Lord Karne wanted the same, but at least he had told me honestly love in marriage was too dangerous on this world to risk. Liking him, and desiring him, could lead me to more, and that would lead to more pain than I could now imagine. I must *not* let my feelings for him get stronger. He didn't want to risk love. Neither did I.

Computer sales slowed eventually. The pile of manor and holding paperwork shrank steadily, because there was no buying, selling, entertaining, or business of any other kind during the winter. In a way I was glad, because that meant I no longer spent most of each day with Lord Karne, feeling myself drawing closer and closer to him.

Life slowed, as it does on other worlds in high summer. My ways of filling time had gone, and there were no summer pleasures to replace them. No winter pleasures, either. The Halareks, personal family and general Family, played riddles, blindman's buff, and chess and told stories. When they weren't doing one of those, the men practiced weaponry in the arena, set up duels, and rode horses while the women did fine needlework and gossiped. Uhl, Arhast,

Koort, and Nemb passed in the same routines.

It was not my way of life. I knew I'd have to live like this every winter for the rest of my life, but this one had come too soon. I couldn't accept the children's amusements that the adults so enjoyed. Lord Karne made a point of spending most evenings with me, but chess, or long talks into the night, or bedplay weren't enough. I needed exercise and fresh air. I needed useful work. As the winter wore on, I felt more and more on edge. I grew more and more short-tempered. When the Thaw finally came, late, it rained and rained and I still could not go outside. And there was the Thawtime Council to prepare for.

I came to my room to rest before dinner on a very trying day. It had started badly. Donna, who usually dressed my hair, was so sick she couldn't get out of bed. Tamara only knew how to brush. Jaklene thought it beneath her. So I fought with the mess myself. I wrapped it into a makeshift bun and accompanied Kit on an inspection of the kitchen, where I accidentally knocked a crock from a table, and, jumping away from the noise, burned my arm on the edge of an oven. Jaklene and Tamara got into a quarrel after lunch and spent most of the afternoon screeching at each other like angry cats. I sent them to their alcove, which was but little help. I lay down, but the quarrel was still going on and several Blues were dicing boisterously in their assembly room just down the hall. Complete relaxation, which I needed to renew my body and spirit, demanded more will than I felt inclined to put into it. I would have to do my internal physical exam some other time. I got up, took my brush from the top of the wardrobe, and sat down on the side of my bed to try to untangle my hair.

The hair was almost waist-long now and held a rat's nest every few inches. I couldn't brush through to the end anywhere without first yanking to a stop in a knot or six. Jerking through knots was all the provocation my head needed to begin throbbing all across the back. Tears of frustration and pain crept out of my eyes. I hated that length of hair more passionately every moment. My battle so engrossed me that I didn't hear Lord Karne open the door from his room.

He cleared his throat. "I'd like to talk to you while you're alone, Zjhanne. We've been bedmates quite a while. Surely by now . . ."

I spun to face him. At the moment, *he* was the system that demanded preposterously long hair. "You don't believe it can be done, do you? I told you I'd give you no children. I meant it! I won't bring a child into a life of fighting and imminent death, no matter how much you want an heir!"

The brush yanked to a stop in another tangle and jerked my sleeve across the burn. I ripped the brush out of my hair and glared at the long red strands snarled in it. "I'll tell you something else, Lord Karne. I'm not going to wear this—this sign of inferiority any longer!"

I hurled the brush across the room. It crashed into the wall and shattered with a crinkling sound. Then I spun back to the small table beside my bed, threw open the sewing box, and snatched out the big scissors. Lord Karne didn't understand until he saw them what I meant to do. I bunched my hair in one hand and hacked at it with quick sawing cuts. The room was, for him, only a few running strides wide, but that was enough. Lord Karne reached me as the hair reached the floor in a dully gleaming tangle. I shook my head and savored its lightness. I thought for a moment Lord Karne would hit me, he was so angry. But he only wrenched the scissors from my hand.

"What do you think you're doing?"

"Getting rid of some of my troubles, milord."

He snatched some of the hair from the floor and shook it in front of my face. "You do this, after hearing a proposal at the last Council for stricter dress regulations! Look at you! Hardly any hair at all!" He lifted several strands on the shorn side, then let them fall back onto my shoulders. His shoulders sagged. "How will I explain this at Council?"

I couldn't meet his eyes. I'd given no thought to the political consequences. "If—if it embarrasses you, my lord, I'll stay here."

"No—but—I'd planned—" He turned away.

Dear God, I've done something awful again. "What had you planned?"

He faced me, but his eyes evaded mine. "I thought we'd make something special of it, ride over. It would take three or four days, but it would be in the sun and open air."

"Ahem."

We both jumped. Weisman stood in the doorway. "I don't wish to interrupt, milord, but will you need me any more tonight?"

"No. Close up and go to bed."

I looked after the man. How long had Weisman been listening? Perhaps that question bothered Lord Karne, too, for he watched the librarian's departure with a frown, but when the door closed, he turned back to me.

"You've willed your hair to grow before. Do it now."

"No, milord. The hair's off and it's staying off. I'll even it and have Donna curl it—"

"By the Four Guardians, madam!" There was lightning in the golden eyes. "Do you want to flaunt your contempt for me before all of Starker IV?"

"Contempt, my lord? If you can believe that's my reason, I *will* stay here."

"You can't."

There was a flatness to his voice that warned me. "Why not? To ride to Council would have been wonderful, but you'll plainly be more at ease without me." He looked more deflated than angry. I put out a hand to touch his arm. "There wasn't any special reason for me to go, was there?"

He spun away. I heard the crack as he slammed one fist into the other palm.

"Damn it, woman! Can't you see it's a matter of pride?" He left the room without looking back, walking with stiff, angry steps.

A few minutes later Kit hurried in. "What happened? I passed Karne in the hall just now and he— Oh, Zjhanne, your hair!"

Kit, too. I felt suddenly very tired. "Aye. My hair. And because of it I told Lord Karne I'd stay home from Council."

"You didn't! Karne planned the trip just to please you and he's been as excited as a boy about it. No wonder he looked crushed."

"It *was* a wonderful idea. Nothing short of a trip home could've pleased me more." Now I felt deflated. "I guess I made a real mess of it. But he was so upset about this"—I kicked the pile of hair on the floor—"that I really thought it would be better if I didn't go."

Kit's dismay was written all over her face. "The Spring Council is a celebration, Zjhanne, a big party where we can be with our friends for the first time in months. Isn't there anything you can do about your hair?"

I picked the red tangle off the floor. "Maybe I could make a switch of this, then nobody could see the difference." I looked up at Kit. "Do you think an apology would help?"

Kit's mouth turned down at the corners. "I really don't know. A quarrel takes the shine off things. Maybe if you told him what you told me, that it's the next best thing to going home . . ." Her hand flashed out and she gripped my arm with surprisingly strong fingers. "Zjhanne, you wouldn't arrange something? Not when he trusts you?"

I shook my head. "I couldn't, even when I was hating him. Not at the price. And I had a chance, Kit. Now I like him too much to intentionally hurt him or his work."

"But you don't like him enough to give him an heir."

"Are liking and—and desiring enough, Kit? A child is an act of hope and complete trust. The kind of trust that comes only with love. A child should come out of love into love. We fight so much. And he doesn't *want* love."

"I know. But he needs to be loved. You could at least be affectionate, Zjhanne."

"I could. But love's too dangerous. He's—unless he returns it—he won't—he could be killed—love hurts so much, Kit!"

Though I had whispered them, Kit heard my last words and put her arm around my waist. "Try, Zjhanne. You're going to be here for the rest of your life and Karne needs love. You need love." She let her head rest against mine. "Love is worth the cost, Zjhanne. I wouldn't give up one second of the time I had with Nik, even if I knew in advance how soon we'd be separated."

We hugged each other in silence for some time. "Think about what I've said, Zjhanne," Kit finally said, so quietly I almost didn't hear it. "Karne doesn't know how much he needs to be loved. He might not believe he needs it, but he does. Heir or not, Zjhanne, Karne has to keep going. Our sire despised him. Neither Lizanne nor Charlotte cared about him." Kit brushed the back of her free hand across her eyes. "He gets so little encouragement outside, Zjhanne. He needs all the love and support we can give." She looked at the floor. The toe of her shoe rasped against the stone. "And it takes two to make a fight, Zjhanne."

Kit left. I sat on my bed and thought for a long time, then I went to look for Lord Karne. I would try to make up for my clumsiness. I felt guiltier and guiltier with every step, because I knew I'd given him the idea that I didn't want to go at all. At least this much Kit's lecture had done: If Lord Karne wanted me with him, that was enough reason for me to go anywhere.

But Lord Karne was at target practice and had left word that absolutely no one was to disturb him. Absolutely no one. I was sure that order was aimed at me. He knew by this time that I regretted losing my temper very soon after I lost it.

I retreated to the library. Weisman was still busy closing up. He stared at me curiously. I ignored his unspoken questions and curled up in Lord Karne's chair to think. I hadn't known I could hurt him and I cared very much that I had.

CHAPTER 14

I didn't see Lord Karne again until after fast-breaking. He accepted my apology politely, told me briefly what clothes I should take, and disappeared with Tommy, who was to be in command of Ontar again.

The few days before departure filled with details that successfully kept Lord Karne and me apart. Kit and Jemmy were to leave later by flier, so they put off their own packing. Jemmy kept busy, anyway, busy getting in everyone's way.

"It's his first time," Kit said apologetically. "He's so excited he doesn't know what to do with himself."

Tommy watched preparations for the overland ride with wrinkled forehead and troubled eyes. I kept telling myself that what upset him was the lack of entourage—ladies and gentlemen to entertain us. We certainly had soldiers enough to protect us.

Departure day dawned bright and crisp, but with a hint of gray clouds collecting over the mountains. Snow still lurked in hollows and shadows, but most of the ground lay bare and brown. Lord Karne and I followed five Lifesguardsmen and the other five fell in behind. Kit, Jemmy, Tommy, Gareth, Weisman, and the ladies-in-waiting saw us off. Kit and Jemmy stood in the garden and waved until they were to us only tiny sticks on the landscape.

By the time we reached the foothills, a stiff wind was blowing. Gordie tossed his head to catch the wind in his mane and danced a little. The road was gravel, narrow, and eaten away at the edges by frost and water. I could clearly hear the crunch of hooves behind us, but the horses ahead had passed out of easy hearing. Over our heads tall bluish pines waved branches that moaned and whispered in the wind.

The road wound over the crest of a hill. Lord Karne stopped his horse at the top. Far behind, dimmed by the shadow of a cloud, a horseshoe of trees marked the manor garden. Through a break in the trees below, I saw the road and the last horse of our rear guard disappearing under swaying blue branches.

Lord Karne waved his arm toward the right and broke his long silence. "You have a good view of the Desert of Zinn from here. We'll soon cross its only river."

I followed his finger. A thin, pale green line traced the bed of the river. On either side of it the land stretched gray and brown and yellow. The foothills became garbled piles of boulders and crumbling rock as they approached the Desert. On them only a few twisted pines survived. Some of those that had not survived remained, too, tall bare poles only a little yellower than the rocks around them.

"It looks very grim, milord."

"It is. A convict survives only a short time this side of the mountains."

The mountains began pulling back not far from us. It was in the giant bowl they formed that the Desert lay.

"If you drive them into Zinn from the plains, they must have to go a very long way."

"Yes."

"That's very cruel."

"Not as cruel as locking them away. A man would get hungry, especially this time of year, and thirsty until he reached the river, but in good health he could cross Zinn in three days."

Lord Karne swung his stallion back onto the road and began the climb toward the mountains. The long hibernation had ended for the creatures of Starker IV and they let us know we were trespassers. Birds squawked and fluttered apprehensively as we passed and small animals scolded from the trees.

"We go over two passes to reach Council ground." Lord Karne pointed at right angles to the Desert. "It isn't a soft ride, but it's very beautiful." He looked down at me from his big horse and his eyes were unreadable. "Would you call me by my name on this trip, Zjhanne? I want no 'lord' and 'larga' between us."

My heart lurched in panic. Alone together, amid beauty and quiet—"It would be very dangerous to your goals and mine, my lord," I said carefully.

For once I wished he weren't so damned good at concealing his feelings, because I would've given a lot to know how my answer affected him. If it had clearly mattered a lot to him, his request—

But his face gave nothing away. He lifted his horse's reins and nudged the animal forward.

An hour or so later we stopped briefly for lunch and to rest the horses and our own legs, then we rode on. Soon the horse sounds ahead vanished in the rushing roar of falling water. I saw mist and smelled dampness quite a while before water-reflected light sparkled through the heavy undergrowth. A thin layer of mud appeared on the road, first in little hollows and then all the way across the surface. In the roar of the water, even the sound of our own horses' hooves disappeared. Then the forest broke and I looked down. Deep-brown water poured with frightening force over a yellow cliff, swirling and foaming into a bowl worn smooth by centuries of water. It quieted for a moment there, then, gurgling and foaming over the rocks, rushed toward the Desert miles to the east.

I turned to Lord Karne. "It's awesome, isn't it?"

But he was studying the banks on both sides of the ford and didn't hear me.

"Is something wrong, milord?"

He did not look up. "Aye. Too many horses have been by today. Far too many."

"Do we wait for Karl, then?"

Lord Karne shook his head. "If these new riders aren't friends, we may no longer have a rear guard." He paused. "It won't hurt to wait five minutes to find out, though. Come."

Lord Karne rode into the shallow water at the river's edge and headed downstream. I wondered what would happen to a horse and rider who slipped and were caught in the swift, smooth current. Several hundred meters from the ford, Lord Karne sent his horse lunging up a rocky section of bank, motioning impatiently for me to follow.

Under the trees, the ground sucked noisily at the horses' feet. When we could no longer see the river, Lord Karne led back upstream. We dismounted on the downhill side of a heavily brushed mound. Lord Karne untied the roll behind his saddle, wrapped himself in the brown traveling cloak he took from it, then climbed the mound and lay down at the crest, with just the top of his head above it. For several minutes the only sounds were the whisper of the wind through pine branches, the twitter of birds, the rustles and squeaks of small animals. Then, under the roar of the falls, I heard the crunch of hooves, followed by thrashing sounds and shouting, cries of pain and the spitting of handguns.

Lord Karne lay on the mound for only seconds more. He came down quietly. "You stay here, out of sight. That was our rear guard. I don't think I can do anything to help, but I'm going to try. Brad and his men can't be too far ahead of us." He gathered up the stallion's trailing reins and draped them over the horse's withers. "Wait for me on the red rocks downstream. If I'm not there in ten minutes, assume I'm dead and try to get back to the Holding."

He led his horse deeper into the trees before mounting, then he was gone in the swish and crackle of underbrush.

Assume I'm dead. Assume I'm dead, dead, dead.

My mind went blank except for that awful litany. Dying was suddenly no longer an abstraction, an effect of Starker IV's politics and feuds. Death was an evil thing on Starker IV. But for *him*, to imagine *him* lying cold and stiff somewhere—

I hadn't known the idea of Lord Karne dead could affect me so, though perhaps I could have guessed, had I wanted to. I shoved the tangle of feelings away. It was staying alive I had to think about now. Our rear guard had been killed, perhaps the fore guard also. My husband and I were alone against unknown enemies.

I tied Gordie and crawled up the mound. Over its crest I saw a section of road. There were no more sounds of fighting. Three men in green uniforms rode by, leading four horses, each with one of our Lifesguardsmen facedown across its back. A fifth, riderless horse followed, and five more men in green uniforms. The men didn't speak.

I lay very still until their sounds disappeared under those of the falls. I started to get up, then dropped to the ground again when more voices floated up from below. Another group of green uniforms rode out of the trees. They dismounted, with much creaking of leather and jingling of tack, just across the clear space. A young man posted himself on a boulder beside the road and lit a pipe.

Creeping backward down the mound, I prayed the Lharr wouldn't meet these men on his way back. I led Gordie deep into the woods before I mounted and followed our trail of bent and broken brush back to the river's edge. I rode to the red rocks and waited, counting the seconds in my head, very fast at first to make up for the minutes I'd missed. The falls drowned all sounds from above.

Fifteen minutes passed by count. Start back, he had said. But what about him? I couldn't leave and never know what had happened to him. Another five minutes passed, then five more.

Gordie threw up his head, ears pricked. Seconds later I heard something, too. Someone was riding in a hurry through the trees on the other side of the river. Hooves thudded dully on pine needles, birds fled shrieking. I couldn't see who it was, only a shadow among the trees. I backed Gordie into the willow bushes along the bank.

The Lharr burst out of the bushes on the other side and looked quickly upriver, his eyes flicking over my hiding place. His face was pale, and scratched by whipping branches. He kicked the stallion down the bank and they hit the water already moving downstream. He hadn't seen me. I kicked Gordie to the edge of the river.

"Karne!"

The rushing water must have covered the sound, because he didn't turn or stop. He would leave me behind.

"Karne, wait!"

I jabbed Gordie hard. He leaped off the bank into the water. He stumbled. The water just ahead ran deep and dangerously fast. My heart's pounding made the scene pound before my eyes in rhythm. But Gordie righted himself and stood trembling.

Karne had turned. When I looked toward him, he was just sliding his gun back into its sheath. He jerked his reins and the stallion heaved up the bank and came pounding back. He skidded to a halt above me. His eyes were spots of lightning in his startlingly pale face.

"I nearly killed you just now! Ten minutes I told you!"

I was trembling with fear, of him, of death, of the lies I was about to tell. My words stuttered out. "K-Karne, my lord, I have no chronometer. My sense of time is very bad. I'm truly sorry."

He was very, very angry, too angry to sense the lie. "You could've been on your way to safety. Go now, before they catch up."

"It's too late. The green uniforms guard the road."

His face went whiter still. "Then God help us!" He waved downstream. "There's a ford down a quarter mile or so. It's a bad one, but we can't go back. Move!" He brought the stallion into the shallow water and we rode east on opposite sides of the river.

The ford *was* bad—deep, rocky, and in a strong current. Gordie had to be coaxed and bullied across it. Icy water swirled around my knees, filled my boots, and tugged at my skirt, but I couldn't pull my legs up because I needed them to urge the horse.

Gordie and I were both badly frightened by the time we struggled into the shallows on the other side. I looked back. The water on either side of the roiling water of the ford flowed with sinuous smoothness. I was glad I hadn't had time to notice what could have happened if Gordie had stumbled.

Karne, his face still unnaturally pale, looked Gordie and me over coldly, then led down the river. We rode without speaking for a long way, he tall and stiff beside me on his big horse.

Dear God, I've done it again, I cried silently. But this time it was different, Lord. I couldn't leave him to take alone whatever happened!

But Karne was rigidly angry and there was small comfort for me in the thought that his anger might be partly fear because he could have killed me.

Karne urged his horse up a rocky bank. "As good a place as any to try getting back," he said shortly.

The hill sloped up steeply and the horses lunged and scrambled to climb it. From the top looking back, our trail looked as plain as if we'd marked it deliberately. I worried about that, but I knew little about such things. Karne turned away from it.

"It'll take them awhile to get here," he said. "*If* none of them know the river like I do. Let's move!"

We found a narrow rock ridge that ran the length of the hill.

Karne slowed his horse to glance back, then he looked down at me. "We have a chance. If we can break through the hills to the plains." But his voice wasn't as optimistic as his words. "When I saw what had happened to Brad and his men I left a plain trail, hoping . . ." His voice fell heavily.

I knew what he meant. He had left a plain trail so I, riding a different direction, would have a better chance to get away. There was pain, knowing I had ruined his plan, and an unexamined joy that he had tried to save me at his own cost. Faintly, shouts drifted to us.

Karne set his heels to his horse. "They've found where we went into the river. It won't take skill to figure we rode downstream."

The stallion plunged off the ridge and down the hill. The brown needle-covered surface under the pines looked clear, but the needles were slippery, and horses soon had to slow so they could keep their feet. The light under the trees was dimmer than it should have been for afternoon. The horses' hooves made a hollow pounding sound, the only sound. The four of us seemed the only creatures in the world. The unnatural quiet, the gloom, the emptiness, frightened me.

The trees thinned. The dimness hadn't been from shade alone. The sun had disappeared under a heavy layer of gray clouds. Shouting again, behind, louder, closer. Karne led us to the edge of the pines. The trees beyond were mostly hardwoods, just lightly touched with green. Horses moved across the slope farther down, plainly visible among the skeleton trees. Karne froze. The riders below wore green uniforms.

"Cut off," Karne muttered under his breath. "All we can do now is try to stay alive. Ride!"

We hit the horses hard. They leaped forward. The soldiers must have heard the pounding hooves, must have seen us, because we had to stick to the edge of the pines to keep the horses on secure footing at that speed. Tree trunks whipped past. The pack below howled. Karne and I pushed the horses harder. Too soon we reached the far end of the hill, the sharp slope toward the river and the Desert, the abrupt valley between us and the hills to the south. Our pursuers came quietly now, moving shadows among the pine trees, visible horses among the bare trees.

"We'll have to run for the river," Karne said. "It'll be dark soon and trailing will be harder."

We needed to move quickly, yet we had to hold back. The slope was too steep and too slippery to take fast. With the sun gone, the river looked dark and sullen. Karne's head swung swiftly from side to side, trying to find a good ford. We lost precious seconds trotting back upstream to a shallow place. Karne spurred his horse into the swirling water and mine followed. Then the horses were surging up the bank and into the trees on the other side.

Our pursuers shouted angrily when they discovered our change of direction. The trees thinned and parted. Behind us I heard the pounding of hooves, ever closer. I followed Karne along a low rocky ridge, aching to run Gordie and not daring to. A wind, funneled down what might have been the river's old bed, whirled over us. River and green soldiers on one side, sharp slope and old riverbed on the other. Dark clouds hung low over the mountains and covered the sky. Always the sounds of pursuit coming nearer. We reached the edge of the ridge. Light had already left the gorge below. The first of Harlan's men rode over the ridge where we had come up and shouted as he sighted us. Karne drew his stunner and took a desperate shot. The soldier disappeared back over the ridge.

Karne set his horse plunging down the rocky mountainside onto a game trail that led to the gorge floor. Gordie followed. Rocks skittered under the horses' feet and clicked over the trail edge and into the chasm. I thanked the Allfather that these horses were more surefooted than the Terran variety.

On the dry floor of the gorge, it seemed night already. It was a small advantage: The Harlan soldiers riding behind us had to come more slowly because the light was bad. Karne slid from his horse. I looked nervously up the trail.

Karne shoved the stallion's reins at me. "Take the horses and wait for me in the box canyon, about half an hour on your left. Here, give me your scarf."

I quickly obeyed. Karne ran back the way we had come, skillfully jumping from rock to rock. He quickly became only a shadow figure that left the trail and clambered down the slope. Stones rattled, broke free, and crashed down to the gorge floor. I closed my eyes and gave a quick prayer for his safety. If I heard him, Harlan's men could, too. Could they see him to know he was alone?

I started walking the way he had said. Gordie picked his way carefully over the rotten stone. I wanted to hurry, wanted to so badly that it was a painful pressure, but the horses were making enough noise already. Besides, would a riderless horse hurry if it hadn't been frightened?

The horses sensed the canyon before I did and strained to get into it. It ended abruptly in a sheer wall down which water dripped with a thin, cold sound. There was grass under my feet and I saw the dim outlines of what must have been a large clump of trees. Wearily I dismounted. Keeping both sets of reins tight in my hand, I lay down on my stomach and pillowed my head on my arms. The short new grass brushed my nose and the slightly damp earth smell comforted. Surely a few minutes rest would be all right.

Someone was shaking my shoulder vigorously. I turned over and sat up quickly. It was too dark to see clearly the face of the man who stood over me, but I knew, after my first panic, that it was my husband. Then I realized my hand was empty. "The horses!"

"Rest easy," Karne said. "They're drinking." His voice was low and tight.

Rain was drizzling down, but I wasn't wet. Karne had laid my cloak over me sometime before awakening me. He helped me up.

"How long have I been asleep?"

"Not long. You needed it."

He walked a few steps into the darkness and returned with two bundles. "There's a game trail near here that will take us out of reach, but we've got to go quickly and without the horses. They could never make the climb and we must be safely hidden before the moon rises. We don't dare count on clouds for protection."

He slipped into the straps he had rigged for his pack and helped me with mine. He took my hand and led me back to the mouth of the canyon. It was very quiet, with only sound of the wind and the soft hiss of rain as it fell on the rocks.

"The soldiers will wait for light. They suspect a false trail but they have to be sure. Even with Torches, tracking on a night like this is nearly impossible. But tomorrow—tomorrow may be very bad."

Little streams of water ran along the cracks in the rocks underfoot and flowed in thin sheets down the gorge walls. We crossed the open floor cautiously, freezing when a rock rolled noisily, trying to avoid slipping. We came to the packed earth of the game trail. Light from the bright white Torches of the Harlan soldiers almost reached us. They were so close, so close!

Karne looked silently up at the black bulk of the mountain in front of us. The rain came harder, rapping on my head and back. Karne turned, looked at me for a moment, his face a shadow, then passed a rope around my waist. "I don't want to lose you in the dark," he told me softly, his arms still around me.

He was so close I smelled the damp of his hair. Then he hugged me hard with a strange combination of fierceness and gentleness. He released me as abruptly and began walking along the rock wall. The rain slid down after us, washing out whatever tracks we left.

We didn't stay at the base of the mountain long. A tangle of boulders connected our path to a narrow ledge several hundred feet higher. We picked our way carefully. A twisted ankle or broken bone would be fatal. With each rattle of rock or scrape of boot against stone, my heart lurched in fear.

Weariness soon blurred the details for me—rain, always rain, and sharp stones cutting into boots not made for walking; river water squishing around my feet with every step; the ruthless enemy waiting and listening below; a wind that got colder and colder; hunger; the frantic need to get off the open slope; the tearing frustration of needing to hurry and being unable to. The steep trail switched back and forth many times, then it became a narrow ledge at the base of a cliff. I stumbled, which sent a stone over the edge. The crash as the stone hit bottom was a long time coming. I froze in place, shivering, too frightened to move. Karne reached back and took my hand. His lean, warm fingers, tightening around mine, roused me and some of his determination reached me through that touch. I blotted out thoughts of the awful drop beside me and followed him.

Just when my aching muscles were warning that they could go no further, we rounded the end of the slope and Karne pulled me behind a huge boulder and into a hollowed place in the cliff. It was almost a cave. He dropped his pack beside his feet.

"We'll rest here till dawn. Try to get some sleep."

I let my pack slide down my back and shrugged my shoulders several times to ease them before I patted the pack somewhat flat and sat down on it. Wind and rain swirled around the boulder in front of our door, but only the cold reached into the hollow. Silver light for a moment touched the rock and then was gone in a gust of rain. I leaned back against the mountain and closed my eyes. My hair and my feet and the bottom of my skirt were wet and my feet and hands tingled with cold. I tried to relax, but hunger twisted my stomach. I willed sleep, but the cold refused to be defeated. Karne's deep, steady breathing said he already slept.

I struggled to sleep for more than an hour. I tried to reach the deep meditative state that allowed sleep to come, but for the first time in my life, I couldn't control my body. The stillness of meditation stayed out of reach while the night got colder and the rain outside turned to slush when it hit the ground. The cold was a torture, a burning pain. My teeth chattered uncontrollably and the memory of my short nap in the canyon was small comfort to my sore muscles.

Karne stirred in the darkness. I tried to stop the chattering of my teeth.

"Zjhanne, bring your pack and come here." His voice was soft with sleep.

I felt my way across to him.

"Put your pack here." He patted the ground beside him. "And take off your boots and stockings."

I obeyed and he rubbed my feet between his warm hands until they, too, were warm. I wrung out my stockings, wiped out my boots, and put stockings and boots back on.

"Open your jacket and bodice."

"Milord?"

"I'm too tired to argue. Just do it."

When I had obeyed, Karne opened his jacket and shirt and pulled me inside, wrapping my arms around him so his bare back warmed my hands. He wrapped his cloak and mine snugly around both of us and pushed my head into the hollow of his shoulder. I snuggled gratefully into the warmth. For a time the only sounds were our even breathing and the drip of rain. I thought Karne had gone back to sleep.

He stirred slightly. "Zjhanne, tomorrow—"

I looked up at him. His tone held more than tiredness. It held a bitter resignation.

"Tomorrow the Desert, more rain, maybe snow. It looks like Richard's won at last. He can do anything now, without worrying that I'll return to challenge him."

I sat away from him just a little. "Don't say that! Don't even think it. You're too tired to think straight. In the morning—"

He stopped me with a kiss. "You're sweet," he said.

Then, slowly, deliberately, he brushed his mouth back and forth across mine. He looked down at me for a long moment, then tangled a hand in my hair, pulled my head back hard against his arm, and kissed me deeply, hungrily. I wanted him and the warmth and comforting he was offering as I'd never wanted anything before. Without words I told him so.

CHAPTER 15

Morning came with gray light and ice-slicked ground. Clouds still covered the sky, but the rain had stopped. Karne rearranged his legs when he saw I was awake. He smiled a little when I sat up and stared sleepily at him.

He touched my cheek too briefly. "We must go, Zjhanne. The Desert's deadly, but it can be defeated. Harlan's men can't be, not by one man."

"Don't count me out."

"You? When the very thought of unnatural death horrifies you? You couldn't kill anyone."

I bent my head so he couldn't see my face nor I his. I'd learned something about myself yesterday, but the knowledge was too new to speak of while watching his reaction. "I could kill someone if it meant saving your life, my lord."

He leaned close as if to catch an echo of the whispered words. "Not your own?"

I shook my head, still not looking at him. "I can't think of a reason good enough to—to take someone else's life for mine. But your life's important to Starker IV."

He considered me gravely. I would have given a lot to know what he was thinking. He picked at his pack. "With luck, we'll be in a guardpost in the hills on the plains side of Zinn in two days. Without . . ."

He squeezed me hard for a second, then, just as abruptly, set me off, refastened his clothes, and stood up. He strode to the boulder and for several minutes looked back the way we had come. I took the time to rebutton my bodice and rough-comb my hair with my fingers. Lord Karne ran his hand slowly through his tousled hair, then shook his head savagely and muttered, "Not a chance." He came back and slung on his pack. "Can you manage?"

"Yes."

He stepped out of our shelter and walked a few steps on the ice. He held out a hand to me. "We'll be all right if we're careful. Sun or rain, this will melt soon."

In the gray light the rocky mountainside was grim, broken and smooth, interrupted here and there by a scrawny bush or dried clump of grass. Trees had grown here once, but some long-past fire had killed them. Giant trunks stood starkly on the lower slopes far below, their yellow wood striped with the glistening black of wind-polished charcoal. At the mountain's foot lay the Desert, barren, gray, and emptiness of rock and brush.

Going down was not as hard for me as coming up had been, except that I was so hungry. The world suddenly swung dizzily and I clutched for something to steady myself. There was nothing in that barrenness to grab. I stumbled and slid several feet down the mountainside on the loose rock. Lord Karne was beside me at once.

"Zjhanne! What's wrong?"

The anxiety in his eyes and the deep concern in his voice shook me even more than the slip. He helped me back to more level ground.

"Fool!" he scolded himself savagely under his breath.

He rummaged in his pack and pulled out three chocolate cubes. He offered two to me. "This'll keep you going till we get low enough to find hoppers. Why didn't you say something?"

"I didn't know you could do anything about it. Besides, you had much on your mind already."

He didn't comment, just stood sucking his chocolate and waiting for me to finish mine. We each drank from the canteen and started moving again. At midmorning, he found and shot a hopper and made a small fire to cook it. The meat was still very rare when he stamped the fire out. Even with blood still running out of it, however, the hopper was good. Probably any food would've been after a day without.

"The Watchers will have seen what little smoke there was," Karne said, spreading the coals and hot ashes into a thin layer with the toe of his boot. "It's foolish to give them time to pinpoint us. We'll eat as we go."

My pack dragged at my shoulders and my boots were rubbing my heels, ankles, and most of my toes raw. I kept telling myself to be thankful the sun wasn't beating down to magnify the discomfort.

In early afternoon, Karne stopped on the warm side of a boulder and brushed a space on the ground beside it free of stones. "Sit and rest, Zjhanne, while I see what I can catch for lunch."

He dropped his pack and ranged off across the slope. His step had none of its usual vitality.

I closed my eyes and leaned against the boulder. Melted ice on the rock and rainwater on the ground dampened me, but my feet could rest. They throbbed painfully and every muscle in me protested movement. I let my mind drift to my husband—his gallant warmth-sharing, his tenderness in lovemaking, his fierce hugs, his concern. Memories spun in my tired brain, a hope and a torture.

My lord, milord, the Lharr, Lord Karne, Karne.

A silly giggle bounced unsteadily inside me. I looked at my dirty hands and broken fingernails, my wrinkled and torn skirt, my wet boots. My rain-washed hair hung in still-damp strings. The giggle bubbled out, a frail little sound. The Lady Zjhanne, Larga of House Halarek. Lord Karne, Lharr of House Halarek. Clearly titles in this waste and in our situation were ridiculous.

But I couldn't keep calling him by his given name. Already it was tearing away the last shred of formality that protected me against feelings I wanted and didn't want. Loving unloved would open me to betrayal far greater, to pain far worse, than I could previously have imagined. This man would be loved with every cell of me and then, when Richard finally killed him—I'd sensed the near certainty of this behind everyone's thoughts, even his—I would know pain beyond my worst nightmares. If Karne let himself love me, his worst nightmares could come true.

Dear God, don't let this happen to us!

But God doesn't interfere in such matters, either way.

A sudden, horribly human scream, abruptly cut off, jarred me back to the Desert. The scrawny black shadows that were the scavengers of Zinn began dropping out of the sky. Somewhere just out of sight something had died.

That scream wasn't Karne's. It couldn't be.

But tales of the wild animals and wilder men of Zinn rushed into my head. Karne had said the convicts headed for the mountains, hadn't he?

I said a quick prayer for calm and was struggling to acquire it when I heard the crunch of boots on rock. I scrabbled backward to hide myself, just in case.

Karne came around the boulder carrying four of the black scavengers. I went limp with relief, even knowing the silliness of my fear.

"It's not hopper, but it's meat," he said sharply, as if I'd protested. "You can't go without something more substantial than candy."

He skinned the birds and again we ate almost-raw meat, washed down with a few swallows of lukewarm water. He shook the canteen.

"We'll have to be careful. I don't expect to reach the river until sometime tomorrow and it's the only safe water around."

He helped me up. We trudged on. Clouds still hid the sun, and thunder rumbled over the mountains. By evening every step was agony for me, although I tried not to show it. I was growing used to hunger, however, if one can ever say one does.

We reached the base of the mountain before it was too dark to travel. We were in the Desert itself.

Lord Karne dropped his pack. "We stay here tonight, in the open. I want to take no chances with animals, or men." He sat down beside his pack.

I stretched out on the ground at once, using my pack for a pillow. We had no fire. The Lharr was sitting, staring thoughtfully into the darkness, when I fell asleep.

Movement awakened me. Lord Karne was pacing up and down our tiny campsite, trying to beat his hands warm against his shoulders without making much noise. My stinging nose told me how cold it was before I was awake enough to see the frost lying thick on everything. Clouds hung more darkly overhead than they had the day before and, if the sun was up, it hadn't been up long. But I wasn't cold. When I sat up I saw why. Two cloaks slid from my shoulders into my lap.

"My lord," I said softly, "you, too, needed rest."

He looked guilty for a moment. "I—I had much to think about. I got up early." He looked away, across the Desert. "Besides, walking keeps me warm."

The cold redness of his hands and his shivering belied that, but I let him have his pride. I walked to him and laid his cloak over his shoulders.

"Thank you for the kindness, my lord."

He spun around, his hands rested on my shoulders a fraction of a second, his hand brushed my cheek, then he bit his lip and turned away.

"Have we chocolate left, Larga?" His voice was as chill as the air.

I dug through our packs and found one piece. Silently I handed him half. He stared back the way we'd come while he sucked the candy.

"There were fires on the mountain before dawn," he said finally. "Harlan, probably. The Watchers would be more careful." He cupped his hands and blew on the knuckles to warm them. "They won't come into the Desert after us, Harlan's men. Richard just wants them to be sure we don't come out."

I watched him. "Can they do that?"

"If Richard wants them to. He could hire enough men to circle the entire Desert if he wanted to."

"But—" I thought of the immensity of the Desert of Zinn.

He looked at me, anger and despair in his face. "And I have all I can do to hire my quota for Council duty in the guardposts."

He pulled a compass from his pack and studied it and the mountain behind us for some time, then he turned and looked out across the frost-covered gray-brown waste of the Desert. He slipped a charge from his pack into his stunner, then picked up my pack to help me put it on. It was very light now, only a couple pairs of dry socks, some gloves, a knife, matches—things I could've carried in pockets, if I'd had any—but every muscle in my stiffened back and shoulders and legs screamed at even that little extra weight. I staggered in spite of myself. Although I steadied myself immediately, I wondered if my feet would bear the weight. They were swollen and already throbbed with pain. But I kept silent about them: Karne had enough to worry about.

Silence was not enough. Karne slid off his pack, though he couldn't hide the difficulty he had in doing it. How much sleep had he allowed himself? I wondered.

He pulled my pack off and began digging into it.

I put a restraining hand on his arm. "My lord, Karne, leave it. You have enough. I can carry it."

"Don't argue!" he snapped.

He took the contents of my pack and added them to his. The pack's plastic he quickly folded into a hood, which he tied gently over my hair with a string from his pocket. Thunder boomed sharply. Karne checked his bearing once more and started toward the lightly green line of the river.

We walked through brittle gray bushes and over sparse clumps of last year's parched grass. The Desert stretched flat and featureless and empty on all sides. Then the black cloud above us split open with a blast of lightning and rain poured down. It swept across the barren ground in icy sheets, beating the crisp grass flat and sodden, beating the little gray bushes into the ground. We kept moving. There was nothing else to do, nowhere to go, no way to protect ourselves. Only when the rain-whipped darkness blotted out his landmark did Lord Karne stop. I moved closer to him, awed by the ferocity of the rain. He put his arm around me and squeezed me against his side.

As suddenly as it had begun, the rain stopped. The clouds overhead thinned a little and I could now see the white glowing place that was the sun. Off to our right, the trees edging the river stood small and sharp against their gray background.

My husband nodded toward them. "About an hour yet, maybe an hour and a half." He smiled at me encouragingly. "Chin up," he said, and kissed my mouth lightly.

For courage, I told myself.

But we were more nearly three hours getting to those trees and without Karne's help, I wouldn't have gotten there at all. In fact, he nearly carried me the last kilometer or so.

Early afternoon though it was, the quiet places of the river still wore a thin layer of ice, as if there had been no rain at all. Karne set me down on a large flat rock and without a word pulled off my boots. He sucked his breath in sharply.

"Zjhanne! Your feet!" With gentle hands he pulled off the bloody stockings. "How long have they been like this?"

"Since yesterday morning."

He looked angry, but he said nothing more. With stinging cold water from the river and a piece of his shirt, he cleaned my feet and daubed them dry with a pair of socks. The water had been cold enough to sting, but the antiseptic he took from one of his pockets stung a thousand times worse. I bit my lip and didn't cry out, but I couldn't stop the tears. For bandaging, he used strips of my petticoat, clean pieces that hadn't been near the ground. When he had finished, he pulled a pair of his socks over the bandages and looked at me steadily.

"You have much courage, my lady wife, more even than I'd thought. I don't know that I would've come as far as you have with feet like that."

He turned away abruptly and walked off into the trees. A long time later he came back, dragging a pile of soggy wood on which lay the bodies of two short-haired gray animals and a hopper. He built a fire and began at once to skin and dress the animals. He spitted the hopper and while it cooked, he scraped its skin and stretched it on a rack. He showed no concern about the column of smoke that betrayed us.

We ate our meal in silence and in silence Karne carried me to the bed he'd made of young branches covered with his cloak. I lay down and he gently tucked my cloak around me. He straightened and turned away.

"But you . . . ?"

He shook his head. "I'll be all right." He sat down against a rock in the reflected warmth of the fire and settled himself for sleep.

He doesn't mean to lie with me, I told myself. Surely the rotten fight we had about this trip doesn't still stand between us? Was his comforting on the mountains a result of despair? Or pity? Even if he's still too angry or hurt to *want* to sleep with me, he should have enough sense to stay as warm as he can.

Whatever his reasons, I knew Karne would definitely not be "all right" by morning. It was far too cold already to sleep without covering and would get colder. I had tried reason last night to get him to lie with me and had gotten nowhere. Tonight I would try an appeal to the instinct of the men of Starker IV to protect their weak and brainless women.

"But *I* won't be all right. My lord—Karne—please. It's so cold. Hold me. Keep me warm." I held up one side of the cloak and began unfastening my jacket with my free hand.

My lord did not turn for a long time. Then he came to me slowly, opening his jacket as he came. He slid under the edge of the cloak and lay down. His hands slid into my jacket, he hesitated, then, abruptly, he wrapped his arms around me so tightly my ribs ached. His body was cold.

Already he's cold, and the night just begun, I thought indignantly.

As he warmed, his hold eased, and we slept.

The next three days passed slowly. The sky remained overcast and the cold deepened. The shallow parts of the river hid under thickening ice. I spent much of each day locked in healing concentration, willing my feet whole again. The multitude of tiny cuts and blisters and festered places required much more concentration than I remembered ever needing before, even the time I broke my arm.

I felt the pressure of time, although Karne never mentioned it.

We ate sparingly, hoarding some of the meat from the gray animals for smoking. Though Karne went out every day, he found no more meat. He caught two fish. He also dragged in dead wood, gathered the tender green tips of a certain desert bush for tea, and cleaned and dressed the skins of the gray animals, which he then made into boots for me. He lined the boots with hopper fur. His busyness could not hide his tension, though. He jumped at small noises. He took frequent trips around the camp's perimeter, though I couldn't see how anything larger than a mouse could hide in the barrenness. He examined the horizon carefully and often.

The morning of the fourth day, he inspected my almost-healed feet, then slid the new boots over them. "I wish we could stay until you're completely healed, but it's too risky. Every night the fires of the Runners come closer. They can be here tomorrow."

He picked me up and set me gently on my feet, then, keeping an arm around me, walked with me a short distance up the riverbank and back. I steeled myself against the feelings that ran through me. His arm was too welcome, too comforting. I stepped away from his grip as soon as we returned to our starting place. It seemed to me he released me reluctantly.

"I'll be quite all right now," I said.

We packed the little we had, carefully stamped out the fire and scattered its ashes. Karne filled the canteen and handed it and the pack to me. Then he picked me up, walked a little way upstream, and carried me across the ice. He set me down carefully on the bank, slung the pack and canteen over his shoulder, consulted his compass, and led out across the strip of trees. He walked swiftly, but he kept an eye on me and when I began to fall back, he stopped.

"Rest a few minutes, Zjhanne. They won't catch us today."

I sank gratefully onto the gravel. Karne eased himself to the ground beside me. Only then, my aching muscles relaxed, my feet relieved of all weight, did Karne's words soak in.

"The Runners? They *will* catch us?"

He shrugged. "Perhaps. In any case they'll be too close too soon. The Watchers must've signaled them as we reached the Desert and they've been coming ever since. They're sure they have us, because they don't hide their fires."

"We didn't either, lord."

"You needed them," he said shortly. "It couldn't be helped."

We sat in silence for a time. Then he rose, looked down our

back trail for a long moment, and started walking toward the distant hills. We walked until dark. Our supper was a few gulps of water. Karne hacked down some bushes for insulation and we curled up on them together.

The next day we saw the Runners themselves for the first time, small figures outlined against the band of trees along the river. We each ate a small piece of the smoked meat and moved on. The Runners had gained on us by their earlier start.

The Runners drew closer all day, three gaunt, dark shadows haunting our trail. Every so often Karne looked over his shoulder at them, then quickened his pace. We didn't stop for food at noon because our pursuers were closing in. We drank a little water as we went.

At last I could go no farther. "Please, Karne, I can't keep up! I'm running to stay with you now."

He stopped and his voice was contrite. "I'm sorry. I'd hoped— The Council's patrols are due soon, so the Runners aren't likely to follow us into the hills. They don't dare let a patrol spot them." Karne tried to sound hopeful, but I read nagging fear in his eyes. "If we can just get into the rocks, we'll be safer."

"I'll try harder."

He set an easier pace after that and I strained to see the rocks he'd spoken of. For a long time I could see only gray brush and brown gravel, right to the feet of the gray-green hills. Then there the rocks were. Black lumps. Specks huddled around the hills. The distance looked impossible. The Runners were closer, their breath floating white in the air above them, their spears tipped toward us.

"Karne!"

He glanced over his shoulder, put an arm around me, and pulled me along. The pain in my feet, the hard muscles of Karne's arm against my back, the hunger that twisted my stomach, the frost-coated gravel, the gray brush, the pursuing shadows, and the hills drawing so slowly closer—it was like a tri-d horror story in slow motion. We stopped looking back.

Finally I stopped, my lungs burning, my breath coming in harsh gasps, my feet a burning agony. "I can't go on. Let's stop, let them have what they want. I'm done in."

Karne's arm tightened and he jerked me into motion again. "We can't. I have only one stun charge left.

"Don't look so surprised, Zjhanne." Then his voice became a little gentler. "That didn't occur to you, did it, that they'll probably kill us for what they want?"

"N—n—no." The words came raggedly between gulps of air. "How could it?"

"Aye, how could it?" There was a kind of bitter despair in his voice.

We struggled on in silence for a time. Karne's eyes still looked at the hills, but his mind was far away.

"Zjhanne, you've read—folk tales. Did anything—strike you?"

"Yes. Characters very superstitious. Charms and magic. Just like—my—ladies."

Karne's arm tightened. "Pray—superstition still lives—among Runners—and—Watchers."

The black rocks stood out from their background now. As the glowing spot behind the clouds that was the sun dropped toward the mountains, I realized the rocks were several times the height of a man.

Karne and I didn't reach the safety of the hills, only the first black outposts. There something swished over our heads and skittered through the gravel ahead of us. It was a wicked-looking spear. Karne dropped the pack, picked up the spear, and turned to face the Runners, thrusting the pack and me behind his back.

"Get behind a rock and stay there," he ordered, not taking his eyes from the Runners.

He stood stiffly with the spearpoint thrust into the ground at his feet. I obeyed. The Runners slowed. They were gaunt, ragged men with faces weathered to wrinkled leather. They halted two or three meters from us and the two taller men, who still had their spears, stood braced with their spearpoints directed at Karne's chest.

I knew Karne feared the Runners, but his stance didn't show it. His hands hung clenched at his sides, true, but his shoulders were straight and he held his head high. I imagined his eyes as they must appear to the Runners—cold and yellow and measuring, like cat's eyes.

I heard the Runners speak, but I couldn't understand their dialect. They demanded something. Karne shook his head. The shortest Runner stepped forward and struck him. Karne flinched and trembled with anger, but he didn't strike back. The Runners demanded again.

Karne again shook his head. "My brother's young and sick, and we have very little," he said.

The Runners stopped him with angry muttering.

Karne shrugged. "I'll bring what we have."

He walked slowly toward me, his proud back defying the Runners' spears. He stopped so his body shielded me from their sight. His face was tense and worried.

"Slip a few matches into your boots."

While I did, he took out the tiny plastic-wrapped package of smoked meat and the compass, then carried the spear and what was left of the pack to the Runners. An argument followed. One of the Runners moved menacingly toward my hiding place. Karne said something sharply. The Runner stopped.

"Hey, boy!" Karne shouted at me. "Look around here."

I stuck my head out from behind the rock. The Runners gasped and drew closer together, but they didn't yield in their demands. Karne walked slowly back.

"They want the meat. I'd forgotten how well hungry men can smell. They're hungry enough to defy even the wrath of a fire-hair."

But the meat was not enough, either. Karne pleaded, but it was no use.

" 'We must have the gun,' they say," Karne told me. "I denied having one, but they threatened to search you for it. We'd better give them the canteen, too. They may soon lose patience with us."

"Won't we need it? Couldn't we hide it and let them search m—"

Karne jerked me toward him with bruising fingers. His face was white and his eyes held both anger and fear. "Little fool! No one would have to search you to know you're a woman. Can't you imagine what that means, out here, to them?"

I suddenly understood and terror gripped me. "What if they—if you—Karne!" and I clung to him.

The bruising grip on my arms eased. "Zjhanne, don't. I'd—" Karne's voice broke and he paused a moment to steady it. "I'd go through Hell, I'd kill you myself, before I'd let that happen to you. Believe me."

I believed him. I watched him walk back, tall and straight and brave, when I was weak with terror. He was so vulnerable. The smallest Runner, who seemed to be the leader, fingered the edge of the Lharr's cloak covetously. The Lharr shook his head stubbornly and straightened his tired back more.

"You have our stunner, our food, our water. Life is all we have left, and if you take our covering life, too, is gone. We came in peace. Let us go in peace. The gods of Those-who-run-the-Desert protect peaceful travelers and lay terrible doom on any who deny such travelers life."

The Runners conferred, the small one arguing against the others and seeming to overpower them. I watched tensely, realizing only afterward that the pain in my palms was from my own ragged nails digging into them. What was going to be a very cold night crept over the horizon and reached out to us across the Desert. Through cloak and jacket I felt its bite. Large flakes of snow began drifting down. The four men stood motionless in a contest of wills as two of the Runners fought the stare of the third and Karne stiffly watched them. The snow swirled lazily around the group. Finally Karne broke the silence.

"To take our cloaks, you must kill us. Yet there's no sacred ground in this place. Our spirits won't have a resting place. They'll follow you, and the fire-hair will take the virtue from your fire, so it no longer warms you."

The Runners began arguing again, their voices quickly rising to shouts. The "leader" jumped about in rage. Karne turned his back and walked slowly toward me. The leader pointed Karne's stunner at him. I stood frozen in horror. Just as the Runner pulled the trigger, one of the others hit his arm. The small one tried again. Nothing happened. The charge had run out.

More enraged, the little Runner snatched a spear. The other two looked afraid, but reluctant to stop him. I tried to warn Karne, but my voice lay trapped in my paralyzed throat. The little man aimed at Karne's retreating back. I didn't want to watch, but I couldn't stop myself. The Runner pulled back his arm and began hurling the spear forward.

"Karne!"

Karne dropped flat. The spear hissed over his head. I sat down abruptly. Karne ripped the spear from the ground before it stopped quivering and came to me.

"The odds are better now," he said grimly.

But the Runners feared haunting more than death and went away.

We hiked over rough ground for hours. My feet hurt terribly. My stomach shrank and screamed protest and shrank and screamed some more, but there was nothing to eat, not even the green things Karne said would be plentiful in another two or three weeks. There was nothing to drink, either. The snow fell slowly and had not collected deeply enough yet on the ground to scoop up. It was just a tantalizing thin layer on the rocks and brush. My tongue felt fuzzy. I wondered if Karne were thinking of food as much as I was. I didn't ask. He had enough burden in the two lives he was responsible for.

How well does a person think without food or water? I wondered. How much farther can we go?

The hunger-weakness in my legs was getting worse and worse with hours of going up a hill, going down, going up, going down. I moved only by the force of will. Karne scraped snow from rocks and offered it to me. There was nothing to say. It was getting dark and Karne still hadn't found the marks he was looking for. He shook his head, puzzled.

"The blazes start a kilometer out from the patrol hut. Surely we couldn't've missed them."

We had spent so much time watching our footing, I wouldn't have been surprised if we *had* missed the markers. Large and small rocks littered the ground and made progress slow and difficult. Where the surface wasn't rock, it was rotten logs and fallen branches and the snow quickly concealed the treacherous places. The cold fulfilled its promise of earlier in the day, biting noses, fingers, even through gloves, and penetrating the heavy traveling cloaks.

"Hurry," Karne urged, striding faster. "If the light goes before we find the marks, we'll be out here all night."

In this cold, that would mean death. I shivered at the thought and forced my leaden legs to move quickly. Only a little light was left when we found the first pink blaze, then two more. Karne walked much faster than I. Soon he was nearly out of sight, then I couldn't see him at all. I panicked. Trying to catch up, I slid on a slanting rock I hadn't seen, twisting my ankle badly. I cried out.

"Zjhanne!" Karne's voice was sharp with anxiety.

"I—I'm all right."

He came back to be sure I was, then stepped out again swiftly. I didn't know how he could do it, as tired as he had to be. He stopped only a short distance farther.

"Do you see a blaze, Zjhanne?"

I strained to see through the gloom and blowing snow. "No. Wait, is that—"

But the light spot was only a patch of fungus.

Karne shook his head. "Let's go back to the last one and try again."

The forest was quite dark now. I scooped up some snow and bit into it. I let the icy wetness soothe my dry mouth and throat.

I felt a wornness under my feet. "This seems to be a path. Couldn't we just follow our feet?"

"It's not safe," Karne told me. "These hills hold the only water between here and the river, so they're a maze of game trails. We could wander forever. We'll try something else. You sit here. I'll range out and find my way back by calling you and following your voice."

"My lord . . ." My voice shook in spite of me. "Karne—"

My husband lifted my hands and squeezed them gently. "Try not to be afraid. This is the only method left us."

He faded into the darkness and stumbled among the rocks. Periodically he called, "Zjhanne," and I answered, "Here." It was night among the bare and ancient trees. The snow I sat on chilled me and the wind cut through my clothes. Then Karne shouted, "I've found it!"

We shouted back and forth until I found him. The blaze glowed faintly on the bark of a broken tree. Karne put his arm around me and hugged.

"The tree leans so much, we must've walked right by when it wasn't quite dark enough for the paint to glow. We can't be far now." His arm dropped until he could take my hand.

We felt our way along the now invisible path. Karne was right. Only two more blazes and we entered the small clearing made for the patrol hut. The building was just a dark lump in the falling snow, but Karne scuffed confidently to the door and ran his hand along the inner edge of the frame. He found the secret latch and pressed. The door slid silently open and we walked in. The door slid shut behind us.

"Wait here," he ordered. "I'll have this place warm in no time."

He walked slowly across the room. I heard him feeling carefully with his feet for objects to avoid. Once or twice he thudded into something, anyway. His boots creaked as he squatted. A moment later the room lit up and warm air shushed vigorously out of vents along the floor. He sank down near a vent and patted the dusty floor beside him.

"Come over and get warm."

I obeyed. We took off our wet outer clothes and sat quietly for a long time, soaking up warmth and resting. Karne pulled me hard against his shoulder.

"That was a near thing," he said finally.

In a rush the knowledge of what could have happened to us broke my intention to be brave and aloof. I buried my face in the hollow of Karne's neck and held onto him tightly. He wrapped his other arm around me and laid his cheek against my wet hair. I huddled there, shaking and crying until I was exhausted.

CHAPTER 16

I didn't remember getting into a bed, so waking up in one surprised me. Stone wall, metal footboard, rough woolen blankets—and snow still falling beyond a window was "down" from where I was. I was in the top bed of a two-high. Karne stood at the radiant stove making breakfast. The friendly smell of hot klag pulled my nose in his direction. I hadn't had any klag for so long!

Karne must have heard me sitting up, for he turned and smiled at me. "Good morning. Are you hungry enough to eat something?"

"Hungry? You have to be joking! Have we eaten in the last two or three days?"

He came to the bed and held up his hands to me. "I'll help you down."

He lifted me down with care and it seemed to me his hands lingered before letting go. Breakfast wasn't any food I recognized, probably some rehydrated synthetic mixture, but it was food and it was good. Karne was very quiet.

"How soon will we be out of this, Karne?"

"When the snow's gone. Four or five days, maybe. It doesn't stay long in spring."

"Can't you send for a flitter or something?"

He looked up from his plate in surprise. "I thought you knew. These posts connect only with each other and Council Command. Starker IV has too many factions to risk permitting soldiers of any House outside contact."

"What about the holding?"

"I'm worrying about it. Lord Richard has something in mind for it, I'm sure, now he thinks us lost, and I can't do anything to stop him here."

We drifted into our own thoughts. Karne stood and went to the window, but his eyes followed me as I cleared the table and put the dishes into the sonic. I felt his eyes as if his hands touched me. Our run through the Desert had changed us, and in ways I didn't want to examine. I don't think he did, either, or he would have said something.

After my redding up, there was nothing else to keep my hands busy, so I curled up in one of the three easy chairs. Karne stayed near the window. His feet shifted restlessly. He looked at me and then away, out the window. I couldn't read the expression on his face. His voice, when he finally spoke, was so low I had difficulty hearing it.

"Zjhanne, I need to know, really know, how you handle dying and death on Fruhe. I ask this, knowing to answer will be very difficult for you. Please answer. I wouldn't ask if it weren't very important to me."

This wasn't an abstract question. He wasn't asking about Fruhe's beliefs. He was asking about himself and me and I didn't want to look at us that carefully. I looked away from him and then back. If an answer was important to him, somehow it was now also important to me. But death, a horrible death—

I had to give him an answer. "On Fruhe, death is always quick." *Always quick. Mercifully quick.* "That's part of the value of being in complete mental control of one's body. There's no disease, really, but the body does eventually wear out. No one has enough energy to repair every cell continually."

I looked at his rigid profile. Damn his Academy training! I needed to know how he was feeling! "My mother was a very beautiful woman when she was young. She thought wrinkles made her ugly, so she decided to make them go away. It took her hours every day to smooth just her face. After a few weeks, she decided it wasn't worth the time. She's still a beautiful woman, only she has fine, soft wrinkles now."

Such a frivolous little story, but it didn't entice Karne to release any of his rigid control. I sighed, then went on with his answer.

"Our Old Ones choose their time of dying—usually when their hearts are very, very tired—and make their preparations: They give away their property, say their goodbyes, and go to a Last Place, where they die within hours. Here—"

I refused to think of what death would be like here, where people planned killings, where they killed for revenge or profit or even, as was apparent from their duels, for amusement. Karne stood at the window still, ostensibly studying the snow.

Anger came at last to my rescue. "Fruhe isn't like this place. Life is precious to us. The Gharr think nothing of killing and being killed. You *murder* each other and it's legal!"

I choked on a lump in my throat and had to stop. This came much too close to my personal nightmares. Karne, dead—

"What does it matter to you how I feel? I'm just a tool, a baby-maker, a—"

He looked at me then, his face full of pain and intense sadness. "I do care how you feel. I care too much. Our situation now says my luck has run out. I'll very likely die soon, my lady wife, by an assassin's hand or in a duel of honor. I can't offer you any protection at all. And what my enemies will do to you—" His voice broke.

I looked away. The pain in his face and the turmoil that roused in me were too much to bear while looking into his eyes.

The rest of the day was an agony of silence and awkward small talk. Karne's painful question had almost laid open feelings and issues neither one of us wanted to look at. I went gladly to bed at fall of dark. In sleep I wouldn't feel so afraid, so confused, so ready to break.

Cold and the sudden pain of turning on sore bones and muscles roused me. I wiggled down in the warm bed and stretched extravagantly, discovering all kinds of new sore spots in the process. Funny how real stiffness always took a day to arrive. I lay still and relaxed my muscles one by one with the speed of long practice. Soon the stiffness was gone.

"Is it time to get up, milord?" That title, any title, seemed safer than his name this morning.

There was no answer.

Gingerly I maneuvered my head and shoulders over the edge and looked down. "Hey, sleepyh—"

There was no one in the bed below. It was empty and neatly made. I looked around the room. I was completely alone. I slung my feet over the side, dropped to the floor, and dressed as quickly as I could, knowing all the time the futility of hurrying. He had probably left hours ago. Then I saw the slip of paper propped against the two-pot on the table. I snatched it up.

Dear my lady,

To get home we need the horses and I can travel faster alone. If, by some accident, I don't come back, wait there for a Council patrol. They'll see you safely home.

Karne

Still holding the note, I wandered to the window. Tall slender bluepines hid the Desert. Snow fell silently, swiftly, and sudden gusts of wind whirled it from the roof in a screen that obscured the trees. A heavy drift lay diagonally across the clearing and piled high against the front door. The situation at Ontar would be as bad for us as Richard could make it, but did my lord have to go out in this?

I craned my neck, trying to see a faint white glow that would locate the sun and tell me the approximate time of day. There was nothing. The wind threw a handful of snow against the window. It clattered against the glass like tiny bits of gravel and, startled, I jumped away.

I looked at my new prison—one room, two doors, two windows, a closet for a shower and toilet, a season's dust on everything. My hand bore a wide gray line now where it had pressed against the dusty window frame. I looked at the note again. No indication of what time he'd return at all.

Four days to get there, I told myself. Maybe two days back. I wished he had said something about how long he'd be. But wishing has no practical uses. I slipped the note into a pocket and looked out the window again. Snow blew diagonally past in a steady stream. Snow—thick, moving, hypnotic. My eyelids drifted down. I was so very tired still. Our escape had sapped more energy than I'd realized. I woke myself when my head dropped forward.

Guilt. There was so much to do. This place was so dirty. I looked again at the gray line across my palm.

So small a room. So much time. Six days. Sleep. Dusting will keep.

I climbed back into bed and slept most of that day and the next, too. I got up only for necessities.

On the third day, I felt much more alert. I went over the room carefully. There was food and a few cooking utensils in a cabinet, but, true to their peculiar ways, the Gharr planners had included only the most primitive cleaning tools, a bucket and broom. I wondered if I would ever stop being surprised at the strange contrasts on this world—radiant ovens, for instance, but not even one domestic robot.

"Men. Shows what happens when they run things by themselves," I muttered.

I filled the bucket, sloshed some water on the floor, and began scrubbing at the dirt with the broom. I took my time. What else would I do with myself? I cleaned everything slowly and thoroughly. It took two days.

I rinsed out the washing cloth one last time, heated a package of spiced meat and beans, sat down at the table, and put my feet up on the other chair. The food had no flavor. Worse, the silence had begun to bother me. It had been almost a year since I'd been so much alone.

I dropped the wrapper and the cooking package into the composter and watched, only half-seeing, as they vanished. There was nothing more to do. I undressed slowly and went to bed.

Morning came far too soon. I lay for a long time staring at the beamed ceiling and wondering what I'd do with myself in the day that stretched bleakly ahead. I tried, in vain, to go back to sleep. Reluctantly, I got up.

Perhaps he'll be back this evening, I thought while I waited for a cup of chocolate to heat. But I knew how unlikely that was.

I held the hot cup between my palms for a moment, then carried it to the front window. Snow lay glittering and still outside. The big blue trees bent with the weight of it. I sipped the steaming chocolate. Nothing moved on the quiet whiteness or in the trees or in the blue, blue sky. I felt I was the only living creature in the sparkling, silent wilderness.

The hours crept away. I dawdled as I swept snow from the back step and the tiny stable behind the cabin. I remade the bed and reinspected the food supply. I sat down at the table with nothing left to do. But sitting permitted mind-wandering and that I couldn't bear. Starker IV was a vicious, violent world, and Richard Harlan's men surrounded the Desert.

I prowled around the room again. In a back corner cabinet I found an ancient deck of cards and, until twilight, I played against myself. Darkness came and the lights went on. I set the table for two and waited. Two or three hours later I served myself, but I could only pick at the food. What could be keeping him?

But the walls had no answer. I stuck my dishes into the sonic. Outside, not even a cloud broke the path of moonlight on the silver snow. I went unhappily to bed.

My sleep crawled with nightmares and I awoke early. Gray clouds again blanked out the sun. I couldn't face getting up to the empty room. I turned toward the wall and concentrated on Fruhe. Home, Mom's serene face, Zjhaques and Sharine pleading for another bedtime story and Mom hustling them into their room. Pieter and his boys. Dad, a reassuring shadow on the edge of every memory. The lake in the park, and the moons floating up out of it. And it worked; homesickness hit with painful force. Months had dimmed the memory of its sharpness.

But I couldn't concentrate enough. When I thought of the park, I remembered the Black Ship and then Karne's golden eyes. With memories of Zjhaques and Sharine giggling over some "just-us" secret came Karne's pleasure in Jemmy and his rare, quick laugh. He would not be shut out. His voice, his quick temper, his gentleness intruded on every memory. I pounded the wall and cried to exhaustion, then I slept.

Morning came again, with its torture of waiting and worry and loneliness. I determined to close out the world, at least for a time, because I had done my last complete physical the first month on this world. It was long past time for another. I closed my mind. After concentration made the room fade to nothingness, I carefully went over myself mentally, millimeter by millimeter, system by system. I dawdled at it. Except for a general tightness of nerves, everything internally was as it should be. I let myself drift back into time. And fear for Karne.

Daylight was fading. The wind had stopped its whispering under the eaves and the big pines hung motionless in the darkening silence.

Karne, come back, come back!

But there was only the icy white silence.

I tried playing cards, but I couldn't sit still. I couldn't eat. I couldn't escape into sleep. I drank cup after cup of klag. I paced from window to window. I looked out in hope and turned back frustrated and afraid. Surely, with horses, he should've been back by now.

The tiny house lit itself. Now I couldn't see outside without turning off the lights, lights Karne might need as a beacon. Out of the darkness my imagination created fears—Karne lying somewhere with a broken leg, or kicked by one of the horses, fallen into a ravine, covered by snow, freezing to death . . .

Or worse, found by Harlan's men. He would die, then, but with excruciating slowness.

Tears slid down my face and dripped with faint plops onto my dress. I bit my lip and wiped the tears angrily away, but the hand that touched my cheek was shaking. I loved Karne Halarek. In spite of kidnapping and common sense and vast cultural differences, I loved him. I laughed rather bitterly, because my cowardly resisting and denying I loved him had spared me no pain at all.

I dropped into the softness of the leather chair. When Harlan's men had attacked on the mountain, or when I heard that scream at the edge of the desert, or now, waiting in fear for his safety—why had it taken the threat of Karne's immediate death to make me admit how empty my life would be without him? I closed my eyes and saw smallness in myself I didn't want to see. It wasn't important any more that he didn't believe in love as I understood it. It wasn't important that he held immense power to hurt me. All that mattered now was that he live.

Karne! Karne! Come back to me!

When I opened my eyes again, it was morning, though I didn't remember falling asleep. Having faced myself made the day no easier, however. Lunchtime came and went and I was frantic with worry. I tried to relax, but I was too tightly wound. That man had shot to pieces years of physical discipline!

Then temper broke loose. I had never lost control of my body this way before, unable to make it relax. I tried again to will calm and failed. How could he do this to me? Did he think I wouldn't worry? I hadn't been as hard as that, had I? Eight days! It took the two of us that long and we came on foot. What did he expect me to do with myself?

I'm imagining horrors and he's probably eating supper by a fire somewhere. My feelings don't matter. My anxiety isn't important. After all, I'm only a woman. Well, I'll certainly tell him—

The back door slid open with a small thump and Karne stepped inside. The angry words I meant to say shriveled inside me. Karne's face sagged, his eyes were glazed, his shoulders drooped as if their own weight were too much for them. For a moment relief overwhelmed me and I could not move.

"Oh, my dear," I whispered, "I've been so worried about you!"

He stumbled toward me, dropping his soggy cloak and gloves on the way. He stopped just short of me, swaying, then he set his hands on my shoulders at my neck and tipped my face up with his thumbs. His hands were like ice. He looked down at me for a moment as if he couldn't believe I was really there.

"Harlan," he mumbled, his eyes never leaving mine. "Dozens of them. Here. On this side." He staggered and his eyelids drooped. "Zjhanne—" He shook his head. The motion disturbed his precarious sense of balance and he nearly fell.

He was so tired! Tenderness for him was almost painful. "Karne, my lord, let me help you."

I tugged off his damp jacket, guided him to the two-high, and helped him lower himself onto it.

"Zjhanne. Harlan soldiers—so close—afraid—" and then he was asleep.

As gently as I could, I pulled off his wet boots and rubbed his icy feet between my hands. I put clean, warm socks on him, tucked the blankets around him, and sat down near the bed to watch him. He was still alive. He was safe again with me.

Oh, my lord, if we'd met another way, on another world . . .

But we had so little time left. Years would be too little, but Karne believed Richard had won and would soon kill him. And I would go empty the rest of my life.

That thought was too painful to face. I went out to check the horses and found that, somehow, Karne had taken care of them before coming in. I came back in, crawled into my bed, and snuggled under the blankets. I could sleep this night. Karne was back.

Karne slept into the next afternoon. I moved about as quietly as I could, setting the table for lunch, dusting at the furniture.

What do I say? I wondered. Do I tell him how I feel? Can I *not* tell him?

I wasn't aware Karne had moved until his arms slid around me and his lips caressed the back of my neck.

"Zjhanne," he said huskily, "I was so afraid for you. It took so much longer than I'd planned. There were Harlan patrols, lots of them, and so near here—

"Zjhanne, Zjhanne!"

He spun me around in his arms, and his mouth on mine told me what his words had not. I freed the love and need I had denied so long and it met his with a force that left us trembling. After a long time he lifted his head a little away and laughed, shakily.

"You've been hiding something from me, my lady."

"Aye, Karne, and from myself, too." The new softness in my voice embarrassed me and I hid my reddening face against his chest.

He laughed again. I loved his laugh. It was so quick and warm and he so seldom used it.

He kissed my ear. "Is my wildcat finally tamed?"

I looked him right in the eye. "Only temporarily, my lord."

He rewarded my defiance with a long, stirring kiss. And another and then another and in a short time we were both in his bed, giving and getting comfort, relief, pleasure, and joy. Somehow, we even managed to fall asleep in that narrow bed and did not wake till morning.

Karne was awake and standing beside the window when I opened my eyes. He opened his arms to me and I flew into them. The sun was shining brightly and water dripped from the eaves onto lines of slush on the ground. The pines had dropped their snow blankets in lumps on the ground and even the big drifts were looking spongy. Karne hugged me tighter.

"The snow will be gone in two days, or three, then we must leave. Let's enjoy every minute we have here, Zjhanne. There'll be so few afterward."

Or maybe none afterward, I added to myself. Depending on what Richard's been doing while we've been gone. "Karne, couldn't we—"

"Don't even think about it." He turned me away from the window and closed his arms around me again. He hugged me so tightly I couldn't tip back far enough to see his face, which is why he did it, I think. "Zjhanne, when I saw Harlan's soldiers—if they'd touched you—I—"

He took a shuddering breath. "It frightens me that I'll have to live with that fear." He hugged me tighter. "Oh, my love, this is why marriage should be only a business arrangement. Emotion ruins a man's judgment." He pressed his cheek against my hair and whispered, "I love you so much, Zjhanne. May the Allfather have mercy on us."

"Is loving me really so horrible, Karne?"

"Oh, no, sweetheart! These last months have been the happiest, unloneliest I've ever had." He kissed the tip of my nose. "But I've been so afraid. I think of Nik and Kit. If Harlan got his hands on you, I think I'd do anything to get you back safe. Like Nik did. That's an awful thought for—after all the years I've worked—"

He didn't mention his own great danger. Deeply moved, I kissed his cheek and held him tight. "Then I mustn't let him catch me."

CHAPTER 17

By agreement, we didn't mention the outside world again until the snow melted. For two days we pretended we were safe and free and without responsibilities. I hadn't known such happiness, or such pleasure, could be. But, even on civilized worlds, such times can't last and Starker IV was not a civilized world. The terrible scars on Karne's body from assassins and wars were proof Starker IV was *not* a civilized world. Karne shook me awake before dawn of the third day and we left quickly, munching a dry breakfast as we rode.

A thin mist hovered just above ground level. In the shadow of large trees and where drifts had been, snow still lingered, but most of the ground was bare. The air felt warm and smelled of damp earth and decayed vegetation. The birds that sing before dawn dropped out of the chorus one by one until only the chirping, squeaking, scolding noises of working birds were left. We saw no other human beings.

Before long, we were on Halarek Holding's side of the hills and the mist became a fog. If it hid Harlan men from us, it also hid us from them and muffled the sounds of our passing. The hush surrounding us subdued even the horses. It was like moving through a dream. I marveled that Karne found his way, even though he knew this side of the hills much better than the Desert side.

As if Karne heard my thought, he turned to me and said, "I've been this way before, twice, at very important times in my life. Landmarks and details from such times stick in the mind."

Once during that day we heard horses and men's voices nearby. We stopped and sat very still until the sounds had been gone some time, but that was the only disturbance of the thick white quietness. At day's end we made camp in a grove of aspens at the edge of the hills. Supper was a packet of rehydrated emergency rations, bed a seat on plasti with a tree trunk for a backrest. It was wet, but it was quiet and beautiful.

Karne roused me while it was still dark. The fog had lifted during the night, although here and there low places still held wisps of it. "We'll be home tonight," he said, "but we're only at the edge of the holding now. Richard's men could still be close."

The Plains of Halarek held no hint of snow. The bushes we passed occasionally were opening tiny leaves. Young green grasses covered the ground. Life hung in the air, warm and exhilarating.

Suddenly, Karne stopped his horse. Seconds later a black flitter dropped to the ground ahead of us. I felt a wave of panic. Then I saw the narrow green bands and the wide, dark-blue band of House Halarek around each wing. A squad of soldiers spilled out and ran toward us. I felt relief, until I saw *how* they were approaching us, spreading to both sides as they came and with weapons ready. The officer in charge slid to a stop in front of Karne, looking startled. He stared hard, then knelt. The rest of the squad followed his example.

Karne nodded and they rose.

The officer's Adam's apple bobbed. "My—my lord! We believed you dead. Lord Jerem has already been installed as you provided."

"Did Council accept Lady Kathryn as Regent?"

The Adam's apple bobbed again. "No, milord. Council acknowledged it was your wish, but Odonnel, Justin, Harlan, Kingsland, Druma, and Gormsby opposed it. The Freemen wouldn't vote, milord."

"Well? Don't stop there, man!"

"Duke Paul of Druma is the young Lharr's Regent, milord."

"By my Mother's Blood! Whose idea was that?"

The officer shook his head. "I don't know, lord. One of the Old Party, surely. With you gone, they're stronger than ever, unbeatable, if you'll pardon my saying, lord."

Karne turned to me. "I have to take the flitter back. Time—"

" 'T won't do no good to go to Ontar, milord," a young soldier of the squad interrupted. "The young Lharr's at Drumanton."

"Thanks, soldier." Karne turned to the officer. "Why didn't you tell me this?"

"I—I've been taught not to interrupt my betters, sir."

"Sometimes you should forget your training," Karne snapped. "Zjhanne, Jemmy's in terrible danger. Get Paul on the tri-d and tell him I'm coming for Jemmy. That worm allied himself with Odonnel. Captain Oroark will know the men I need and how to get them to me fastest. I'll talk to him from the air."

He didn't kiss me, not in front of outsiders, but he caressed me with his eyes for a long moment before he lifted my hands to his lips for a ritual farewell. Warmed but not comforted, I kicked Gordie toward Ontar. The officer rode beside me. Before we had gone a kilometer, the flitter had become a mere speck on the horizon.

Tommy and four soldiers of the Blues, contacted by the flitter, were waiting for me at the stable's lift. Tommy's face showed how glad he was to see me alive, but he had no words. He made a few fumbling attempts, blushed, and offered me his arm. He and his men walked me to my suite.

My appearance sent the staff into chaos. Ostensibly scrubbing or sweeping or dusting or carrying messages, servants swarmed into the halls. I felt their eyes as I passed and heard the excited buzz of questions and guesses begin behind me. Tamara and Jaklene jumped when the door opened. They sat frozen for several seconds, their needlework falling unnoticed to the floor. Then they ran to me and curtseyed.

"Milady, we thought—"

"They brought back Lord Karne's glove and the pack horses and your scarf. There was blood—"

"Where—"

"Stop!" I ordered.

They silenced themselves with such unusual haste that I had to laugh. "You'll find out what happened after I've finished some business for Lord Karne."

The soldiers usually stationed in the tri-d room had gone to Drumanton to meet Karne, so Tommy stationed one of my four Blues as sentry outside the door, sent the techs out, and himself set the tri-d controls for me. He stood in the center of the transmitter's range, so Paul saw him first.

"Peace on your House, milord Duke." Tommy was all captain-of-Blues. His tone was icy without being insubordinate.

Paul nodded acknowledgment. "And in yours, grace and peace,

Captain. What is the purpose of this call?"

"The Larga Halarek has a message for you, milord."

"The—the Larga?" Paul's face grayed and little beads of sweat broke out on his upper lip and along his hairline. Again the life-likeness of the tri-d struck me. I felt I could walk to the wall where Paul appeared, reach out my hand, and feel his trembling. What other method of communication let a man so clearly betray his cowardice?

Tommy nodded. "Aye, milord. Lord Karne said to tell you he's on his way to get Lord Jerem and Lady Kathryn."

"But—but Lord Richard said—you both were reported dead, killed in an accident. He brought evidence. He—"

"What's the matter, Paul?" I heard the sharpness in my voice too late to soften it. "Kit and Jemmy *are* with you, aren't they? They *are* all right, aren't they?"

Paul sagged backward onto the edge of his desk and wiped the sweat from his forehead with a shaking hand.

"Paul! Tell me. Don't just stand there!"

"They're ill, Larga, have been since soon after they arrived. The—the doctor doesn't expect them to live."

I went cold. "What is it?"

Paul's hands fluttered uselessly. "He doesn't know, Larga. He can only ease the pain."

"Who brought them to you?"

"One of my flitters, Larga, with escort from the Families."

"*Which* Families, Paul?"

He averted his eyes and fumbled for a pipe from the stand beside him.

I leaned forward, aching to shake the truth out of the little coward. "WHICH FAMILIES!"

Tommy, who had stepped out of range when I began to speak, stepped back into Paul's view. Paul paled even more.

"Tell her, my lord." Tommy no longer made any pretense of respect. "Tell her Odonnel, Gormsby, Justin, and Harlan brought the young lord to you. Tell her they put me under Council arrest because I protested. Tell her Lady Kathryn and Lord Jerem spent the day after Lord Jerem's installation at Justin Holding."

I swallowed hard. *Dear God in Heaven! Jemmy's only six years old! These barbarians are willing to kill a child in their clan wars!* "Paul, how could you let them have Jemmy at all? Why didn't you insist they bring him directly to you? Why didn't *you* bring him to Drumanton personally, if that was really where he had to be?"

Paul licked his lips. He wouldn't meet my eyes. "I tried. Really I did. But the Houses voted against me and the Freemen said it was Family business. Then Harlan's men took me bodily off Jemmy's flitter." He paused and then added bitterly, "I can't insist on anything. If I put up a fight, Garren promised an embargo on industrial diamonds. Odonnel's my other liege lord. He can do that. Not many worlds still use the diamonds, but they keep my House alive.

"You know he'd do it, too," he continued petulantly, looking at me for agreement. I gave him no help. "Now the young Lharr's dying and I'll be blamed, because as Regent I have most to gain from his death. Of course, there'll be no investigation of his dying. Lord Richard doesn't want that." He turned away and terminated the transmission.

I just stared stupidly at the empty wall where he had been.

Tommy put a hand hesitantly on my shoulder. "Larga, it would be best if you walked through the manor. It would occupy your mind and it would quiet rumors among the serfs."

I followed him out of the tri-d room. Three Blues fell in behind. Halarek relatives, off-duty soldiers, and domestic servants had assembled in the Great Hall, on Tommy's orders, I supposed. I hadn't seen them all together before. The number staggered me. They filled the Hall and packed the galleries. I stopped just inside the door.

"What do I do, Captain?"

He shrugged. "Say something. Anything. Your voice is what they want."

I walked to the center of the Hall. Remembering I was Karne's representative, I straightened my shoulders more and looked around with my head high. "Members of the House and servants of the Family, you see me alive and safe. Lord Karne has flown to Drumanton to bring back Lord Jerem and Lady Kathryn. Everything shall be as it was. Go in peace."

I watched the household file out of the Hall. They might believe what I said, but I knew nothing would ever again be as it had been. If Lord Richard could manipulate Council into such an unjust thing, he was so strong he could do as he wished with House Halarek.

The gathering in the Hall wasn't the end of my duties. Many serf-servants couldn't leave their work, so to each such workplace I had to go. It seemed so silly, to visit them all, as if they were frightened children. I, with Tommy and my guards, visited the kitchen, the clinic, the 'ponics plants, the guards at the flitter pad. We even visited the stables and spoke to the grooms, trainers, stableboys, and tack-keepers. The process enlightened me about peasant attitudes and beliefs in Terra's pre-industrial age. Not that I would ever be able to publish my insights.

At last we started back. On the way, we passed a row of colored doors. Unlike the wooden doors in the rest of the manor, these were plastex-laminated. I stopped and touched the slippery surface of one.

"What are these doors for, Tommy?"

"They go to the storage and delivery areas under the house. The blue is medical, green is gardening, black goes into Ontar itself, red is weaponry, yellow is clothing and linen, gray—"

"That's enough. I was just curious."

Tommy nodded and started moving again. "Most of the serfs don't read, you know. This makes finding the right storeroom possible."

A soldier met us outside my door. He saluted smartly, then drew Tommy aside. They conferred quietly, then Tommy brought the soldier back to me and beckoned the escort closer so they, too, could hear.

"Sims here says word has just come to General Wynter that Old Party forces, mainly Harlan's, surround Drumanton. The Lharr will have to fight his way in. Wynter's sending Centen Gregg and his Century to help. With luck, they'll arrive before Harlan discovers he'll need more men."

I drew a deep breath to help collect my wits. Karne's life was in danger from Lord Richard. Again. And so soon after our narrow escape in the Desert. Well, he had warned me.

The men, except my sentry, saluted and left. Once I was inside my room, my ladies assaulted me with words. Even quiet Donna managed to put in a few. Finally I clapped my hands together sharply.

"Quiet! If you must know the whole story *now*, tell the young man outside to come in. I'm sure he won't mind telling you all the details. I must write a letter. Don't bother me before I'm done."

"Madam, a letter is quite impossible." Lady Agnes stiffened and glared at me down her long and elegant nose. "You know the rules—"

"Lady Agnes," I said, being as gentle and sweet as I could manage, "you do your duty with amazing zeal, but I think you came back from your vacation too soon. You still look tired. You'd better go back to your daughter's until you look better. I'll order a flitter for you."

I left Lady Agnes with her mouth hanging inelegantly open, went into Karne's room, and closed the door behind me before Lady Agnes could get her wits back together.

This room was a place I knew too little of. When Karne came to me for coupling, he came to my bed. I sat down on the edge of his big bed and surveyed the room. It was stark compared to mine. There were no rugs, no tapestries, no window. The only decoration was a battle scene painted on the wall. The one night I spent in his bed, Karne had told me Egil Olafsson, a friend from the Academy, had painted the battle scene for him years ago. His blue-eyed friend, Egil Olafsson. Then Karne had kissed my blue eyes shut and—

The other furnishings were a large, hide-covered chest, a soft leather chair, a plain desk, a night table with a worn book on it. It was a businesslike room. I sat at the desk and scribbled what I hoped was an encouraging note to Karne.

How I love you, my lord, I thought as I sealed the letter and sent it to the men leaving for Drumanton.

I leaned my elbows on the desk and examined the room some more. Add a rug on the floor and a tapestry on a wall and I could like this room myself. My room could be a sort of sitting room, someplace I could enjoy my window, yet not be confined to the company of those chattering women all the time. Besides, partners in a proper marriage belong in the same bed. I smiled a secret smile. It was not for proprieties I wanted the Lharr Halarek in my bed, nor he me in his.

I slept that night in his bed. It was a kind of comfort for me. I got up in the morning, sure Karne would like the new sleeping arrangements. The moment I slid from the bed and my feet touched the cold stone floor, I promised myself that the room's rug would go on *my* side of the bed.

I slipped into my room, dressed quietly, and brushed out my hair. What a pleasure short hair was! I had had so little time before to savor the pleasure of brushing it, or of looking at the collection of pins and combs and nets I would never use again.

Two days later, our rooms, arranged and cleaned, I stood in the connecting doorway, admiring them. A page rushed in with the news that Karne was almost home with Jemmy and Kit.

"How long?" I demanded.

"Less than half an hour, Larga Zjhanne. You're to call doctors and nurses up from the clinic."

Doctors! My heart stopped for a moment. Then I forced myself to the intercom. Of course. Jemmy and Kit were very sick. And there would be wounded.

In twenty minutes I'd made all the provisions I could and was standing anxiously behind the blast shield at the flitter pad. One by one black troop-flitters appeared against the cloudless blue sky and floated down the shaft. Two, three, four of them—Wynter had obviously decided that a transport was too good a target and had sent Gregg's Century in twenty-five men units. I twisted the trailing edge of a sleeve. Was that all? Where was Karne's own flitter? Then an electric blue flitter dropped into the shaft. It settled on the pad and then the massive doors above slid across and shut out the sky. The green light over the control-room window began blinking. It was safe to come out from behind the shields. I hurried forward, motioning impatiently for the black-robed doctor and his assistants to follow.

Soldiers poured out of their ships. Some ran to the medical technicians, who stood at one side with litters, to show them which ships held the wounded. The others encircled the blue flitter. Its cabin door slid open and Paul, pale and trembling, stepped out and looked around. His wife followed. No friendly faces greeted them. I felt a twinge of pity, but only a twinge. Then Karne stepped out and I forgot everything else. A bloody bandage wrapped his head, his tunic was torn and dirty, and he wore a crude splint on his right forearm. Jemmy's small body lay limp in his arms.

Karne motioned the doctor to him with his head and nodded curtly to me. "Take care of Kit, Zjhanne. I'll be in to help you later if I can."

A soldier boosted me onto the wing. I stepped into the cabin. Kit lay on a pallet between two seats. Her face was flushed and dripping with sweat. She breathed shallowly and rapidly. Take care of her? What could I do? I didn't even have a cool cloth for her forehead.

Soon two techs lifted Kit to a litter and, because the litter moved much faster pushed than it could go by itself, one tech set the control for "hover only." On my orders, they pushed the litter to my room. Since I didn't intend to occupy the bed there again, it seemed a very good place to put Kit. She would be in the room next to me instead of across the hall. Karne came upstairs, briefly, to look in on Kit and to give me a quick kiss. I tried to get him to let the doctor see to his hurts.

"They can wait, Zjhanne. When Jemmy's taken care of, and the seriously wounded . . ."

"How's Jemmy?"

"Taking him to the clinic was the quickest way to get the oxygen and equipment Dr. Othneil needed." Karne's voice caught. "He doesn't expect him to live till fast-breaking."

I saw the tears in Karne's eyes and looked away to spare him embarrassment.

Jemmy hung on despite the poison, but there was little hope he'd recover. Karne, soon joined by Baron von Schuss, spent nearly all his time at Jemmy's bedside. I sat in my quarters with Kit, who cried out in her delirium against the men who had held her captive.

From her ravings I pieced together what had happened. First Harlan's men had killed Jemmy's uhl-uhl slowly and painfully while the boy watched. Then Lord Richard had taunted Kit, repeatedly, with his successful plan to trap Nik and with the details of what he planned for her, for Jemmy, and for her beloved brother. For her, he planned to finish what Karne and Nik's rescue had prevented before. And all the time she had watched Jemmy become sicker and weaker.

I didn't leave my quarters for the first two weeks after Kit and Jemmy came back. I learned from the sentry outside my door that Lord Richard had somehow found out Halarek was sending reinforcements and he had been ready. The cost to Halarek had been great, perhaps greater than the House, already financially unsteady because of the Black Ship, could afford.

"If it hadn't been for some unexpected help from House deVree," the sentry said in conclusion, "none of us would've come back."

Karne ate by Jemmy's bed, slept there, or stayed awake watching all night. Sometimes I saw him in chapel, where he took short breaks to join me in prayer for Jemmy and his mother. Those moments were a precious bond between us, too.

When Karne did come upstairs to bed, he looked so worn and sad that I ached to comfort him, but there was nothing I could say or do that was more than temporary comfort. His vigil began to affect his health. Early in the second week, one of Jemmy's nurses came to me in her off-duty hours. That was unusual enough. But it wasn't Jemmy she wanted to talk about.

"Lord Karne's head wound isn't healing properly, Larga. You must make him rest or he'll collapse."

I touched her arm lightly in thanks and then laughed ruefully. "*Make* him rest? Perhaps that's something a wife can do among Freemen, but among the Families . . . Believe me, I've tried. But thank you for caring."

The nurse curtseyed and left.

Into all this worrying and waiting came a tri-d call for Karne from the Earl of Kingsland. Karne wouldn't leave Jemmy to receive the call, but sent me.

"Kingsland's been Halarek's enemy since Ingold arranged for his sire to have an 'accident.' There isn't anything he has to say important enough to take me away from Jemmy right now. You find out what he wants."

Ingold Kingsland was a handsome man, in a rather hard way. He bowed politely when I told him I was Karne's delegate to receive anything he had to say.

"As your lord wishes, Larga," Ingold intoned smoothly.

The phrasing got my back up, as I'm sure he meant it to. I would not let him provoke me into saying something he could use against Karne. I *would* not.

"Paul IV Druma has been formally charged with attempted murder, Larga, and has been sentenced to death by Garren Odonnel, his liege lord." He paused.

"Who did he kill?" I asked, ever so politely.

"The Lharr Jerem Halarek."

So this was the game they would run, that Jemmy had been legally installed. "Lord Jerem is still living, my lord. He has no murderer. And should he die, his illness was acquired on Justin Holding. Hundreds of witnesses will attest to that, milord."

Ingold stood staring at me, his thoughts chasing each other furiously across his face. He was not used to a woman thinking faster than he, perhaps?

In the end, he ignored the technicalities I'd brought up and went on to the other matter he wanted to tell me about. "House Harlan is calling in the military service his serfs and vassals owe him and making up an army to march against Ontar, Larga Zjhanne. He intends to capture the fugitive and punish Lord Karne for sheltering him." Ingold cocked his head a little to one side. "Did you know it's illegal to shelter a fugitive from Council, milady?"

I looked at him as blandly as I could manage. "Is it? It's done so often here."

"Do you understand what I'm telling you, Larga?"

"It sounds like the Old Party is selectively enforcing an unobserved law, my lord."

"The point is," he said, "that Lord Karne has broken a law. Not only has he broken it, but he has told Council by means of his secretary, Frem Weisman, that he doesn't intend to give Druma back to his overlord for justice."

"Lord Karne is Druma's liege lord, too," I put in.

"The point is, Larga," the earl said with exaggerated patience, "that your husband, by his refusal, has brought war upon himself. I realize war is something your people don't understand, but that's what this means."

I thought of the ruins of Clarridge and half a hundred other cities, still glowing more than a hundred forty years after the War. *No, my lord, we understand war far better than you, with your stunners and beamers and impregnable cities.*

". . . so Harlan has to give you a week's notice before he attacks," the earl was saying.

"Thank you for the warning, Lord Ingold. I have nursing duties to attend to. We have many wounded." I terminated the transmission and left the room.

As soon as the earl had disappeared, I returned to place a call to the Duke deVree.

"Peace be on your House, my lord," I said as soon as he appeared.

"And on yours, peace, Larga Zjhanne. What can I do for you?"

I summarized my conversation with Kingsland and explained Karne's preoccupation with Jemmy.

DeVree sighed. "I'll do what I can, but with Paul under sentence and the Lharr and Baron von Schuss occupied with the boy, it won't be much. I can assure you, though, that Council will force Richard and Garren to give you forty days. It's the law. A week is laughable." He didn't look like he felt like laughing. "The Freemen will continue to say the fight's a Family problem. I just hope the fools see the truth before it's too late, for us and for them. The Lord be with you."

"And with your spirit."

The content of deVree's call hadn't been much, but that the duke would commit himself to do anything at all in the matter was a giant step forward for him. After eight to ten years of clinging to the fence between the factions, it sounded as if the Duke deVree were coming down on our side.

Instead of telling Karne myself, I sent for Wynter and told him what I had learned. His sharp military mind would come up with useful ideas for Karne by the time he had walked down two levels from tri-d room to clinic.

Later, as I sat in the library trying to ease my loneliness and anxiety with a book, Karne tapped softly on the door and then came in. I dropped my book and ran into his arms.

"Karne! I've missed you so!"

His arms squeezed me hungrily and the kiss that followed told me more eloquently than words what I wanted to know; he still loved me. I leaned back within his embrace and looked at him. His face had lost its healthy color and was thinner than ever. Tenderly I ran a fingertip over the new lines around his nose and mouth and touched the bluish circles under his eyes.

"Let me take your place tonight, milord. You need sleep badly. You aren't recovering as you should."

"No, sweetheart. Dr. Othneil says that if Jemmy survives the night, he'll live. I must be with him."

"Karne, let me—"

"Don't argue!" he snapped. He shook his head hard once and winced with pain. "I'm sorry. I shouldn't've yelled. I'm getting edgy, what with Kingsland's announcement on top of Jemmy's condition. I only came up to say I'm sending you to safety with my aunt, Deaconess Alba, at her Retreat House. With a neutral relative and in a religious community, no one will harm you."

"But what about Kit? She's too sick to be moved."

Karne sighed. "Kit can't go. She'll have to take her chances here."

I touched his arm. "Let me stay, too, Karne. I want to. I *belong* with you."

"Zjhanne, don't—!" He stopped, looking bewildered by the anger, then lowered his voice to normal volume. "I don't know what's come over me." He sighed and I ached for his weariness. "My heart, too, says you belong here. But my head says no. You mustn't be caught here. This fight will go on until—

"Only one will survive this time, Richard or me. I want you to be safe." The sadness in his voice and eyes said he believed Richard would be the survivor.

I knew Karne would die if he began the battle feeling defeated. That much I had learned of this world. I gripped both his arms tightly. "Karne, it must be *you*. You can't let yourself believe anything else!" I dropped my grip and looked away. It was not fair to inflict tears on him now and I knew I was going to cry. "Karne, without you—"

He took my head between his left hand and the palm of his cast and shook it gently back and forth. "Don't you cry. Don't you dare cry. Oh, I see one. It's sneaking out under your lashes. It's sliding. Ha!" He softly kissed the side of my nose. "I caught it." He licked his lips loudly.

The fun never reached his eyes, but I assembled a shaky smile for him.

"That's better." He stroked my cheek just once with his good hand. "Now, run upstairs and pack enough clothes for at least a month. You're leaving tomorrow morning, as soon as we know how Jemmy—" He took a deep breath. "I'll bring you back to me as soon as I can, believe me. Go on now." He turned me toward the iron stair and started me on my way with a loving, left-handed swat on the behind. "Say goodbye quickly tomorrow," he called after me. "Halarek can't afford for me to weaken."

I turned to reply, but he'd already gone back to Jemmy.

Packing was easy. Without Karne or the Lady Agnes to please, my clothing needs were simple and my three women and I made quick work of it. Kit awakened during this, but was in no condition to comprehend more than that I was still alive. I spoke to her reassuringly several times, but she obviously didn't hear me. Kit's nurse laid cool cloths on her forehead and wrists and began talking to her in a steady, soothing monotone. Comfort was all we could give her. The doctors had done what they could; the rest Kit had to do herself.

Too soon it was morning. I sent my trunk down after fast-breaking and said goodbye to all my women. Tommy met me at my door and escorted me toward the pad. Karne met us as we stepped out of the lift at level 2.

"Captain Oroark, leave us," he snarled.

Tommy looked blank.

"Leave us!"

"Yessir!" Tommy snapped a salute and headed for the pad on the double.

Karne watched until the pad door had closed behind him, then he turned to me. "He's dead. Six years old and he's dead."

"Oh, Karne." I reached out to him.

His eyes were dull and dilated. With horror and bewilderment I saw hate smoldering in them. I let my hands fall before they touched him. His hands gripped my shoulders with fingers like claws.

"If it weren't for you, he'd still be here! If it weren't for your damned stubbornness I'd have an heir and Jemmy wouldn't've been such a tempting target!"

"My lord—"

"Shut up!" He shifted one hand to my arm and propelled me along the hall to an empty room in the servants' quarters. He slammed the door behind us and we were alone in the tiny room, his anger and grief like a red fog around us.

"It's a lovely plan, isn't it?" he snarled. "Get Jemmy and two Houses have no Heir, two Houses because the baron can't have children. If I'd had an Heir, Harlan would've been careful to keep House von Schuss legally neutral. One less for my side. But the baron won't stay neutral now. He no longer has a reason to. Paul is under sentence. That's a third House. Harlan's ready to attack. He's set this up. With Paul and Emil and me dead, Starker IV falls into Richard's hands and retreats three centuries. Soon after, boom!

"You'll be around to see that, madam, because once I'm dead, you'll never again leave the Retreat. And Richard *will* kill me, if he deigns to meet me at all. He's had a lot more practice at dueling than I have."

"Stop! Stop!" I struggled to free myself from his punishing grip. "You can't mean what you're saying."

"On the contrary, madam," he retorted dryly, "I mean every word." He propelled me back through the door and down the hall, still with that cruel grip on my arm.

I hung back, I tried to free myself, I set my heels, only to be jerked into motion again. "Please, Karne, don't send me away. Not while you feel like this. I love you. I loved him. Don't blame me. Please!"

He acted as if he didn't hear me. The sentry at the pad saluted and swung the gate open for us. Tommy looked up from his inspection of a one-man flitter. Karne walked me to its side, but he wouldn't look at me. He dropped my arm when we reached the wingtip and stepped stiffly back. Tommy looked from one of us to the other questioningly. I waited, but Karne neither moved nor spoke. Apparently he didn't intend even to say goodbye.

I drew breath with difficulty and thick black spots danced before my eyes. I willed the spots away. We couldn't part like this! I put my arms around Karne and held him tight.

"Please, Karne. I don't want to leave. If you die, I want to die with you. Please . . ." But it was like embracing and talking to a statue. A tree would have been more responsive.

Don't shut me out like this, my heart cried to him.

Karne pulled my arms roughly away and put them at my sides. "You shame me with such display," he said, his harsh voice a stranger's.

A roaring began in my ears, followed by blackness. My will came aware too late to stop myself from falling. It was Tommy's arm that caught me. Tommy who helped me onto the flitter's wing. Tommy who explained the controls. Tommy whose deep-brown eyes told me goodbye so much better than his fumbling tongue. The heavy doors above slid open and everyone stepped behind the blast shields.

"Karne, take care," I cried before Tommy closed the flitter door for flight.

But if he heard he gave no sign. There was nothing left to do but press the red button and go.

CHAPTER 18

The flitter hovered for a minute above the garden. Four black escort ships rose and joined mine.

"Milady," Tommy's voice crackled out of the cabin speaker, "we'll go with you two hundred kilometers, to the edge of the holding, but in radio silence. The lever at the far end of the control panel raises and lowers your shield. Throw it when I sign off. Is this clear?"

"Yes."

"The Lord be with you."

"And with your spirit."

I threw the lever and watched as the trees below blurred for a moment. Enclosed within the flitter's blast-proof shield, I experienced an awful sense of finality. The feeling frightened me.

It was his exhaustion speaking, and his grief, I told myself.

But there was that look of hate. In my grief and bitterness and humiliation, I couldn't convince myself that I hadn't just seen the end of our marriage. A long battle, a brief friendship, and a briefer marriage. I willed away the tears that crowded my eyes and watched the mountains I'd come to love slide away, fading from blue-green and brown to black to purple to misty blue-gray. Here is home, their solid, familiar shapes told me. Here is home, home, home.

I watched them until even my imagination couldn't see them standing across the horizon. Then Tommy and his Blues dropped away and I flew on toward the equator alone. Kilometer on kilometer, hour on hour, the strange, featureless plains of Starker IV flowed under the flitter.

At last, on the horizon, a small square bump with towers appeared. Soon I could pick out the walls, the moat, the heavy gate. I recognized the fortress that was the Retreat House from its picture in a history book. It was a rare survivor of the planet's brief surface civilization. A thousand years it and its eleven siblings had stood, deserted, before apostles of The Way restored them and turned them into Retreat Houses, half for men, half for women.

The flitter descended rapidly and I prepared myself mentally to meet the abbess. When the flitter touched down, I waited. After several minutes, the massive gate in the Retreat's wall split and half slid into each wall. Three gray-robed deaconesses strode out. When they were within speaking distance, I climbed down from the flitter and curtseyed.

"Peace be on this house."

The deaconesses bowed and replied in unison, "Grace to you, and peace, Larga Zjhanne."

A tall austere woman stepped forward. "Come, the abbess waits. A lay worker will shed your flitter."

A small serf woman ran out of the courtyard and climbed into the flitter. I and the deaconesses walked into the Retreat.

The courtyard was quite plain. Paved with graystone, it enclosed a small orchard and an herb garden. There were no frivolous plants. A portress swung open the heavy door to the building itself and my guides and I walked up a broad stone staircase and down a quiet, cold hallway lit by real torches. A few women in hooded gray habits passed, slipping by like shadows. They bowed their heads in our direction, but said nothing.

"If anyone wishes to be spoken to, she will lower her hood," one of my guides said. "You do not speak to anyone with her hood up."

I had dreaded a month with only women for company, but it might not be quite so bad if they didn't chatter all the time. The austere deaconess stopped before a door that stood slightly ajar.

"Deaconess Alba, the abbess, is in there."

The three women lifted their hoods and went away. I entered the room hesitantly. Light from a window slit fell across a large oak desk. When the gray-robed figure at the desk raised her head, I curtseyed politely and waited for her to speak. The abbess's dark eyes, shadowed by her hood, regarded me gravely and disapprovingly for several uncomfortable minutes. Then the abbess lowered her hood and the light revealed a stern, aging face framed by a tight braid of gray hair.

"I'm surprised my nephew would permit his wife to dress so brazenly. He must have gone far down the road my brother was traveling before he died."

I wondered what the abbess meant. My plain, fitted dress looked no different to me than the dresses of other women of my rank and class. Perhaps styles had changed since the abbess had last been out in the world. Abbess Alba rustled through the papers on her desk.

"Ah, here it is. Karne commits you to my care for the duration of this Family argument. That means you must respect the rules of the Community. And *that* means, to begin with, you cover your horrid lack of hair with some modest head covering. I'll send the wardress with you to select something. The rules are simple. You'll find a little folder listing them on the desk in your room."

The abbess jerked the bell rope by the desk. A serf came in.

"Show the Larga her room," the abbess said. "And bring her a selection of wimples suitable to her rank."

The serf bobbed obediently and led me quickly down the hall and up two broad flights of stairs.

The stairwells and halls were remarkably bare. Even Druma manor had a few tapestries Paul brought out for special occasions, and his was the poorest House. Here there were no decorations at all.

My room was small and as stark as the hallways. Its furnishings consisted of a narrow bed, my trunk, and a small desk and chair. Two narrow, uncurtained windows looked out on the courtyard and the ancient outer wall.

"Meals are at 800 and 1500 hours, milady," the serf-wardress was saying, "in the refectory downstairs. Any lady up here'll show you. The bell will chime once. Worship is four times a day—the bell chimes three times—in the chapel across from the abbess's office."

"Does mail come here?"

"Daily, milady. And it goes out three times a week. Letter materials are in the desk. The tri-d's down the hall, across from the Common room." The serf pointed vaguely.

"A shower?"

"Aye, milady, back by the stair."

"Thanks. As for the wimple, just bring anything blue or white that I can wrap around my head. Leave it outside the door, because I think I'll take a nap."

The serf backed and bobbed out the door. I sat on the bed. It was quite as hard as it looked. Without even taking off my cloak, I lay back and pressed the heels of my hands against my eyes. Everything had suddenly gone wrong, when it had seemed finally to be going right. I lay there for many minutes, until I could bear the images of Karne standing stonily by the flitter no longer. I went to the shower, hoping the stream of hot water would ease away the knots in my body and my mind, but for once, a shower was no help at all. I gave up, wrapped my absorbent bathrobe around me, and plodded back to my room. A green wimple lay on the floor in front of the door.

I lay down again and willed my tension away, then held that willing just on the edge of consciousness for half an hour or so. More relaxed, I began the physical check I had had no time for at the manor. Halfway through, my consciousness touched new life. I stopped, stunned. The days of waiting in fear and worry at the patrol cabin, the intense relief and joy after Karne came back safely—I had neglected my internal controls.

I checked again, though about such discoveries there can be no mistake. He was there, the son, the heir, the Heir, that could save Karne's life. Richard would benefit little from killing Karne now, because Halarek Holding would still have a lord. Had I subconsciously selected male, knowing how desperately Karne needed a son? Had I "forgotten" to do a physical check after we returned to the manor to give this new life time to grow? Whatever had happened, a baby boy was now in the making and I could offer him to Karne as a gift of love. Was it too late? Would Karne have said what he did if he'd known? Would he believe me now, feeling as he did? I had to find out.

I padded to the desk and went through its drawers. Plasti sheets, stilos, tapes, galactic stamp books, sealing wax—any way to send a message I wanted was there. I sat down with the recorder, inserted a tape case, pulled a ring, pushed the small sliding switch, and began.

"Dear my lord, I have such wonderful news . . ."

But I didn't need a playback to hear the stiffness and formality of my words. I'd never liked recording and the sting of Karne's parting words further inhibited me. I pulled out a plasti sheet and stylus and struggled to compose a letter that way. He must believe the child was there! I tried to read the letter as he would, angry, grieving, blaming. I reread it, heat-sealed it, and dropped it into the mail chute.

Who handles his correspondence now? I wondered.

The following afternoon an intercom announcement roused me from a book. "Tri-d declaration of state-of-war, one minute."

The Retreat Houses rarely permitted tri-d watching, because it was a distraction for the worldly. A state of war. I didn't need a tri-d cast to tell me whose. I slid into my shoes, threw the wimple around my head, and hurried to the tri-d room. More gray robes than I'd seen before except at meals already stood looking toward the screen. A few lay workers and serfs hovered around the edges of the group. Light wavered across the screen, then steadied, and the blue-green mosaic outside the council chamber solidified out of it. The Duke of Harlan and the Lharr Odonnel appeared and walked to the center of the screen.

The Lharr Odonnel lifted his chin and brushed a tiny wrinkle from his tunic. "People of the Gharr, we come to swear to you that the murderer of the young Lharr of Halarek shall not escape punishment. I, Lharr Garren Odonnel, have sentenced Paul, Duke of Druma, my vassal and the boy's appointed guardian and heir, to death for his crime."

He paused and Lord Richard spoke. "Unfortunately, Karne Halarek, former Lharr in House Halarek, snatched the murderer, Lord Jerem, and Lady Kathryn from Drumanton and took them to Ontar before the sentence could be carried out. He refuses to give up Druma to his liege lord for justice. Because of this, we now lay siege to Ontar."

"How can such a pleasing face hide such a lying soul?" I didn't realize I had spoken aloud until the deaconesses around me turned to stare disapprovingly.

The Council chamber wavered and disappeared and the library at Ontar replaced it. The picture focused on Karne's gray and drawn face. So close, so real, and so far away! I longed to hold and comfort him. The invisible transmitter pulled back and Baron von Schuss, Kit, Paul, and Frem Weisman came into focus.

Karne stood straighter with obvious effort. "Milord Duke fails to mention that the young lord came sick from Justin Holding to Drumanton. I requested an investigation of the poisoning, an investigation Harlan's control of Family votes in Council denied." Karne's voice dragged with fatigue.

For an instant the picture flashed back to the Council room and Richard Harlan's face. "Lies," he sneered. "All lies. He'll protect Druma at any cost."

Then Ontar came on screen again. Karne leaned toward his distant audience. "You of the Families and minor Houses who want your children to survive, help us. Freemen, forget your 'neutrality' and fight for our world. There will be no more freedom if Harlan is allowed to rule."

A pause of many minutes followed. Then the screen lit again, showing a room in someone's house. Chairman Reed, Councilman Duval, and several other Freemen clustered to one side of the picture. The invisible Lord Richard cleared his throat impatiently. The Freemen spread out and Chairman Reed stepped toward us. I could almost believe one step more would bring him into the front rank of deaconesses.

Chairman Reed looked out at his audience. "If you of the Houses permit, the Freemen will mediate this dispute. However, if you don't accept our offer, both sides must give the full forty days for non-combatants, especially women, to get to neutral areas, the Retreat Houses, perhaps, or to places you set by agreement. Any Family or minor House that wishes to stay out of this feud must declare its position before the end of that period. No Freeman may shelter any of you."

"Frem Chairman," Richard snapped, "forty days was the limit in the days before the War and flitters."

Reed's face stiffened. "That is the time allowed by law, milord Duke. Your law. Accept it and pull your forces away from Ontar and Drumanton or Council shall be forced to embargo all your off-world freight."

"Freemen have never interfered bef—"

"We are not 'interfering.' " Reed's face grew even harder. "We only require that the rules made by the Families be obeyed and we shall enforce them."

After a long pause, Lord Richard's disembodied voice came into our room and Reed's. "You give us no choice. We'll pull back three kilometers and will permit women through our lines."

"*Anyone* who wishes to remain neutral may leave within the forty days, my lord."

"But Frem Chairman, that would mean that even the Lharr Halarek could leave if he wished."

"It does." Then Reed added, dryly, "He wouldn't, though, as I'm sure you know."

Richard continued to press Reed for some yielding, perhaps to suggest to the large audience that even the Freemen bowed a little to his power. "If he must let men through, I insist they carry white flags."

"Insisting on such a change isn't within your power, Lord Richard." There was just the slightest suggestion of satisfaction in Reed's tone. "White flags are used only *after* a war begins. Anyone until then may leave when and as he pleases. It's the law."

"That's absurd, Frem Chairman! Halarek could set all sorts of spies on me. They could walk through my lines, count my men, and report to him from some other holding."

Reed nodded. "He could, but he won't. Not even his enemies, most of them, would credit Halarek with such dishonorable use of the truce. You know the rules, milord," Reed added. "Abide by them in full." And he ended the transmission.

After that broadcast, I expected some word from my lord. There would be war. Surely that changed things. Then I remembered that in the beginning, before Jemmy died, the coming war was the reason Karne was sending me to safety.

A week passed and then another. Women from the Families streamed into the Retreat, filling every room. Three weeks passed, surely sufficient time for Karne to have received my letter and answered it. Then the forty-day truce. Surely Karne would send some word. But nothing came.

I became desperate to see him, to at least hear from him. The odds were against him. Everyone said so. Lord Richard's bold manipulation of the Families and his brazen declaration of war said so. I had to make Karne listen to me.

Sending a letter had failed. I saw no reason why Karne would answer a tape if he would ignore a letter. Would he refuse to talk to me by tri-d? I sent a request to the abbess to make a tri-d cast to Ontar. She would not even discuss the matter with me. I would have to return to Ontar, then.

I was so sure that the abbess would refuse permission for me to leave that I didn't even ask her. I went out to the flitter sheds and tried to start my flitter. Nothing happened. Even the clock on the control panel was dead. I don't know what I would've done if it had started, because I knew nothing about steering one of the things. I didn't even know if its controls had been set for a return to Ontar manor. I sank into the pilot's seat, curled around the life within, and cried until my eyes had swollen nearly shut and sobs came convulsively.

My lord, my life, what have I done to deserve such treatment from you?

I sat in the flitter for a long time, submerged in pain and bewilderment. It was hours before I could control my emotions and get out.

I had just started up the stairs to my floor when a serf tugged at my sleeve and pointed to the abbess's office. The last person I wanted to see at that moment was Karne's stern aunt, but Alba *was* the abbess.

Abbess Alba looked up as I entered. "Perhaps you didn't read the rules regarding temporary guests, Larga," the abbess said coldly. "You may not leave the Retreat until this war is over or until such time as your husband calls you back. Fortunately, Lord Richard foresaw that some women might try to break the truce by going back, so he sent a man to disable the machines."

I stared at the woman, aghast. How could she trust her nephew's mortal enemy?

"There's no need to stare at me, Larga. Lord Richard was obviously right. You shall stay here. If my nephew wants you, he'll send for you. Until that time, he expects you to behave like the Larga of Halarek, not like a crazy, willful foreigner. You may go to your room now and meditate on your willful nature." The abbess lifted her hood and turned away.

I swallowed my anger. The abbess had signaled there would be no further talk. To argue would be pointless. It would also worsen Alba's already low opinion of me. I spun away and returned to my room.

In the weeks that followed, very little news of the fighting came into the Retreat. I entered the life of the community to the extent of wearing the shapeless gray habit and hood. At least the habit would eventually conceal my pregnancy and the hood hid my face and saved me from conversation. Still, I clung to only the edge of Retreat life. I went to chapel and took communion, but only once a week. I did not read the Holy Book and meditate on what I read. I did pray.

Even when among the other Family women, such as at mealtimes, I was alone. Always there was an unstated distance between us. I could trust no one. There was no one I dared talk to, tell my fears to, tell of the son I carried. There was no one to help me untangle the emotions that kept me in a state of confusion and uncertainty.

Had I delayed so long that Karne no longer cared whether I gave him an heir? Surely not. House Halarek meant too much to him. Did he blame me still for Jemmy's death? Hate me still? Love me still? Round and round and round with no way out of the circle of questions and doubts that began and ended in depression and despair.

On the chance that somehow my letter hadn't gotten through, I forced myself to try again. And again. Still no word. Trapped by the circle of questions, doubts, depression, despair, I reduced still more my contacts with the other women. I left my hood on even during meals. I paced the battlements for hours and spent more hours staring across the dry plains toward home. Summer marched across the plains, through the courtyard gardens, and on to the north. Harlan's green-clad soldiers threw a "protective" guard around the Retreat. I wondered if they had Council permission to do that or if Lord Richard no longer bothered with Council.

In the refectory sometimes I heard the war discussed. Druma Holding was completely in Lord Richard's hands (Odonnel's, really, but it amounted to the same thing), and House Harlan was slowly claiming Halarek Holding, hectare by hectare and kilometer by kilometer. In the on and off fighting, Ontar city and manor were often besieged. Yet I knew none of this should affect the mail. The Gild handled all mail and no one bothered the Gild.

I became more convinced that Karne just didn't want to communicate with me, and with this conviction brought a deep bitterness. I had been so sure he loved me and that in love we could work out anything. I was alone, abandoned. All I had now to show for my certainty about being loved was the child.

When the leaves in the orchard began yellowing, I carefully composed a letter to First Merchant Tremo. Then in Fruvan, spoken slowly for his foreign ear, I recorded my composition:

> "I cannot reach my lord. Is this his wish? Should I call for off-world help? Surely your contacts and Dad's could save him. If you judge this a good idea, will you see to it?"

I flipped the switch to off and thought. I had to know.

> "I want the truth, Sam, whatever it is. If Karne should be dead, or just dead to me . . ."

I couldn't go on with that. I signed off with "Give him my love," ran the message back, sealed and addressed the tape, and dropped it into the mail chute as I went to chapel.

After a week, one of the younger deaconesses knocked at my door and stuck her head into the room. "I'm sorry to disturb you, my lady, but Abbess Alba wants to see you."

Alba met me at the door to her office. "A Gildsman was here to see you." She must have seen the happiness I felt at this news, for it meant something of mine had finally reached someone. She frowned and continued sternly. "I couldn't permit him to speak to you, of course, and sent him away."

I turned angrily to leave, but the abbess stopped me with a hand on my shoulder. "He did say the matter was urgent and concerned my nephew, so I let him leave this. Here"—the abbess pressed a tape case into my hand—"I hope it's good news."

The gentleness of the abbess's last words surprised me and the abbess, too, apparently, because she walked abruptly back into her office and shut the door firmly behind her.

The tape had very little news. Sam hadn't been permitted into Ontar and not even rumors were getting out.

> "I did what I could, Larga. I sent your letter to the manor by Weisman. He had been trapped in the city by the last siege and took refuge in the Gildhall. He swore by his love for his lord he would get through. When Harlan pulled back for a few hours, Weisman left for the manor."

Advent came, and the fall rains, and then frost. With each day, my bitterness increased and my thoughts turned more savage. In return for believing and loving again, I'd been betrayed again. He'd used me. "Let her think you love her," the men in my life said to themselves, and set out to convince me. And I believed them. Lance now had the wealth he had always dreamed of. Karne would soon have the son he wanted. I was twice the fool this time. Worse than twice, because Karne had never pretended he believed in love between man and wife. In fact, he had said several times such love was a bad thing. Each time the bitter train of thought ended in the same place: Why couldn't I stop loving Karne, then? I had stopped loving Lance. Why couldn't I stop the hurting?

My days flowed into each other as featurelessly as the raindrops on my windows. I kept to my room except for meals and the long, solitary walks on the fortress wall. Raining or not, I didn't care; the walking was a kind of release. The women of the Families were becoming bored and wanted someone new to talk to, but

I refused to see them. They reminded me of a life I'd have to forget.

But every day the physical reminder of that life grew and with it the conflict between my heart's unshakable faith in the love Karne had felt and my pride's repetition of his betrayal and desertion. Every day refectory conversation reported the weakening of Halarek positions or the incredible violence of another serf uprising. The war was destroying all the Houses.

Christmas came, but without gaiety or celebration, only an extra candle-lit service Christmas Eve. Even on the holy day, my lord sent me no word. Two days after Christmas, as I sat by my window listening to chill wind howl outside, someone knocked at my door. I didn't answer, hoping whoever it was would go away. Another knock. Then the door whispered open. I turned angrily, with biting words ready, but they died unspoken. Kit stood in the doorway, white, and leaning heavily on Donna.

"Peace, Zjhanne." Kit's voice was just a thin thread of sound.

"I have no peace." I turned back to the window. After months without any word, did Kit expect an enthusiastic welcome?

"Milady—"

"Hush, Donna! Help me sit."

With faint swishes, Kit and her maid crossed to the desk. I heard the rustlings of Kit sitting down.

Kit took several deep breaths and then her husky voice said, "I bring word from your lord, Zjhanne."

My hands clenched on the stone edge of the window. I choked on the words. "He's waited overlong. I no longer care what he has to say."

"Overlong?" Kit's voice shook with outrage. "Overlong? What sort of woman are you, that two weeks is overlong?"

"Two weeks?" I heard the harshness in my short laugh and couldn't make myself care. I turned to look at Kit. "Lady Kathryn, I've been alone here for more than four months, without even one letter from my lord, or from you, the people I believed cared something for me. After so long, and such anguish, I have no caring left."

Kit looked at me hard for a long moment. "Can you care nothing about causing Karne's death?"

Time stopped and blackness rushed in as the blood left my head. I clutched behind me for the window edge. "He's dead? How?" The words came out in a harsh whisper.

Kit shook her head. "He's not. Yet. Aunt Alba said you'd isolated yourself. But not soon enough, Zjhanne, not before you'd destroyed everything."

"Destroyed?" A whisper was all I could manage. I felt very faint.

Kit stood slowly and walked toward the door. "Come. I'll show you. You must be the only person on Starker IV who doesn't know."

CHAPTER 19

Kit led me to the tri-d room. The Council chamber already filled the screen. Council members sat quietly, waiting with an unusual intentness. Karne sat in the prep table, but soldiers in a mixture of uniforms, all Old Party Houses, stood around him as if he were a criminal. Chairman Reed pounded the meeting to order.

"Lord Richard, you called us together on a most urgent matter. Please explain your charges in full."

"Lords and Freemen, for many months I've suspected what I now can prove. I've called you here to try and to convict Lord Karne, former Lharr of House Halarek, for treason against Starker IV."

Everyone in the tri-d room gasped, even though, according to Kit, they all knew why the meeting had been called. Karne's pale face tightened at the shameful words, but he showed no other signs of emotion. That he revealed even that much gave a clue to the depth of his pain. My heart ached. Such a terrible humiliation for him! Of all the people on this world, Karne was the least likely to commit treason against it. I felt as if I were about to suffocate.

Lord Richard, having waited for the full effect of his charge to soak in, continued. "My evidence covers the period of his lharrship and after—"

"Milord," Reed broke in sharply, "we are Freemen and members of the Houses here, not serfs. Don't try playing games with words. Karne Halarek is as much Lharr as he's ever been. The installation of Lord Jerem upon news—false news—of Lord Karne's death was obviously a mistake. Besides, according to Lord Karne, it was *your* soldiers who pursued him into Zinn while trying to kill him and the Larga. It was *your* soldiers who brought the evidence of Lord Karne's 'death.' You, too, are on trial here, milord, so try no more such tricks. You will give the Lharr his proper title and stick to facts."

"The matter of the title can be taken up at some other time," Richard conceded smoothly. "If there is another time. However, to the case before us. A man is responsible for his own actions, of course. As you all know, by ancient law, he is also responsible for the actions of his wife. By this law do I accuse Karne Halarek. I bring the charge before Council only because, unlike the rest of us, Karne Halarek has no other liege."

Again he paused for effect. Many of the deaconesses turned to look at me, then just as pointedly turned away. Lord Richard tapped a finger thoughtfully on a stack of papers and tapes on the Harlan table, his eyes never leaving the circle of the Nine.

"As you also know, the Lharr brought into his House a woman from a world of the old Empire. He thought our lives would improve if we eased our restrictions on women. So he allowed his Larga much freedom. She was unworthy of such trust, just as any woman would be. His mistake dooms them both." He faced Karne directly. "Lord Karne, when did you last hear from the Larga?"

"I don't think that's anyone's business."

Lord Richard gave the other Families a "see what I mean" look and then continued. "I know for certain, milord, that you've heard nothing since she left you several months ago."

"It has been one hundred sixty-five days, milord. And she didn't 'leave' me, I sent her away."

"Then you knew."

"Stop playing guessing games, Richard, and get to your point!"

"You knew your wife was plotting with her leman against Starker IV. They've called for an off-world invasion."

Karne sprang to his feet. "That's a lie!"

"Would you recognize the Larga's voice, milord?"

I hated Lord Richard's smooth, confident voice like I'd never hated anything before. He was being so clever, too, not calling anyone names or using emotional words. His unadorned report of why Karne had selected me showed he didn't intend to antagonize anyone by showing his hate for House Halarek. But then he didn't need to. That hatred had been going on for three or four generations.

"Then if I may play a tape . . . ?" Lord Richard bowed to Chairman Reed.

Reed nodded. Lord Richard pointed his ringed hand at one of his relatives. "One of my aides, acting on my orders, searched the quarters of First Merchant Sam Tremo."

There was a sort of horrified murmur in the Council chamber. A lord of the Nine had dared to invade a Gildhall!

Lord Richard ignored the sound. "Among the First Merchant's belongings was a very interesting tape, which I'll now play for you. We're passing the sound through a translit because the tape was recorded in Fruvan, which is nearly as good as a cipher."

I sat frozen as my own words incriminated me.

"Sam, my love, call for off-world help. Karne should be dead. Will you see to it?"

Disbelief, then terrible pain wrenched Karne's face. Everything inside me twisted. He was betrayed again, by another wife, after he had broken all his own rules and let himself love me. The reality of tri-d doubled my helpless anguish. I ached to reassure him, to explain that this was a horrible distortion of the truth.

"I don't know that you've told anyone, my lord," the duke continued, "but you *were* wounded by an assassin just about a month ago, weren't you?"

The deaconesses near me inched away. They believed Lord Richard's implication.

I would not let these women see my pain, any more than Karne was letting the Council see his. But I wept inside.

The Council chamber hung in deadly silence for an age, then exploded into sound. Chairman Reed pounded and pounded for order. At last the noise quieted to a mutter.

"I know it ain't none of it true," Donna whispered quickly in my ear.

"Is that the Larga's voice, Lord Karne?" Reed did not look as if he had any pleasure in the question.

Karne, love, don't believe Richard, no matter what "evidence" he presents!

Karne's voice came low and hoarsely. "Aye."

"Louder, milord," the Marquis of Gormsby sneered.

Reed asked gently, "Do you accept this as proof of her involvement in a conspiracy, Lord Karne?"

Karne slammed the prep table with his fist. "No! By the Four Guardians, no!" His voice was low and frighteningly intense.

"Never! Not in a thousand years! She's not like that. She couldn't do it. No Fruvan could." He shook his head as if to clear it and whispered, "She *wouldn't* do that."

Richard smirked. "May I bring witnesses, Frem Chairman?"

Reed nodded and the duke brought out witnesses—witnesses to my visits to Sam, witnesses to Tommy's constant companionship. Lord Richard brought to the stand servants who'd seen me go into Ontar with Tommy, Halarek soldiers who told about our horseback riding and schlakball together. Then Lord Richard called Tommy himself, who had to be reminded of his duty under the law first, and made him admit we had gone to the Gildhall twice, that he'd seen Tremo take my hand in a familiar way, that the First Merchant and I had talked in a language he couldn't understand. Then a Harlan soldier came forward and swore he'd seen Tremo enter the Retreat House where I was living.

The moment that soldier resumed his seat behind the Harlan table, Richard turned to the Council. "I sent men to arrest Tremo yesterday," he told the Council. "Unfortunately, he resisted arrest, was seriously injured, and is unable to be here today. But the two soldiers who arrested him can testify."

The two soldiers swore that Tremo admitted speaking to me in Fruvan so Tommy wouldn't know our plans, that we'd been friendly on Fruhe, that he'd visited me at the Retreat. I wondered what the Gild would do about this drastic violation of its neutrality. I wondered what Richard had had to do to Sam to force him to lie. I felt quite sure Sam had not been injured while being arrested, but later.

Lord Richard next presented pieces of evidence given him by "a friend of Starker IV"—the Gild receipt for the Rom tapes, the letter I once thought Weisman had sent to my family, the letter from my mother. Lord Richard then called Lady Agnes, Jaklene, and Tamara to testify. Each lady eventually admitted seeing me close myself into the Lharr's room to write a letter, alone, the day the two of us returned from Zinn.

"To whom was this letter going?" Richard asked each of them.

Each answered, "I don't know."

Richard leaned closer. "She didn't say, nor did she read it to you?"

"No, milord, but—"

"That's all, thank you. Next."

Richard patted each woman comfortingly on the arm as she left the stand and the green stone in his ring flashed with every pat.

Harlan green. The death of House Halarek.

Tamara was the last. She looked across the room pleadingly at Karne as she left the witness box.

Karne stood and faced the chairman. "That night she sent a letter to me." His voice was clear, but shaking a little.

"You'll get your turn," the duke said smoothly. "Next witness."

Weisman took the box. He trembled visibly.

"Tell the Council, Frem Weisman, what you did the night the Lharr and Larga returned from their mountain trip."

" 'Mountain trip'!" I couldn't help blurting.

"SHHHH!" the rest of the Retreat hissed.

Weisman wet his lips. "I went to the Gildhall, milord."

"Why?"

"The Larga gave me a letter. She said it was very important. It had to go right away."

"Who was the letter for, Frem Weisman?"

"I—I don't know, milord."

Richard clucked disbelievingly. "Come, come, sir. Your 'curiosity' is notorious. Don't tell us you didn't even look at the address."

Weisman glanced at Karne, at the duke, at Chairman Reed, at Karne again. He licked his lips. "It was addressed to Pieter Verlith, Gildhall, Fruhe-base, milord."

"The liar! The miserable little liar!" I shook my fist at the weasely little man.

The deaconesses turned en masse and gave me an angry stare.

"Tell us who Pieter Verlith is, Frem Weisman."

Weisman licked his lips. "Her brother, milord. He called her from his starship one night, offering to take her home. I know because I brought the message to her."

I wondered how Weisman knew that, since he had been unable to learn either of the galactic languages. And if he had had the conversation translated, why he didn't mention my refusal to go.

Richard turned smoothly toward the ranks of benches containing the men of the Nine. "Her brother captains a starship, Councilmen. One such ship could land an army larger than any two of us here have. The offer to take her home had to have been a code for something else, since she's still here. That's all, Frem Weisman."

So, Weisman hadn't told Lord Richard about the refusal, either. Or he hadn't heard it. Or Lord Richard chose to skip over it.

Karne's eyes were yellow flames in his pale face. He chewed his lower lip and ran a shaking hand through his hair. That familiar gesture pulled away what few tatters of pride I still protected myself with. He was betrayed and trapped and it was my fault.

Weisman had left the stand, but he stopped in the aisle beside Karne. "Milord?"

Karne looked up at that pleading tone.

"Milord, I didn't want to tell. Truly. I wouldn't have violated your trust, except that he"—he pointed a shaking finger at the duke—"threatened my sister and her child if I didn't tell the truth. Please, milord . . ."

Karne nodded wearily and Weisman hurried out of the room.

Lord Richard had witnesses in the dozens and the bits and pieces they gave totaled a convincing story. Karne sat with frozen face and watched his dreams and reputation crumble. The minor witnesses had been called to add plausibility to the evidence of Weisman and the witnesses before him. When the duke's parade was done, Chairman Reed called a recess, which only prolonged my agony.

Such a skillful frame. Would anyone believe me after it? Would Karne? How could he? The whole case was aimed at the prejudices of Gharr males—ownership of the female, anger at female faithlessness—and at the fear of off-world contacts.

Chairman Reed strode back down the aisle through the Freemen's section to his desk and rapped the session to order.

Karne rose. "I request that an impartial expert, Freeman or Gild, examine the tape."

Reed nodded. "Granted. Isn't it, milord Duke?"

Richard bowed with elaborate courtesy to the chairman. "Of course, honorable Chairman. He won't find any splices in it. That's what he's hinting."

"Thank you, milord." Karne bowed with elaborate, mocking courtesy to Lord Richard. He turned to the rest of the chamber and his voice was brittle. "May I assume the tape is the most damning evidence in your eyes, lords and Freemen?"

Heads nodded and a murmur of assent filled the room.

"Then I request that, until the genuine, untampered state of the recording has been proven, all the remaining evidence be considered explainable and innocent."

The muttering that followed this attested to the thoroughness of the duke's presentation.

"That's a lot to ask, milord," a lord of one of the minor Houses protested.

"The sworn testimony—" began one of the older men on the Justin back benches.

Karne held up a hand. The protestors quieted. "But it's all circumstantial testimony, testimony my lady could counter, were she here." He paused, looking down at the surface of the Halarek table. When he looked up again, the lines in his face had drawn tighter. "If you are unwilling to do that, at least divide the charge. Separate the evidence that appears to come from the Larga's own lips from the evidence that comes through milord duke and his spies. You know Lord Richard believes he has good reasons to hate me and might, in trying to destroy me, slant evidence."

"We know about the blood feud, Lord Karne," Reed's voice cut in, dryly.

"Let's put the separation to a vote," shouted someone on the back benches of Gormsby.

"Aye."

"Aye."

"Aye."

"Gentlemen, gentlemen." Reed rapped for order and the tri-d view shifted to him. "All among the Families in favor of separation, please stand."

The Old Party lacked one of defeating the call for separation.

The Earl of Justin rose. "Frem Chairman, I protest the vote of the Duke of Druma. He's under a charge of murder and should have no vote."

Chairman Reed stared at Justin for a long moment. "Your point is well taken, milord. The Duke of Druma's vote will be stricken." Reed glanced at the clerk to be sure it was done. Then he looked slowly around the entire chamber. "Freemen and minor Houses, weigh the choices. They're more important than they look."

The counted vote split the Freemen and minor Houses evenly. The tension in the Council chamber, and in the Retreat, was tangible. I held my breath, not understanding the point of the issue at all, and watched Chairman Reed. If he voted with the Old Party, whatever Karne was working so carefully, so desperately for would be ruined and we would die in Richard's trap.

The chairman laid his gavel on his desk and looked right into Karne's eyes. "I vote with Halarek."

Karne wobbled and rested a hand against the edge of the table to steady himself. For the first time, a little color crept into his face. He raised his head and with a glimmer of hope in his golden eyes, he looked straight out at me. I thought my heart would stop. I clutched at Kit.

"I promised him you'd watch this, no matter what it took to get you here," Kit murmured.

Karne turned back to the chamber. "You can't know my thanks, Frem Chairman." He pinned the duke with a look. "Richard, your 'evidence' today, except, perhaps, for the tape, is all circumstantial. But this isn't the first time you've tried to cast doubt on my lady's honor. Many here remember that the first time any of you met the Larga, at Justin's hunt, Lord Richard made sly implications about my lady's faithfulness to me. I challenged him then, but he arranged that no tourney took place. You know how he evaded my challenges after that. A man with a just cause doesn't run from judicial combat, Richard."

Richard turned white with fury and opened his mouth to speak. I sensed there was a subtle insult in being addressed without his title. Karne turned to Reed and continued.

"By right, I may be my lady's champion and challenge Richard of Harlan to prove his charges in battle." At the chairman's small nod of agreement, Karne turned, stretched out his arm, and pointed directly at the duke. "Richard, Duke of Harlan, I, Karne, Lharr Halarek, name you coward and liar and challenge you to prove your charges on my body, *à outrance*."

Utter silence.

Richard went whiter and his hands clenched against his sides. House Halarek was not yet ruined, he could not evade this challenge, and there was a slight chance he would not survive such a duel. He had well and truly cornered Karne Halarek, but he had not, apparently, sufficiently considered all the consequences of so cornering him.

Chairman Reed cleared his throat. "It *is* your right, Lord Karne. If the duke wins, his charges are considered proven."

Karne stood a little straighter. "I know that, Frem Chairman. Most of you already think them so. If I don't fight, my lady and I die anyway. This way, at least, I die a man."

Another long silence. Then Reed pounded on his desk. "This session of the Council is adjourned, the Duke of Harlan, the Lharr Halarek, and their aides excepted."

The screen went blank, but the image of the emptying chamber with Karne, Richard, Gormsby, Tommy, Emil von Schuss, and the Lharr Odonnel standing with Reed in its center stayed with me for long seconds afterward. I felt drained. I was sure I couldn't move. But I was just as sure I couldn't endure one moment longer the cold scrutiny of the deaconesses who remained in the room and who made no attempts to lower their voices as they discussed what they had seen.

"The Lharr's such a good man. It's too bad he has to die this way."

"Aye, he made a bad mistake, marrying that woman with her newfangled ideas and bullheaded ways."

"The duke's killed a lot of men?"

"Aye, more's the pity. Youngsters many of them."

"Halarek's no youngster."

"Well, I still don't think he has much of a chance. I've seen the duke in a tourney."

"Then why would he have avoided duel before?"

"The duke isn't one to take risks unnecessarily."

I could bear no more. I stumbled to my feet. "I'm going to my room," I muttered to Kit. "Come when you can." I ran clumsily out the door, accidentally brushing against two lay workers as I went.

"Humph!" one snorted.

"I wonder if Alba'll let the tourney tri-d here," the other said.

The hall tilted and I pressed against the wall. Karne had chosen to die fighting and the battle would be watched for *amusement*!

Karne, Karne, what have I done to you? Why was I so blind?

My room was only a little distance away, but the floor kept swinging crazily. I inched along the wall until I reached my door and pushed blindly through it. I dropped onto the bed and tried to close myself in protective concentration, but I was too upset.

Think! I told myself. Think! You've got to get home.

Dear God, if Richard kills him, what will I do with myself?

Steady, you're going off again. Think about flitters, think about slowing your heart, think about careful breathing, think about the soldiers out there . . .

"Larga Zjhanne, Larga Zjhanne." Donna shook me. "We couldn't come faster. What're we goin' to do?"

I looked past Donna to Kit.

Kit took a deep breath. "You know that by custom you should be there to watch him fight. But we also know we'll do well if we get you past Harlan's guards and into the flitter before dawn, let alone to Council ground by then."

"Dawn." I put my hands over my face. There was so little time and so many soldiers outside. How could we escape? Yet to see Karne cut, burned, bleeding, dying—

"Kit, what does *à outrance* mean?"

"Essentially, 'to the death.' One or both, it doesn't matter. One must die."

I couldn't stop myself from asking, "Will it be Karne?"

Kit looked away. "I can hope not, pray not, but Richard is well practiced and Karne's left side is still stiff from the assassin's burning. It would take an extraordinary effort for him and I don't know whether he has that now. What does he have left to fight for? The holding's broken up, the Family separated, and he has barely enough money to feed the staff, even after selling off a lot of land and orak to keep things going. Harlan's had all our exports embargoed and the local price for orak isn't very good. Karne doesn't even believe he has you anymore." Kit looked at me again, her eyes bright with unshed tears. "Yes, I think he'll die."

Everything was coming too fast. I writhed inside trying to bear the blows, but they came so fast, so fast. In less than an hour my careful emotional conclusions about betrayal and desertion had been shattered, then reversed. *Karne* was the one betrayed and deserted.

"Kit, don't fling these little bits at me. I can't stand it. I wrote and wrote and cried and cried and Karne didn't reply. What was I to think except that he'd left me here to rot?"

Kit shook her head. "I can't understand what went wrong, but the results are too good for Richard for it to be an accident." She glanced nervously at her chrono. "I'll tell you what's been happening after we leave. We have to think of a way out of here. Soon."

"But the assassin they talked about. What about the assassin?"

"He escaped through a moving bookcase, just like you said Tane's murderer did. So far nobody's found how to make it open."

Richard's man, or men, in our house. And Karne was there alone. Karne was not only going to be killed, he was going to be shamed and disgraced first, and it was all my fault. Without my self-concern, Richard would have no charges to humiliate Halarek with. He would have had to fight Karne on some basis more closely tied to his own honor.

"Kit"—a whisper was all I could manage—"after what I've done to him, can he still love me?"

"Let him tell you." Kit handed me a recorder with a tape case already in it. "He made this last night, hoping that you wouldn't ignore it, as he thinks you did the others, if *I* brought it."

My hands trembled so much that at first I couldn't slide the play-back switch. At last the reel began turning.

His voice. After so long without hope.

"Dearest Zjhanne, why don't you answer my letters? Why won't you come home? Did you say you loved me only for revenge? I deserved it—" Karne's voice broke and there was a pause on the tape. "If you're so afraid of having a child with me, I'll name a cousin heir. Only come home! I need you."

CHAPTER 20

Joy and grief and an increased urgency about getting home hit me all at once. "He still loves me!" I whispered.

I had to go to him. But there was no point in asking the abbess for permission to leave. Alba's rigid, legalistic mind would demand a letter with Karne's seal making a formal request for my return to Ontar. And even if by some miracle Kit and I could persuade the abbess to give permission herself, I had no reason to believe Harlan's soldiers would honor it. Yet Kit had gotten in.

I turned to my sister-in-law. "Kit, the truce is long over. How were you allowed out of Ontar? Or into here?"

"Councilman Duval got safe-conducts for us. But there are only two. Besides, once you're recognized, your chances of getting to Ontar are nil. You'll be held for execution."

I looked out at the empty plains. "And if I stay here?"

"Council troops, or Richard's, will come for you after the duel."

After the duel. When Karne was dead. Never to hold me in his arms again. Then I would be executed. Death for both of us on circumstantial and manufactured evidence. I straightened my back and squared my shoulders. If I were doomed no matter what I did, I would be with my husband, or as near him as I could get.

I turned back to the room. "Donna, does your safe-conduct have your picture on it?"

Donna fumbled with the wallet hanging from her belt and pulled out her safe-conduct. She looked at it carefully. "No, milady. It's just for 'serf woman, servant to Lady Kathryn von Schuss.' Least that's what the soldier read as we was comin' in."

I took the little woman's hand and willed her to look up. "Donna, I ask a favor of you. It's too dangerous for me to order you to do it. Will you change clothes with me and stay here in my place? In my habit, if you stay in the room most of the time, you ought to be safe for a few days. If we live, my lord and I will bring you home before that. If we don't, you may have some unpleasant times. Lord Richard may even kill you."

I glanced at Kit, who nodded agreement. I looked at Donna again. Donna understood. I let go of her hand, so not to exert even that little coercion. "It's a big gamble for you, Donna, because the duke has all the advantages. No one believes either the Lharr or I will be alive tomorrow."

Donna fell on her knees and kissed my hand. "Larga Zjhanne, I'd do anythin' for you. Even if they was to tear me limb from limb. You and the Lharr are the first people that treated me like I had feelin's."

Hot with embarrassment, I extricated my hand. "If we live, you'll be a Freewoman, Donna."

We exchanged clothes then. I looked at myself critically in the room's small, foggy mirror. "I'm taller than Donna, Kit. Will the guards notice?"

Kit's mouth twisted wryly. "Well, one of them did comment on how cute she was . . ."

"We'll have to wait, then, till the guard changes at 1800. It'll be nearly dark by that time, too."

And my love will be hours nearer to death and I still so far away!

Kit made a small relieved sound. "That's one reason to be glad winter's begun again, that darkness will help hide the change. No one usually notices a serf, but it's best to be safe. And if we then fly without lights, Lord Richard's men on the holding won't see us until we're dropping through the pad gates." She turned to the maid. "Donna, help your lady with that turban."

It's true, what I'd read, that people didn't notice serfs. I myself had never noticed how different a serf's headdress was from everyone else's, so I couldn't wind it on properly. Donna had to make the peculiar folds for me.

At last I was dressed. I turned slowly all the way around for the others to inspect her. "Will I pass?"

"Well . . ." Kit frowned. "You have sort of let yourself go to pot."

It was a moment before I saw the tired twinkle in Kit's eyes.

"It will probably drop off after a month or two at home, though, won't it?" Kit added.

"Oh, Kit!" I hugged her. "I wrote Karne, but until now no one knew."

The humor vanished from Kit's face. "No one except the person who snags your letters, and Richard."

That sobered me, too. I dropped my arms and stepped back. "Yes. Except for them."

Kit eyed me carefully. "You really do look out of proportion, though."

I pulled out a generous handful of the dress's bodice. I hadn't realized I'd lost so much weight. "What if I stuff this some?"

They tried a towel inside.

"If you slump, you'll pass," Kit finally decided.

The sun now hung low, but it was still several hours until its last light would fade. We spent those hours in silence, each of us locked in her own thoughts. I hated every minute of inactivity, every second that separated me from Karne.

He still loved me!

At last, with horn-blowing and shouting, the shifts changed outside. My tension increased, but I felt relieved, too. At last I could do something. I reminded Donna for the last time to keep her hood up and her face averted whenever she had to leave the room and to take occasional walks along the walls, in full sight of the Harlan patrols. Then Kit and I ventured out into the quiet hallway. Everyone else was at chapel or getting ready for the nightmeal.

Slump, I reminded myself. Walk slowly and a little behind Kit. Keep your head down humbly.

Kit walked very slowly. My every cell cried to her to hurry, but I bit back my impatience, knowing that Kit had strained her endurance to its limit just to come. Hours it seemed we walked through the hall, down the stairs, and out the main door. Step by slow step we walked across the empty courtyard to the flitter sheds. With every step in that courtyard, I felt the eyes of the sentries on the walls above us. I waited for one of them to shout an alarm.

We entered the flitter shed at last. A soldier stood watch just inside the door. Kit's flitter was just a few steps beyond him and it carried von Schuss, not Halarek, colors. I hoped we looked more confident than I felt. Kit beckoned imperiously to the soldier. I swallowed the lump that suddenly had appeared in my throat.

"Soldier, assist me into my ship." Kit spoke with the authority of years of ordering people about.

The soldier stepped a pace toward her and saluted smartly. "Sorry, milady. None of the flitters may leave. Council orders."

Kit stiffened and her voice grew icy. "Soldier, I came on safe-conduct, in this ship, this morning. I must be home early tomorrow. Get me your superior."

"Milady—"

"Now!"

"Yes, milady. I mean, no, milady." The soldier saluted and hurried away.

My stomach clenched with apprehension. This arrogance wasn't like Kit. I was sure she was overdoing it. What if the sentry suspected we weren't supposed to leave? What if he'd seen through my disguise? Was that why he was so long returning? He suspected us? Suspected me? If we were found out—

The appearance of a middle-aged officer with a graying mustache interrupted my spiraling panic. Kit took the offensive at once.

"Sir! This delay is inexcusable! Our Council safe-conduct guarantees passage out whenever I want to go. Even Lord Richard would not go against Council in this way. I wish to leave at once!"

The graying man bowed. "Milady, I regret the inconvenience, but we are at war. May I see your passes, please?"

Kit thrust them at him. He examined them carefully. "They're in order, of course, milady. I'll enable the ship at once. Just a wire disconnected, milady. May I assist you onto the wing?"

He lifted her onto the flitter, then climbed onto the wing, leaving me to struggle onto it as best I could. I shouldn't have been surprised. Of *course*, he would never even consider helping a *servant*.

And I had to struggle. Luckily, the officer's attention was on the small wire that had been disconnected to keep the flitter on the ground and not on the maid whose bulk shifted and squashed suspiciously as she pulled herself onto the flitter. The wire took forever for the officer to find and then fix.

Finish! I cried at him inside my head. Get it done and get out of here! It's hours already before we can get home. Karne may die without knowing—

Dear God, don't let him die before I can tell him I love him.

The officer finished. He left. I sat in the seat beside Kit, as I could not have done while the officer was with us. The big shed door slid open and two soldiers carefully rolled the flitter out, taking their sweet time getting out of blast range afterward. The engine coughed and died, coughed and died. I was beside myself. Kit sat back for a moment, took a deep breath, then tried again. This time the engine coughed, sputtered, and settled to a businesslike hum. The flitter lifted and I went limp. The first step on our long trip back. I looked down at my hands. While my mind had been occupied with worrying, my hands had been shredding a section of hemline.

Kit adjusted a few instruments slightly, then reclined her seat. Her skin seemed transparent. Her eyes closed, and she lay there so quietly that I wondered if she were still conscious.

Kit spoke, without opening her eyes. "Karne's lost so much. You are his life, but the child will be a comfort to him." Then she remembered the isolation I had been living in. "But you don't know, do you? The manor house is all we still hold, and that's precarious." She shifted with the soft shushing of cloth against the contours of the seat. "We're finished without the Freemen and they still refuse to see what will happen to them if Richard takes Halarek. Because it involves Family honor and Family feud, they believe they can stay out of the quarrel. They didn't even examine the quality of Richard's 'evidence' against Karne! I keep praying they'll wake up. Just four days ago, serfs rioted in Londor, a freecity near Odonnel Holding, and killed about a hundred and fifty Freemen and their families, as well as some of Odonnel's worthless kin. If that doesn't convince them—"

She reached over and laid her hand on my arm. "But I've told you too much bad news already." She patted me, then returned her hand to her lap. She sighed. "Try to get some sleep, Zjhanne. Tomorrow will be easier to face if you're not worn out."

I pulled the towel out of my front and reclined the seat, knowing it would be next to impossible for me to rest. Always images of Karne dying or Karne dead spun through my head the moment I closed my eyes. Dead.

I looked over at Kit. "If Karne wanted me home, why didn't he come for me?"

Kit snorted. "You know a little thing like a war wouldn't have stopped him, if he'd been sure of you. But he wasn't sure. He was afraid, I think, that after the awful things he'd said to you, you'd refuse to see him. He couldn't have taken that. Then, later, there were the threats of charges of treason and then the charges themselves. You were safer in the Retreat."

Kit's voice dragged with drowsiness. She snuggled into the seat cushions, then sat bolt upright. "Thinking of those charges makes me think of Richard. It's only four hours to dawn. I'm going to take some revenge now, while I'm alive to enjoy it. I owe it to him. By the Four Guardians, I owe it to him!"

She sent a vary-frequency call to House Harlan and insisted on speaking to Lord Richard himself.

The Harlan com officer looked at her coldly. "I'm sorry, madam, but his lordship is resting for the tourney. He does not wish to be disturbed."

"Wake him!" Kit snapped. "This is not a message to be delivered to a minion. This is urgent and he'll have your hide when he finds out I wanted to speak to him and you didn't call him."

The com officer hesitated, clearly torn between orders and fear of the punishment that would fall upon him if Kit were right. But he tried to keep up a pretense of hauteur. "Whom may I say is calling?"

"The Lady Kathryn von Schuss."

The man gasped and disappeared. In a few minutes the rumpled, handsome face of Richard of Harlan came onto our viewer.

"My would-be lover awakens," Kit said softly, but not so softly that Richard could not hear her.

Richard stared at her in silence for a minute or two.

"You're ready to come to me now your holding's lost, Kathryn?"

Kit's mocking laugh would have decimated the ego of a less confident man. "Dream on, Richard."

"Your brother's withdrawing and didn't have the guts to tell me himself, then." Richard spoke as flatly as if his wish were fact.

Kit smiled at him sweetly. "On the contrary, you failed lover of Halarek women. Karne doesn't know I'm talking to you. No, I wanted to tell you our good news all by myself."

Richard's face lost its arrogance. It even reddened, which surprised me. Kit was taunting him, not only with his attempt to rape her, but with the brief time Karne's second wife had been his lover before she returned to Karne. I was very glad we were far from the duke's reach.

Kit's voice went on, relentless, gloating. "The Larga and I, and Karne's son, are returning to Halarek Holding, Richard, though perhaps not to Ontar. You know the Council won't even consider executing the Larga, if it even comes to that, until *after* Karne's heir is born. Halarek Holding still won't be yours, milord." She laughed insolently at the fury that convulsed Richard's face. "Sleep well, milord."

She switched off, then sat forward and studied her reflection in the window. After several seconds she said softly, "Kathryn, I didn't know you had such meanness in you." She lay back, sighed contentedly, and closed her eyes again.

I squirmed until I found a comfortable position for sleeping. Death haunted my dreams, death as it never was on Fruhe, death that was painful and bloody and violent. I saw Council soldiers forcing me to attend the duel. I saw a parade of killings—Nik, Orkonan, Kit, Jemmy, Tommy, Baron von Schuss, Karne. Over and over I saw them die, horribly.

Would they really have made me watch Karne duel, knowing how such an ordeal would affect a Fruvan? I couldn't even face the *thought* of his death? How, then, could I sit beside Karne's body? And I would have to. The Gharr hold wakes. A wake would set memories of cold, rigid features and a stiff body among the memories of his smile and grace and glowing eyes.

I can't do it. I can't!

"Father-of-all, Karne is young, and he has so many dreams," I finally whispered. "Don't let him die."

But I knew God seldom made miracles and it would take a miracle to save an injured and defeated Karne from the expert duelist who was his opponent.

A shrill alarm startled me out of my thoughts and I was grateful. Kit stirred and fumbled groggily across the control panel.

"Sensor alarm. Almost to the shield," she mumbled.

Kit turned off the alarm and sat forward to look out the window, then she patted her cheeks briskly for a few seconds. When she turned on the communicator and spoke softly into it, her voice was wider awake. "Hello, the House. Hello the House. Is anyone there? This is Cat. I repeat, this is Cat. Is anyone there?"

A half-sun hung red on the horizon and sent thin shafts of light across the faces of the mountains. The silence from the house made that glow seem ominous. Dawn meant Karne was now fighting for his life, and for mine.

At last a very young voice answered. "We read you, Cat. You'd best stay out. The shield fell for a few minutes an hour ago and some Harlan men got in through the skylight. They're hitting us hard. You'll be safer in the hills."

Kit flipped the "wait" switch, which shut off our signal. "Which will it be, Zjhanne, house or hills?"

"What will they—what will happen to Karne?"

Kit rubbed fingers slowly across her cheekbones. "It's his right to be brought home for burial, win or lose."

Burial. Death. Dead, whether he won or lost. Death coming at me from all sides. I was suffocating in it. "Doesn't the victor survive, either?"

"*À outrance* isn't like an ordinary tourney. If the first round kills no one, the men change weapons and go at each other again. After several changes . . ." Kit choked and shook her head and turned away. "Don't count on seeing him alive, Zjhanne. It'll be easier if you don't. I know."

She was talking about Nik. I felt dizzy with fear.

Lord, Lord, help me. I have to be able to think. To be a widow before I've been truly a wife—give me the strength to do what I must this day.

I waited until I had some sort of control over my panic, ragged though that control was, before I spoke. "I want to be with him, Kit." *I want to be with him, but I don't know that I have the courage.*

"I hoped you'd say that." Kit turned the "wait" switch off. "Clear us to come in."

"Aye, milady." The young voice was reluctant. "But you really shouldn't. I'll open the doors when you're directly overhead. Longer than that and Harlan men'll be jumping in."

I looked down. Huge holes and small, smoking craters dotted the plains and the lower slopes of the foothills. The manor garden had ceased to exist. I decided the shelling must have been aimed at retreating Halarek soldiers, because no weapon could penetrate the house. Only starvation or treachery could do that. Tiny figures in Harlan green and Odonnel's black and white checks swarmed around and among the holes.

The flitter dropped lower. Here and there I thought I saw spots of red. I shook my head. It must be the sun reflecting from something. Then the flitter was over the pad doors. The air below shimmered for a moment. When it cleared, a deep-blue oval seemed suspended in the air above the manor. The shield was open. The pad doors slid apart and the flitter floated down the shaft. After it had set down, the door to the com center slid open and the young soldier who had spoken to us walked quickly toward us. He saluted, then turned to me, extending his hand. In his palm lay a heavy ring set with a green, green stone out of which a gold snake curled.

"I found this on the shield controls, Larga. I thought it might be the Lharr's. He stopped in as he left to say goodbye."

How like Karne, I thought as I accepted the ring. On his way to his last fight, he stops to say goodbye to the men who've served his House.

I glanced at the ring, then closed my hand on it. "It's not the Lharr's, soldier, but thank you. It looks valuable. I'll see that it's returned to its owner."

The young man saluted again and went back into the com center. Kit moved slowly toward the door into the manor house and I followed. Our heels echoed loudly in the empty pad. No sentry stood at the door. Inside, no soldiers patrolled the hall. I stopped, suspicious. This was not the way Halarek was run.

"Where is everyone?"

Kit looked around. She rubbed the back of her neck, weariness in every line of her. "They were here when I left. Maybe the house has been evacuated since."

"But would the com center still be manned then?" It didn't seem logical. "Why don't you find an empty room here in the servants' hall and rest, Kit? You can't move fast enough to risk wandering around where there are no Halarek guards."

Kit nodded weary agreement and turned slowly down the corridor.

"Who's in charge now, Kit?"

Kit stopped and looked over her shoulder at me. "Well, Wynter's in charge of our defense, Tommy's seconding Karne at the duel, so I suppose Weisman is in charge of the servants and Captain Gregg of the soldiers that are left here. Weisman and Gareth took over the work you and I used to do."

I thought of Karne, and of Weisman at the trial, and took a deep, shuddering breath.

Kit looked at me with concern. "Take care of yourself, Zjhanne. There's still Karne's child to live for." She turned and moved slowly away.

My heart cried for her, who no longer had even her son.

I walked quickly to the lift, pressed the call button, and waited for the lift to come down. When the door slid open, I stepped in, touched the button for level 5, and turned out the light. Level 5 was probably Harlan's goal, too, so I would have to be extra careful, because the child's bulk eliminated most of my speed and agility. The lift stopped silently and let me out.

I entered our suite through my ladies' sleeping room, just because it was the closest door. Someone had hurriedly searched the room. The door from it to my old room was closed. I moved quietly and leaned lightly against the door, listening. Everything was quiet. I put my hand on the latch. Something clanked metallically on the other side. Weapons? If so, whose?

I lifted the latch very carefully and opened the door a hair. Through the crack I saw Harlan green. I swallowed hard and shut the door more carefully than I'd opened it. My heart beat so loudly as I backed away that I was sure the soldiers could hear it if they were listening. I slipped into the hall and hurried back to the lift, but not quickly enough. As the lift door slid shut, I caught a glimpse of a green uniform and the uniform a glimpse of me.

"Halt th—" The door amputated the soldier's shout, but through the little window in the lift door I saw his mouth still moving.

I punched "2" and "lock," so no one else could stop the lift. Could the soldier run downstairs faster than the lift could travel? Would he be waiting for me below?

When the lift stopped, I looked through the little window. I saw no one. I touched the "open" switch and looked out into the hall. For the moment I was alone, but I wouldn't be for long. I thought of Kit and decided not to risk looking for her. It would be better if Harlan's men knew of only one woman loose in the manor. The pad door stood ajar, unguarded still. Where were our Blues? I hadn't heard even sounds of fighting. And what could I do now? I had to get out of the manor. No, I would check the clinic first. Not even Harlan could stop the Council from bringing Karne home. I would think no more about what the sight of my dying, or dead, husband would do to me. If there was any life left in him, he had to know I loved him still.

I walked cautiously past the kitchen. It lay silent, without even lingering odors. The 'ponics workers were gone from the 'ponics sheds, too, something that never happened. And where were the Blues patrols? Surely, even in the short time I had been in the house, I should have seen or at least heard one patrol! The funereal emptiness of the house frightened me. It could only mean the house was no longer ours at all. The comtech was still there because he was safe in his locked room. I was on my own. There would be no rescue if I ran afoul of Lord Richard's men.

I passed the main lift and stood in the open door to the clinic. Beds, equipment, and machines stood as they always had, but here, too, there was not one human being, neither injured nor staff.

Around the corner to my left, I heard the faint hum of the lift starting. I went to the corner and looked down the hall. A demand light blinked angrily from level 5. Harlan's men were on level 5. I swallowed, then licked dry lips. It would be only minutes before they were also on level 2, looking for me. Every muscle in me tightened with fear. Where could I go? Not into the warren of the manor's servants' quarters; I could too easily be trapped. But, if Harlan men held the Lharr's suite, House Harlan controlled the upper levels already. The comtech had told me the shield had fallen, briefly, and Harlan soldiers had come in through the conservatory skylight. Of course they held the upper levels. Unless the spy in the house had also let them in some other way. There was always the spy to consider.

The lift began descending. Its blinking light indicated it was at level 4. I had to leave before they arrived. My brain raced, but I couldn't think of a safe place. The flitter was still on the pad, of course, but I didn't know how to fly it. I couldn't run upstairs to hide and there were no staff and no Blues to protect me where I was. I cursed the Gharr Families and their bloody feuds. Lord Richard would destroy me if he caught me, just because I carried House Halarek's heir and I didn't know how to save myself or the baby.

The lift light blinked for level 3. I could almost feel that lift, full of Harlan soldiers, descending. I had to hide, somewhere. I once had promised Karne I wouldn't let Lord Richard catch me. There was only the city left to me, and that, too, was probably Harlan controlled. There were many bolt-holes in the city, though.

I ran down the stairs to level 1 and the running made me acutely aware of the difference the baby made. I had no speed at all. I ran by the stables and Gordie nickered a greeting. I turned a corner. There was the row of colored doors I remembered. I stopped in front of them. Which one? Which one had Tommy said led into Ontar? For one terrible moment I couldn't remember anything. I heard men shouting, back where the lift was. I shut my eyes, trying to remember the day Tommy had shown me this level. The black door. It had been the black door.

Please, God, let it be open!

I turned the knob, pushed, and stumbled into a dark stair landing. I shut the door quietly and stood against it, waiting for my eyes to adjust to the darkness. Men began pounding on the doors at the far end of the corridor. Even through the thick plastex I could hear their rough voices shouting and the boom of their fists. I licked dry lips. Luckily they had come around the other end of the hall.

The stair ran straight down into darkness.

CHAPTER 21

A faint glowing line outlined the door at the foot of the stair. I hesitated only a moment. Whatever the cause of that strange light, I had to go down the stairs and open the door. I felt my way carefully down the rough and uneven stairs. House Halarek didn't seem to feel a pleasant entrance was necessary for tradesmen and serfs.

The glow was from the strange, cold "night" light of the alley on the other side of the door, let through by the poor fit of door to frame. The narrow alley was littered with paper scraps and unidentifiable bits of other refuse. Deep shadows around trash bins and in doorways could have concealed most of a squad of soldiers.

Four or five meters to my right, the alley ended in a blank wall. As I watched, a large rat scurried from one shadowed corner to the other. I saw no people. I couldn't ask the way to the Gildhall and its protection, then, and in moments Lord Richard's men would burst through the black door above in pursuit. I stepped into the alley and walked to my left. I dared not spend what energy I had left running until I had to. The faint swish of my dress and the rustle of rats in the trash were the only sounds. Then I heard male voices and heavy feet on the stair.

I hurried to the street at the end of the alley, turned onto it, and ducked into the nearest deep doorway. I waited in the shadows, heart pounding. The men came closer with the brilliant glare of Torches and the slap and clank of jostled weapons—the careless noisiness of confident men. I pulled myself as far into the shadows as I could, held my breath, looked away from the street, and prayed for invisibility. The men passed. The light that lingered behind them revealed the green of their uniforms. I waited until sounds and light had faded.

"You 'nt want to meet 'em either, eh, missy?"

I jumped and cried out. A shriveled old man had materialized at my elbow.

He put a bony hand on my arm. " 's only old Bill. 'e won't 'urt you. Been too much 'urt 'isself. You better get outta sight, though,'cause they'd do more'n just kill a pretty woman like you." He squinted up at me. "Why're you out? All 'ouse people was warned but old Bill. 'e was in town, worse luck."

"I—" I remembered my serf's clothing just in time. "Nobody told me, either, and now I can't go back."

"Where's your man? 'is job's to protect you, you almost a mother an' all."

My man. *Dear Lord of all, do I still have a man?* "He—He would if he could, but he's fighting now."

"With the Council or with the Lharr?"

"The Council?"

"You 'aven't seen the red uniforms yet? They showed up this morning."

"Who do they fight for?"

"Old Bill didn't stay to ask. Bill'd be with the Lharr, though, if 'e weren't so twisted an' old. 'e don't like 'arlan at all, racked 'im for stealin' bread for 'is kids,'arlan did. Old Bill run away here and 'id till 'e was free." The old man shrugged his skinny shoulders and began walking away. Then he stopped. "Old Bill's got eats at 'ome. You 'n' the youngin're welcome, if we don't get nailed on the way. When'd you last eat?"

"Sunset yesterday."

"The Guardians 'ave mercy!" The old man beckoned me after him and hobbled off.

I followed and was later glad for it: Several times we met Harlan soldiers, who apparently took me for Old Bill's daughter or wife. The soldiers passed the two of us without a second glance. No one else was abroad in the city. Everyone had followed the orders to get away from the manor.

The effects of fear and hunger slowed my feet and my brain, my stomach grumbled rudely, and I began realizing how little rest I'd had between nightmares on the flight home. "Is it much farther, Bill?"

" 's just outside the manor walls, missy, only a little way."

He turned into a narrow, damp alley and passed through to the dingy street beyond. I wondered absently as we passed them if the rusted gates between the manor and the city could still be closed. Not far from the alley Old Bill shoved open a sagging wooden door and hobbled inside.

"Come in, come in." He motioned impatiently. "Ain't safe to stand outside."

I stooped and entered. The room smelled musty and old. A pile of coals on the other side of the room showed thin edges of orange and pink. They provided no light. Bill rummaged in the dark, muttering. Then he squeaked quietly in triumph and a few seconds later an ancient oil lamp brightened the room. I lowered myself gingerly onto a battered, dusty box and watched the old man prepare his "eats." This was a side of Gharr life I'd never seen and now I regretted it. Perhaps I could have done something. There was much that needed doing.

Across the room a large gray cat stared at me with slitted yellow eyes. Apparently deciding I wasn't worth noticing, he extended a front paw, spread the toes, and began carefully licking between them.

Some time later, a heavy, greasy smell roused me. Bill was holding out a plate of fried potatoes and beans.

" 'tain't much."

I smiled at him. "It's enough. Thank you."

I began eating, ignoring the hardened, dried food from previous meals that hid under the potatoes. The old man hunkered down by his fire to warm his hands. Smoke rose slowly and vanished into the city's central air-conditioning. Soon Bill's head nodded and he fell asleep. I leaned against the wall and prayed for Karne's life, then wondered if the Lord would listen to a prayer for one man to kill another.

Lord Richard was said to have killed many men in combat. Everyone was sure he'd kill Karne, too. I thought then of Karne's coming back to that empty house to die. He wouldn't be like Fruhe's Old Ones, dying confident that they were loved. He doubted that. I tried to imagine the bitterness of such a homecoming, and the effort made the struggle inside me more painful. Much as I wanted to remember Karne alive and vital, I couldn't let him die wondering or, worse, believing I no longer loved him, had never loved him.

He's already dead, one side of me argued. Everyone says Richard will win. Don't expect to see him alive. Kit told me that. Often neither fighter survives. If he's dead, gone forever, how can anyone expect me to add the frozen lifelessness of his face to my memories of him?

But he doesn't know you love him still, another side argued. He believes you deserted him. Your proof of your love and trust is the child and Karne doesn't know about him.

I'll never get to him. There are too many soldiers between us. And I promised him Richard wouldn't catch me. And the Council wants me for adultery and treason. I have a choice of executions. No. I'll wait with Bill until things settle a little, then I can try to reach the Gildhall. What's the use of running into a trap when it won't help him?

What if he isn't dead? It's a tiny chance, but you can't let him die alone and believing you've betrayed him.

In the end, Karne's belief that I'd betrayed him just like the others became more important than the danger of soldiers, more important than the ghastly memories of his death that would torture me the rest of my life. My comfort of mind later was not more important than any comfort I might be able to give Karne now. He had lived too long without love. As for the death sentences—

I brushed aside the thought. I couldn't afford to be caught. I got up awkwardly. The cat glanced at me and yawned. If—

But there wasn't any point in hoping. "Bill?"

The old man was just finishing his share of potatoes and beans. He looked up, chewing vigorously.

"I'm going back, Bill. I must be there when the Lharr's brought home."

He looked at me sharply. "Be you the Lharr's leman, then?"

"Aye."

Bill got up stiffly. "Bill 'opes 'e takes good care o' you an' the youngin. That off-worlder sure hasn't done much for him in the way of kids." He began to kick dirt onto the fire. "We'll go soon's I smoor the fire."

"There's no need for you to go. You've done enough. I'll be careful."

"Missy—"

"It's too dangerous, Bill. Nobody with any sense would try it. The Lharr, if he lives, will remember you."

The old man looked skeptical and shrugged. "There be still soldiers, Missy. 'ow'll you miss 'em?"

I looked away from his bright, knowing eyes. "I'll find a way. I have to find a way."

He shrugged again and resumed his hunched position by the fire. I slowly opened the sagging door. A rat scurried away. I ducked out into the deserted street. Cautiously, I started back, walking as quickly as I could.

I had been on the streets under the manor house several minutes before I saw bright light flowing out of an alley not far ahead. I stopped. The light got brighter. Where could I hide? I searched my memory. Men's voices approached. Oh, why hadn't I paid more attention to what Bill and I were passing!

The light was even brighter and now I heard the swirling of air through a hovercar. They must be just around the corner! I whirled despairingly, unable to remember even a doorway. The tunnel was brighter now. I could see a pool of shadow where it had been too dark to see shadows before. I threw myself into the shadow with a whimper of fear, only later realizing it could have been a stairwell or an open lift shaft I was throwing myself into. The hovercar sound came toward my hiding place. Why were the soldiers so quiet? I heard no clank of weapons, no raised voices. Had they seen me? Were they listening for me to betray my hiding place? I inched back from the opening and bumped into something that slid, whirred softly, across joints in the masonry. I grabbed frantically and caught what felt like a broomstick seconds before it would have clattered into the corner of the closet. My heart pounded so heavily I could see my pulse in my eyes. The car stopped outside. Soldiers talked in low voices, then the car floated past and gradually the light from the Torches on it faded. They had been Council troops. Council planned to execute me.

I waited in the dark, listening, until I couldn't hear the car or see the light anymore. Cautiously, I slid to the door and looked out. There was darkness, only darkness, out there, except for the pools of cold, weak light around the luminous "streetlamps." I slipped into the passage and continued on my way.

Only a little beyond the intersecting alley, someone in the shadows hailed me. "Halt! In Lord Richard's name!"

A Torch flared. I still stood safely in the dark outside the circle of light. A Harlan soldier peered into the darkness.

"Come out and identify yourself," he ordered.

I hesitated, then ducked and tried to run past him, but I couldn't move fast enough. The soldier grabbed me as I went by. I tore free and ran around the nearest corner. Then hair fell onto my shoulders and into my eyes. The soldier had grabbed my headdress. Seconds later he began shouting, "The hair! It's the Larga Halarek!"

"After her, you idiots!" shouted another, deeper voice. "She's worth our lives in trade!"

I dodged around corner after corner, not caring if I lost myself if only I lost my pursuers. The baby's bulk made me slow and awkward. The musty air was hard to breathe. The footing was rough and uneven. I stumbled into walls and cracked toes on loose stones. I was struggling for air. I had to stop, gasping.

Karne, my lord, my life, my love, forgive me if I fail you. I've tried.

One direction seemed as good as another now. I smothered the sounds of my breathing as best I could and listened. Men marched somewhere behind me, but the rattle of their equipment and the thud of their feet were still far away. I would run away from their sounds, then, and upstairs, if I could find a way. Upstairs was where they'd carry his body. But that thought struck at what strength I had left and I pushed it away. Behind me the tramp of feet in step came closer, but it fell too evenly to be men in pursuit.

I began moving again, cautiously. The footing here was slippery. Puddles gathered along the base of the walls. Every few feet a trickle dripped loudly into a puddle. The air smelled of cold, wet stone. Then, ahead, Torchlight brightened the corridor. More patrols. They didn't talk. Only their light and the sounds of their boots betrayed them.

I drew back from the intersection just as a soldier turned a corner farther down the hall. The glare of his Torch blanked out the color of his uniform to my eyes, now used to dimness. Assuming the worst, I edged away, but I couldn't go very far back. Behind me were the men who knew me for the Larga Halarek. My hands clenched and I bit my lip in the agony of deciding. The light behind was getting brighter. The soldiers in the adjoining corridor were so close I could hear the creak of their boots as well as the rattle and slap of their equipment. I edged farther away. Perhaps they were Harlan soldiers cleaning out the last of the enemy. Perhaps they were Halarek. Or Council. But they didn't sound victorious. They didn't shout or laugh or even talk. No, they were probably sneaking away.

The soldier with the Torch stopped at the intersection. I shrank against the wall. He came toward me. I panicked for a moment, freezing a second before I ran. The Torch-bearer saw me move and shouted. Someone began to run toward me, then someone else.

I dodged back the way I had come and ran. Partially blinded from looking into the light, I bumped into the wall several times before my eyes adjusted again. Each time I stumbled I lost time, while the men behind me could see where they were going. I had a small lead, but in my condition I couldn't outrun them. I'd have to outwit them. Ahead now, the men I'd originally been trying to escape, or others like them, were indistinguishable black figures against their lights.

I was trapped! What could I do? Were any of them friends? If only I knew!

I forced my legs to keep up a lumbering run in spite of weariness that made my feet like lead blocks. The men ahead shouted. My pursuers responded with a shout. Did that mean they were on the same side? I dodged into a narrow alleyway. It twisted and turned and my hunters were close, very close. They were reaching out for me. Their fingers brushed my arm and shoulder. My lungs burned with the strain of pulling in the stale air. I stumbled on a loose cobble and nearly fell. One of the soldiers jerked me upright with a wrench that made me gasp.

Caught! And the grip was a cruel one. The soldier twisted my arm behind me and shoved me toward the bright lights in the main passage. His three companions fell in behind.

"It's only a serf woman, squadman," my captor said as he pushed me into the light.

Silence followed our arrival. I blinked at the brightness.

"Fool," someone growled. "Look at her hair, not her clothes. It's the Larga herself."

My captor dropped his cruel hold and stepped back. I could see the color of their uniforms now. They were Council red.

The squadman made a small, I thought a mocking, bow. "This way, milady. The captain'll know where you're to go."

Well, at least the Council's sentence would be more humane than Richard's. I'd face it with all the courage I could muster, as if Karne could know. He'd have no reason to be ashamed of me. I straightened my tired shoulders and lifted my head as they marched me down the alley.

"Looks like the place's pretty well cleaned out," one of the soldiers behind me remarked.

"Yeah, men don't fight much once they know their lord's dead."

My last hope died. I thought I would fall, but my captors caught me, more gently this time.

"They should be here somewhere," the squadman muttered under his breath.

We rounded a corner and suddenly I was among familiar dark blue uniforms. It was so unexpected, so unhoped-for that I felt numb with the shock of it. And they were *my* Blues. They wore my green shoulder patch.

"Captain?" The squadman's voice suggested he couldn't see the captain yet, either. "Captain, we found the Larga." He smiled at me a little crookedly. "She must've thought we were Harlan,'cause she led us a merry chase."

The captain was coming out of the shadows toward the rear.

"Tommy!"

He broke into a run and I stumbled to meet him, crying with exhaustion and relief. He put his arm awkwardly around my shoulders.

"Orby," he snapped, "get a litter from the other party. Jenkins, tell Lady Kathryn we've found the Larga unharmed. Brach, the household will be coming back now. Be sure a way is clear for the Larga's litter."

"The—the house," I managed to croak through shock and a dry throat, "it's crawling with Harlan men."

Tommy's arm tightened just a little, as if to reassure me. "It *was*, milady. Except for this level, the house is clean now."

I looked at him. "You were there. Is Karne—is he—?"

Tommy's face was troubled. "I don't know. We heard Harlan's men were here and Lord Karne sent me back before the tourney was over. But he was fighting well when I left. He had to see you again, he said. Too, the news that the Freemen had finally mobilized to help us buoyed him. Lord Richard is dead. That's all I know for certain." He turned his head toward the men following. "Orby! What's taking you so long?" He seemed to sense my impatience. "Can you walk, milady?"

I nodded, but I trembled so violently that I had to stop after only a few steps.

Tommy tightened his encircling arm. "Relax. You've strained too much already for a woman in your condition. The litter will be here soon."

It was and Tommy gently helped me into it. Some of the Blues pushed it to hurry it upstairs. Tommy walked alongside, talking to keep me calm.

"The duke came to the tourney quite upset," he said. "Brach 'persuaded' Harlan's seneschal to tell us what had happened.

The seneschal told him Lady Kathryn had called the duke in the wee hours of the morning. The seneschal didn't know what Lady Kathryn said, only that the duke immediately afterward ordered his men to attack and capture Ontar manor. She shook the duke out of his calm, milady."

Tommy turned then to respond to a soldier's touch on his arm. I closed my eyes and took several deep breaths to try to calm my inward agitation. It helped very little. Then I examined the child. The running and jouncing hadn't bothered him at all. With that fear gone, I concentrated on resting, since I would need every crumb of my strength for the ordeal ahead, and I prayed with all my heart that my husband was still alive.

I was feeling a little better by the time the procession stopped at the door to Karne's room.

The sentry there stepped forward and saluted briskly. "The Lharr isn't here yet, milady."

Tommy nodded curtly. "Thank you, soldier. Dismissed."

"Yessir!" The soldier saluted enthusiastically.

That stirred something I knew I should remember, something that needed doing. It hovered at the edge of my memory. I forced myself to think clearly.

"Soldier."

"Milady?"

I fumbled in a pocket for the ring. "Here. If there's no one in the library, leave this in plain sight on the desk. Then put a sentry on each door. No one is to enter. Absolutely no one." I looked at the Blues around me. I had trusted them with my life daily for months. The traitor spy wasn't one of them. "Say nothing about this."

"Aye, milady."

Tommy sent two soldiers with the sentry, posted two more at the doors to Karne's room, and dismissed the others. He then carefully guided the litter to the corner between the doors to the library stair and to my old room. He perched uneasily on the edge of Karne's desk and stared down at his hands. He clearly didn't know what to say under the circumstances, and I was too tired to help him.

Perhaps a quarter of an hour later, the sentry in the hall knocked briskly. "Weisman here to see the Lharr, Captain."

Tommy's dark eyes met mine for a long moment. I shrugged.

"Just a moment," Tommy answered. He pushed himself off the desk and brushed some dust from his uniform, then he opened the door. His body blocked my view, but I heard Weisman's high, confident voice.

"Captain Oroark, I have important information for Lord Karne."

"The Lharr isn't here yet." Tommy's voice was courteous but cool.

"I'll wait."

Tommy hesitated. "The Lharr is like to be on the edge of death."

Weisman did not move. I heard him impatiently tapping his pen against something hard. Tommy nodded slowly. "All right, but you're to keep quiet until Dr. Othneil says the Lharr may talk to you."

Tommy stepped aside. Weisman stepped forward. I sat up and got carefully out of the litter. Weisman's mouth fell open and his face paled. His pen tapped more rapidly against his ring, the ring with the green stone and the gold snake.

He licked his lips. "On second thought, I'll come back later. If he recovers I'll tell him. Of course I shouldn't bother him until he's recovered." He turned toward the door.

He knew I knew! "Stop him!" I cried.

Tommy's hand shot out. The guard at the door sprang forward. Tommy gripped Weisman by the collar and turned him around. I pointed at the white and trembling man.

"Captain Oroark, arrest this man for treason and murder."

"Nonsense." Weisman plucked at Tommy's hand. "She's overwrought, Captain. Nothing could make me betray the Lharr. I've been with him since he came of age. I've been with House Halarek close to twenty years."

Tommy twisted the collar so it cut into Weisman's neck. "Not so fast, Freeman," he said in a quiet, dangerous tone. "I'd like to hear more."

"What do you mean? Unhand me! I'm the Lharr's private secretary." His voice contained the proper mixture of rage and indignation, but he ceased struggling.

I walked slowly toward them, willing my exhausted body to act steady and alert. Weisman must not see my weakness. "Look at that ring, Captain. You saw me give it to the sentry. You heard my orders and saw to it that they were carried out. A soldier found it on the shield controls this morning, Frem Weisman. You lowered our shield for Harlan."

Involuntarily, Weisman's hand covered the ring. "She's talking crazy," he blustered. "This ring was a parting gift from a former employer."

I looked Tommy in the eye. "Captain, the Duke of Harlan showed me a ring like that at my wedding and explained that he gave it to people he especially wished to honor. I think I know what you've done to earn his 'honor,' Frem Weisman."

"There are lots of ringmakers." But Weisman's eyes were darting from side to side.

"Who handled all Halarek mail, Captain? Who told Harlan we were riding to Council? And how could Weisman testify to what I said to Pieter unless he was eavesdropping the night I told the Lharr? Pieter and I spoke Fruvan. You don't speak Fruvan, do you, Weisman? As a matter of fact, you can't speak any language but Rom as I remember. And the ring on the shield controls? Careless of you. You've sealed your own death warrant."

"No!"

Weisman tore free of Tommy's grip and sprang toward the door to the library stair. Tommy caught him in three strides and brought him back to me in a most uncomfortable hold.

"When you missed your ring, what did you do?" The hatred I suddenly felt for this man, whose ambition almost destroyed everything Karne had spent ten years building, surprised me. Hatred. Me. "You probably looked first in the control room, but it wasn't there? You should have suspected then that someone had found it and would suspect its owner of opening the shield. Where did you look next? Your place, the library. But the library doors were guarded. So you used the moving bookcase. You're the only person who knows how to make it work, Frem Weisman. You've just proved that you tried to assassinate the Lharr and that you killed Orkonan. You probably arranged for the Larga Charlotte's murder, too."

Weisman just glared.

"Why?" Tommy asked. "The Lharr is a good lord. How much did the duke pay?"

In Weisman's white face I saw the explosion coming.

"Twenty years! I've worked here twenty years. For nothing! Ten years earned me the secretary's job, but the old Larga gave it to Orkonan. After that, what right had this House to my loyalty? I have skills and I sold them." His voice rose to a shout. "I thought if Orkonan died—Orkonan's place was *mine*! Mine by right of years of work and you took it! You! A *woman*! An off-worlder. Over *me*!"

He snarled and sprang at me, hands clawed. Tommy hit him neatly with the edge of his hand. Weisman crumpled to the floor. Tommy prodded him contemptuously with his foot.

"Sentry!"

The young man popped his head around the edge of the door. "Sentry, search this carrion, then drag him out of here and lock him up in the tightest, most uncomfortable place you can find. He's just admitted he's the spy who's been selling Halarek to Harlan."

Tommy and the sentry searched Weisman, then manacled his hands. In their search, they found the original of the tape I had sent Tremo. Had he been planning on giving it to Lord Richard after his victory in the duel?

Only moments after the door had closed on Weisman and his escort, it opened again for Jenkins and two Lifesguardsmen. An angry voice followed them in.

"My lord, don't be a fool!"

Behind the guardsmen floated a litter. A thin gray man in a black robe came through the door still lecturing angrily. I recognized Dr. Othneil by his voice as well as his uniform.

"You'll be committing suicide!" the doctor snarled. "You can't make a tri-d transmission. You wouldn't live to finish it!" He saw that he was getting nowhere. "By my Mother's Blood! I never saw such a man!"

Everything went black for me for a moment. Karne was still alive! I trembled with joy, so much that I was afraid I wouldn't be able to walk to the litter. But I knew how stubborn my husband could be and I didn't want to lose him.

The litter had come fully into the room. Karne lay so still and looked so gray I wondered how he could think of getting up. The doctor saw me hesitating and beckoned me to the litter.

"See," he told Karne tartly when I stood beside him, "you should have more faith."

I knelt beside the litter, afraid to touch Karne's still, pale body. "My lord, obey the doctor. I wouldn't have you leave me."

"Zjhanne," he whispered. "Zjhanne, you came!"

The wonder in those words hurt me. He *had* doubted.

He raised his left arm stiffly and let his fingers brush my cheek. His face was so white and strained, his eyes so dark . . .

"You weren't there and I thought—" He summoned a faint smile and held out his left hand to me. His eyes never left my face. "Words can't say how glad I am to see you. Are you well?"

I held that precious hand against my cheek a moment. "Aye, lord, now I'm with you again. But I must let the doctor see to you." I started to get up.

His grip tightened painfully. "Don't leave me."

"My lord, I'm not leaving—"

"Please!"

How could I leave him then, no matter what it cost me? I looked up at Othneil. He nodded shortly, then motioned four guardsmen forward. Karne let my hand go reluctantly. With amazing speed and gentleness, the guardsmen lifted him into the open bed. Yet, despite their care, the pain was too much for conscious bearing and Karne blacked out. I turned to the doctor in panic. He smiled thinly.

"The pain is very bad. He's gravely hurt. But he'll live if you make him follow my orders. If you can do that, he ought to be up and around in about three months."

Karne's golden eyes opened. They held a weak glimmer of laughter. "Three months. A good portion of the winter. I'll be at your mercy for a long time, my lady."

"Years and years, my lord."

Othneil motioned to his tech, who rolled forward a formidable cart of equipment. The doctor selected a knife and began the swift removal of his emergency dressings.

"Zjhanne!"

I thought there was a note of fear in Karne's voice. I set a hand on his unhurt shoulder. "I'm still here, sweetheart."

The doctor looked at me, hands poised, waiting. I sat gingerly on the edge of the bed and gave Karne my hand again. I looked only at his face while the doctor worked. To watch the doctor would've been more than I could've endured. Watching Karne's face was enough. He bit his lip until blood trickled down his chin. I leaned to wipe it away and just that movement caused him pain. He squeezed his eyes shut and took a sharp breath. I looked at the doctor.

"Couldn't be helped." He went back to work. "Can't risk putting him to sleep."

Karne tried so hard not to make any noise, but the pain was too much for his will. He crushed my hand. His harsh gasps and sharp cries tore at me. Tears streamed down my face and I didn't even try to wipe them away. I didn't completely trust the doctor's assurance, either. Karne's pain seemed so excruciating. I talked to Karne continuously, keeping my voice steady by will, praying that somewhere in his flickering consciousness, he would hear my voice and hold tighter to life.

"Love, stay with me. Hold on for our sake, for your son's sake. The worst is over now, Karne. Lord Richard is dead. You can be free. We're young. We can bring Halarek Holding back. You're what's important, Karne, you. What would the Gharr do without you? What would *I* do without you? Hold on, my dear lord, hold on!"

I repeated the words like a litany. They were a charm that tied him to me, though he wandered deep into hell.

After an eternity, the doctor sighed and straightened. "He'll come round in a little bit, Larga. Don't stay long. And give him this when you're through." He poured a milky liquid into a cup. "It'll let him sleep." He walked around the bed to pat my shoulder encouragingly, then left with his tech and his cart and the guardsmen.

Gently I loosened Karne's hand from around my numb fingers. I lifted and dropped my shoulders to loosen them a little. I felt in every bone and muscle the strain and weariness of what seemed hours of running.

"Are you leaving me, Zjhanne?" Karne's eyes opened slowly and he looked as if he didn't see me clearly.

"Just changing positions a little. Did I hurt you?"

He shook his head the tiniest bit. "Not lately. Promise you'll never go away like that again, even if I try to send you."

There was such loneliness, such wary hope in that request that I longed to hold him tight. But he was too much hurt. I had to satisfy myself with caressing his cheek ever so gently instead. "Never, my lord. If I left you, who'd raise our son? We have a chance to make a truly new life for him here. We'll bring the holding back, different and better than it's ever been."

"Are you teasing me, Zjhanne? About the son? You didn't want to make a child with me."

"No, my lord. I wouldn't tease you about something so important. Here." I pressed his hand firmly against my belly. "This is no joke. He's as real as I am."

The child cooperated and kicked me just then.

Karne took that in in silent wonder for a moment.

"You trusted me so much, Zjhanne?"

"I loved you so much. We've both learned. We can work our problems out. I know we can."

"A son." Such joy lit his thin, tired face that it shook me. "I prayed for one to come home and I got two." He closed his eyes for a moment. Then, "Come kiss me, wife," he ordered softly.